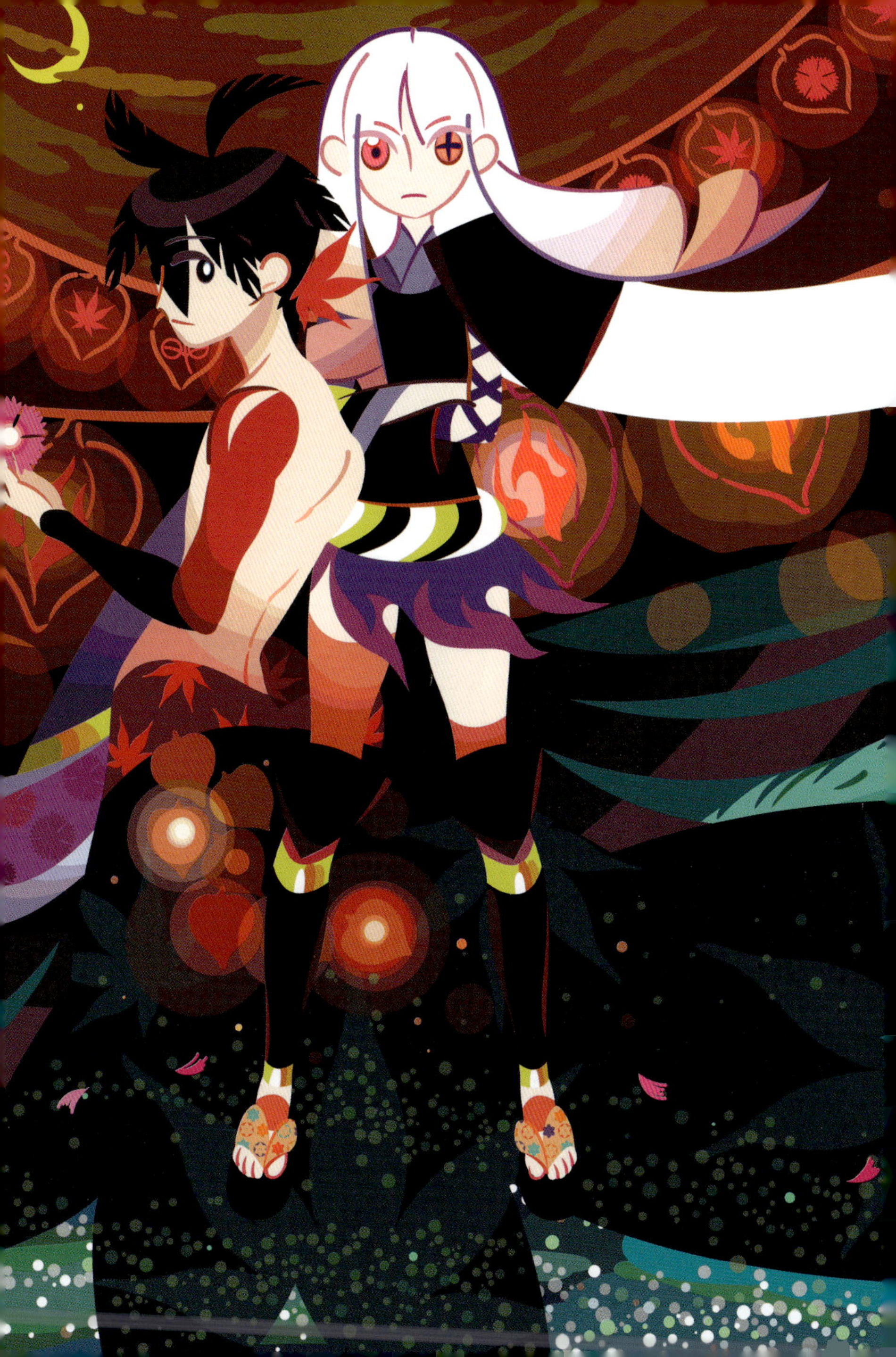

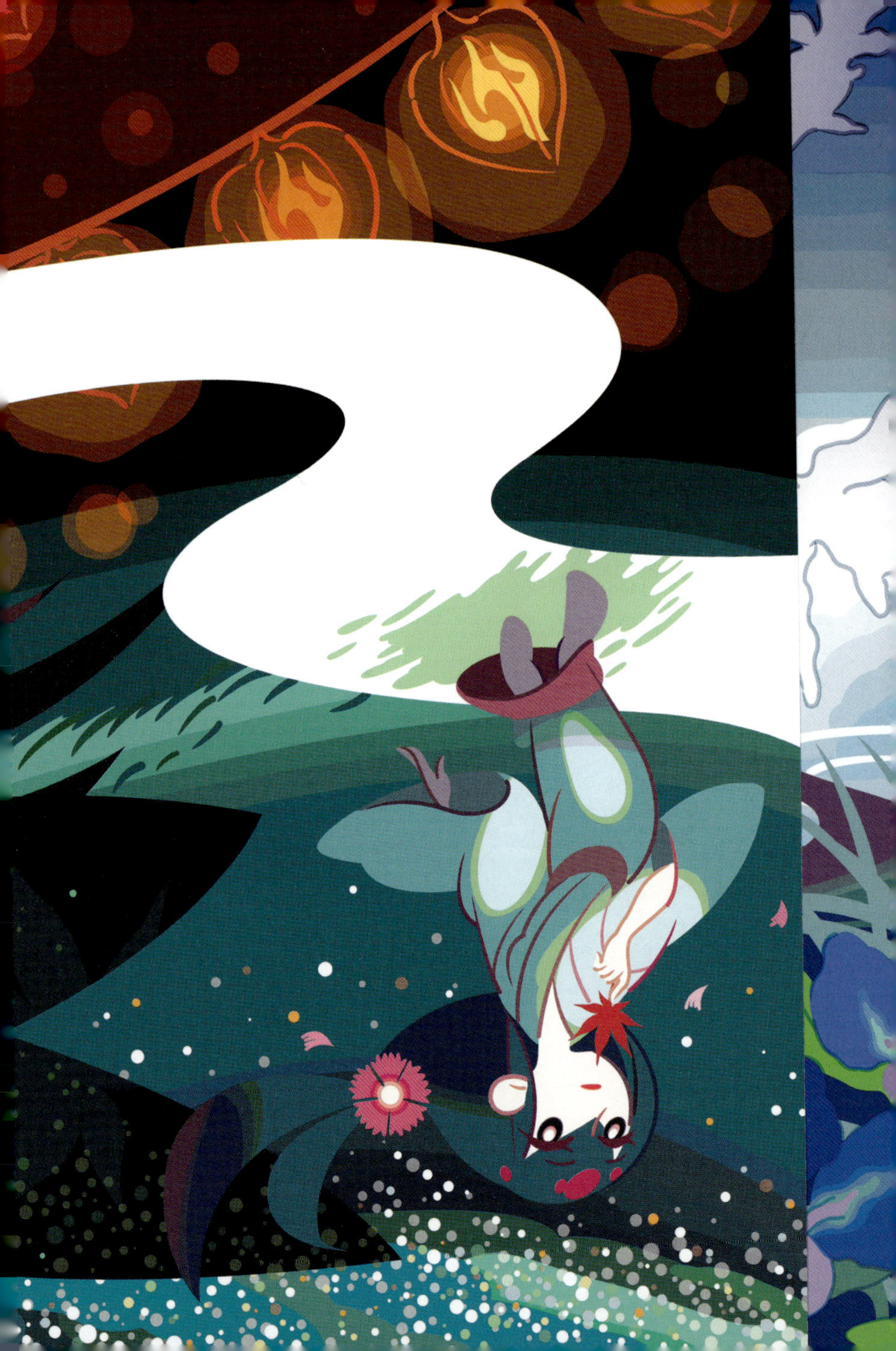

KATANAGATARI
Sword Tale

3

NISIOISIN

Art by take

Calligraphy by Hiroshi Hirata

Translated by Sam Bett

VERTICAL.

KATANAGATARI
SWORD TALE: THREE

Katanagatari Dai Nanawa Akutou Bita
Katanagatari Hachiwa Bitou Kanzashi
Katanagatari Dai Kyuuwa Outou Nokogiri

© 2007 NISIOISIN
Illustrations by take
All rights reserved.

First published in Japan in 2007 by Kodansha Ltd., Tokyo.
Publication rights for this English edition arranged
through Kodansha Ltd., Tokyo.

Published by Vertical, an imprint of
Kodansha USA Publishing, LLC., 2019

ISBN 978-1-947194-91-5

Manufactured in Canada

First Edition

Kodansha USA Publishing, LLC.
451 Park Avenue South, 7th Floor
New York, NY 10016

www.vertical-inc.com

TABLE OF CONTENTS

BOOK SEVEN — AKUTO THE EEL

Prologue		003
Chapter One	Gokenji Temple	009
Chapter Two	Emonzaemon Soda	033
Chapter Three	Shichika Hachiretsu	047
Chapter Four	Nanami Yasuri	061
Chapter Five	Shichika Hachiretsu Redux	073
Epilogue		095

BOOK EIGHT — BITO THE SUNDIAL

Prologue		109
Chapter One	Schemer Mansion	113
Chapter Two	Mansion Negative	131
Chapter Three	Umigame Maniwa	147
Chapter Four	Skytron	165
Chapter Five	Lake Fuyo	179
Epilogue		195

BOOK NINE — OTO THE CURED

Prologue		207
Chapter One	The Heartland School	213
Chapter Two	Zanki Kiguchi	229
Chapter Three	The Follower	241
Chapter Four	Oshidori Maniwa	257
Chapter Five	Shangri-Oto	275
Chapter Six	Blind Shogi	293
Epilogue		305

NOTE ON THIS ENGLISH EDITION

This volume collects the third trio of a dozen-part series. The cover art was for the original Book Nine, while Books Seven and Eight's have been included as a gatefold.

Where appropriate, the transliterations provided in the footnotes add bars called "macrons" above vowels for a closer approximation of the pronunciation, including for names and words that appear without them in the main text. A syllable with "Ō" is supposed to sound more like *boat* than *bot*. A repeated consonant like "CC" should be construed in the same manner as in *Rebecca*.

BOOK SEVEN

AKUTO THE EEL

第七話
悪刀・鐚

序章
一章 ── 護剣寺
二章 ── 左右田右衛門左衛門
三章 ── 七花八裂
四章 ── 鑢七実
五章 ── 七花八裂・改
終章

本文憑画/竹田英史
版面設計/植田弘史
構成協力/野嶋ツナト
本文使用書体：FOT-筑紫明朝 Pro L

PROLOGUE

■   ■

About a month ago.

Togame the Schemer, Grand Commander of Arms of the Yanari Shogunate Military Directorate, Owari Bakufu, and Shichika Yasuri, Seventh Master of the Kyotoryu had just realized that the ship which they had boarded was traversing the Sea of Japan bound not for Owari Castle, but for Ezo—realized, one might add, considerably too late.

Meanwhile, on Mt. Shirei[1] in Mutsu—which like Mt. Odori, where they would shortly find themselves, and Lake Fuyo in Edo, had been designated as a Level One Disaster Area.

At the summit stood a woman, looking unbelievably exhausted.

In fact—

She was the only thing left standing.

Every other mortal present—lay crumpled on the ground. Some face down, others facing the heavens—easily over a hundred fallen bodies clothed in white.[2]

The Sacred Guardians[3] of Mt. Shirei.

In order to protect the Level One Disaster Area that was their mountain, these stewards lived under the harshest of conditions where not even a single tree could grow. They had no ties to the local government, much less the bakufu, yet were held in the same high regard as Izumo's storied Three Goshin Regiments. An independent order—

But they had been annihilated to a man.

And the woman who had been their ruin—

"...Whew."

—Sighed, sounding ever more exhausted.

This woman—could sigh with the best of them.

Unfazed by the bodies of the Sacred Guardians dressed in white, whom she had *scattered* all along the trail like breadcrumbs in a fairy tale from overseas—she gazed into the little shrine[4] before her.

The tiny shrine built at the summit of Mt. Shirei.

Ensconced therein—she saw the sword.

"Hmm, what kind of sword is this?" she mused. "But I guess this must be it. *I can sense it...* Poor thing—set up on a pedestal, all the way up here. Ugh, I can totally relate."

Softly—she reached out her hand.

Her fingers only grazed the outside of the shrine—but it exploded as if gunpowder had been employed. She blew the thing to bits.

[1] 死霊山 SHIREIZAN "Dead Spirit Mountain"
[2] 白装束 SHIRO SHŌZOKU often worn when practicing religious rites
[3] 神衛隊 SHIN'EITAI "god guards" neologism playing on 親衛隊 SHIN'EITAI private guard
[4] 祠 HOKORA an altar not much larger than a person, built in the likeness of a shrine

Leaving nothing but the consecrated sword—

"Hah. Great—I kinda like it. I had my doubts about Soto the Twin—but this one is nice and light, and just the right size, too... Good enough—or bad enough for me?"

She laughed merrily.

"After all, this is Akuto the Eel."[5]

Kiki Shikizaki, the legendary swordsmith who effectively had reigned over the Age of Warring States.

His swords, the Mutant Blades—feared and revered.

Standing a cut above the rest—there were a precious twelve.

And among the Twelve Possessed—was Akuto the Eel.

"Well then. According to Miss Togame, each of the Twelve Possessed has its own unique characteristics, based around a single principle—for Zetto the Leveler, it was *hardness*...and for the last one, Soto the Twin, it was *heaviness*... so what about Akuto the Eel?"

Fixated.

Focused.

Rapt.

She strained her vision—peering down at the katana perched atop the rubble of the shrine.

Eyes.

Fast on the sword.

Looking at—over—through—into—and out for it.[6]

Observing—and examining[7] it.

"Oh. Okay, now I get it," she finally announced. "In that case—this katana suits me perfectly. A sword may not choose who to kill, but a sword will choose its owner. Does this mean that Akuto the Eel has chosen me? That would be so good—bad, I mean."

She reached out her hand.

Picking up the sword—like it was hers.

Just as she had said a moment earlier, perhaps this was not a proper sword. To say the least, its shape was not what usually comes to mind when one speaks of *katana*.

It looked more like—a throwing knife.

The projectile daggers wielded by a ninja.

But this was a creation of Kiki Shikizaki, a swordsmith unbeholden to formalities, and there was surely more than meets the eye—a fact hit home by other Mutant Blades like Zokuto the Armor and Soto the Twin.

It may be shaped like a mere dagger, but this sword was grand as any.

The woman—could sense it.

The perfect size for her small hands and slender fingers, almost as if it had

---

[5] 悪刀 鐚　AKUTŌ BITA　"The Wicked Sword: Farthing"
[6] 見る—視る—観る—診る—看る　[all] MIRU　see—look—watch—examine (medically)—attend to/nurse
[7] 観察 診察　KANSATSU SHINSATSU　study carefully　diagnose

been forged with her in mind—indubitably,[8] this blade was a katana.

"Alright...now that I have something to show for myself, I may as well catch up with Shichika. Not like I know where he is, though, or what he's up to, but that doesn't matter. Considering the mess I've made, he'll catch wind sooner or later, if he hasn't heard already... As long as I wait out in the open, in plain sight, they'll come to me. They'll find me. Maybe not Shichika—but Togame will for sure."

In that case, she thought things over.

"Maybe I'll try Gokenji[9] Temple—the holy land of swordsmen. A place like that should be easy enough to find, even for somebody who gets lost as easily as me... Who can miss a giant buddha? Why not get in the mood and partake in the Katana Pilgrimage? In which case I'd better—ahem, *badder* strike[10] while the iron is hot."

The woman turned about.

Carrying the dagger in one hand, she went back down the trail—without batting an eyelash at the bodies of the Sacred Guardians fallen by the wayside.

Huh?

A hand grabbed her by the ankle.

It was one of the fallen soldiers dressed in white, a youth, somehow still breathing, and miraculously conscious. If he had laid low, he may well have lived to see another day—but his loyalty was with Mt. Shirei, and so he seized her ankle.

"W-Wait," he said. "D-Don't...take it away. You can't take it away... The mountain can't survive without that sword... We need it, to protect the mountain..."

"..."

The woman turned toward the young man whose hand was limply clasped around her ankle, but saying nothing—

She simply looked at him.

That look.

"I-I'm not only saying this for our sake... I'm saying it for yours, too... That sword is more than *any single human being* can handle... It's not just one of the Twelve Possessed of Kiki Shikizaki...but the evilest of them all."

He strained his voice—struggling to speak.

"P-Please... Take anything else, anything you want, just leave the sword—"

"..."

The woman.

In answer to his plea—sighed ever so, ever so...

Deeply.

Then—narrowing her eyes, she turned her icy stare on him.

---

[8] まごうことなき MAGOU KOTO NAKI an archaic way of saying "unmistakably"
[9] 護剣寺 GOKENJI "Sword Protection Temple"
[10] 善は急げ―いえ、悪は急げ ZEN WA ISOGE—IE, AKU WA ISOGE "tarry not to do good—or rather, bad" the first half is a common axiom, and the latter half the character's improvisation

"Who said that you could lay your hands on me—dill weed."[11]
Using her free foot—she stomped on the young man's head.
Again. And again. And again.
Ignoring his reactions—she stomped away.
"Weed. Weed."

Before long—the man's head was flattened.[12]

Obliterated—no more than a puddle of blood, a puddle of flesh.

Somehow his hand still clasped the woman's ankle—but she broke his grip with a merciless toss of the foot.

Not caring that her straw sandals were bright with blood, she set off on the trail once more—as if nothing had happened.

At this point, there was no one on the mountain left to—interrupt her progress.

No.

Forget Mt. Shirei—you could search the whole Japanese Archipelago and still find none. Twenty years earlier, at only seven, she had been the strongest in Japan. Two months back, her younger brother Shichika had vanquished Hakuhei Sabi, foremost master of swordplay of his day, making himself number one—but she had been there first.

Nanami Yasuri. Head of the Yasuri.

Sickly and genius.

Boasting immaculate[13] eyes that let her emulate all and sundry that they took in, she was, in the history of the Kyotoryu, a most freakish[14] blade.

In the fourth moon of the year, she had put an end to Chocho Maniwa, Mitsubachi Maniwa, and Kamakiri Maniwa—the three bosses making up Bug Unit Maniwa; in the fifth moon of the year, she had wiped out the Itezoras, who had made Mt. Ezo their home; and in the sixth moon of the year, she had massacred the Sacred Guardians of Mt. Shirei—and now that she had laid her hands on Akuto the Eel, she was heading for Shikoku.

To meet up with her little brother—

Her beloved little brother—

"I guess it's been six months by now. I hope he's had the chance to grow up... heh. Anyway, I feel so good—"

That sickly genius Nanami muttered to herself, making her way back down the path—mashing the white-clothed bodies of the Sacred Guardians into pulp, without a thought.

"Bad, I mean," she amended with a sadistic[15] smile.

[11] 草　KUSA　grassy plants in general, or pesky wild plants specifically
[12] 失われた　USHINAWARETA　lost
[13] 究極　KYŪKYOKU　superlative; ultimate
[14] 異形　IGYŌ　"strange shaped" aberrant
[15] 邪悪そうな　JA'AKU SŌNA　"wicked-seeming" foul

■ ■

And now the family showdown that you've all been waiting for!
    Brother versus sister—Shichika Yasuri versus Nanami Yasuri!
    The strongest in Japan against his predecessor!
    Can the Seventh Master of the Kyotoryu overmaster his older sister?!
    Would the sickly genius murder her own younger brother?!
    The ultimate face-off, a few pages off!
    A flowery battle, a florid family feud!
    A period piece that knows no peace—period!
    Book Seven of the Sword Tale, where the Seventh Master meets his match ♪

CHAPTER ONE

GOKENJI TEMPLE

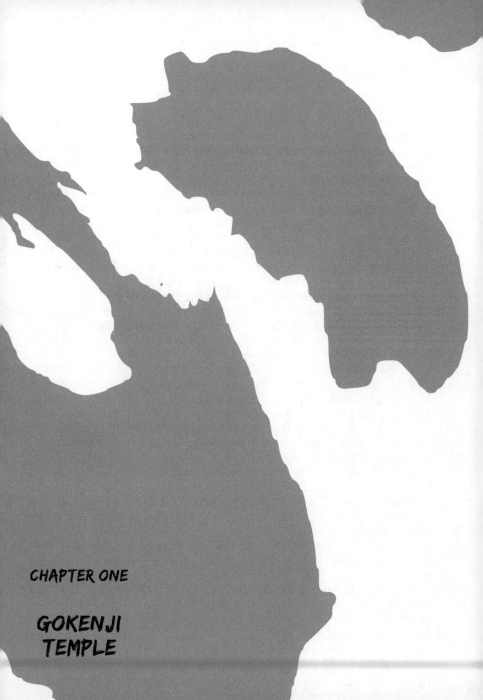

■ ■

The sacred status of Seiryoin[1] Gokenji Temple on Mt. Sayabashiri[2] in Tosa needs no introduction—every year, thousands upon thousands of swordsmen, from the east and west, make the trip across the waters to Shikoku to partake in the Katana Pilgrimage.

At the center of this holy site is the Katana Buddha.

The gigantic buddha erected by the Old Shogun, as the annals now refer to him, who prevailed over the Age of Warring States and unified the nation—and promptly launched the Great Sword Hunt, that appalling piece of legislature which made all swords under the sun government property. The hundred thousand blades seized by the law were melted down to produce the Katana Buddha, the literal embodiment of the spirits of all swordsmen.

Swordsmen crossed the nation just to catch a glimpse of it.

Ostensibly the statue had been built, in the wake of chaos, as a memorial to peace, that such horrific conflict need not ever be repeated, but today it is a well-known fact that the Old Shogun's motivations were more complicated—indeed, his motives were apparent even then.

He was really hunting swordsmen.

That none might threaten[3] his supreme authority—

He robbed the swordsmen of their swords.

To rid their kind from all Japan.

And while he managed to achieve his superficial goal and forge the giant buddha, the Old Shogun, who had managed to unite the nation, failed to rid the warriors from the land—however.

Very few knew that this objective was also a ruse.

Official motive—building a giant buddha.

Ulterior motive—hunting down swordsmen.

But the Old Shogun's true motive was to round up all the swords of Kiki Shikizaki.

To collect all thousand of the Mutant Blades made by that legendary swordsmith, who reigned over the Age of Warring States—such was his plan and obsession.

He succeeded—one might say ninety-nine per cent.[4] Including the Mutant Blades in his possession at the onset of the hunt, the Old Shogun wound up with nine hundred and eighty-eight Shikizaki blades to his name—and if that isn't ninety-nine per cent, what is?

[1] 清涼院　SEIRYŌIN　"Cooling House"
[2] 鞘走山　SAYABASHIRIZAN　"Sharp Blade Mountain"
　　　鞘走る　SAYABASHIRU　to slip out of a sheath　鞘　SAYA sheath　走る　HASHIRU run
[3] 揺るがす　YURUGASU　shake
[4] 九分九厘　KUBU KURIN　nine and nine-tenths (out of ten)

Yet try as he might.
The twelve remaining swords evaded him.
Regardless of the legislation he enacted, or however many troops he deployed—at best, he ascertained their owners or their whereabouts.
Which is no surprise.
These twelve swords epitomized[5] the Mutant Blades of Kiki Shikizaki—they were masterpieces of such consummate perfection that the nine hundred and eighty-eight swords the Old Shogun did manage to collect were considered mere prototypes for the remaining dozen.
Ultimately a failure, the Great Sword Hunt was the undoing of the Old Shogun and led to his demise. Lacking a proper heir, he was forced to cede his power to the present-day Yanari Bakufu—nevertheless.
Gokenji Temple, whose grounds encompass the Katana Buddha, remained a sacred place.

■　■

As part of their training, the priests of Gokenji Temple were schooled in swordplay—nay, more than a part of their training, this swordsmanship was the most conspicuous and characteristic practice of their order. As to be expected from a school headquartered on hallowed ground—the Gokenjiryu[6] was seen as matchless and unparalleled. While a sizeable fraction of Katana Pilgrims sought to join the priesthood through apprenticeship to their school, only a chosen few received the honor. The gate to their order was narrow, and the walls were high—it was not rare for some foolhardy young swordsman to show up, knocking down the door,[7] only to be booted down the footpath before he even drew his sword.
Gokenji was the home to around two hundred priests.
All of whom, though holy men, were warriors[8]—whose chosen weapon was the sword.
Most of their kind favor the spear—but at Gokenji Temple, brandishing anything except a sword would be unthinkable.
Toward the end of the seventh moon.
In the middle of the day.
At the Fifth Hall—westernmost of the five dojos on the compound of Gokenji Temple.
We find four souls.
Priests of the order—nowhere in sight.
All four souls present being temple outsiders.

---

[5]　札付き　FUDATSUKI　"tagged"　notorious
[6]　護剣寺流剣法　GOKENJIRYŪ KENPŌ　the Gokenji school of swordplay
[7]　道場破り　DŌJŌ YABURI　"dojo busting"　challenging the strongest members of a school
[8]　僧兵　SŌHEI　"priest soldier"　warrior monk

One among them dressed in monkish robes[9]—so oversized they hardly made a dignified impression. And yet some aspect of her feeble, willowy appearance made the unflattering garment immaterial, setting her well above the rest.

That icy stare.

Almost transparent skin.

Nanami Yasuri—Head of the Yasuri.

Standing across from her, facing her head-on—there was a lanky guy with tousled hair, stripped to the waist, dressed in a hakama. Unencumbered by his usual arm guards and leg guards—ready to rumble.

The Seventh Master of the Kyotoryu—Shichika Yasuri.

Sister versus brother.

Reunited for the first time in over half a year—and facing off in the dojos of Gokenji.

Both empty-handed.[10]

But these two scions of the Kyotoryu, the swordless school of swordplay—were armed fully even when their hands were empty.

Shichika assumed Form Seven—the Kakitsubata.

Nanami just stood there.

But Shichika knew better—he knew about his sister's stance on *forms*. How *formlessness* was *form* for her. He knew about her personal addition to the Kyotoryu, Form Zero, the Ichijiku—while he had failed to comprehend its workings, he knew of her peculiar, unique form and its ferocity...

Shichika watched Nanami's every move, eyes fixed upon his sister and not so much as blinking. In turn, Nanami leveled her icy stare on Shichika—

Observing and examining him.

Her little brother.

In six months, how has he changed and grown—
And how far has he fallen?

" ... "
" ... "

The air was thick with tension—meanwhile, the other two souls present watched them over by the walls. One of them, as you have probably guessed, was Togame the Schemer, Grand Commander of Arms of the Owari Bakufu Military Directorate. Her brash and brilliant kimono, highlighted by her long white hair, was perhaps not the most suitable attire for a temple visit, but there she leaned against the wall. She was watching Shichika Yasuri—her sword—face off against his older sister, Nanami Yasuri, out on the planking in the middle of the hall.

Noticing something—she addressed the man beside her.

"Lieutenant Emonzaemon,"[11] she whispered.

The man she had spoken to was watching the siblings in the center of the

[9] 法衣 HŌI "holy garb" 法 HŌ law; dharma, i.e. 仏法 BUPPŌ Buddhist teaching
[10] 手ぶら TEBURA unequipped; also, visiting a host without a gift or souvenir
[11] 右衛門左衛門どの EMON ZAEMON DONO "Sir Righty-Lefty" a joke on archaic male suffixes
　　　　　　　　　　どの DONO (honorific) lord; rendered as "lieutenant" for this character

hall as well—but when Togame uttered his name, he turned his eyes on her.

A thin man.

Dressed in nothing quite so brash and brilliant as robes worn by the Schemer, but nevertheless wrongly for a temple.

Indeed, his outfit was wrong for the entire era.

He wore a coat and trousers.[12]

Upon entering the dojo, he took off a pair of shoes, rather than sandals.

But to top it all off—Emonzaemon wore a mask that covered half his face.

And scrawled across the mask—the word "NON-NINJA."[13]

"What is it, Madame Schemer," Emonzaemon said—he, too, in a whisper.

"We made it here. You've served your purpose—you're free to head back to Owari. Wouldn't want to keep that precious princess of yours—waiting."

"*No need*[14]—don't worry about me, Madame Schemer. I'm enjoying the opportunity to witness this event firsthand. I'm not so cheerless[15] as to turn back now. Unless, Madame Schemer, my presence is some kind of an inconvenience to you."

"An inconvenience. Hah!"

Togame grimaced at the thought.

"Don't flatter yourself—neither you nor your precious princess—could do anything to inconvenience me. Frankly, I'm surprised that you have nothing else to do. I meant only to suggest there might be better ways for you to spend your time than sitting on the sidelines."

"*Not at all*—don't fret, Madame Schemer. *Simply sitting here with you*—is all I need to do today. Learn more about your sword firsthand—and I'll have done a full day's work."

"..."

Togame clicked her tongue.

She had no more to say and turned her gaze back to the action at the center of the dojo.

Of course, however softly they may have tried to speak, it was one giant open space, which meant that everything Togame and Emonzaemon discussed had made its way to Shichika and Nanami.

Shichika, however, did not move a muscle—[16]

Not so for Nanami.

"...Whew."

She sighed.

That sigh—which suited her so well.

"Get your act together, Shichika—look how bored our audience is getting. Can't you hear them chatting over there? Don't just stand there staring at me, make a move."

---

[12] 洋装 YŌSŌ Western (i.e. European) clothing 洋 YŌ ocean, i.e. overseas
[13] 不忍 SHINOBAZU "un-enduring/hiding"
[14] 不要 IRAZU unnecessary archaic syntax and a verbal tick echoing "Princess Negative"
[15] 枯れて KARETE dried up; lifeless
[16] 身じろぎ MIJIROGI flinch

"Same old sis," responded Shichika.

Without breaking from the Kakitsubata.

"Quit talking down to me. I know you're strong and all, but it's not like I've been sitting around the hut the past six months. This fight won't be a repeat— of last year."

"No?"

Nanami smirked.

She had no form to break from—and yet it seemed as if her posture had relaxed.

"I suppose that I can sort of *see* it—but let me ask anyway. What have you been up to for the past six months?"

"Well, first I fought a swordsman named Ginkaku Uneri, in Inaba Desert. That guy was a master of iainuki—so fast you couldn't even see him draw his sword."

Shichika did what he was told—and caught Nanami up on what had happened.

"Then came Meisai Tsuruga in Izumo—who used a style of swordplay called the Sentoryu. It actually has a lot in common with the Kyotoryu. She put up a good fight—and after that came yet another swordsman, Hakuhei Sabi...the strongest swordsman in Japan. He put up a good fight, too, but I won in the end."

"Ah," Nanami interjected[17] without suggesting she approved. "I suppose that means that you're the strongest swordsman in Japan now?"

"That's right. I had to fend off a whole bunch of challengers—but let's not count those guys. My next big fight was with a guy named Kanara Azekura, down in Satsuma. His armor class made him unbeatable, until I cracked him like an egg. My last fight was against Konayuki Itezora, who was a little girl but had this monstrous strength. Still, I won without a scratch!"

Shichika lied to his sister.

The heat of battle got the better of him.

But nothing got past her.

"Show me a liar, and I will show you a thief,"[18] she chewed him out. "*One look at you* and I can tell you hurt your left arm not that long ago—Konayuki Itezora's doing, I suppose? Still...it seems to have completely healed."

"Just a flesh wound," whined Shichika, flustered at being called out on his lie, but he didn't let it hamper his bravado: "I've come into my own—way stronger than the first time that we fought each other. Don't underestimate me, or you'll get hurt."

"Hurt?" Nanami looked puzzled at his choice of words. "We're not here to play games, Shichika—this is the real deal. Kill or be killed."

"Kill..."

Was it because Shichika was showing signs of hesitation?

---

[17] 相槌を打つ AIZUCHI WO UTSU to chime in while another person is speaking; literally: (an apprentice) getting in hammer blows between the (master) smith's strikes
[18] 嘘つきは泥棒の始まり USOTSUKI WA DOROBŌ NO HAJIMARI "Once you lie, you start to steal"

"Don't tell me you've gone soft," Nanami snapped.
"S-Soft?"
"Ugh, I was afraid this was going to happen. Oh boy...who's to blame for this? Ginkaku Uneri? Meisai Tsuruga, Hakuhei Sabi, Kanara Azekura, maybe Konayuki Itezora? Or perhaps..."
That stare.
Turning slightly—Nanami eyed the Schemer leaning against the wall.
"Is this *your doing*—Miss Togame?"
"..."
Togame stared right back—saying nothing, not shying from her gaze, simply facing her.
"You've got some nerve," Nanami admitted. "But no matter. Listen, Shichika. I'll say it again—this is not a game or contest. It's a real fight, to the death. I aim to kill you—and ask you to do the same. If you're too soft for that, at least come at me—aiming to die."
"I told you not to underestimate me, sis," warned Shichika. "I've never fought someone as strong as you—but I'm stronger than you now. If we fight each other, fight for real, you're definitely the one who's gonna die."
"Exactly—that's more like it."
"Look, if you'd just give up that Shikizaki blade...Akuto the Eel, we can end this before anyone gets hurt. Just hand it over to Togame and everything will be okay. Why do we have to fight each other, anyway?"
"What a foolish question." Nanami laughed—sneered. "When two swordsmen chance upon each other, what reason have they not to fight?"
"Sis, you're not a swordsman."
"I suppose you're right."
Nanami floated[19] forward.
"Like you—I am a sword."
"..."
"Are you so different? But Shichika—I figured you would need a reason for us to fight. That's why I went to all the trouble of tracking down the Twelve Possessed of Kiki Shikizaki and finding you. Is that not clear enough for you? *If you want the sword—you have to take me down*. Okay? Dad didn't raise you to ignore whoever owns you for my sake."
"Fine, then," said Shichika. "What the hell—why not. Just don't say I didn't warn you. Hey, Togame."
"Hm?"
Naturally, the Schemer perked up when Shichika called her name.
"Give us the signal," he said. "From the top."[20]
Here goes, she thought.
Shichika was not the only one who had misgivings about the match—but after a moment's hesitation, she raised one hand high, up toward the ceiling...

---

[19] すぅ、と　SUU, TO　onomatopoeia for smooth, silent movement
[20] 仕切り直し　SHIKIRI NAOSHI　poising anew, in sumo

"May the best sword win—fight!"

As Togame cried the words, Shichika leapt forth.

Launching from the Kakitsubata, in a straight line for Nanami.

No—not exactly a straight line.

What makes and *brakes*[21] the Kakitsubata is its kaleidoscopic footwork. By the time he made it to his sister, standing there in no stance in particular, he'd pulled off a total of twenty-four feints both big and small.

For someone with his legs, Nanami was about five steps away—this was the maximum number of feints imaginable.

He knew—

Shichika knew how strong his sister was.

He wasn't planning to pull any punches.

He'd go all in, at full speed, from the get-go.

"Shichika," Nanami addressed him casually.

As if her brother wasn't charging at her.

"I know we're in the middle of a battle, but for old time's sake—I'll let you know that you messed up."

Fixated.

Her eyes observed Shichika's movements.

"First off...it doesn't matter one bit if your six months of experience battling all kinds of enemies has made you stronger than me. I have my eyes—eyes that devour all—and once I see you move, your strength becomes my strength."

Watch and Learn—this was her genius manifest.

The *martial talent*[22] let her pick up any move by seeing it in action.

Her father, Mutsue Yasuri, had forbidden her from taking part in any kind of training—but thanks to her genius, she had made the Kyotoryu hers without moving a muscle, just from watching her family practice.

She was the Kyotoryu, yet she was not the Kyotoryu.

Left out of the school, she was the school personified.

Nanami Yasuri.

But the power of her vision went beyond acquiring the moves of others—nothing could get by her.

No trick, no motion.

No weakness.

Seeing through it all, without exception—Nanami Yasuri watched and learned!

"...then!"

Of course Shichika knew.

He'd spent most of his life beside his sister, and her eyes were a fact of life. Not even twenty-four feints sufficed—she must have seen every last one of his feints for the fake it was.

And that was only the beginning.

---

[21] 緩急自在　KANKYŪ JIZAI　readily changing speed
[22] 戦闘技術　SENTŌ GIJUTSU　"battle technique"

His sister knew everything about him.

She knew every move the Kyotoryu had—and knew them better than anybody in the history of the school. The ins and outs. The pros and cons.

She knew exactly how to fend him off because she understood all of his moves—except for one!

The Last Fatal Orchid—*Shichika Hachiretsu*.

He called it a secret move, but it was no such thing, having no history or place in the tradition. He had thought it up himself, only six months ago, back on Haphazard Island.

The spectacular move deployed all seven of the secret moves at the same time—

Fatal Orchid One: Kyoka Suigetsu
Fatal Orchid Two: Kacho Fugetsu
Fatal Orchid Three: Hyakka Ryoran
Fatal Orchid Four: Ryuryoku Kako
Fatal Orchid Five: Hika Rakuyo
Fatal Orchid Six: Kinjo Tenka
Fatal Orchid Seven: Rakka Rozeki

And he had only shown it to his sister *once*!

If he had any chance of taking her down—this was it!

Shichika was certain.

Certain that this move would work against Nanami.

So what if she was a genius or had immaculate eyes? She couldn't see a weakness that *wasn't there*.

This move, which he'd thought up on his own, was truly—

The Last Fatal Orchid of the Kyotoryu!

"Kyotoryu *Shichika Hachire*—"

"And another thing."

Just like that.

As he was about to hit her with the move—Nanami, cool as can be even at that instant, resumed her lecture.

"Forget what's happened in the past six months—you're still way weaker than me."

Watching by the wall.

On the sidelines of the gung-ho battle[23] for the strongest sword in Japan—Emonzaemon and Togame had absolutely no idea what happened.

They saw everything—up until the moment Shichika tried to unleash his secret move.

But it came after.

As if removed[24] from space and time—the next few moments were a total blank. What the hell had happened in this dojo?

The only certain thing was the result.

---

[23] 好対戦　KŌTAISEN　good match
[24] 切り取った　KIRITOTTA　sliced out

Akuto the Eel

Shichika was stuffed in the ceiling—all six-plus-feet of his substantial body.

Having busted through the panels, he was stuck up there, supine, although the question of whether he was facing up or down might be a matter of semantics.

Apparently conscious.

He gazed straight down at his sister—in a daze.

But she didn't bother looking up.

She merely—

"...*Whew.*"

Sighed and clapped her hands together.

Pam.

There was no way that this sound had rattled the dojo enough to free him, but Shichika tumbled from the ceiling to the planking of the floor—though thanks to his marvelous reflexes,[25] he spun in midair several times and landed safely[26] on all fours, without a sound.

While the same could not be said for the poor ceiling, his back was unscathed.

Sturdy guy.

But—dazed nevertheless.

"Huh?" he peeped. "S-Sis...what the heck was that?"

"Exactly what it felt like, dummy," Nanami answered plainly. "I grabbed the waistband of your hakama and chucked[27] you up into the ceiling—that wasn't any move. Just brute force."

"..."

He knew what happened—knew exactly.

It made sense that Togame and Emonzaemon missed it, over by the wall, but he understood it all too painfully. Although she had caught him totally off-guard, he'd done this once himself, using a feat of strength when no move would suffice—*but he was Shichika.*

Nanami may have been part of the Kyotoryu—but she was different.

As small and as weak as Togame the Schemer.

And sickly to boot, in no condition to be fighting battles—she merely made up for all of that with *her pure genius*!

With genius to spare!

"Th-That makes no sense. Since when do you have the muscle[28]—to toss me up into the air?"

"You really are an idiot, you know that? It doesn't take a genius to comprehend that you haven't just been messing around for the past half a year. But Shichika—it's not like I've been biding my time on the way here either... You mentioned that you fought Konayuki Itezora. Of the Itezoras. In that case—*this monstrous strength* should ring a bell for you."

[25] 運動神経　UNDŌ SHINKEI "motor nerves"
[26] 成功した　SEIKŌ SHITA succeeded; pulled off
[27] ぶん投げる　BUN'NAGERU toss violently
[28] 腕力　WANRYOKU "arm strength"

"...?"

"Ah!"

Shichika seemed like he still wasn't getting it, but Togame cried out so loud that Emonzaemon, beside her by the wall, spun round to see what was the matter.

"N-Nanami—were you the one who wiped out the—"

"Precisely.[29] Keen as ever, Miss Togame."

"Whoa, watch out, Shichika! Nanami has Konayuki's monstrous strength—no, not a pipsqueak[30] like Konayuki—she took on the awesome power of all those grownup Itezoras when she wiped out their village!"

"V-Village?" Shichika's eyes went wide. "But how—I thought their village was buried in an avalanche?"

"An avalanche can't happen on a mountaintop," Nanami gibed.[31] "I'm surprised that anyone survived... But considering you wound up with the sword I left for you, things turned out fine. In answer to your question, Miss Togame—yes. I'm the one who brought the Itezora village to its ruin."

"I knew a monster crushed Mt. Shirei..."

Shichika's voice trembled as he spoke—

As if he couldn't believe his own ears.

As if he couldn't believe his eyes.

"How come—you had to destroy their entire village?"

"Huh?"

"Come on, sis—you could have just taken the sword. Same goes for Mt. Shirei—and for this temple, too! Why'd you have to wipe them out? Thanks to you, poor little Konayuki—"

When they found Konayuki Itezora.

The little girl—was all alone.

"You've started saying some pretty goofy stuff, you know that, Shichika?" Nanami gibed—again. "What's all the fuss *about uprooting a few weeds*? Weeding is fun. Don't tell me, Shichika, that a sword—ought to choose who to kill."

"..."

"Miss Togame, I'm afraid that allowing Shichika to join you—was an error. I'd thought I could rest easy..."

Nanami shot Togame a sidelong glance.

Without flinching, Togame brushed her off.

"You're the one making the mistake, Nanami. I'm free to use my sword however I see fit—am I not?"

"Of course you are."

That was wrongheaded of me, and uncalled for, Nanami backed off—more readily than you might think.

"But that's neither here nor there[32]—listen, Shichika. This just goes to say

---

[29] ご明察　GOMEISATSU　"bright observation"　a polite way to confirm a correct guess
[30] 童　WARASHI　(archaic) child
[31] ぴしゃり　PISHARI　onomatopoeia for slapping shut
[32] 閑話休題　KANWA KYŪDAI　"nix the chit chat"

that on my way here to Gokenji Temple—I, too, have been through hell and back again.[33] I'm not the person you left on the island. Starting with the members of Bug Unit Maniwa—I've had the chance to fight all kinds of people, including the entire Itezora Clan and the Sacred Guardians of Mt. Shirei, not to mention the warrior monks of Gokenji Temple. And I've *absorbed* every single one of them," Nanami said. "*With my eyes.*"

"You fought the Maniwacs too, sis?"

Shichika gulped.

Bug Unit Maniwa...she must have meant the three Maniwa Bosses that Hohoh Maniwa had mentioned disappearing—Chocho Maniwa, Mitsubachi Maniwa, and Kamakiri Maniwa.

In other words, Nanami was no longer only versed in swordplay—she knew ninpo.

"No—no frigging way."[34]

What could be—more frightening.

Hoisting himself up off the floor—Shichika cussed his sister out.[35]

"There's gotta be some things you can't learn by watching them—how the hell can you just look at someone and absorb their monstrous strength?"

"Don't ask me—I just can. It did take a few small adjustments to my *insides*. The only other thing I'll add is that the monstrous strength of the Itezoras goes beyond mere brawn like yours. It's much closer—to a kind of ability.[36] That doesn't mean there aren't some things that I can't watch and learn," Nanami ceded, "but just one look was all it took to figure out that Last Fatal Orchid of yours."

"..."

"Although its shortcoming—escaped me until I tried it out myself."

"Sh-Shortcoming?"

"Ah, so you hadn't noticed. That's nice, Shichika—sounds like you've been fending off a bunch of chumps. Not one of them caught such a glaring shortcoming."

"What—shortcoming..."

Indeed.

Monstrous as the strength of the Itezoras may have been—it was no sufficient explanation for the spectacle a moment earlier. Before Nanami had a chance to subject Shichika to her monstrous strength, he was already unleashing Shichika Hachiretsu.

"That's why I left the island. I had to find you, so I could set you straight—but after this uninspiring display, I've changed my mind. *Don't waste my time—figure it out yourself.*"

Limbs limp, hands dangling at her sides—in Kyotoryu Form Zero, the Ichijiku, Nanami advanced nonchalantly toward her brother.

[33] 戦火を潜り抜け SENKA WO KUGURINUKE "dove through the fires of war"
[34] 無茶苦茶 MUCHA KUCHA a total mess
[35] 毒づく DOKUZUKU spit venom
[36] 能力 NŌRYOKU talent

"Nkk..."

Shichika rushed into Form One, the Suzuran—but failed to hide his panic and distress.

Seeing him like this—Nanami sighed.

Sighing with the best of them.

"Relax—it was cruel[37] of me to say this was a proper fight. You're in no condition to be facing off against me. I'll admit you've gotten stronger in the past six months—but I could stop you with my pinky finger."

With that—Nanami raised her right pinky finger and came toward Shichika.

"...Agh!"

This provocative—nay, humiliating language—enraged Shichika.

Making light of Shichika was bad enough—but she was putting down everybody— Komori Maniwa, Ginkaku Uneri, Meisai Tsuruga, Hakuhei Sabi, Kanara Azekura, Konayuki Itezora—all the enemies that he had fought along the way.

All the worse coming from his sister—but who else?

He couldn't let this slide.

"Like you're so big and strong!"

But Nanami had foreseen—even this outrage.

Losing his patience, Shichika broke from the Suzuran, a defense stance, and came barreling at Nanami. She had a way of making moves so slowly that it wore you down. If anybody should have known this, it was Shichika—but she had pushed him past his limit.

Lots to learn.[38]

Shichika had a long way to go—

One look—and she could tell.

"Here's a medley[39] of our strike moves, from the Hinageshi to the Jinchoge."[40]

This time—not even Shichika understood what happened.

He had no idea what hit him.

And if Shichika, on the receiving end, had no idea, then Togame and Emonzaemon, over by the wall, would have been clueless—

The sounds of impact rattled through the dojo.

Before you could count to five—

Shichika lay crumpled on the floor.

Face up this time—no doubt about it.

Tup.

Nanami placed her foot on Shichika's belly.

"I tweaked the Harlequin Butterfly, for good measure."

He had taken every single hit, unable to evade her, but remained conscious, and somehow *wasn't even injured—just lying on the floor.*

"If I hadn't removed the weight from all my strikes—you'd have died two hundred and seventy-two times over, before you even hit the floor."

[37] 大人げなかった OTONAGE NAKATTA "not grown up" childish
[38] 未熟 MIJUKU unripe
[39] 混成接続 KONSEI SETSUZOKU interlinked
[40] 沈丁花 JINCHŌGE "The Daphne" small, fragrant evergreen shrub

"..."
Shichika was conscious.
Conscious—and yet speechless.
He was at a loss for words.
He could have been dead—
Two hundred and seventy-two times over?
That's what she said.
Not like he'd had the chance to count—but now that she had given him a number, it sounded plausible that she had battered him that many times.
The thought of it—sent shivers down his spine.
"What's wrong, Shichika?"
Nanami took her foot off of his abdomen.[41]

Togame, the referee, had yet to call the fight, but anybody watching would have known who won. The difference in ability was so extreme that you could argue there had been no contest in the first place.
Too soon—for the real deal.
Just like the year before, when the siblings battled on Haphazard Island...
"If you have something to say—come on and say it."
"You're the liar, sis." She had pushed him—so he spat it out. "Whatever happened to just using your pinky?"
"I'm afraid that you weren't listening to me. What I said was 'I could stop you without even using my pinky finger,' which is exactly what I did."
"..."
She told him off so confidently, he dropped it.
Alright, so he had lost his cool and acted like a rookie.
But he wasn't about to beat himself up about it.
He could care less.
But—but.
"Sis—what the hell was that?"
"What?"
"Don't josh me—you couldn't possibly have *strung together* all those moves... There's no way that you have the energy for that. *In your condition*—you're not hitting anyone two hundred and seventy-two times."
"Oh, that."
Nanami nodded.
As if she'd forgotten.
"I can see why you'd have your doubts—even with eyes like these, I can't make myself healthy on my own—"
"..."
Nanami Yasuri had a feeble constitution.
She lacked both energy—and stamina.[42]
The sole blemish to her genius.

---

[41] 腹筋 FUKKIN stomach muscles
[42] 持久力 JIKYŪRYOKU staying power

Her sole weakness—or so it seemed.

"It's like this, Shichika."

To show him what she meant—she pulled open her robe.

Bare to the waist now—just like her brother.

Exposing her bony, pallid body—delicate and slight, devoid of any trace of muscle.

Breasts that made sense for a woman her age.

And thrust between them, in the middle of her chest—*a single dagger.*

Stabbing her—so as to pierce her heart.

"Wha... S-Sis!"

"Calm down. You know how odd the Mutant Blades can be. I'll have you know, this is the only way to wield Akuto the Eel, one of the Twelve Possessed of Kiki Shikizaki. *Charged with lightning, and plugged into my heart, this dagger zaps away my sickness.*"[43]

Like an electric shock.

Akuto the Eel—*revivified* her body!

Digging into her[44]—the dagger took away the pain and soothed her maladies!

Behold!

If this blade could heal the billion maladies festering in her body—then it was truly something else!

"D-Do you mean to say—"

"Indeed, unlike your Last Fatal Orchid, I am now without a weakness or a blind spot."[45]

With these words.

Nanami fixed her clothes and turned her back on Shichika, who simply lay there on the floor—and headed for the exit of the Fifth Hall of Gokenji Temple without so much as waving to Togame and Emonzaemon over by the wall.

On her way out, she called back to her brother.

"Stop daydreaming[46] and we might do this again."

Shichika Yasuri versus Nanami Yasuri.

The battle over Akuto the Eel—had been postponed.

But the suggestion of there being any hope the second time around—was cruel enough to be abusive.

■　■

Back in Ezo atop Mt. Odori, a Level One Disaster Area, when Hohoh Maniwa—one of the Twelve Bosses of the Maniwa, and effectively the head of the entire

---

[43] 強制的に癒される　KYŌSEITEKI NI IYASARERU　coerced into healing
[44] 苦無　KUNAI　a joke on how the characters for ninja knife literally mean "pain" and "none"
[45] 死角　SHIKAKU　"dead angle"　puns on 視覚 SHIKAKU "sense of sight," Nanami's strength
[46] 顔を洗って、出直して　KAO WO ARATTE, DENAOSHITE　wash your face, then come back

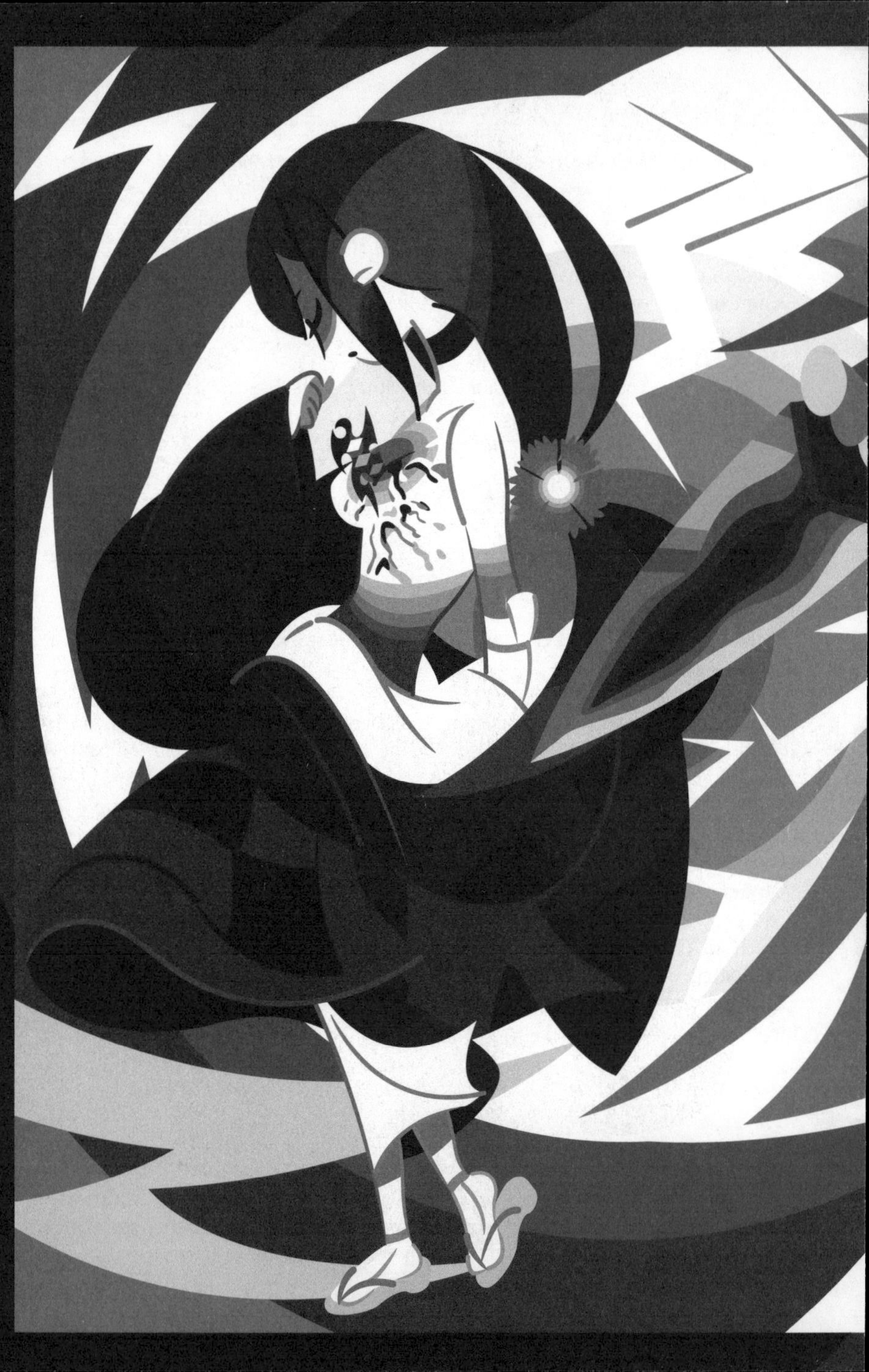

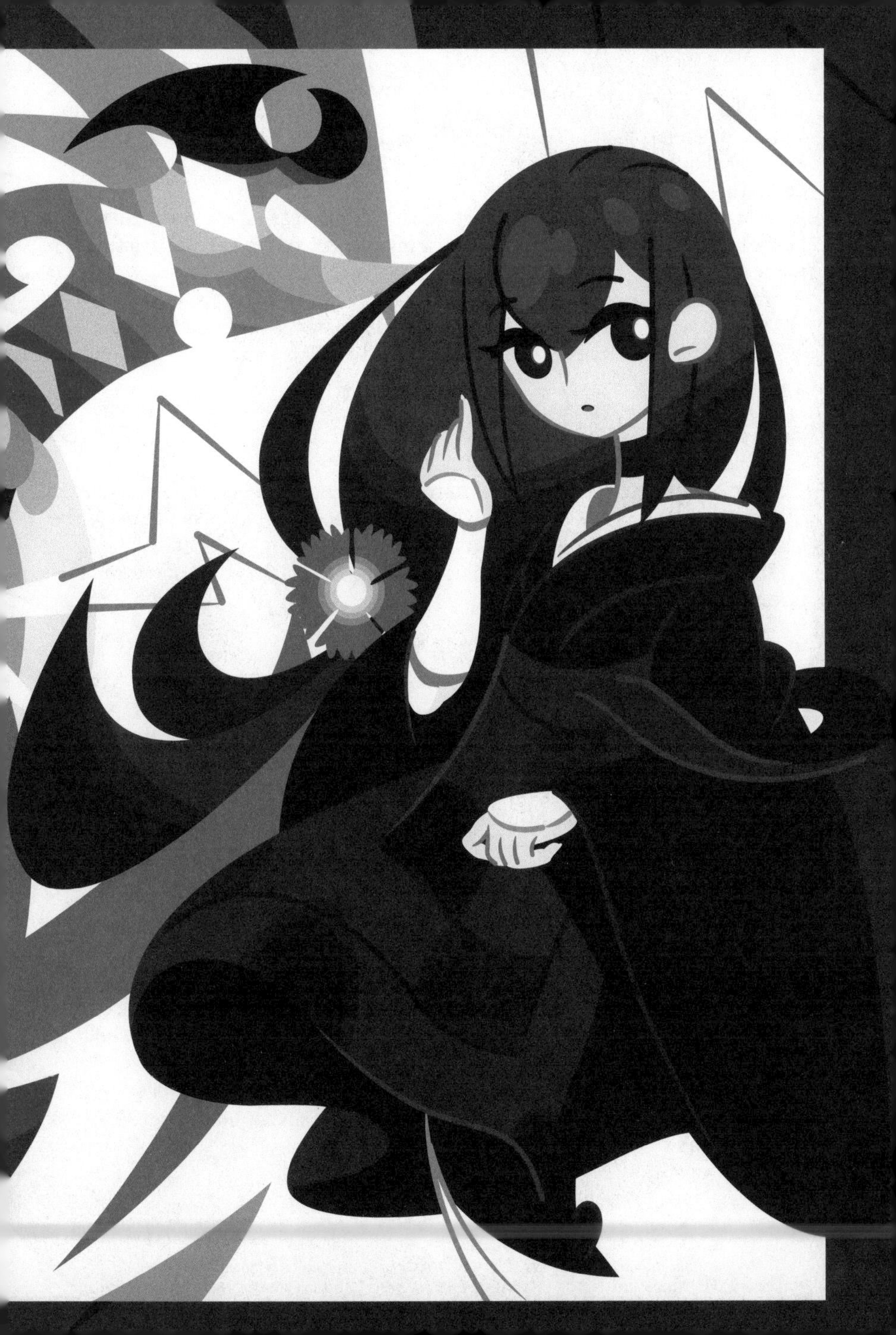

ninja clan—had told them that a "monster" had besieged Mt. Shirei, Togame had scrapped her plan to head back to Owari. Instead, at the harbor in Ezo, she and Shichika had boarded a boat bound for Tosa in Shikoku so that they could chase this monster.

While the voyage down was not exactly a direct route,[47] eventually they made it to a port in Shikoku—where a man in curious dress was waiting for them.

This was the first time Shichika had seen a man wearing a suit.

And on his feet he wore a kind of footwear he had never seen before.

What's more, he wore a mask that covered half his face—and on the mask was the word "NON-NINJA."

This strange getup caught Shichika's eye, but not his interest—while Togame practically exploded when she saw it.

"What the hell are you doing here!" she screamed.

"*Not a word*," he rejoindered. "There should be no need to explain, Madame Schemer—I have some business with you. It's been far too long, but—you're beautiful as ever."

"Skip the pleasantries—hey, Shichika! Get this man out of my sight this instant!"

"A-Are you sure?"

Even Shichika was hesitant to follow this outrageous order.

"*No good*—come now, Madame Schemer. What reason would we have to fight?"

"Cut the crap. Do you honestly think that I don't know of the resurgence[48] of your precious princess? I'm liable to think that you've been on our tail—"

"*Not far off*—that's basically the truth. But this time, I am only here as a liaison—which doesn't mean my eyes aren't open, so to speak, but we have bigger fish to fry. And when I say we—I mean the both of us."

"...?"

"Hey, Togame—who the heck is this guy?" Shichika finally interrupted, no longer able to endure being excluded from the conversation, but Togame seemed bothered by the question.

"Lieutenant Emonzaemon Soda,"[49] she said. "I told you all about Princess Negative on the boat. He's her trusted aide—or rather, sword[50]... They call him 'Emonzaemon the Non-Ninja.' He's a former ninja, and the only person who that nasty hater Princess Negative can deign to trust."

"*Not correct*—you've got it wrong, Madame Schemer. The Princess trusts not even me. As loyal as I am, she denies me—that's what makes her Princess Negative, and what makes me fit to serve her."

"...Weirdo."

---

[47] 最短距離 SAITAN KYORI shortest distance
[48] 復権 FUKKEN return to power
[49] 左右田 SŌDA "left right field" another joke on name conventions
    echoes the affirmative そうだ SŌDA "that is so" despite all the motifs of negativity
[50] 腹心 懐刀 FUKUSHIN FUTOKORO GATANA "belly heart" "pocket katana" both mean "confidant"

"You should talk."
With that—Emonzaemon started walking.
Not so much as bidding them to follow.
But considering the circumstances—like it or not, they had to follow him.
Messenger of Princess Negative.
This was no incidental meeting[51]—at the very least, there had to be some link between Emonzaemon waiting for them portside and the monster who had taken on Mt. Shirei.
They kept a safe distance behind him—so that Shichika, a few steps ahead of Togame, could cover[52] her and keep an eye on the Lieutenant—in case he tried anything funny.
When they had strayed far from the harbor into town, Emonzaemon finally spoke up.
"It's too bad that you keep having to turn back from Owari, Madame Schemer. The Princess misses you."
"Get real, Emonzaemon. When and where did you learn to jest? Have you been banished to the backwater[53] and found someone who truly understands you?"
"*Not one*—I need not find another. No one but the Princess understands me. I mean it when I say she misses you—why don't you catch the next boat home and surprise her with that stunning hair and pretty little face of yours?"
"Is that what you've sailed all the way to Shikoku to tell me?"
"Please."
"I can't see a ninja like you making the Katana Pilgrimage."
"*No ninja*—as you just mentioned, I am not a ninja—only a former ninja. Can't you read my mask? These days I make my living as a swordsman—and what's so strange about a swordsman visiting Gokenji Temple?"
To be sure, Emonzaemon had two katanas slung from his waist, although they didn't exactly match his bespoke style.
A pair of swords—one big, one small.[54]
Shichika had spotted them the second they stepped off the boat.
—*Those can't be Shikizaki blades.*
They don't have any lifeforce.
Normal swords.
"What's so strange, you say... Lt. Emonzaemon, do you really mean to tell me that you're making the Katana Pilgrimage?"
"Effectively, I am. But Madame Schemer—I do actually have a message for you from the Princess. An order from on high.[55] As you continue with your Sword Hunt..."
"Does this involve what happened at Mt. Shirei?"

[51] ただごと TADAGOTO commonplace occurrence
[52] 庇う KABAU protect
[53] 左遷 SASEN "send leftward" relegate to a lower position
[54] 大小二本 DAISHŌ NIHON the customary combo of a long and short katana
[55] 上意 JŌI the will of an authority

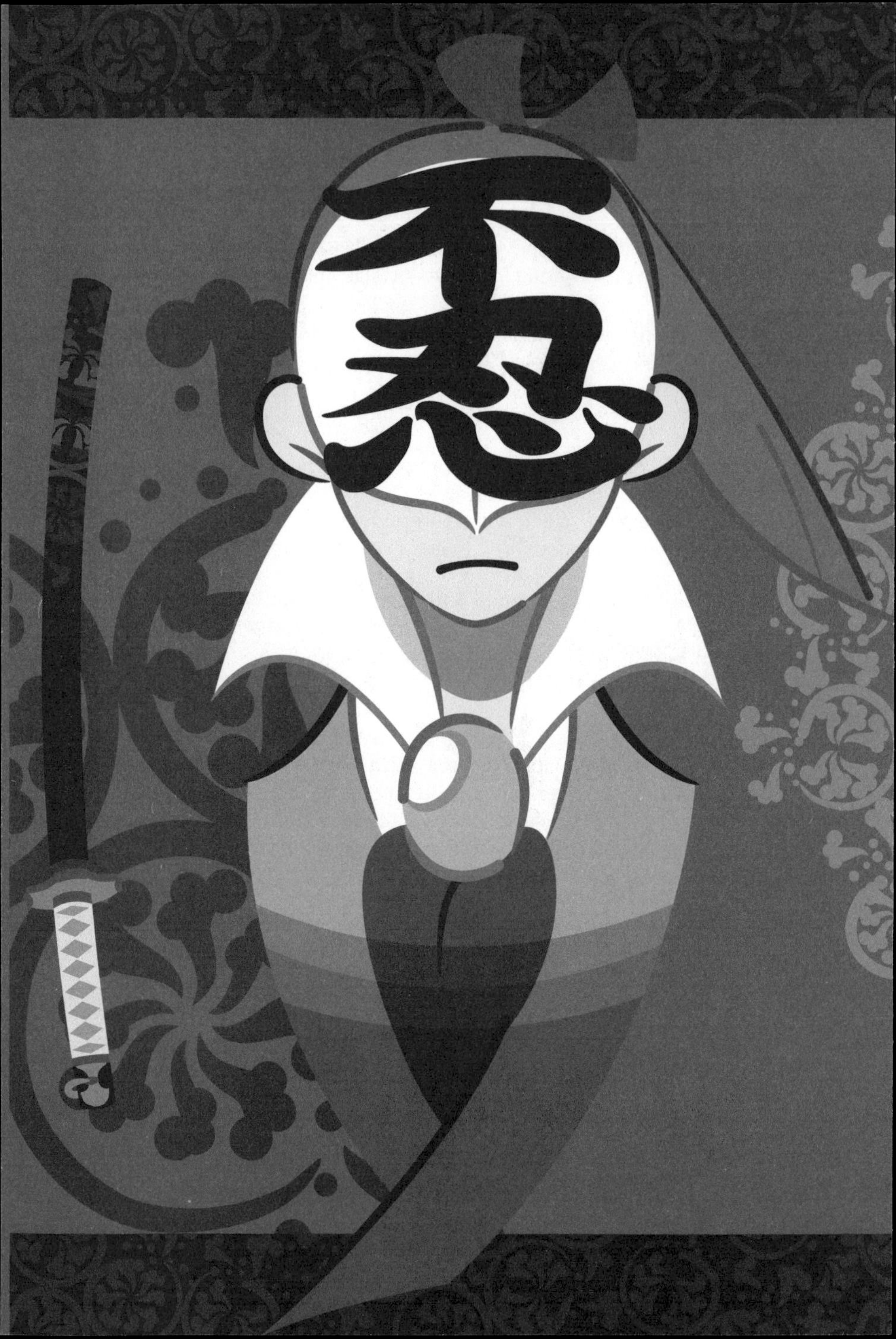
忍

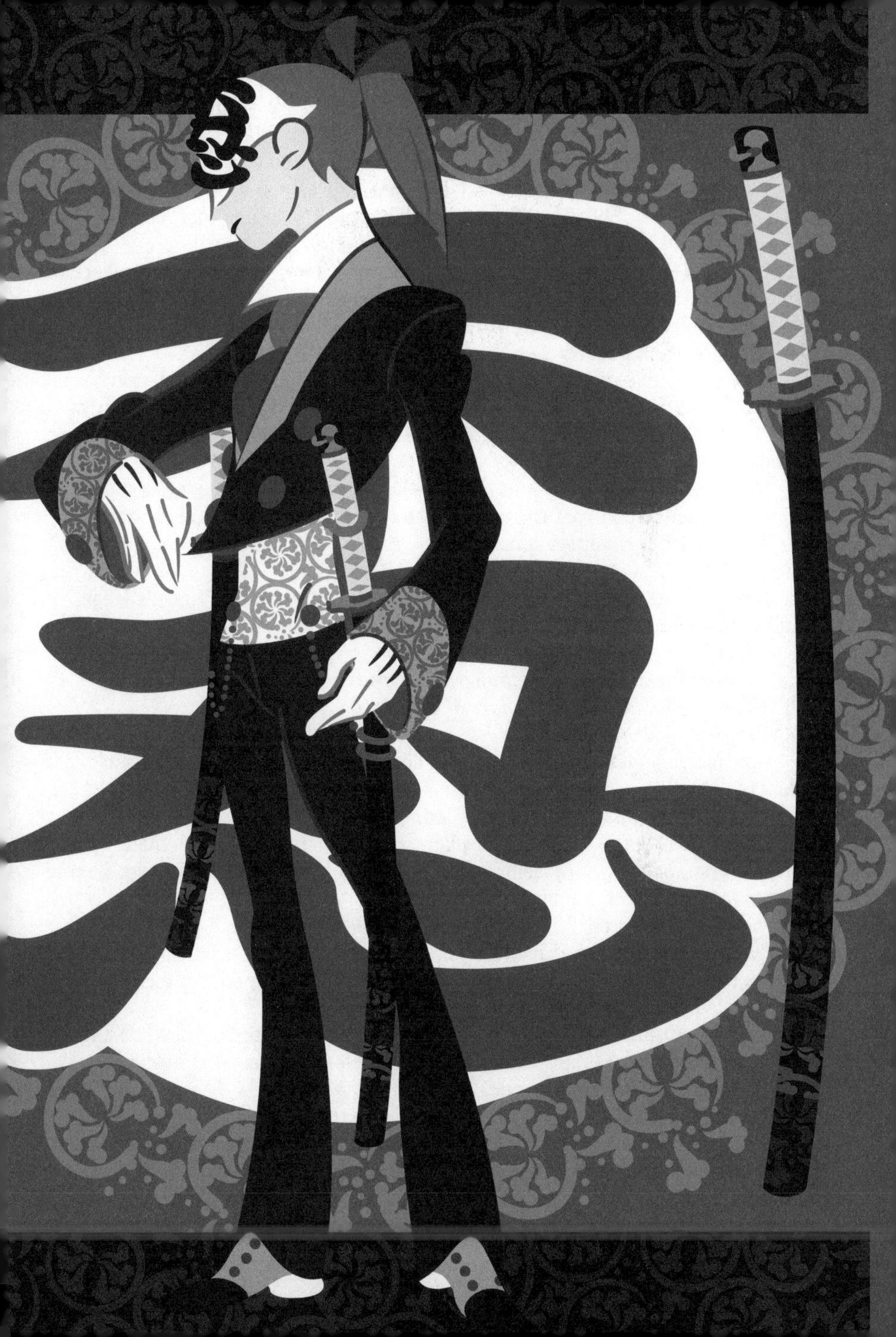

"In fact, it does. You are to catch and—if necessary—finish the butcher. It would appear this butcher also has one of the Mutant Blades of Kiki Shikizaki you've been hunting—so essentially, you're being asked to do your job."

"Thanks for the reminder," said Togame, "but as you well know, that is exactly why we're in Shikoku. We were just about to try to find that *monster*—or, as you say, the butcher."

"*No need*—finding the butcher won't be necessary. I know exactly where to find the butcher... That's why I've come here. That I might save you from going to the trouble."

"Impressive... Fast as ever."

"*No dice*—flattery will get you nowhere, Madame Schemer. I won't soon forget the countless times that you've besmirched the Princess's credibility."

"Fair enough—in that case, why not kill me off? Assuming you can take on Shichika."

"As much as I admire his allegiance—*not this time*. I'm not confident enough in my abilities to confront the swordsman who disposed of Hakuhei Sabi."

The barbed formalities continued.

Shichika was getting pretty bored.

It seemed as if Togame had something of a history with Princess Negative and Emonzaemon—but he was not about to ask her to elaborate.

—Still.

Between the Maniwacs, Hakuhei Sabi, and Princess Negative...

Togame sure has her fair share of enemies.

Did everybody hate her?

Considering what she was trying to accomplish in the bakufu, it wasn't that farfetched.

"So, where's this butcher of ours hiding?"

"*Not hiding*—the culprit is in plain sight. Out in the open—that flagrant murderer is on Mt. Sayabashiri, staying at Seiryoin Gokenji Temple...having commandeered[56] the temple."

"C-Commandeered?" Togame asked. "What do you mean?"

"Exactly what I said," Emonzaemon answered. "Having cut through half the warrior monks that call the temple home...and when I say *cut*,[57] I mean it—the butcher is pretending to be some guest of honor."

"I suppose that isn't beyond a monster who blew the top off of Mt. Shirei in no time," admitted Togame, "but Gokenji Temple...that makes it even worse."

"Worse? Why is that, Togame?"

"I mean, Gokenji is a place of worship. Women are forbidden[58] from a portion of the compound. If the butcher is behaving like a guest of honor—he must have access to the innermost reaches of the compound, which as a woman I do not."

---

[56] 乗っ取った　NOTTOTTA　taken over
[57] 惨殺 斬殺　ZANSATSU ZANSATSU　murder savagely　murder with a blade
[58] 女人禁制　NYONIN KINSEI　"no girls allowed"

"*No need*—don't worry, Madame Schemer. At this point, their custom of barring women past a certain point is moot.[59] For the butcher whose might has brought Gokenji Temple to its knees, this monster—is a woman."

"I-Is that so?"

"*Nanami Yasuri.*"

With these words—Emonzaemon Soda turned.

Leveling his gaze on Shichika.

"She is the one who plunged Mt. Shirei, a Level One Disaster Area, into ruin, the one whose fist has closed around Seiryoin Gokenji Temple, holy land of swordsmen—and the owner now of Akuto the Eel."

"Huh?"

This news baffled Shichika Yasuri.

At any rate.

In three more days—he would have his moving[60] family reunion in the Fifth Hall of Gokenji Temple.

---

[59] あってなきがごとし ATTE NAKI GA GOTOSHI "there, but as good as not"
[60] 感動の KANDŌ NO emotional sounds no less sarcastic in original

CHAPTER TWO

EMONZAEMON SODA

■ ■

In a corner of the town built up around Owari Castle, and cloistered in a copse of trees, we find a residence fit for a samurai—and known to some as Mansion Negative—within one room of which a woman, posture rigid, paused in thought.

As if waiting for something.

But just then, a voice issued from the ceiling—

"Your Highness," the voice said. "I've returned—it is I, Emonzaemon Soda."

Hearing the voice overhead, the woman said, "You're late," negging[1] him from the get-go.

Princess Negative.

Inspector General of the Yanari Shogunate—

Nobody knew her actual name.

"Every single time. Do you realize how long you've kept me waiting? Fool."

"...I'm terribly sorry."

"And? What happened in Shikoku?"

Princess Negative cut to the chase.[2]

Waiting might have been her job, but it would seem that she had finished for the day.

"That silly rumor that's been going around about Mt. Shirei—how much of it did you bring to light?"

"As it so happens—all of it."

"All of it? So the entire thing's—a lie?"

"The entire thing—is true."

Thus spoke the voice in the ceiling—Emonzaemon.

"This goes beyond the incident at Mt. Shirei. As much as it dismays me to convey this information—Nanami Yasuri, the sister of the Kyotoryu...is an absolute monster."

Thus Emonzaemon apprised his superior, Princess Negative, of every single thing he witnessed[3] in Shikoku—on Mt. Sayabashiri in Tosa, at Seiryoin Gokenji Temple, the holy land of swordsmen.

At first the Princess grinned at the absurdity of the tale—but by the time that it was finished there was no trace of a smile on her face.

Princess Negative was weary.

"You and I have been together quite some time. Among the many things I'm proud of is the startling fact that I have never once gone easy on you... But now, I cannot help but sympathize[4] with you—I'm sorry that you had to come here with that crazy story."

[1] 否定的なことを言う HITEITEKI NA KOTO WO IU say something negative, i.e. put down
[2] 本題に入る HONDAI NI HAIRU bring up the main topic
[3] 見聞き MIKIKI "see and hear"
[4] 同情 DŌJŌ "same feeling"

"Your Highness, I am not worthy of your sympathy," Emonzaemon said ceremoniously.

Princess Negative rubbed her forehead[5] with her finger.

"Did you say—she wiped out the Itezoras?" she asked. "How on earth did she manage that? Am I correct this was before the *sister* acquired Akuto the Eel?"

"Indeed—which only goes to show it's not the Mutant Blade that makes her such a monster. As I mentioned, she has also mastered many of the ninpo stylings of the Maniwa—"

"In which case, we can assume that she has taken on the tactics of the Sacred Guardians of Mt. Shirei, and the swordplay of the warrior monks of Gokenji Temple... Fighting only makes her stronger. She doesn't even need to lift a finger—with those eyes."

"Quite right, Your Highness," Emonzaemon assented meekly. "It would seem—that we're in a bit of a fix."

"A bit of a fix? I'm more than glad to see the best-made plans of our little Schemer go awry, but I will not tolerate us being dragged into the mess she's made. How could we let this happen? Those schemes of hers keep throwing us for a loop. Whether they get her anywhere or not aside—I mean, it's a good thing that she's dragged the Kyotoryu to the surface, but I'm afraid she's dredged up a monster in the process."

"Your Highness—Nanami Yasuri is also of the Kyotoryu."

"But what about that Mutant Blade of hers?" the Princess probed. "I would think the Eel disqualifies her from the Kyotoryu."

"..."

"Anyway, how did it go? This duel between Shichika Yasuri and Nanami Yasuri—you say they've scheduled a rematch, but does Shichika have any chance of winning?"

"None," Emonzaemon answered succinctly, betraying no uncertainty whatsoever. "This isn't just about Shichika Yasuri. That woman—cannot be stopped."

"Not even—by Hakuhei Sabi, for instance?"

"No. While Sabi truly was a genius—he was nowhere near as genius as Nanami Yasuri. If...it pains me even to imagine this, but even if a swordsman who surpassed her genius were to challenge her—*those eyes of hers* would make his *every strength* her own, post-haste."

"*Watch and Learn...*"

Seeing.

Seeing everything.[6]

Seeing through things.[7]

Seeing into things.[8]

---

[5] 眉間　MIKEN　"space between eyebrows"
[6] 見切り　MIKIRI　figure out　切る　KIRU　slice
[7] 見抜き　MINUKI　unmask　抜く　NUKU　remove
[8] 見定め　MISADAME　determine　定める　SADAMERU　decide

Seeing beyond things.[9]
Seeing to the end of things.[10]
Seeing made them hers.[11]

"Fighting is all about compatibility[12]—strength and weakness being two sides of the same coin, even the strongest enemy can be beaten, if they meet their match... But I'm afraid this maxim does not hold for Nanami Yasuri. Were she to ever meet her match, her enemy would automatically meet theirs."

"Quit joking," Princess Negative laughed.

At this point, what else was there to do?

"I have to ask you, then, for my own erudition. If it was you—how would you take on Nanami Yasuri?"

"*Not fighting*," Emonzaemon said, brushing off this unkind question from the Princess. "I am not foolish enough to take on a foe I have no chance of beating—I would much rather put my effort into avoiding confrontation altogether."

"Just the sort of answer I'd expect from an ex-ninja. But what would you do if you found a conflict unavoidable?"

"I would buy myself some time," replied Emonzaemon. "Enough time—to make sure that you had a chance to flee."

"Gold Star,"[13] said Princess Negative—before delving into thought.

You could see it in her face.

"Of course, I'd just as soon avoid a conflict—but if Nanami Yasuri has Akuto the Eel, we cannot simply look the other way... A dagger that revitalizes and replenishes—*I'd heard of this before*, but that makes it no less of a threat. Wielded properly, it can be used to raise an undead, undefeatable[14] army. But I thought that no single human being could exercise its full potential. I'm quite impressed that Nanami Yasuri could pick up Akuto the Eel with zero guidance... I suppose we have her eyes to thank for this as well?"

"I'm afraid so," Emonzaemon admitted. "But be that as it may—how can the Eel revitalize its owner? Saying it is one thing—"

"Hello! This is a Mutant Blade of Kiki Shikizaki. At this point, do you really need an explanation? If I had to say, I suppose it works a lot like acupuncture."[15]

"*Aku*—puncture?"

"Hence the name,"[16] said Princess Negative. "Anyway, atop Mt. Shirei, they kept the Eel inside a shrine that it might fill the mountain with vitality, although it wasn't actually thrust into the earth... Apparently not even the Sacred Guardians knew how to wield the Eel correctly. It took true genius to realize this was necessary. Still—even locked up in the shrine, it worked its wonders. But

---

[9] 見通し MITŌSHI prognosticate 通す TŌSU push through
[10] 見極め MIKIWAME ascertain 極める KIWAMERU master
[11] 見取る MITORU "look take" perceive puns on 看取る MITORU attend to a dying person
[12] 相性 AISHŌ affinity
[13] 花丸 HANAMARU a circular floral design used to mark a student's job well done
[14] 不死不滅 FUSHI FUMETSU "not dying, not perishing"
[15] 針治療 HARI CHIRYŌ "needle therapy"
[16] 薄刀『針』 HAKUTŌ HARI "The Thin Sword: Needle" (the original puns on an earlier Mutant Blade)

without Akuto the Eel—its source of life—Mt. Shirei will fall apart."
"Mt. Shirei—a Level One Disaster Area?"
"Just as she massacred the Itezoras of Mt. Odori... We can only hope she has her way with Lake Fuyo in Edo as well."
"How mischievous of you."
"Mischievous? I suppose—but I'm not so sure we'll have the last laugh. Now that this monster has armed herself with such a menacing weapon—left unchecked,[17] she could overthrow the bakufu. Weren't the Yasuris banished to that island? Who needs a better reason to resent the government?"
"It would seem the Schemer—plans to stop her."
"I wouldn't count on her for anything—that woman never thinks of anyone but herself. She let on like the Sword Hunt was the best thing for the nation, but the only thing it benefits is her career. By the way, how is Togame? That old busted[18] girl."
"She's fine. In fact, a bit too fine—along the way to Gokenji Temple, she kept on kicking me and claiming that it was an accident."
"She has a childish way about her..."
"She got depressed after the battle in the dojo...but if there's one thing you can say about Togame, it's that she always bounces back."
"And hatches another one of her schemes," said Princess Negative. "Well, I'm glad to hear she's in good health. Otherwise our rivalry would be no fun. But the way things stand—it's like our hands are tied. I can't imagine where we'd go from here..."
"For the time being, why not start by figuring out what Nanami Yasuri meant by the weakness of the Last Fatal Orchid?"
"The weakness of... Oh, you mean Shichika Hachiretsu? That's easy. I figured it out just by listening to you. She must have seen it instantly."
"Y-You mean you see it too?"
Emonzaemon was blown away.
"I can't be absolutely sure," demurred the Princess, "but considering the details of your report—it seems to me that any effort to offset or overcome this weakness is in vain. Faced with the overwhelming strength of Nanami Yasuri."
"Indeed... I personally can't think of what this weakness might entail, but if Shichika Yasuri wants to beat his sister—he needs to fundamentally revise his strategy."
"Not his strategy," the Princess sneered. "His scheme. Togame calls herself the Schemer—because scheming is the only thing she knows. Last time around, she kept her mouth shut, watching quietly from the sidelines, perhaps to keep her sword from losing face...but next time, you can trust things will be different. I am certain she will try some kind of scheme—and act like it was all part of the plan.[19] There's just one thing I can't quite understand. This sister of

---

[17] 最悪　SAI'AKU　worst (case)
[18] 不愉快　FUYUKAI　unpleasant
[19] 仕上げをごろうじろ　SHIAGE WO GORŌJIRO　"behold the finish"
　　　shortened from a longer expression, the gist of which is: "the proof is in the pudding"

the Kyotoryu—Nanami Yasuri. *What's her agenda? What is she trying to do?* What makes entrenching[20] herself in Gokenji Temple absolutely necessary? I know that other countries fight over their holy lands, but that rarely ever happens here. I simply can't figure it out—but I fear that it spells trouble."

"Shall I head back?" Emonzaemon asked the Princess. "If the Schemer's scheme allows them to take down Nanami Yasuri—I should like to have a front-row seat."

"Perhaps... No, let's hold off. That woman hates you and me to death—we don't want her to lose her focus. Ordinarily, I wouldn't be so generous, but this time we have no choice... I know their odds of winning are one in a million, but that Schemer always seems to find the one way out."

"Speaking of losing focus," said Emonzaemon, as if he just remembered something.

Nay.

This former ninja—could not possibly have forgotten.

"We would do well—to consider what her nemeses, the Maniwa, are doing. The Schemer tells me they've made some kind of an alliance, or an armistice—"

"Ah yes...the Maniwa. But haven't they already lost over half the bosses? Let's see... Nanami Yasuri wiped out the entire Bug Unit, taking out three more—she sure does like cracking skulls—then last month, at Mt. Odori in Ezo, a couple more...which leaves them with, what—four? Those guys are a lost cause. Forget about them."

"I'm afraid that would be premature—not if Hohoh Maniwa's still with us," Emonzaemon answered Princess Negative's dismissive[21] jab in a grave tone. "That ninja is running the show—if all the bosses perished, but for him, the Maniwa would still give you a run for your money."

"I see. Coming from you, that's quite the warning—but as long as the alliance stands, she should be in the clear. At the very least, I don't expect they'll show up in Shikoku—if they aren't acting up, we'll look the other way. Now, I trust you told that nasty woman to hurry back home to Owari as soon as she can manage?"

"I did. I'm sure Owari is their next stop—once they've dealt with Nanami Yasuri and Akuto the Eel."

That being said.

The odds of this were pitifully[22] low.

Could they actually deal with Nanami Yasuri—and Akuto the Eel?

"Yes," said Princess Negative, as if she had detected her lieutenant's mute apprehension. "In that case—I will wait."

---

[20] 立てこもる TATEKOMORU hole up
[21] おざなり OZANARI slapdash
[22] 著しく ICHIJIRUSHIKU manifestly

■ ■

Although not designated as a Level One Disaster area like Mt. Odori in Ezo, Mt. Shirei in Mutsu, and Lake Fuyo in Edo—the greenwood[23] spreading from the pediment[24] of Mt. Fuji were known in this era of Japan as dangerous terrain, to be entered at your own risk.
Greenwood.
Just as the word suggests—it was a world of green.
In contrast to your average forest—this was a place where plants, not animals, held sway.
Through the churlish heat and moisture of this vegetative realm—two men walked without breaking a sweat.
The first was young.
Tall and slender, long black hair cascading down his back. Expressionless, and yet his eyes possessed a glint of violence.
The second, a squat fellow, looked even younger, to the point he could have passed for a mere boy. Noticeably cautious, he plodded after the expressionless man ahead of him.
Though it would seem that they had not a thing in common—their outfits were the same.
Sleeveless ninja garb.
Chains wrapped around their bodies—both of them.
Yes.
The man walking ahead was one of the Twelve Bosses of the Maniwa—Hohoh Maniwa.
And the man behind him was another of the Twelve Bosses—Pengin Maniwa.
The Divine Phoenix—and *Pengin the Breeder*—walked together through the greenwood at the base of Mt. Fuji.
"I wonder—how things are going?" asked Hohoh out of nowhere.
Though startled, Pengin managed to respond.
"Wh-Wh-Wh-What do you mean?"
"You know, down in Shikoku. I'm sure by now the Schemer and the Kyotoryu have made it to Gokenji Temple—"
"You mean the family showdown..." Pengin said. "Not once did I suspect this...that the monster who destroyed Mt. Shirei was the sister of the Kyotoryu..."
"It wasn't just Mt. Shirei. Mt. Odori also met its ruin—when the sister of the Kyotoryu, Nanami Yasuri, came to town. That is, according to the intel that you gathered in the aftermath."
"Y-Yes..."

[23] 樹海　JUKAI　"sea of trees"
[24] 裾野　SUSONO　"skirting fields"　gentle slope at the base of a mountain

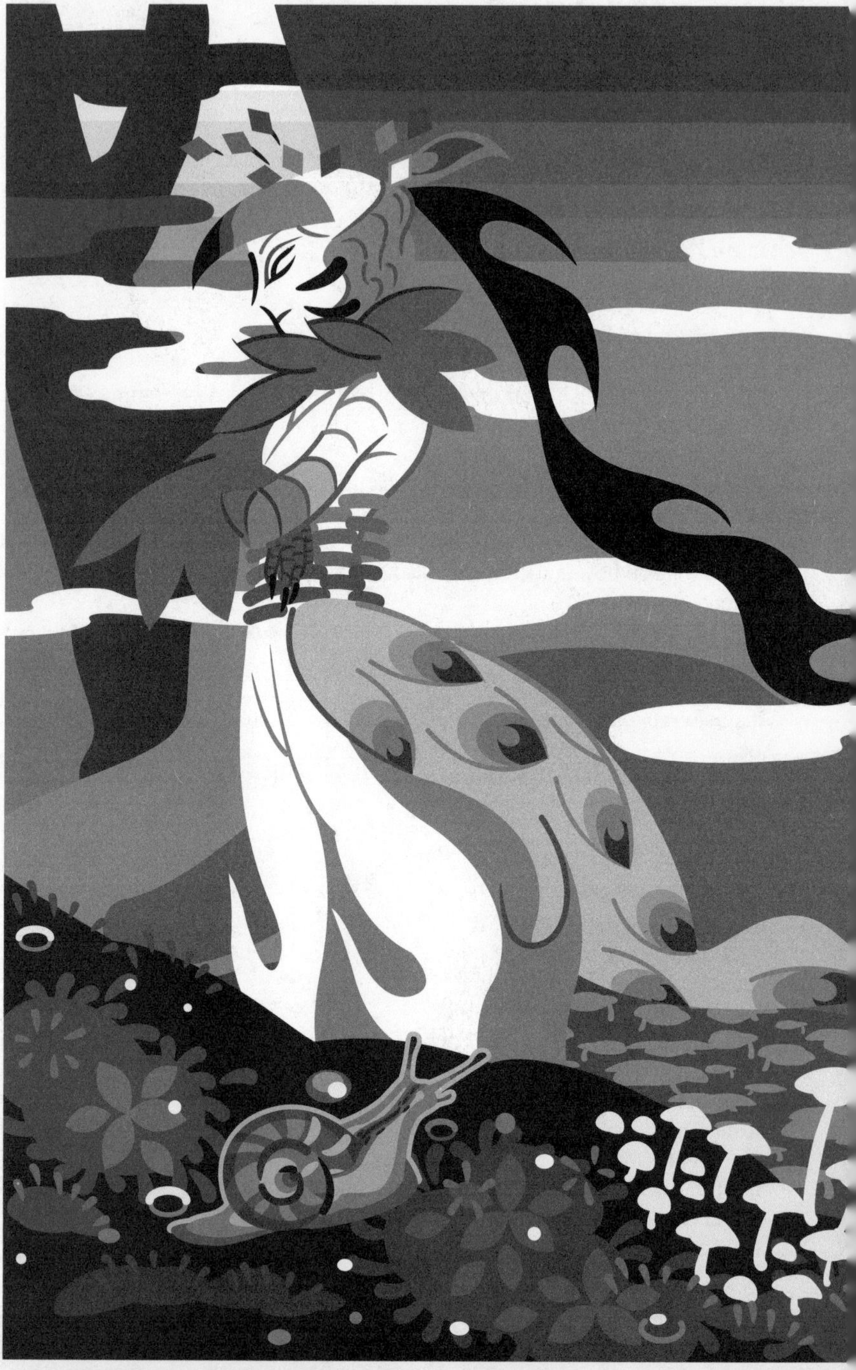

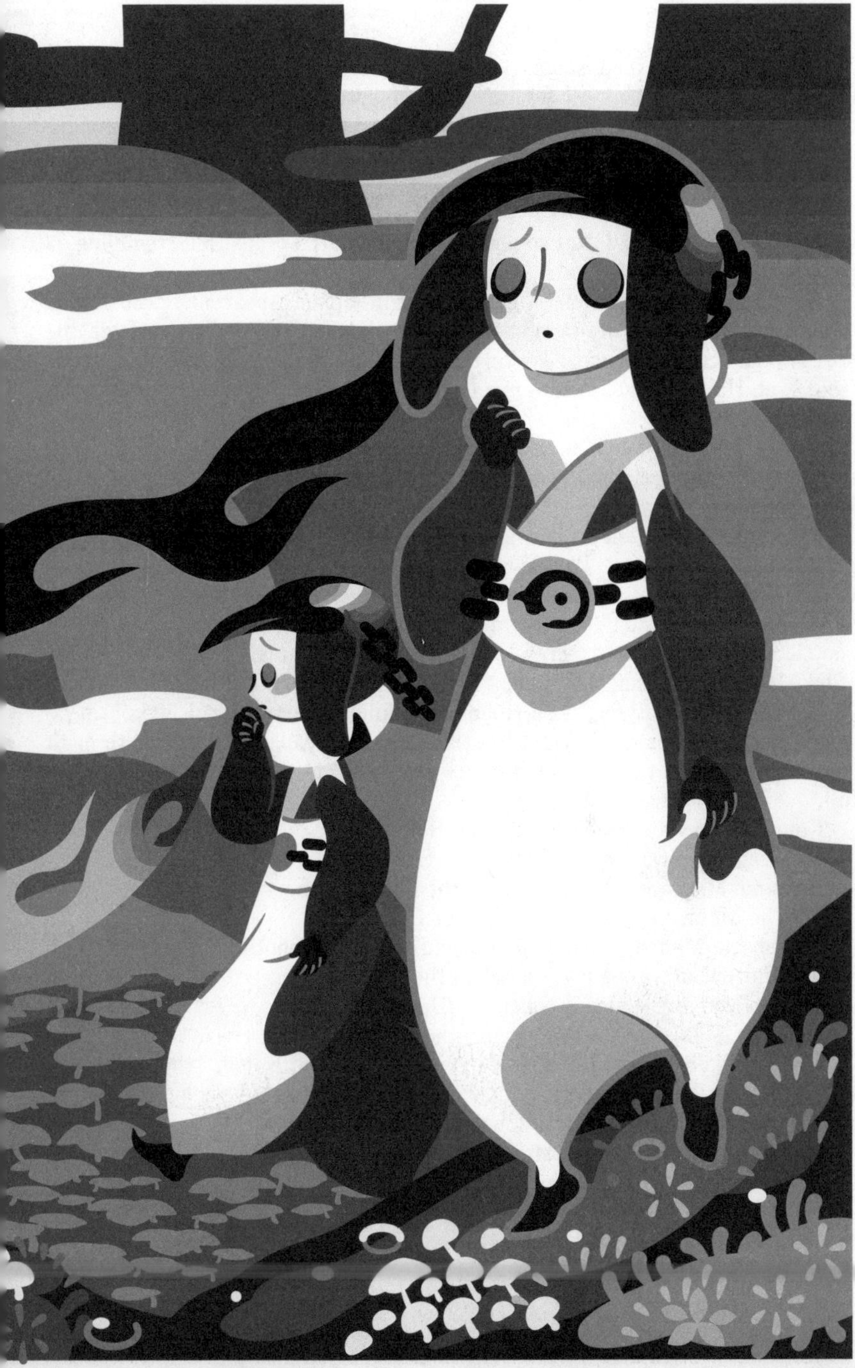

"But that's not all. It seems Nanami Yasuri killed every member of our brethren in the Bug Unit—I say this like it's news to you, when you're the one who found it out. Honestly, Pengin, sometimes I marvel at your powers of reconnaissance. Well done."

"It-It-It's...nothing, really."

Shaking.

Pengin hung his head. Not so much shying from the praise, but trembling all over, terrified.

"Nanami Yasuri—was once the strongest in Japan." Apparently accustomed to this sort of thing from Pengin—unshaken, Hohoh trudged on through the greenwood. "Still," he said. "We're talking about someone in another league from even Hakuhei Sabi. Assuming all of your intelligence is true, I gotta say, our hands are tied."

"I hate to break it to you...but every word of it—is true." Though his voice trembled, Pengin spoke with conviction. "I suppose by now—she's brought Gokenji Temple to its knees."

"What better person to roll into the holy land of swordsmen—no, not a person—she's a monster. Well now, what to do about the Schemer. Any warrior worth their salt knows that no plot[25] or scheme gets past an actual genius."

"B-But the Schemer—is no warrior. She might come up with something good... She better, or we're screwed... Out of the four remaining bosses, not one of us would stand a chance[26] against her...including you, Sir Hohoh."

"Thanks for clarifying," said Hohoh, smirking at this unvarnished observation. "But you're absolutely right—if that mad dog Kyoken was still with us, it would be a different story...but maybe even Kyoken would have had her paws full."[27]

Komori Maniwa—a.k.a. Komori the Hell-Made.
Shirasagi Maniwa—a.k.a. Backwords Shirasagi.
Kuizame Maniwa—a.k.a. Kuizame the Sand Trap.
Chocho Maniwa—a.k.a. Flying Butter Chocho.
Mitsubachi Maniwa—a.k.a. Mitsubachi the Sharpshooter.
Kamakiri Maniwa—a.k.a. Kamakiri the Head Hunter.
Kyoken Maniwa—a.k.a. Kyoken the Dogged Scourge.
Kawauso Maniwa—a.k.a. Kawauso the Nosey Otter.

"Of the Twelve Bosses of the Maniwa," proclaimed Hohoh, "there are only four survivors. We cannot spare another loss—which means we have to let the Schemer eliminate the monster for us."

"Shichika Yasuri may be strong...but up against a genius—he's bound to suffer."

"This is a family feud[28]...but if things don't work out in our favor, and that monster winds up siding with the Schemer—the Maniwa have no hopes for the

[25] 秘策 HISAKU "secret plan"
[26] 太刀打ち TACHI UCHI "(exchange) broadsword strikes" compete, match the mettle
[27] 無理だった MURI DATTA "found it impossible" [a canine joke seemed a permissible liberty]
[28] 骨肉の争い KOTSUNIKU NO ARASOI "fight of flesh and bone" warring between blood relatives

future."

Pengin gave this a moment's thought.

"That strikes me...as unlikely," he opined. "I would imagine that the Schemer and Nanami—would have an awful hard time getting along."

"Yes—you have a point. That's right, you've met the Schemer, haven't you? Hmm. Let's not forget, we also have to worry about Princess Negative. Either way, we only have so many options. I'm sure that Umigame and Oshidori have been fighting the good fight[29] since we split up. So long as this alliance with the Schemer is in play, we'll have to keep on questing for the swords—whoa."

Hohoh stopped midstride.

Before a wind cave at the foot of Mt. Fuji.

"I think we're here."

"Y-Yes..."

"Leave it to Pengin the Breeder—every last one of your leads has legs."

"On the contrary...we wouldn't be here if it weren't for your *left arm*. Or wait—" Pengin shook his head. "I guess technically—*Kawauso's arm*."

"Yeah." Hohoh swung his left arm in a circle, as if to confirm its existence. "He wasn't called the Nosey Otter for nothing. I was worried about the accuracy since *it was attached only recently*—but it looks like there's no need."

Kawauso Maniwa—one of the Twelve Bosses of the Maniwa Ninja Clan.

The ninja who had met his end the month before, on Mt. Odori in Ezo.

Whose ninpo, dubbed the Infovac, enabled him to glean the history of objects.

And now his ninpo—*was in the hands of Hohoh Maniwa*.

Since his left arm—was Kawauso Maniwa's left arm!

"*Life Line*.[30] Man, that pirate's was garbage[31]... Makes me appreciate just how marvelous this new arm really is."

"I'm sure that Kawauso...would be proud. Even in death, he has become a part of you, and taken on new life—"

"Let's hope you're right."

Hohoh sounded concerned.

Long story short, the two of them had made it this far—through a synthesis[32] of Pengin's information network and the late Kawauso's Infovac.

Last month, to make up for Kyoken running amok, Hohoh renewed his stake in the alliance by felling his own brother, Kawauso, but it was not a total loss.

Although Kawauso was dead.

Hohoh had taken on his ninpo—thus.

That former ninja Emonzaemon had been eerily correct in his prediction—the Maniwa were alive and kicking.

Ever a menace to the Sword Hunt of the bakufu—

"Come on. I think *it's here*, inside this wind cave."

---

29 頑張って GANBATTE hanging in there; hustling also the most generic of exhortations
30 忍法命結び NINPŌ INOCHI MUSUBI 命 INOCHI life 結ぶ MUSUBU to tie (a knot), connect
31 役立たず YAKU TATAZU useless
32 合わせ技 AWASEWAZA combination of two different moves

"Yes," Pengin nodded. He sounded quite sure—and went in first.

Hohoh crossed his arms and followed close behind.

"Still...I don't get it."

Even once they had both slipped into the cave, the two of them had pep in their step.

Not worried about their footing or where the cave was taking them, as if it was their backyard—they carried on at normal speed.

"D-Don't get...what?"

"Well, Nanami Yasuri—from what you've gathered, she's a genius, and has immaculate eyes, right?"

"Y-Yes... Watch and Learn, they call it... There is no move or form that she can't figure if she sees it once, and master if she sees it twice—she sees it all. As much[33] for swordplay as for ninpo... Most likely she knows every trick in the Bug Unit book by now."

"Hmm. I bet you're right. But hold on, Pengin—something's fishy."

"Fishy?"[34]

"The ninpo that I used to make Kawauso's mine, the Life Line, may take a different route, but it has lots in common with Nanami Yasuri's Watch and Learn. Same goes for Kyoken Maniwa's Foaming Mouth—it usurps another's form and memories. Not to mention Komori Maniwa's Body Melt, which let him morph his body in the shape of whomsoever he pleased."

"Okay?"

Pengin looked perplexed, not getting what Hohoh wanted to say.

Life Line.

Foaming Mouth.

Body Melt.

And—Watch and Learn.

Indeed, these moves had something in common.

"Of course, the finer points show just how different they are—my Life Line, for instance, starts with killing off your counterpart, whereas the Foaming Mouth presumes its user is dead. Meanwhile, the Body Melt can only imitate the vessel.[35] None of them approaches Watch and Learn."

"...Nope."

The technique was extraordinary.[36]

Nanami Yasuri—Watch and Learn.

"But here's my issue, as somebody whose ninpo has a thing or two in common. Does Nanami Yasuri...really need to watch or learn?"

"..."

Totally lost, Pengin failed to even summon a response.

"Like—isn't Nanami Yasuri phenomenal already, without all these extra moves?"

[33] 等価 TŌKA equivalent
[34] 不自然 FUSHIZEN unnatural 不 FU non- 自然 SHIZEN nature
[35] 器 UTSUWA container
[36] 並外れた NAMIHAZURETA exceptional 並み NAMI average 外れる HAZURERU be removed from

"A-Ah."
Pengin finally understood what Hohoh had been driving at.
"Th-That's what you mean..."
"Yeah. 'Course—her Watch and Learn does let her size up her opponent and identify their weaknesses, I guess. But matching the enemy in terms of strength is what it's supposed to be for. It started when she was a girl. Her father wouldn't teach her anything, so she had to watch and learn for herself—with those *eyes* of hers. But now, no one as strong as her needs them. Tricks only make sense when they make up for a weakness. The strongest—have no use for them."

"And yet, she's gone to lots of trouble...amassing all these different abilities. The monstrous strength of the Itezoras, for instance..."

"Like I said—I don't get it. I latch onto the lives of others because I am weak. Kyoken took over other people's bodies because she wanted to be stronger. And Komori changed his body because it was convenient to do so—dirty deeds are how a ninja makes a living. I sap power from others to make up for what I lack, my ninpo has its roots in inability.[37] But this applies to all ninpo, across the board. Take my other move, Decapitation Cycle, or your own fearsome ninjutsu, Pengin—at the end of the day, it's all about making up for weakness. The Schemer might say that ninjutsu is merely a way for the strong to torment the weak; in reality, it has a lot in common with her schemes. It's just a matter of whether you make up for weaknesses or let your weakness stand. But Pengin, what the hell is Nanami Yasuri doing learning other people's moves, if she's already as strong as she can get?"

The eyes of Nanami Yasuri.
Did they really change the score?
Not like this question had a chance of being answered. Pengin didn't even try, and Hohoh had nothing else to say—thereafter, they walked on in silence.
Wordless, through the wind cave in Mt. Fuji.
Eventually, they made it.
At the dead end, embedded in the wall—they found a lacquer scabbard holding a sword.
Sword.
It was a Mutant Blade—one of the masterworks of Kiki Shikizaki!
"It's so beautiful it's almost terrifying," said Hohoh, giving his...that is, Kawauso's left arm another spin. "When the cat's away, the mice will play,[38] am I right? No sooner do we renew our alliance with the Schemer than we hit the jackpot. Is it me, or is that woman the goddess of fortune?"

"I guess this means—we have one sword."

"Yep," said Hohoh, reaching out to grasp the katana embedded in the wall. "But this is only the beginning. When we're through, the Maniwa will hold all of the Twelve Possessed of Kiki Shikizaki—with no sword left behind."

---

[37] 非力　HIRIKI powerless
[38] 鬼のいぬ間に洗濯　ONI NO INU MA NI SENTAKU "doing laundry while the ogre is gone"

Hohoh gripped the hilt.

With his left hand—obviously.

Unclaimed by any owner, the sword was waiting for them, in the back wall of a wind cave at the foot of Mt. Fuji.

But which of the swords was it?

Bito the Sundial? Oto the Cured?

Seito the Garland? Dokuto the Basilisk?

We will soon find out.

While Togame the Schemer and Shichika Yasuri, Seventh Master of the Kyotoryu, dealt with their surprise challenge in Shikoku—the Sword Tale was marching on.

CHAPTER THREE

SHICHIKA HACHIRETSU

■ ■

A week had passed.

Following the battle in the Fifth Hall, Emonzaemon Soda zipped back to Owari—but the same could not be said for Togame the Schemer, who had pushed[1] the Sword Hunt, and Shichika Yasuri, Seventh Master of the Kyotoryu, who stayed on, just like Nanami Yasuri, as special guests of Seiryoin Gokenji Temple.

After Nanami Yasuri had brazenly occupied this holy site, the temple shut its doors and sent all of the pilgrims packing—without offering those who protested[2] any kind of explanation.

How could they possibly explain?

But as a result, Gokenji Temple had more vacancies than it knew what to do with. Its warrior monks, once numbering two hundred strong, had been decimated—at the hands of Nanami Yasuri.

Few of the survivors could fight.

All that was left were older monks and new arrivals[3] who had just begun their training—in other words, only those who had declined to challenge Nanami had survived.

Their ranks had been essentially wiped out.

Those unfit for survival had been culled from the holy land.

Now dominated by a genius—the fittest.

After all, this was the holy land of swordsmen, and a swordsman lives to fight. Thanks to Nanami Yasuri, the place had become all the holier—and yet the bakufu could not simply look the other way.

In addition to pushing the Sword Hunt.

Togame was also responsible for having pulled the Kyotoryu, once banished to Haphazard Island, out of hiding—and thus she was obliged to act.

"..."

Now.

Faced with the grave facts of a tremendous gap in skill—Shichika Yasuri had been in a funk[4] all week. Rising without enthusiasm, eating without tasting his food—he was going through the motions with a blank stare, in a daze.

He made no attempt to see his sister, who was under the same roof.

When Togame tried to talk to him, he barely even answered.[5]

Today, for instance—he had been laid out on his futon for the majority of the day.

[1] 名目　MEIMOKU　(ostensible) reason; pretext
[2] いぶかしむ　IBUKASHIMU　to doubt
[3] 小坊主　KOBŌZU　"little monk"　aspiring acolytes who are still children
[4] 落ち込んでいた　OCHIKONDE ITA　felt depressed　落ち込む　OCHIKOMU　to fall into
[5] 生返事　NAMA HENJI　"raw response"　vague reaction

Staring at the ceiling.
"..."
Last year.
After he fought Nanami for the first time, back home on the island.
Following the death of their father Mutsue—Sixth Master of the Kyotoryu.
—*Was I this down?*
Shichika wondered.
Yes—he'd been depressed back then, too. That match had ended without contest; Nanami brushed him off like a mosquito.
No.
He felt even worse.
Last year, he hadn't expected to prevail.
But this time—he actually had.
He and Togame had deflected crisis after crisis[6]—he was sure they could deflect his sister's gaze.[7]
Those eyes.
Nanami Yasuri's—menacing eyes.
Thought he could easily evade them, huh?
In the heat of battle—he had made a total fool of himself.
In front of Togame.
And in front of her enemy.
His bumbling[8] performance—was mortifying.
—*Sis must think that I'm a total hack.*[9]
And he thought she was proud—look where his pride had gotten him.
Had he learned nothing last month, when he lost to Konayuki Itezora?
The match had yet to be decided—
But Shichika had been defeated, no matter how he looked at it.
That had been nothing but defeat.
He was so weak, for Nanami—that she'd done no more than brush him off like a fly.
Why.
—*Why'd I ever think I had a chance against her, when I had none at all?*
What was I thinking—hoping to make life easier for her?
That's how it was back on the island.
Sis.
She never needed any help from me. Who was I kidding?
Me, do something for her?
"..."
BAM.
While Shichika was lost in thought—or at a loss for what to think—someone in the hallway slid the paper door open with undue force.

[6] 死線を越え SHISEN WO KOE "cross the line of death" to undergo a harrowing experience or lethal trial
[7] 視線をも、越え SHISEN WO MO, KOE "cross, too, the line of sight" pun on the above idiom
[8] 無様 BUZAMA "no style" clumsy, unsightly
[9] 見下げ果てられて MISAGE HATERARETE "looked down upon in the extreme"

Who else but Togame the Schemer.
Naturally, they were staying in the same room.
For the past week, Togame had shown Shichika an attentiveness that was unlike her. To the best of her ability, she was trying to be sweet towards her poor sword, who had been brushed off by his own sister.
Although Togame had something to see to—
When she had a chance, she went back to the room and tried to console Shichika.
You could even say she was devoted, as unlikely a descriptor as that may be for her.
Trouble is, it backfired on Shichika, who felt even more miserable—a classic case of cruel to be kind—but.
Right here, right now.
At this moment, at least—that wasn't an issue.
Standing like a demoness in the open doorway—she looked furious.
That's Togame for you.
This was a look—that felt familiar.
"T-Togame?"
She didn't answer.
Just barging into the room, and lunging at sleepy Shichika—
"Cheeriohhh!"
She booted him in the face.
Because Shichika was something of a masochist—no, because he was so loyal to his owner, he never shied from these blows (or abuse).[10] This particular foot strike,[11] however, he probably couldn't have dodged if he tried.
Her aim was true.
She gave him—everything she had.
"Hmph!"
Togame spun off of her kick and clipped[12] Shichika another, square in the face. With the ball of her heel, as if to seal his lips. Not what you might expect from the Schemer, who shunned both weaponry and martial artistry on principle, but there it was: a marvelous flurry of attacks. This being Togame, who had no muscle, against Shichika, whose muscle was over the top, the result was no disaster—but under normal circumstances, kicks like that were liable to knock your teeth out.
"You've gotta be...kidding me!"
"? ? ? ?"
Shichika had no idea what hit him, no idea what was happening—Togame roared, foot planted on his face.
"Who are you to take advantage of a random act of kindness... You think you can just mope around this place forever? Imbecile!"

[10] 攻撃（暴力）　KŌGEKI (BŌRYOKU)　attack (violence)
[11] 蹴撃　SHŪGEKI　kick neologism in lieu of 襲撃 SHŪGEKI assault
[12] 叩きつける　TATAKI TSUKERU　smack against

"H-H-Huh?"

"Lose once or twice and you start acting like it's the end of the world! Do you realize how many days you've been like this? Shichika! Eyes on me."

Togame pointed at herself with her thumb—and struck a pose.

"Do you have any idea how many failures I have under my belt? Not like I'm proud about it, but the number's nothing close to one or two. More like hundreds, thousands! And I've never wallowed in despair like this! Know why? Because I always beat them in the end!"

You should be ashamed of yourself!

Togame dug her foot—into his face.

He was ashamed alright.

Embarrassed.

But only—because he lost against Nanami—not because he was depressed.

Look at him, though.

Feigning remorse, feigning regret.

How embarrassing was he?

"Get up!" shouted Togame—finally lifting her foot from his face.

Rattled by her intimidating demeanor, Shichika sprang to his feet.

Whereupon Togame cuffed him upside the head.

Short as she was, she had to hop off of her tiptoes, which seriously compromised the form and efficacy of the hit.

Besides, she botched her landing.

Although she fell down on her butt, she stood right up again.

"Just once!" she said. "I'm only going to ask you once—and no matter how you answer, I won't hold it against you.[13] This one time, I pledge not to twist your arm.[14] Just answer me!"

Togame asked him:

"Shichika—Are you prepared to fight Nanami again?"

"..."

It would have been a lie to answer yes.

This was nothing like his rematch against Konayuki Itezora.

The first time he lost to Konayuki, Shichika was dying for another chance—but the circumstances with Nanami were incomparable.

Losing to her was categorically dissimilar from any other loss.

They'd postponed resolving their match, but why fight her again?

He was sure to be defeated.

This time, he might even wind up dead.

To pretend that the postponement changed anything was cruel enough to be abusive—and yet.

Togame.

If Togame the Schemer could face this cruel suggestion without giving up hope...

---

[13] 咎める TOGAMERU scold despite echoing the speaker's name
[14] 無理強い MURIJI'I force unreasonably/impossibly

"Yes," Shichika answered, as clear as day.

Minutes earlier, he probably would have given her a flat-out no—but even if his answer was a lie, at this point he could see no way around it.

Lying—was by now one of his moves.

"Good," said Togame.

Not beating around the bush.

That was Togame for you.

Acting like herself again.

"In that case, I'll set about hatching us a scheme—a genius scheme, fit for that genius sister of yours... For starters, your Last Fatal Orchid—Shichika Hachiretsu—has a weakness."

■　■

Fatal Orchid One: Kyoka Suigetsu
　Fatal Orchid Two: Kacho Fugetsu
　Fatal Orchid Three: Hyakka Ryoran
　Fatal Orchid Four: Ryuryoku Kako
　Fatal Orchid Five: Hika Rakuyo
　Fatal Orchid Six: Kinjo Tenka
　Fatal Orchid Seven: Rakka Rozeki

And the Last Fatal Orchid, Shichika Hachiretsu, unleashing the other seven at the same time—but for the record, the only foe this secret move had ever felled was the first of the saga, Komori Maniwa.

Other than that, Shichika had only tried the move out at a dojo in the Capital, to show Togame.

It had barely seen the light of day.

"So you needn't feel down just because its weakness has been revealed, let me assure you," said Togame. "Someone was bound to discover its weakness sooner or later, even if it wasn't Nanami."

For the first time in days, Shichika rolled up his futon and stuffed it in the closet. Then he and Togame laid out cushions and sat across from one another.

"I thought...it was unbeatable."

"How can I put this, Shichika... You only thought this secret move up half a year ago... No wonder it's still rough around the edges."

"Well, when you put it that way, sure."

Shichika scratched his head.

Now that he had been tasked with the rematch, the gears inside his head were slick with instinct—in this respect, he was a model of the simple man who lives to get the job done.

"So, what's the deal with this weakness?"

"Under ordinary circumstances I would second what Nanami said and say figure it out yourself, but this time I'll make an exception. I'm going to be straight up[15] with you—Fatal Orchid Four, Ryuryoku Kako, is getting in the way."

"Th-The way?"

Togame had been straight up alright, but she was so direct he missed the point.

"What part of—how is Ryuryoku Kako getting in the way?"

"Let's walk through this step by step. What's the basic premise of Fatal Orchid Four?"

Two months ago, in Satsuma.

This was the move Shichika had used against Kanara Azekura, in their battle at the Basket—the armor-piercing Fatal Orchid of the Kyotoryu.

Among the Seven Forms of the Kyotoryu, it was the only time he made a fist—launching from Form Four, the Asagao, this blow bypasses[16] the surface.

No buckler or block can shield you from its impact, which demolishes your insides but leaves your skin unscathed—theoretically, the move could blast someone on the other side of the planet.

"I mean, I guess it didn't work against Kanara Azekura and Zokuto, with his unparalleled armor class. Still, though, it has to be one of the most useful moves in all the Kyotoryu. 'Course, it's for specific situations... Of all the moves to wind up getting in the way—"

"I'm not debating pros and cons[17] here, Shichika. Why don't you show me Ryuryoku Kako—go ahead, let's see it."

"...?"

Shichika looked plenty skeptical, but he had no good reason not to do the move. To begin, he stood up from his cushion and assumed Form Four, the Asagao.

Feet parallel and sideways—Shichika bent deep at the knees, to lower his enormous body.

Torso twisted as far as it would go.

So that he nearly turned his back on Togame.

One hand made a fist, which he covered with the other, open hand—

"Okay, from here—I snap back—and drive my fist!"

Fatal Orchid Four—Ryuryoku Kako.

His body spun back from the impact—but the fist remained stuck to its target.

Although in this case, he was shadow-boxing,[18] so the fist wasn't stuck to anything—

"...Well, how's that? Pretty cool move, if you ask me."

"Don't talk back to me.[19] No one is taking jabs at Ryuryoku Kako. It's a fine

---

[15] 単刀直入　TANTŌ CHOKUNYŪ　"plain sword, simple entry"　to the point
[16] 打撃透徹　DAGEKI TŌTETSU　"penetrating hit"
[17] 有用無用　YŪYŌ MUYŌ　"useful useless"
[18] 空振り　KARABURI　"swinging at the air"　in baseball and other sports: a swing and a miss
[19] 噛みつく　KAMITSUKU　snap (your jaws); bite

move, one of your best. But can't you see—it's different from the other six Fatal Orchids. You just showed me yourself...it forces you to *pause*."

"...?"

Pause.

Twist your body to an unnatural degree—and pause in that unnatural pose. The move required *preparation*.[20]

"Oh..."

"See it now?"

Once Togame saw that Shichika had understood, she had him take a seat and went on, speaking patiently.

"Look, I'm not saying that the prep work, in and of itself, ruins the move—even if Ryuryoku Kako didn't work against Kanara Azekura, your execution was flawless. It's just that *mixed up with all the other moves—things get messy*."

Fatal Orchids one through seven.

Combined and synchronized—Shichika Hachiretsu.

But the pause inherent to Ryuryoku Kako tripped up the synchronicity.[21]

The pause meant there was an opening.[22]

It was that simple.

All that Nanami had done—was take advantage of the opening in Fatal Orchid Four, Ryuryoku Kako—and use the monstrous strength of the Itezoras to heave his body up into the ceiling of the dojo.

That was the whole shebang.[23]

"Right...I know I said *all at the same time*...but Shichika Hachiretsu has seven separate moves, and I only have so many arms and legs, so strictly speaking, they aren't really hitting at the same time. It might not be, strictly speaking, a consecutive strike, but it's like a medley of attacks—"

"Which is why Nanami countered with a medley of her own."

The Kyotoryu—

A medley of moves, from the Hinageshi to the Jinchoge.

Two hundred and seventy-two hits in a row.

"Regardless, that sister of yours totally babies you. She may have told you to think for yourself, but then she practically handed you the answer."

Not the sort of thing Nanami would have been glad to hear, considering Togame gave Shichika no chance to think before she spelled it out—but anyway, she had a point.

The merits of Fatal Orchid Four Ryuryoku Kako aside, the move was no good mixed with all the others. Anyone with a mind to catch him with his guard down would find a chance in the split-second that he made the necessary pause.

"How big is it?" asked Shichika.

"Huh?"

"I mean the opening—you think this break in Shichika Hachiretsu is big

[20] 下準備 SHITAJUNBI preliminary steps 下 SHITA under/below 準備 JUNBI prepare
[21] 同時性 DŌJISEI simultaneity 同じ ONAJI same 時 TOKI time 性 SHŌ disposition
[22] 隙 SUKI gap; imperfection common term and concept in martial arts
[23] それだけのこと SOREDAKE NO KOTO that and nothing more

enough that anyone could get a hit in?"

"Hard to say—far be it for me to judge, having no proficiency in the martial arts to speak of, but if I had to guess, it's not like you're wide open. Apparently it worked on Komori Maniwa. And you made a show of it at the dojo in the Capital. Apart from Nanami—I dare say that the likes of Hakuhei Sabi could make it through."

"Yeah... Good thing I didn't try it, when we fought on Ganryu Island."

By the way, the move he used to take down Hakuhei Sabi had been Fatal Orchid Three, Hyakka Ryoran,[24] playing off Form Three, the Tsutsuji.

"Alright—so Shichika Hachiretsu won't cut it as a Fatal Orchid. Not with a glaring weakness like that."

Shichika made no attempt to hide his disappointment.

This was understandable, since he himself had devised the Fatal Orchid. Worse, if Shichika Hachiretsu was off the table, he couldn't use his catchphrase, or whatever you might call it. Right when he was finally warming up to it.

"If I cut out Ryuryoku Kako and make it just the other six—that throws the balance off entirely. I'd have to call it Mutsuka Shichiretsu,[25] which doesn't have the same ring[26] to it."

"Easy, Shichika," Togame said. "I found a way for you to overcome this weakness."

"Huh? You did?"

"Of course I did—I'm Togame the Schemer! I've got it all figured out. Why else would I sound so high and mighty?"

"Because you're always high and mighty?"

"Cheerio!"

Another kick.

Shichika let her hit him.

The conversation went on as if nothing had happened.

"Don't you think you've been a little careless[27] about the order of the seven moves? What should I expect, when the whole point is that you do them at once—but from what I gather, you're just doing them whatever way feels most convenient at the time."

"Hmm...I guess I hadn't thought about the order much."

Take, for example, the time he used the move against Komori Maniwa on Haphazard Island—since he was already in Form Two, the Suisen, he started off with Fatal Orchid Two: Kacho Fugetsu, and went on down the line, through Fatal Orchid Three: Hyakka Ryoran, Fatal Orchid Four: Ryuryoku Kako, Fatal Orchid Five: Hika Rakuyo, Fatal Orchid Six: Kinjo Tenka, and Fatal Orchid Seven: Rakka Rozeki, finishing up with Fatal Orchid One: Kyoka Suigetsu.

---

[24] 百花繚乱 HYAKKA RYŌRAN "Splendor of a Hundred Flowers"
[25] 六花七裂 MUTSUKA SHICHIRETSU subtracts one from each of the number characters in 七花八裂 SHICHIKA HACHIRETSU also echoes 難しい MUTSUKASHII difficult
[26] 語呂が悪い GORO GA WARUI words that don't sound good together
[27] 無頓着 MUTONCHAKU unconcerned

But nothing was holding him to that exact order.[28]

The move was flexible on principle.

He could mix and match the Seven Fatal Orchids—in five thousand and forty different ways!

And every one was Shichika Hachiretsu.

He thought that any combination would be fine—and that the order didn't matter.

"It's just like you to see this so simplistically[29]—but you need to change your way of thinking. Shichika Hachiretsu showcases all seven of your best attacks at once. The move has fabulous potential—it just needs some tightening up."

"Alright, so what should I do?"

"It's obvious. If you put Fatal Orchid Four, Ryuryoku Kako, *at the beginning*, it all works out."

"..."

"*Stopping halfway through the sequence is the problem*—so just do Ryuryoku Kako first, before your wheels are spinning."

"Oh...good idea. Then I can blow through the other six—no problem."

It was an elementary solution—but it made perfect sense.

As a result, he would always have to begin Shichika Hachiretsu with Form Four, the Asagao, which nixed the marvelous convenience of being able to unleash the move from any stance—but also the Last Fatal Orchid's weakness.

From five thousand and forty different ways—to seven hundred and twenty.

But no worse than that.

"It sounds—easy."

"Because it is."

However.

Togame may have seen beyond the weakness and proposed a workable solution—but her face was far from cheerful.[30]

"It also means—we can be sure Nanami sees it coming."

"Yeah, I bet."

The eyes—of Nanami Yasuri.

She could pick up any move just by watching it in action and see through any weakness.

In which case—it would come as no surprise if she saw through their countermeasure.

In fact, it would be much more of a surprise if she missed it.

That sister of his.

"At the end of the day, I'm never beating sis unless we find a way to counter her eyes—but if we could, we wouldn't be in the mess we're in. There's no use trying to blind her or use a smoke bomb or something. She'd see us coming a mile away."

---

[28] 型　KATA　form; fixed sequence (in martial arts)
[29] 大雑把　ŌZAPPA　overlooking details　大 DAI big　雑 ZATSU miscellaneous　把 TABA bundle
[30] 晴れやか　HAREYAKA　radiant　晴れ HARE clear skies, sunny

"Her eyes, huh?"

Togame snorted.

"As a matter of fact—I've hatched a scheme for that as well."

"What? You have?"

"While you were down in the dumps, I was working my butt off.[31] When I wasn't caring for *my poor little sword*."

Her voice rang with irony.

But irony was lost on Shichika.

He took Togame at face value: it put him in good spirits knowing she was confident enough that he would bounce back to devote herself to working out a scheme.

That helped explain why she had been so angry.

Seriously—how much longer was I planning on just moping around?

When Togame really does believe in me.

"Ugh, lose the creepy smile. Who cheers up when they've been insulted? What kink[32] is this now..."

Togame could not read his mind.[33] Without getting up, she used her knees to scoot back.

The heart of a sword cannot be fathomed by its owner.

"So, Togame—you already have a plan for beating sis?"

"Well, with everything I heard about Nanami's eyes on our way here, I figured I should get one started. There's a million ways to blind a person, but this is Nanami we're talking—we can assume that she's prepared for almost anything."

"Prepared? That's not the way it works, Togame. She doesn't have to see it coming. *Once she sees me*—she'll know exactly what we're up to. We can't use any strategy without giving it away."

"Exactly," said Togame. *"We just won't give ourselves way."*

"..."

"Not even Nanami can cope with an *invisible scheme*. If she can't watch it—she can't learn it, and she can't see through its faults... But we'll only have one chance."

It was that kind of a setup.

"If you screw it up, we can't try it again—or anything else, for that matter."

"...So everything's ready?"

That was why.

Togame had booted him—to help him snap out of his funk.

Her patience had been wearing thin.

But on the flip side—that usually meant she was ready to go.

"Nope." Togame shook her head. "I still need to work out the ending[34]—

---

[31] 一生懸命　ISSHŌ KENMEI　as if one's life depended upon it

[32] 特殊な性癖　TOKUSHU NA SEIHEKI　special (sexual) proclivity

[33] 心中　SHINCHŪ　innermost thoughts
　　　vs. 心中　SHINJŪ "suicide pact between lovers," spelled the same but pronounced differently

[34] 最後の詰め　SAIGO NO TSUME　endgame　最後　SAIGO very last　詰み　TSUMI checkmate

before I can set this scheme in motion, Nanami and I have some negotiating to do."

"Y-You're going to negotiate with sis?"

He remembered.

The two of them had talked back on Haphazard Island, half a year ago—

It was a match made in hell.

"Whoa, don't remind me..."

Shichika had been in a pickle.[35]

Back then, he had mostly brushed it off, but now that he had a capacity for feeling, he wasn't looking forward to a second confrontation.

"I can see why you're concerned—but this is the moment of truth.[36] I'll ride it out somehow—after all, negotiation is my specialty."

On that note, Togame stood.

"We mustn't tarry—by now Emonzaemon has made it to Owari. If I had it my way, the rematch would already be over. How soon can you fight?"

"How soon?" asked Shichika. "If you want me to—tonight."

"Yeah?"

"Luckily, or maybe not so luckily, I made it out alive, without a scratch—I'm ready to go basically anytime. I mean, after spending most of the week in bed, my body feels a little crunchy, so I'd like to stretch a little first. Fighting this second might be tough."

"That's fine—I'm not ready for you to fight this second either. Well then, let's plan on doing it tonight. As long as Nanami is cooperative... I'll break down the particulars after the negotiations, but let me just say, Shichika—if you want to beat Nanami, then at the very least, you'll need to retrieve Akuto the Eel from her breast."

Needless to say.

"That sword invests her genius, harrowing on its own, with endless supplemental energy—Akuto the Eel's powers are quite fiendish. An atrocity.[37] Bear this in mind, as you work out your battleplan."

"Right... Happy as I am to see sis feeling better—it isn't exactly healthy. First off..."

Shichika paused.

This had been on his mind, under the muck of his depression.

For the past week.

"I gotta say—the Eel's not right for Nanami."

"What do you mean? What better weapon for a sickly genius like Nanami? Talk about a sword picking its owner. Exemplary, really—it isn't one of the Mutant Blades of Kiki Shikizaki for nothing. Or is this about the Kyotoryu? Are you saying that it's wrong for her to use a sword?"

"No—that's not what I meant. It's way more personal[38]...I meant it's not like

---

[35] 板ばさみ　ITABASAMI　"squeezed between boards"
[36] 正念場　SHŌNENBA　crucial stage (in kabuki etc.)　正念　SHŌNEN (Buddhist) right mindfulness
[37] 鬼に金棒　ONI NI KANABŌ　"demon with a staff of iron"　double threat
[38] 根本的　KONPONTEKI　at the root; basic

her. Is that thing really boosting her energy?"

"I won't pretend to understand what's just a feeling on your part. All I can say for sure is that you have no chance of winning, so long as Akuto the Eel remains a factor. That and Nanami's eyes—we need to focus all our resources on cutting these two out of the equation.... Now, if you'll excuse me."

"Huh?"

Having said all she had to say, Togame slid open the door, to Shichika's stupefaction.

"Y-You're leaving now? To go see sis?"

"I need to see her now, if the rematch is tonight."

"Oh—right, that makes sense."

"Shichika," Togame said, standing in the hallway. "I had thought it best to hold my tongue, but this is for your own good. What made you hide from me that Nanami was stronger than you?"

"Well."

She'd sprung the question on him out of nowhere.

But after an unamicable[39] silence—he responded.

"Sis isn't one to show off. She doesn't even think she's strong—to her, it's more like everyone else is weak."

"I'm not asking about Nanami. I'm asking about you."

"Fine."

Shichika turned away.

Averting his eyes from Togame—

"I just wanted to be your sword, okay?"

"..."

"If you'd known sis was stronger—why wouldn't you have chosen her?"

"...Fool," Togame muttered.

Then she laughed, ever so slightly.

"I'm only gonna say this once, so listen up. Who knows how I would've felt six months ago—but at this point, you're the only sword for me. One or two defeats can't change that. *Do I have to spell everything out for you?*"

Togame closed the door.

Leaving Shichika to bask in a strange feeling—some of which he let out with a little tumble.[40]

After which he spread his arms and legs[41] and thought things over.

Thinking through—his battleplan.

On the assumption that Togame would succeed in her negotiations.

---

[39] 不貞腐れた　FUTE KUSARETA　sulky　不貞　FUTEI　unchaste, faithless　腐る　KUSARU　to go bad, rot
[40] でんぐり返し　DENGURI GAESHI　forward or backward roll
[41] 大の字になって　DAI NO JI NI NATTE　stretch out one's limbs, like the character 大　DAI　big

Proceeding down the hall.

Dragging the hem of her brash, brilliant kimono on the floor, Togame headed for Nanami's chamber, each footstep resolute.

Once Togame had decided on a strategy, it was firm.

She had fanned the flames[42] of Shichika's heart.

The only thing left undecided—was the winner.

"..."

However—there was something Togame failed to comprehend.

"What on earth...is that Nanami Yasuri thinking?"

Her question—

Mirrored what was on the mind of her archnemesis,[43] Princess Negative, back in Owari, who asked herself, at almost the same time:

"If she showed up just to warn him of his weakness, why not spit it out? I don't see any need to be so tedious... She had to pick up Akuto the Eel, of all the Twelve Possessed! Why make her brother fight her when he has no chance of winning, after having babied him? Don't tell me she actually believes that two swordsmen, chancing upon each other, have no reason not to fight—"

---

[42] 焚きつけた TAKITSUKETA stoked 焚く TAKU burn; kindle; light (木 KI tree 火 HI fire)
[43] 忌み嫌う IMIKIRAU detest

CHAPTER FOUR

NANAMI YASURI

■ ■

The fact that Nanami Yasuri had come into possession of Akuto the Eel was inarguably a hassle for Togame the Schemer, but that being said, had things gone differently, allowing for the sword to remain at the summit of Mt. Shirei—collecting it would never have been easy.

Mt. Shirei was a Level One Disaster Area.

It had been wrested from its shrine by none other than that genius Nanami Yasuri, who did her work in a matter of minutes.

Akuto the Eel had been safeguarded in the most treacherous of climates by the Sacred Guardians of Mt. Shirei, men dressed in white—whose ranks would have posed a stubborn challenge to both Shichika and Togame.

Yet the men were not warriors.

Nor hunters like the Itezoras.

They simply—*had the ability to see.*

Apparitions.

Ghosts. Ghouls. Spirits.[1]

Specters—phantoms.[2]

Questions of proper nomenclature aside, the Sacred Guardians of Mt. Shirei had the ability *to see people who were dead and gone.*

They call it—necromancy.[3]

It may sound crazy—but remember Kyoken Maniwa, who waylaid Shichika Yasuri and Togame the Schemer last month on Mt. Odori? How could she have taken over thousands of bodies over the centuries *without something like a soul to do the work?*

This was about—*persistent presence.*

While there may not be an afterworld—there is a dreamworld.

And the presence of memory.

Is the presence of the departed.

The presence—of dreams.

Along those lines, consider the Infovac of Maniwa Kawauso, "The Nosey Otter." It may come across as superstition,[4] but perhaps it has some philosophical[5] basis after all. Furthermore, while Kawauso Maniwa was from Maniwa Village, born and raised, his father's side had roots in Mutsu—so they say.

You can imagine just what Princess Negative would declare:

"There's no such thing as ghosts—but I don't doubt those men can see them."

[1] 幽霊、亡霊、心霊　YŪREI, BŌREI, SHINREI　"wretched spirit" "lost spirit" "inner spirit"
[2] 霊魂―人魂　REIKON—HITODAMA　"spirit soul" "human soul" will o' the wisp
[3] 交霊術　KŌREIJUTSU　communication with spirits
[4] 迷信　MEISHIN　"errant beliefs"
[5] 理論的　RIRONTEKI　theoretical

Anyway.
While Nanami Yasuri was making short change[6] of the Sacred Guardians of Mt. Shirei—you can be sure that she had watched and learned their *methods*.
With those eyes.
Just as she had gleaned the Maniwa Ninpo.
And the monstrous strength of the Itezoras.
She observed—their necromancy.
Since warriors they were not, their skill did not immediately prove useful to Nanami, but on the boat sailing from Mutsu to Shikoku—
She tried it on for size.
And was visited by her father—Mutsue Yasuri.
And her mother—Migiri[7] Yasuri.
Not misty images—but clear as day.
"Huh."
Nanami nodded comprehendingly.
"Okay...so this was how it works."
Soon she heard the departed speak.
The first voice was her father, Mutsue.
—Nanami.
My dear—
Sweet Nanami—you're far too—
Far too—way too—
Strong—
Too strong for me to teach—
I must not—must not make you any stronger—
You—
You're a monster—
You should never have been born.
Migiri chimed in.
—Poor thing.
Poor little—girl—
Poor girl—
If you—
If only you could die, it would be over—
But you can't die—and can't live either—
Trapped—in a life you never asked for—[8]
I wish—
I wish you could just die.
"Boh-ring."
Nanami switched off the move.
It was boring the hell out of her.

---

[6] ないがしろ NAIGASHIRO not take seriously
[7] みぎり MIGIRI suggests: 砌 MIGIRI moment, season 見切り MIKIRI abandonment, resignation
[8] 生きぞこない IKIZOKONAI "a failure at living"

This was—only memory.
There inside her all along.
She didn't need a special move—to see them.
She saw them.
Thought about them constantly.
"Enough,"[9] she said under hear breath.
And so—the two visiting figures disappeared.
Disappeared—like phantasms.[10]
"Thanks but no thanks—I don't need you to remind me."
Thus.
Nanami Yasuri refrained from toying with the methods of the Sacred Guardians of Mt. Shirei—for the remainder of the voyage.
She was on her way to see her little brother.
Who accepted her.
He was the only person in her family—who accepted her.

■ ■

"Sounds good. Or maybe *bad*—but in any case, I understand."

Her proposal so readily accepted—

Togame the Schemer was perplexed, even if it was exactly what she'd hoped for, and it was written all over her face.

"You seem surprised," Nanami said. "But I'm at least as surprised as you, Miss Togame. It's been about a week now. I figured you and Shichika had given up and gone home."

"Listen to that," Togame snapped, but she had no leg to stand on.

They may not actually have run home with their tails between their legs—but they may as well have, what with Shichika down in the dumps for a week straight.

However, that being said.
Where would Shichika have gone?
Haphazard Island?
Now literally deserted—no one there.
"..."
They were inside—Nanami's chamber.

Though women were normally forbidden access to Seiryoin Gokenji, the temple had given her this room. She had been treated like a queen, but this should come as no surprise, since she had waltzed onto this sacred ground as if she owned the place. She had the nerve[11] to act as if the monks of venerable

---

[9] 消えろ KIERO disappear
[10] 夢幻 MUGEN "dream visions"
[11] 怖いもの知らず KOWAI MONO SHIRAZU "knowing nothing scary" fearless

Gokenji Temple were only there to serve her—indeed, nerves were not an obstacle for Nanami.

After giving Shichika a swift[12] kick in the butt, Togame marched right down the hall to see Nanami—although she knew where she was staying, she had refrained from seeing her, like Shichika.

She needed time—for *preparation*.

And certainly couldn't allow Nanami to perceive that she was being schemed. Couldn't allow it—*to be seen*.

But now, Togame was prepared—and Shichika had rallied.

All that remained were the negotiations.

Propositioning for a rematch—but her wish was granted readily.

When Togame gave her terms.[13]

"I understand," Nanami had answered promptly.

She may not have explicitly assented, but she had answered without hesitation.[14]

"Well—I would be much obliged if you would think it over...."

"I have no reason to refuse—I am a sword."

"I hate to say it, but Shichika had a point. How can one sword own another?" asked Togame. "Tell me, Nanami—apart from besting you in battle...is there anything that we can do to get you to hand over Akuto the Eel? I know that I can't speak for you or Shichika, but personally, I'd rather not condone a showdown between siblings."

"So kind of you—as always," Nanami noted with a thin smile. "That's exactly why I trusted you with Shichika in the first place, which makes it even harder to express my disappointment. It's just, it's just—Miss Togame. I never thought—you would start treating Shichika *like he was human*."

"..."

Togame withheld comment.

Unperturbed, Nanami continued.

"He's gotten rather—tame. Back on the island, he was, how can I say...a sharper sword. It's like he's a rusty blade now."

"Rust," Togame snorted. "I mentioned this when we met on the island, but the last owner of Hakuto the Whisper was named Hakuhei Sabi—and he took pride in the literal sense of his surname. He called himself 'a broken sword, scarred with rust.'"

"Broken sword? Even better—I mean, *badder*," said Nanami. "In that case—maybe I'll break Shichika in half."

"Cut the violence."[15]

"The violence? How do you mean? What's on the schedule tonight aside from violence? This fight will be the absolute epitome of violence—a battle to the death."

[12] 強烈 KYŌRETSU intense, powerful; heavy (hit)
[13] 文言 MONGON wording (of a document)
[14] ふたつ返事 FUTATSU HENJI "reply twice" i.e. はいはい HAI HAI yes, yes (to demonstrate eagerness)
[15] 物騒な BUSSŌ NA troubling; dangerous

"I gather that the swordfight cannot be avoided?"
"What reason have I to avoid it?"
"Well, then. I rest my case."
Togame was done negotiating.
The rest was to be settled between swordsmen.
She had no right to intervene—from here on out.
"Oh, by the way, Miss Togame."
This time.
Nanami was the one asking the questions.
"Has Shichika already run his mouth?"
"…"
It was all too plain what she meant.
Unfortunately, the answer was yes.
"Unfortunately—he's told me both his secrets."
"Oh my."
Nanami held her hand over her face.
To hide her wry smile.
"Although—I'm not all that surprised…"
"Can I assume—you've heard about *my past*?"
"Sure, but it's not the sort of thing to discuss here at Gokenji Temple. I may have taken over it, but it's still under the bakufu's jurisdiction."

Togame's past.

The origins—of this young woman who had risen, out of nowhere, to the highest echelons of government.

And her father?

Mastermind of the Rebellion.

Kaoyaku of Oshu—Takahito Hida.

Sworn traitor of the Yanari Bakufu—

While the Hero of the Rebellion, who smote down Takahito Hida, thereby ending the Rebellion—was Mutsue Yasuri, father of Nanami Yasuri and Shichika Yasuri.

For Togame the Schemer, this made the Yanari Bakufu, her current employer, an enemy of her family—whom they massacred—and Shichika and Nanami the offspring of the man who killed her father.

Strange connections.

But Togame had ventured over to Haphazard Island well aware of these connections—call it a historical inevitability.[16]

"We both—carry the burdens of our fathers," Nanami said.

"Yeah—suppose you're right."

The Hero of the Rebellion, in its wake, found himself banished to an island.

Dragging Nanami and Shichika into the fray.

"By the way, Miss Togame—do you know why my dad was banished?"

"Yeah. I heard that he offended a senior official in the House of Tetsubi, one

---

[16] 歴史的必然 REKISHITEKI HITSUZEN historical necessity vs. 偶然 GŪZEN coincidence

of the six daimyos who had taken power—"

"Right, that's what happened, but know what, Miss Togame? In actuality—it wasn't my dad's fault."

"Huh?"

"It was my mom's," divulged Nanami. "In fact, she came from the House of Tetsubi—not like any of that matters now. Like I said before, I have no grudge against the bakufu."

"...What are you driving at?"

"Because it involved the Tetsubi, they had to keep it under wraps, so I'm not sure what it says in the official record, but my dad *was suspected of killing my mom*... Honestly, with a charge like that, he's lucky all they did was banish him. It's a wonder he wasn't beheaded—or at the very least forced to commit seppuku. But he was the Hero of the Rebellion after all.[17] So they went easy[18] on him."

"He killed her?"

The words fell out of Togame's mouth.

Before she had a chance to censor herself.

"Mutsue Yasuri—killed his own wife?"

"At this point, the truth is underwater—choked in duckweed.[19] Which is appropriate, considering her last doctor was a quack."[20]

"Is this a good time for a pun?"

"It's as good—or *bad* a time as any."

Togame had the basic facts—she knew that Nanami and Shichika's mother had died.

She'd discussed the matter with Shichika a few times.

But her understanding—was that Migiri Yasuri had succumbed to illness.

Shichika didn't even remember her face—

"I remember her. Back then, I may not have had the *eyes* that I have now, but my memory is crystal clear."

"I bet."

"My mom was a handful. That she died before her sickly daughter might have been divine punishment—she could have lived to be a hundred. My dad raised my brother as if he wasn't missing anything without her. So Shichika must not have given it much thought...but when it comes to women,[21] don't you think he's more than a little obtuse?"

"Hah...I think that every day."

"Oh, so you've been thinking about how you're not enough woman for him?"

"I never think that!" Togame screamed.

---

[17] 腐っても大乱の英雄　KUSATTEMO TAIRAN NO EIYŪ　pun on　腐っても鯛 KUSATTEMO TAI
　　　"even a rotten sea bream has its value" = "a diamond in a dunghill is still a diamond"
[18] 温情　ONJŌ　"warm feelings" lenience
[19] 藪の中　YABU NO NAKA　"in a grove" lost in the bushes　a common expression
　　　also the title of a short story by Akutagawa that Kurosawa's *Rashomon* is based on
[20] 藪医者　YABU ISHA　"hedge doctor"
[21] 母性や女性　BOSEI YA JOSEI　maternity and women

Because she did think that.
Nanami chuckled at the sight of her.
Her evil laugh, the first since her arrival at Gokenji Temple.
It truly sounded—evil.
Despite Shichika's remark that Akuto the Eel was not right for his sister, seeing her behave this way, the vicious sword seemed made for her.

"Enough about my mom—you said that he's told you both his secrets, Miss Togame. Does that mean that you know—about how Dad died?"

"Suppose I do."

Unlike the fact that Takahito Hida, an enemy of the state, was actually her father, there was no reason to fear mentioning this matter—but it was not the sort of secret to air in a place of worship.

"You mean how Shichika murdered Mutsue."

"Yup," Nanami nodded. "Well, how did you react?"

"How, you ask... I'm not in a position to pass judgment, am I?"

Hero of the Rebellion.

When she first heard that Mutsue Yasuri had died...that the man who killed her father, took the head of Takahito Hida right before her eyes was dead—Togame would be lying if she said that she felt nothing.

But when she heard that Shichika had done the deed—

Her first reaction[22] was surprise.

After which—she gave up thinking on it.

Deeming it impolitic.[23]

"What kind of a Schemer would I be if I waded into a martial school's private affairs?"

"A martial school's...private affairs?"

Nanami gave Togame a quizzical look, then said, "Oh. Miss Togame, is it possible you've misunderstood something? Are you under the impression that it had something to do with inheriting the family tradition, or the apprentice becoming the master—you think that's why Shichika killed Dad?"

"Isn't it?"

That was exactly what she thought.

She'd taken this for granted.

But come to think of it—Shichika had never said as much.

She'd arrived at the conclusion on her own.

"Then—did Mutsue have some kind of fatal accident while they were training?"

"Nope," Nanami said. "That boy. If he had to tell you, he could have at least explained what happened—anyway. Now that you know, I may as well tell you the rest. Shichika killed our dad—*for me*."[24]

"Wha?"

---

[22] 先に立った SAKI NI TATTA "stood ahead"
[23] 考えてはいけない領分 KANGAETE WA IKENAI RYŌBUN a domain one's thoughts mustn't intrude upon
[24] ため TAME purpose same "for" as in "I can trust a man who works *for* love" (Book One)

Togame was baffled.
For Nanami?
"I'll admit he went too far—but Dad finally noticed my ability to watch and learn. After nineteen years of keeping it a secret from him..."
"Ah yes. To keep your genius in check, Mutsue vowed to teach you nothing—right?"
As a result, Nanami had acquired her ability to watch and learn.
And Shichika had known it—
But not Mutsue.
Interesting.
"Right. But Shichika couldn't keep a secret."
"..."
Not if his life depended on it, Togame thought with a smile.
But she wiped the smile off her face—
When she heard the next thing Nanami said:
"Dad tried to kill me. While I was sleeping."
Casually, like she was talking about a stranger.
"And I didn't mind dying."
Like this was someone else.
"Once Shichika knew, he put an end to Dad."
Casually she said this.
It had nothing to do—with the school's lineage.
Nay.
He'd killed him—in cold blood.
Togame was at a loss for words.
"B-But—"
She pulled herself together.[25]
"Shichika thought the world of Mutsue—"
"He's a sword," Nanami said. "Just like Dad—and just like me. Don't expect us to behave like everybody else. Not when we were brought up on that sandbox[26] of a desert island. And in fact, Shichika thought Dad was an awesome father, aside from when he tried to kill me. Dad was his master, and he barely even remembers Mom."
Nanami went on.
"Shichika doesn't even realize Dad killed—could have killed—Mom. All the same, that boy accepted being exiled along with his father. I suppose that makes him good-natured?"
"..."
"But as to why I'm going on about this—you get it, right, Miss Togame?"
"To a Yasuri..." said the Schemer. "To a Yasuri, killing is a fact of life, *even among family?*"
"Exactly," Nanami smiled.

---

[25] 気力を振り絞って　KIRYOKU WO FURISHIBOTTE　"squeezing (the last drop out of) one's spirts"
[26] 箱庭　HAKO NIWA　"(ornamental) garden in a box"

A truly wicked smile.
Her father could have killed her mother.
Her father could have killed her too.
Her brother killed her father.
That was the Yasuri family for you.
In which case.
If she killed her brother.
Or if her brother killed her.
It would only be natural!

"So if you'd prefer not to witness a showdown between siblings, you can hop along back to Owari. Either me or Shichika—whoever wins the fight will find you there."

"Are you saying that if you win—you plan to help me on the Sword Quest?"

"Sure."

Nanami nodded, surprisingly. Then she elaborated on the dubious pledge, as if to confound Togame.

"If you don't complete your Sword Hunt, we'll never clear our father's name. Restoring his honor—was part of what you promised you would do when you took Shichika."

"This is true..."

That conversation too.

Took on a new dimension—in the context of the current conversation.

Not only had her father almost killed her.

He hadn't even given her a proper upbringing—

And yet she wanted to restore his name, to what it was before he had been banished.

The Yasuris—retainers of the House of Tetsubi.

What kind of a family were they?

"If Shichika should die along the way, I'll have no choice but to replace him. To clean up my little brother's mess—"

"Who are you to blame the mess on him?"

It looked like their diplomacy had devolved into banter.[27]

"I thought the air here on the mainland was too rich for you?" quipped Togame. "Akuto the Eel was obviously a lifesaver, but I'm amazed at how you got through Ezo and through Mutsu without it. Even Shichika almost died of frostbite on Mt. Odori."

"I'd do anything for my little brother." Nanami was unperturbed. "Although I have to say, I'm glad that I found Akuto the Eel...yes."

"How did you cross over to the mainland anyway? I thought you didn't have a boat. Oh, right, I forgot you were ambushed by the Maniwa—did you sail over in their vessel?"

"No, I walked over the sea. Using the ninpo Harlequin Butterfly."

"Of course," groaned Togame.

[27] 軽口 KARUKUCHI "light mouth" joking around

The Maniwa are always getting in my way...

Because the Bug Unit had paid their visit to Haphazard Island before she and Hohoh shook on their alliance, she had no right to complain—but still.

"Come what may, I intend to use no sword but Shichika. This idea of going on a journey with you? Thanks, but no thanks."

"Don't be silly. Swords are disposable," Nanami said. "If one breaks, you just replace it with another."

"..."

"As long as you don't mind, I have a question."

Nanami—looked at Togame.

Looked at her—with those eyes.

Fixated.

Focused.

Rapt.

"When your Sword Hunt is over—what will you do with Shichika?"

This was not the time or place to bring that up.

Which is why Nanami left it at that[28]—but Togame did not need her to continue.[29]

The Kyotoryu had been her father's enemy.

What would she do with Shichika—the Master of the Kyotoryu?

"You can forget about me, just take good care of Shichika. I know I said swords are disposable—but since you want to treat him *as a human*—"

"That's up to me," Togame said and sat up,[30] ending the conversation. "I don't need your advice, I'll do things however I see fit. My only wish for Shichika—is that he finds another cause."

"Find a cause? I'm not sure what you mean by that."

"So it seems."

"I hope that you'll say more. Cause, huh. Well then, Miss Togame, let's see what you've got up your sleeve.[31] Including for this evening."

It was unclear what she saw, watching Togame with those eyes.

Unclear what she saw—when she saw through her choice of words.

But it made Nanami nod.

"Last week, you managed to restrain yourself...but tonight I'm sure you plan to get involved. Or maybe not involved yourself—but try something involved."[32]

"Gee...I wonder," said Togame, who had taken to her feet.

"Don't bother," Nanami said.

Provocatively—caustically.

Nanami was different from Shichika.

---

[28] みなまで言わない MINAMADE IWANAI leave certain things unsaid
[29] 言わずもがな IWAZU MO GANA needless to say
[30] 腰を浮かす KOSHI WO UKASU "float one's hips"
[31] お手並み拝見 OTENAMI HAIKEN "show me what you've got" common taunt in manga, etc.
[32] 手を出す[...]出すのはあくまで知恵 TE WO DASU [...] DASU NO WA AKUMADE CHI'E
extend one's hand vs. only provide wisdom (wordplay on two idioms that both use 出す DASU put out)

In mind games[33] also—her genius shined.

"No strategy you hatch—can ever make it past me. The second it catches *my eyes*—I'll make it mine too. My will has no bearing on the matter—I don't even have to want to. Whether I like it or not, I watch and learn. That's all there is to it."

"Hmph. You make it sound like you've been picking tricks up that you'd just as soon have done without."

The Sacred Guardians of Mt. Shirei.

Their ability—to sense the spirits of the dead.

Like her father.

And her mother.

"..."

Togame had no way of knowing what had happened. She simply drew her own conclusion from Nanami's choice of words—an all-too-vivid demonstration of the strained dynamic shared between the two of them.

The Schemer continued.

"Strategy, you said—but I deal only in schemes. No matter how cute your eyes[34] get, mark my words, I'll find your blind spot."

"Good for you...or *bad* for you. I'm good too—or *bad*. Well then...I'm looking forward to it."

Nanami was done talking.

She did seem to be looking forward to it.

To beholding one of Togame's infamous "schemes."

"See you down at the Fifth Hall after dinner?"

"Right. Oh...wait. Not in the dojo," Togame said.

Offhand, as though she'd just remembered.

"No?"

"This showdown shouldn't happen in a dojo. It demands a proper battlefield. I can't countenance another vague ending like last week's. This is the one and only rematch, no more chances. To make sure there's no confusion over who's the winner—I'd like to have you battle where the Buddha can lay eyes on you."

"The Buddha?"

"Where else?"

Laughing boldly, Togame announced the venue for their rematch:

"I mean that trophy cast from the one hundred thousand swords that the Old Shogun plundered via his foul decree, the Great Sword Hunt—tonight, you'll fight in front of the Katana Buddha."

---

[33] 心理戦 SHINRISEN psychological warfare
[34] おめめ OMEME diminutive term for eyes, generally reserved for small children and pets

CHAPTER FIVE

SHICHIKA HACHIRETSU REDUX

■ ■

The Katana Buddha.

Though it had been a curiosity for the majority of their journey, Shichika did not seek out the Katana Buddha in the entire week since their arrival at the hallowed grounds of Seiryoin Gokenji Temple.

The second they had shown up he had dropped everything and fought his sister, and we all know about his sorry state after the fight.

He gazed up at the Katana Buddha—in all of its enormity.

Your typical giant Buddha stands over sixteen feet high, but the Katana Buddha stretched at least a hundred feet into the air. It was so tall you could barely see the top, and so unnecessarily enormous, even grasping its true size gave you a headache.[1]

Quite aptly for a statue cast from a hundred thousand swords, its four arms each gripped a katana, while its furious expression, so unfamiliar on a Buddha, was the very face of war.

Built so as to encompass the gargantuan Buddha, the Inner Sanctum of Gokenji Temple was ginormous[2] in its own right, and propped here and there by girthy pillars.

Night had come.

Outside the temple, tucked within the steep folds of Mt. Sayabashiri, all was black—inside, however, it was bright as day.

That the Katana Buddha might be always bathed in light, the courtyard of the Inner Sanctum had been lined with candlesticks. Hundreds of candles brimmed the Inner Sanctum with an orange light.

Burning for the Katana Buddha.

Sending up their wagging orange light—from all directions.[3]

And standing in this light—Shichika regarded the Katana Buddha.

The Great Sword Hunt.

That notorious decree of the Old Shogun.

He amassed one hundred thousand swords, from every corner of Japan.

Plundering the souls—of one hundred thousand swordsmen.

Shichika was raised to be a sword, and thought himself a sword today.

So facing the Katana Buddha—he felt something.

Something altogether different from the lifeforce that he sensed when faced with any of the Mutant Blades of Kiki Shikizaki—but felt something all the same.

An impossibly imposing impact.[4]

[1] 骨が折れる　HONE GA ORERU　"bone-breaking"　a hassle
[2] だだっ広く　DADAPPIROKU　excessively expansive
[3] 四方八方　SHIHŌ HAPPŌ　"four directions, eight directions"　every which way
[4] 圧倒 圧巻 圧力　ATTŌ AKKAN ATSURYOKU　overwhelm highlight pressure　圧する　ASSURU press

"I hate to mar your first impression," Nanami said, standing before him, "but the Katana Buddha...is chock full of impurities. Maybe it's odd to speak that way of gold and silver and other treasures,[5] but the point is that it wasn't purely fashioned from katanas. When you add it up, a hundred thousand swords would never be enough to make a statue this enormous."

Hearing this—Shichika looked at his sister.

"No use for dreaming—huh, sis? Why try to disappoint me?"

"I can't believe I need to spell it out for you."

Nanami sighed.

A sigh that suited her exceptionally well.

"You know as well as anyone that dreams are useless to me. My body makes dreams unnecessary—out of the question."

"Not anymore though—right?"

"Right."

Nanami was dressed in monkish robes.

Though no longer fully bared, her chest must have held that dagger, Akuto the Eel.

The change was so minute that only Shichika would have noticed, but Nanami's face had taken on a bit of warmth. Pale, to be sure, but with a hint of health that bore the promise—he could see it—of a full recovery.

Health.

The one thing that Nanami—and Shichika—wanted for her more than anything.

If either of them had a dream, then this was it.

And yet something—was awry.

What was it?

He couldn't put his finger on it, but he sensed it.

It wasn't right for her.

Seeing Nanami bearing Akuto the Eel—

"I guess you could call me Nanami the Heel,"[6] she jested. "Hey, if you want to spend your whole day sightseeing, be my guest—but Shichika. You've got some nerve to stand in front of me like some kind of a tourist."

"I wasn't doing it on purpose, sis. Can I just ask one thing, though?"

Nanami refused. "Don't even bother. The answer hasn't changed. I'll only give you Akuto the Eel if you defeat me, I won't simply hand it over. If you want to round up this sword for your owner—you're going to have to take me down."

"..."

"Kill or be killed,"[7] Nanami said—and stood there.

Her form was formlessness.

Kyotoryu Form Zero—the Ichijiku.

"I'm happy to do the killing—"

---

[5] 高価な金属　KŌKA NA KINZOKU　expensive metals
[6] 悪刀七実　AKUTŌ SHICHIMI　"The Wicked Sword: Spice" pun on 悪党 AKUTŌ villain 一味 ICHIMI gang
[7] 殺す気で来なさい　KOROSU KI DE KINASAI　come at me intending to kill, i.e. pull no punches

"Sis."

"Please, don't disappoint me. We're here because you asked me for a rematch—come on, assume your stance."

Hearing this—Shichika did as he was told.

And took position.

He straddled his feet, parallel, one ahead of the other, sinking into his knees and bending at the hips, to make his upper body lean slightly forward—his hands pointed like spears, his elbows at right angles, parallel again and offset, like his feet. His weight on the front leg, as if to tumble forward.

Kyotoryu Form Seven—the Kakitsubata.

Nanami Yasuri and Shichika Yasuri.

Both choosing the same stances as the week before.

"Hmm."

Nanami—glared at Shichika.

Watching, with those eyes of hers.

Fixated.

Focused.

Rapt—

"Seems like you've sharpened up a bit, knocked off a little of the rust. Still soft... Not mushy, but not solid either. Which reminds me, how'd things go with Shichika Hachiretsu? Did you find a way to make up for its weakness?"

"'Course we did. I didn't think of it myself," admitted Shichika, "but we came up with a perfect fix."

"Really. I should hope so—otherwise there'd be no sense to have a rematch."

"Sis, you're about to witness Shichika Hachiretsu as you've never seen it before. You won't be able to brush it off like last week."

"Maybe not."

While Shichika gritted his teeth, ready for battle—

Nanami's expression was relaxed.

In the Ichijiku, even the face was normal.

Same face that she made every day.

Natural posture.

Natural as ever—

"Miss Togame," she addressed the Schemer, there by the wall like that other day.

The only other person present in the grand hall—Emonzaemon was long gone, but not even the monks of Gokenji Temple were around. As both their witness and their referee, Togame kept as much distance as possible to ensure that she was not embroiled in the fight.

"Yes?" she answered, still leaning against the wall, with her arms crossed.

"Go ahead and give the sign, please—there's no use putting on airs."

"I thought I'd give you two a chance to speak, since this might be the last chance that you have."

"Here we go[8] again," Nanami said—laughing wickedly.

An apt laugh for the owner of Akuto the Eel.

"Don't fret—I'll *make sure* this is the last time that we speak. We won't have another sloppy bout like last time—right, Shichika? Remember how things were when you killed Dad?"

"Yeah, I remember," replied Shichika, holding position. "What about it, sis?"

"Never mind. I realize that I've yet to thank[9] you—but I'm not exactly thankful, so don't hold your breath. You could've let Dad—kill me."

"..."

"You should've let him kill me. I don't belong among the living."

"Come on, sis—"

"You come on," Nanami said, "and kill me."

Once again—she eyed Togame.

Not giving Shichika a chance to protest.[10]

"I've made myself clear, so go ahead and give the sign...or are you trying to buy time? Do you need another moment for whatever scheme you're working on?"

"...Okay, okay."

Togame clicked her tongue like she was fed up.

She closed her eyes and raised one hand, like she'd stopped caring.[11]

"Go ahead and kill each other. You're siblings, but you're swords. Who am I to try and stop you. May the best sword win—"

She let her hand fall through the air.

"—Fight!"

That very instant.

Togame the Schemer's scheme—activated.

■　　■

Of course, Nanami Yasuri had some ideas about what sort of chicanery[12] Togame the Schemer might attempt. If she was honest, Nanami was significantly more concerned about Togame, tasked with working as the referee, than with Shichika, her actual opponent.

She suspected firearms.

What if they shot at her with guns set up outside, or off behind the pillars holding up the Inner Sanctum, or from behind the gigantic Katana Buddha?

But her suspicion was not the same as fear.

A fact all too apparent in light of her rumble, back on Haphazard Island,

---

[8] この期に及んで　KONOGO NI OYONDE　"this late in the game"
[9] お礼　OREI　gesture of gratitude
[10] 返事を待たずに　HENJI WO MATAZU NI　without waiting for a response
[11] 半ばやけくそ　HANBA YAKEKUSO　half out of desperation
[12] 仕掛け　SHIKAKE　contraption; contrivance

against Mitsubachi Maniwa, one of the Twelve Bosses of the Maniwa Ninja Clan—whose Blunderbuzz had one-hundred-percent accuracy, able to nail a target from two hundred feet away... Yet Nanami had seen through it all too easily, and turned its powers against him.[13]

Nanami did have firearms on mind—but this also assured her that they would not come into play.

It would be far too typical a scheme.

Togame would never try something so trite.

So what did she have up her sleeves?

Nanami could not begin[14] to speculate.[15]

Nay—*she had no need to speculate.*

Nanami could simply—*watch and learn.*

Speculation be damned—she had *those eyes*.

She could watch and learn.

Seeing.

Seeing everything.

Seeing through things.

Seeing into things.

Seeing beyond things.

Seeing to the end of things.

Seeing made them hers.

Looking at—over—through—into—and out for it.

Observing—and examining it.

Hence.

Regardless of what trickery Togame the Schemer tried to pull, Nanami was ready to fight back—however!

"—nkk!"

Once they had received the signal, Shichika launched from the Kakitsubata, charging full speed for Nanami—but without making even one of the twenty-four feints he had made last time.

Nanami saw that much.

But once she had seen it—*the vision crucial to her strength went black.*

Nay.

That wasn't possible.

At times like these, Nanami would not even allow herself to blink—both of her eyes were open wide.

What had gone black—was the Inner Sanctum.

Once brimming with the orange light of hundreds of candles—swallowed in darkness.

Because the burning candles—had gone out.

Hundreds of candles—all at once.[16]

---

[13] 逆手に SAKATE NI "backhand" turn the tables
[14] 皆目 KAIMOKU "(even) all eyes" ironic considering her power of vision
[15] 見当 KENTŌ "look & hit (strike true)" i.e. guesswork (as above, involves seeing as metaphor)
[16] 一斉 ISSEI in unison

"...nkk! ...nkk!"
—*So that was her scheme!*
Nanami understood immediately.

Why Togame had asked for them to battle not in the Fifth Hall, but the Inner Sanctum, where Nanami may manage, but Shichika would find it hard to negotiate the pillars and the various other obstacles—that was why!

She understood why she had asked for them to fight at night, too.

And in a place where oh so many candles were no oddity, but *a necessity*—none other than the Inner Sanctum of Seiryoin Gokenji Temple, at the very feet of the Katana Buddha!

If it had been the dojo, she would have seen it coming.

There, candles, even hundreds of them, would have only served one purpose—shedding light on Nanami and Shichika—and would have been impossible to miss. But candles in the Inner Sanctum served a higher purpose, namely illuminating the Katana Buddha.

—*The Katana Buddha.*
Did his presence—
Baffle even me?
For the past week.
The Schemer—*had been hoarding[17] candles.*

Then she'd *swapped out* the candles of the Inner Sanctum with her own collection.

Not rigging them with any special mechanism, however—since Nanami would have noticed any trickery.

These were run-of-the-mill candles.

She had merely modified their lengths.

So once all of them were lit—*the candles would burn out at exactly the same time.*

If it was possible to estimate how long a candle will burn before going out.

It was equally possible to make two candles burn out at the same time.

Or hundreds of candles, for that matter—

It could be done.

And the Schemer—*made it happen.*

Using candles of the exact same length would have stood out, so she must have mixed things up with candles of all different shapes and sizes and materials. Moreover, since she could only light one at a time, she had to gradually reduce their length so that the last one finished at the same as the first—

As agonizing as this mathematics and their realization[18] sound—the Schemer must have done it all alone.

Not calling on the temple monks for aid.

This temple was under Nanami's control.

The monks she lorded over with an iron fist had seen their holy land usurped,

---

[17] かき集める　KAKI ATSUMERU　scrape together; amass
[18] 作業と計算　SAGYŌ TO KEISAN　operation and calculations

and could hardly be regarded as her friends—but neither could they be expected to voluntarily abet Togame's schemes.

The candles went out in a flash.

Followed by total darkness.

The veil[19] of night.

Needless to say, Nanami was not completely blinded by the darkness, but the sudden *shift from light to dark*, as if the sun had fallen from the midday sky—shrunk her field of vision instantaneously.

All she had to do was watch.

And she could see through any scheme.

But she couldn't see through schemes—*she couldn't see!*

"Nkkk...gh."

Nanami was not so much surprised or confused—

As she was overwhelmingly impressed.

In this case, perhaps the difference was a matter of semantics—but the source of her reaction was the sheer scale of the ruse that the Schemer had cast *over their simple duel.*

Nanami asked her whether she was buying time—but had not thought that she was *really* doing such a thing. While listening to Shichika and Nanami hash it out, and following up with a few comments of her own—

Togame had a clock ticking inside her head.

Keeping time—with lunatic[20] precision.

Eyes never drifting toward the candles.

After giving the signal, she dropped her hand—out like a light.

May the best sword win—hah.

It was a truly—loveable performance.[21]

Even in Nanami's eyes.

Utterly fascinating!

"...Whoahhhhhhhhh!"

Shichika too.

Shichika Yasuri, the Seventh Master of the Kyotoryu.

Obviously Togame filled him in beforehand that the candles would burn out immediately after she had signaled them to start the fight—sending the effulgent Inner Sanctum into darkness.

Knowing in advance had only saved him from the element of surprise; Shichika could not escape the darkness either.

This scheme was indiscriminate,[22] affecting everyone, not just Nanami.

But knowing that his field of vision would go black—gave Shichika a foothold in the fight. Which is precisely why he charged full speed for Nanami, without adding a single feint.

[19] 帳 TOBARI burial shroud
[20] 常軌を逸して JŌKI WO ISSHITE "beyond the norm"
[21] 惚れ惚れする手際 HOREBORE SURU TEGIWA "crush-worthy handiness"
[22] 無差別 MUSABETSU "no difference-separation" 差別 SABETSU (racial, etc.) discrimination
無差別攻撃 MUSABETSU KŌGEKI indiscriminate attack (heedless of civilian casualties)

Leaping through the darkness—Shichika landed at Nanami's feet.
And inside her reach—took Kyotoryu Form Four, the Asagao.
His answer to the darkness.
Something that Nanami, depending solely on her vision—could not possibly have done.

"Alright, sis, here I come—"

The weakness of Shichika Hachiretsu—was in the pause preceding Fatal Orchid Four: Ryuryoku Kako. Togame had alerted him, and even told him he should launch the sequence of attacks from Ryuryoku Kako, so he could rip through all the others in one go—but Shichika kept on thinking and added to the strategy.

He was fighting for Togame.

For the owner of Shichika Yasuri, sword that he was.

Thus he arrived at a conclusion.

If any of the Seven Fatal Orchids could be said to have a pause, Ryuryoku Kako was the culprit, but all of the other six had some kind of a pause or windup. It was just that Ryuryoku Kako was the most conspicuous—in which case.

Among the five thousand and forty possible permutations[23] of the Seven Fatal Orchids, there had to be a combination more efficient than the rest—

An order of attack that bested any other combination.

Shichika had thought hard.

As bad at thinking as he may have been—he tried like crazy.

Tuning his Last Fatal Orchid to have *minimum interference*—and *maximum ferocity*.

The ideal combination.

From five thousand and forty—down to seven hundred and twenty.

And again—down to a single sequence.

Fatal Orchid Four: Ryuryoku Kako
Fatal Orchid One: Kyoka Suigetsu
Fatal Orchid Five: Hika Rakuyo
Fatal Orchid Seven: Rakka Rozeki
Fatal Orchid Three: Hyakka Ryoran
Fatal Orchid Six: Kinjo Tenka
Fatal Orchid Two: Kacho Fugetsu

Unleashed in this specific order simultaneously, the Seven Fatal Orchids went beyond a medley—they formed a maelstrom![24]

This was it!

Last Fatal Orchid of the Kyotoryu—Shichika Hachiretsu Redux![25]

---

[23] 順列組み合せ　JUNRETSU KUMIAWASE　ordered sequence
[24] 混成接続ならぬ強制接続　KONSEI SETSUZOKU NARANU KYŌSEI SETSUZOKU
　　　"not a mixed connection but a forced connection"　bolted together rather than just interlinked
[25] (改)　(KAI)　revised, remodeled

Akuto the Eel

■ ■

Complete darkness is easy to say and hard to find.

For over time—the eyes become adjusted to the dark.

Starlight wafted through the windows here and there around the Inner Sanctum—this particular scheme was only advantageous in the moment after all the candles had burned out.

In darkness of the Inner Sanctum of Gokenji Temple.

All that remained to be seen—is who had won.

And Togame the Schemer could see for herself.

Shichika Yasuri—held his guard.[26]

Nanami Yasuri—lay face up, a short distance away.

This genius that had been labeled a monster.

Lay with her back on the floor.

"Hey, Togame."

Togame had been at a loss for words at this display, but snapped out of it when Shichika called her name.

"Wh-What."

"Look."

Togame looked.

Shichika held up his hand—gripping a dagger.

Akuto the Eel.

Struggling in the darkness, or perhaps attacking her and meeting no resistance, Shichika had wrested the sword from her breast.

"Here's another one—check."

Shichika lobbed the dagger at Togame. Lacking the reflexes to catch it, she allowed its point to sink into the floorboards—then prized it free.

A faint numbness wiggled through her fingers.

The blade was charged—with lightning.

It was unclear how it worked, but one thing was for sure.

"That makes seven."

Zetto the Leveler, Zanto the Razor, Sento the Legion, Hakuto the Whisper, Zokuto the Armor, Soto the Twin... This made seven.

"What about Nanami? Is she—dead?"

"Nah, she's the same as ever, she'll live. Even in the darkness, she found a way to block me, and Shichika Hachiretsu Redux, my new Last Fatal Orchid, only found so much purchase. It took everything I had to yank out Akuto the Eel. But I gotta say, her defense was less than perfect—she probably couldn't see that well."

Shichika turned over to his sister—prostrate and motionless.

"It was kinda like this after Sabi... It sorta feels anticlimactic... At least half of it was thanks to your idea. Anyway, I guess we won? But wow...take her eyes

---

[26] 残心の構え　ZANSHIN NO KAMAE　"mind-remaining stance"　ready to receive a counterstrike

by turning out the lights. You sure think up some crazy stuff, Togame. This time you really cooked us up a banger."[27]

"I had no choice against someone as strong as her. You wouldn't believe how much it cost and what a pain it was to come up with a scheme that Nanami and the monks wouldn't catch on to—but it was all worthwhile."

"Yeah—seems that way."

"Still, that was quite the gamble. Everything was riding on that one shot. If you had missed with Shichika Hachiretsu Redux, it would have all been over. But it seems like you picked the winning set of numbers for the sequence."

"I dunno though, I think it still needs lots of work[28]—but we can save that conversation for another day. Can you call us down a doctor, Togame? Without Akuto the Eel, I'm scared that sis won't last."

"Right, the air here on the mainland is too rich for her... Got it, then—Shichika!"

When Togame screamed—Shichika burst into action.

Togame's eyes—were on Nanami, of course.

Prostrate in her monkish robes—but moving.

Or so it seemed—from where Togame stood.

"...!"

Shichika assumed Form Seven, the Kakitsubata, and faced his sister.

But Nanami did not so much as shiver[29] where she lay—

"Uh, Togame—"

"Eyes on her—it can't be true..."

However.

If it were true—they were in serious trouble.

That scheme would never work a second time—and she was fresh out of ideas.

It had been one hell of a gamble.

They could dispossess Nanami of the Eel—but they could never strip[30] her of her genius. Togame was at a loss for schemes, and Shichika no better.

If it wasn't over yet—

"...Phew."

Indeed.

Still lying on her back—Nanami *heaved a sigh.*

A sigh only Nanami could have sighed.

"Looks like—I underestimated you."

Then—no rush.

Not rushing—Nanami sat herself up from the floor.

When she was hit or perhaps when she tumbled to the floor, her monkish robe had come undone—baring her chest.

And in the middle of her chest.

[27] 大掛かり ŌGAKARI elaborate device, plan
[28] 研鑽 KENSAN practice with an aim toward mastery 研 KEN hone 鑽 SAN bore (a hole)
[29] 微動だにしない BIDŌ DA NI SHINAI not make even the slight movement
[30] 剝奪 HAKUDATSU "peel away" rob

A yawning gap.
Left by Akuto the Eel.
Hollow—not a drop of blood.
The shape of nothingness[31] itself.
The shape—of darkness.
Perfect darkness, impossible by definition.
"Akuto the Eel? You do realize that bogus sword *tempered*[32] my strength—*in revitalizing me, it slowed me down*[33]... As for Watch and Learn... Taking on the moves of others—*made me weaker by design.*"
Looks like, she muttered.
Looks like—I was wrong.
Nanami Yasuri—stood up.
"I was wrong...to try and *live a little longer—to fight you head-to-head in my condition.*"
"Huh?"
Watch and Learn.
One would think—the skill would make a person stronger.
That it would mean the acquisition of additional strength.
However—
A genius like Nanami Yasuri.
Took on the skills of others—to become weaker.
In order to be weak.
A weaker being.
Governing[34]—her strength.
That she may live.
Nanami Yasuri watched and learned not to increase her strength—but to survive.
And thus—she watched and learned voraciously.
Maniwa Ninpo.
The monstrous strength of the Itezoras.
The necromancy of the Sacred Guardians of Mt. Shirei.
The Gokenjiryu of Seiryoin Gokenji Temple.
And yes.
Even the methods of the Kyotoryu!
"S-Sis..."
No wonder Akuto the Eel didn't suit her.
That it seemed like a bad fit—as fitting as it seemed to be.
The Mutant Blade, the work of Kiki Shikizaki, inarguably revivified Nanami—but only because it contained her strength.
To Nanami, Akuto the Eel worked as a handicap.[35]

[31] 虚無　KYOMU "hollow nothing" void　虚無的 KYOMUTEKI nihilistic vs. 虚刀流 KYOTŌRYŪ
[32] 調整　CHŌSEI　modify, arrange (to suit the circumstance)
[33] 沈静化　CHINSEIKA　pacify, quiet down　as in the cognate　鎮静剤 CHINSEIZAI sedative
[34] 制御　SEIGYO　control e.g. 制御棒　SEIGYOBŌ　control rod (in reactors)
[35] 拘束具　KŌSOKUGU　restraint

A handicap she needed—to survive.
To make her weak enough.
"Alright, come on, Shichika," Nanami said.
And took her position—or lack thereof.
Kyotoryu Form Zero, the Ichijiku? Not even that!
This time—she was standing there, and nothing more.
Even Togame, a stranger to the martial arts, could see—and perhaps see all the better.
This was everything and nothing.
Nothing—just Nanami Yasuri, being herself.
Like Konayuki Itezora, back on Mt. Odori in Ezo, she was not working off a pattern. Yet Nanami was no amateur—but a genius!
"I'm still alive. Hurry up and kill me please."
"But sis—"
Shichika—was shaking.
Completely spellbound.[36]
Even without using her eyes—Nanami was capturing the essence of Shichika Yasuri.
He was terrified.
And overwhelmed.
Togame could not sense it.
But Shichika, being *halfway strong*, took the full brunt of the fearsome energy radiating from Nanami.
"Enough!" Togame cried in a voice that echoed through the Inner Sanctum. "What's the point? We have Akuto the Eel! Call it a day! You have no reason to go on fighting!"
"*Quiet.*"
Nanami—spoke softly.
And moved again.
Turning toward Togame, she appeared to merely whip her sleeve—but *something else* had happened here.
Her hair.
Togame's hair of white—fell to the floor.
It had been snipped off.
In a straight line—just above her shoulders.
"...nkk!"
The line cut clear across her slender neck—
Lopping off her signature white hair in such a clean and perfect path that she was lucky she hadn't lost her head as well.
On the floorboards of the Inner Sanctum.
The hair sat in a pile—at Togame's feet.
A pile of white.
"Wh-What the... H-How did you—from over there?"

[36] 呑まれていた NOMARETE ITA "swallowed" figure of speech for feeling cowed

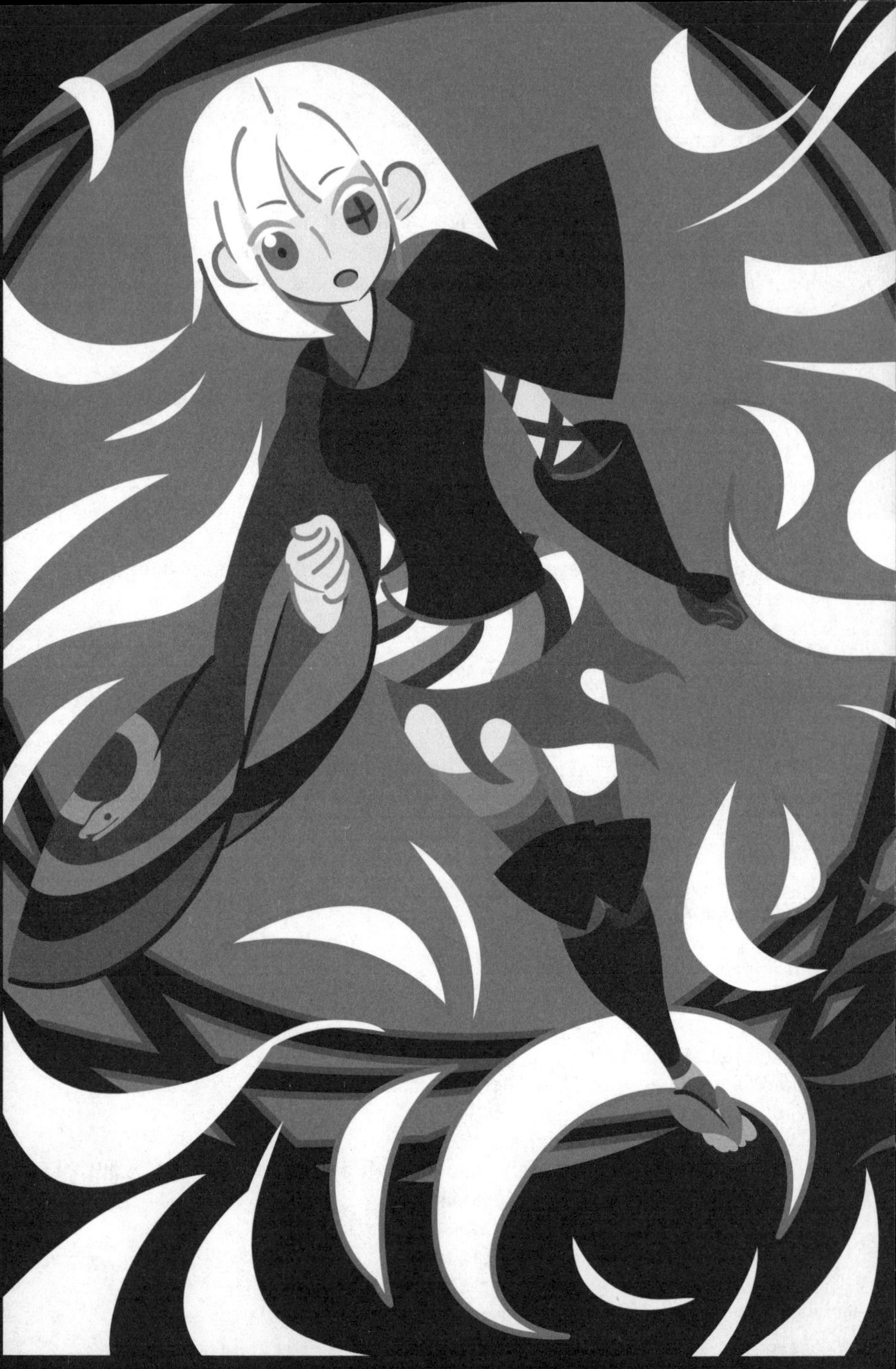

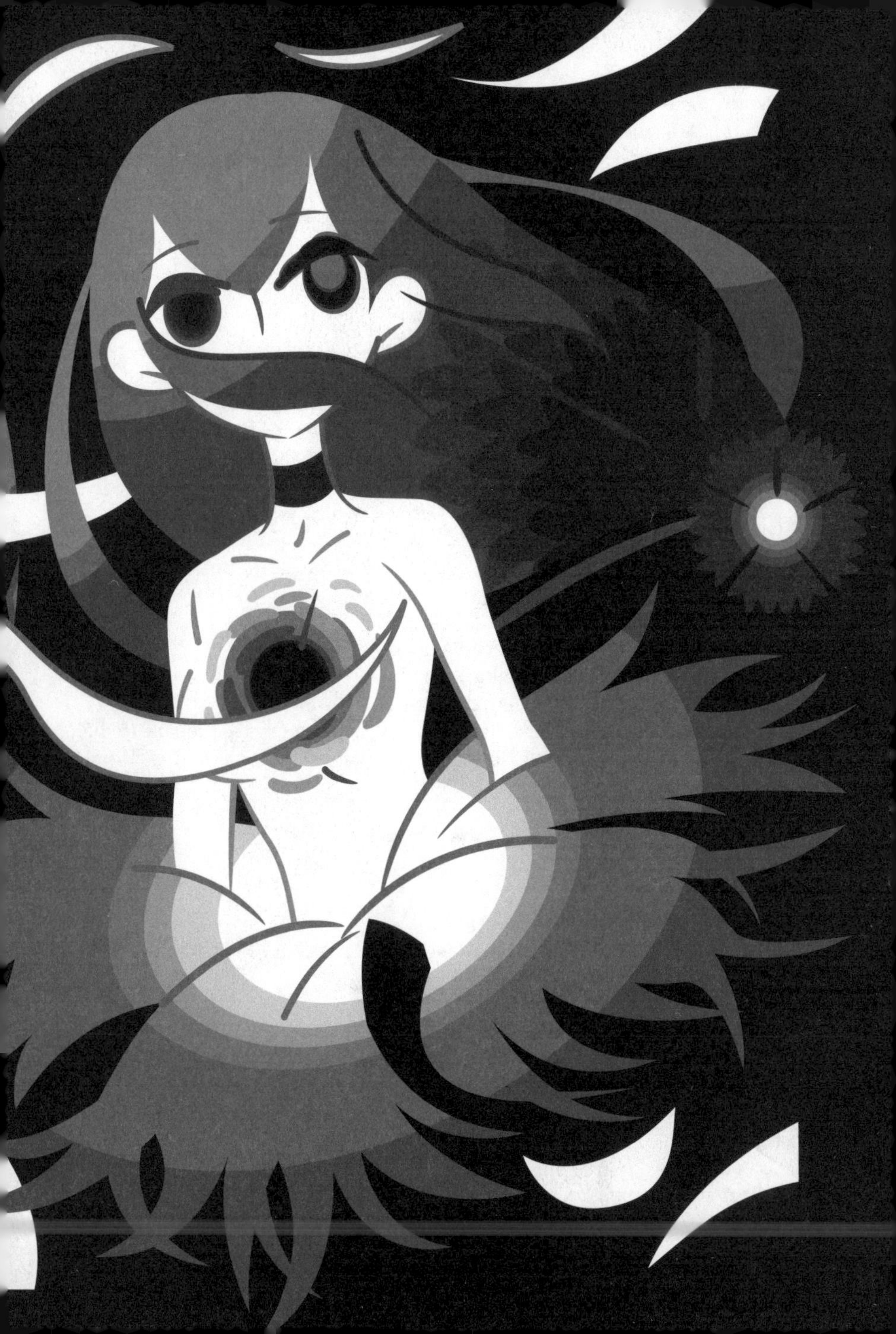

"*Make no mistake—your head is next.*"
Nanami—laughed.
Her laugh sounded evil to the core—tireless[37] in its wickedness.
Losing Akuto the Eel—had made no difference.
"There, Shichika...now you have a good reason to fight."
"You cut...Togame's hair."
No longer shaking—Shichika had frozen.
His eyes were clear of trepidation.[38]
Ferociously—he glowered at his sister.
"That I cannot forgive—Nanami."
"Have a fetish for long hair? That's one more thing—for you and Dad to have in common. You're both disgusting. So guess what."
Shichika's indignation—had failed to get a rise out of Nanami.
"Rather than pluck you like a weed, I'll pick you apart[39] like the flower you are."
"Go ahead, but that won't be easy—*if you're torn to smithereens,* sis."
Togame held her tongue.
They may have captured Akuto the Eel—but the battle wasn't over.
In fact, they were only getting started.
The family showdown!
The erstwhile strongest in Japan against her successor!
Nanami Yasuri versus Shichika Yasuri!
No plots or schemes, and may the best sword win—*fight!*
"I am Shichika Yasuri! Seventh Master of the Kyotoryu—prepare to die!"
"And I am Nanami Yasuri! No school or loyalty—*prepared to die!*"[40]

■ ■

She was ready to end it then and there.
But she could see[41]—that this would not be possible.
Nanami couldn't help but see.
—*Ahhhh.*
The instant she had taken her first step, the foot that held her weight collapsed. And not only her foot—her whole body *came apart.*
Separating—unraveling.
The skin tore from her body, flaying her alive, exposing flesh that bled from every vein.
Blood sprayed.

[37] あくまでも AKUMADEMO "to the very end" derived from 飽きる AKIRU get bored
[38] 憶する OKUSURU to flinch, shrink, quail
[39] 散らして CHIRASHITE scatter petals falling are a traditional image for getting killed in action
[40] 来ませい KIMASEI come (for me) archaic locution
[41] 悟った SATOTTA realized not explicitly Buddhist here vs. 悟り SATORI enlightenment

With a body like hers.
—*I saw this coming.*
I knew my body—could never stand up to the full force of my strength.
It had been obvious.
That's why—she'd tried to learn everyone's moves.
Her father's—and Shichika's.
In order to be weak.
A weaker being.
That she may live—
Her mouth filled with the taste of blood.
She was collapsing on the inside, the same as on the outside.
Her veins had ruptured.
Her flat muscles went to tatters,[42] and her thin bones snapped.
Nanami Yasuri unbridled, her true self.
Incapable of taking—but a single step.
Neither plucked like a weed.
Nor scattered like a flower.
She tumbled—like a ripe fruit.[43]
All on her own.
—*Just one hit.*
I thought I might last long enough to get in one hit, at least...
Was she paying[44] for the ill-begotten energy that Akuto the Eel had afforded her? Even so—
"..."
As she collapsed, her vision blurred.[45]
She happened to be facing Togame, whose enviable[46] tresses had been cropped short at the shoulders so that she looked just like a little kid[47]—
But it was with a pained frown that the Schemer greeted the crumbling mess that was Nanami.
—*Ah.*
Was that...unnecessary?
Did Miss Togame see this coming, and rub me the wrong way to provoke me—screaming like that?
Yet another scheme, at that stage?
Predicting that my body couldn't stand up to the full force of my strength, did she aim to wear me down, if only by that much?
Putting herself on the line.
When she could have died.
Unlikely.

---

[42] 千切れ　CHIGIRE　break into "a thousand" pieces
[43] 実　MI　fruit　second character in　七実 NANAMI　"Seventh Fruit"
[44] つけ　TSUKE　bill, tab; figuratively, comeuppance
[45] 狂う　KURU'U　screw up; go crazy
[46] 見目麗しい　MIME URUWASHII　"lovely to the eye"
[47] 童子　DŌJI　very young child; monk too young to shave his head

But maybe—that's what having an agenda means?
The point of any—still eluded Nanami Yasuri.
But she chuckled anyway.
Another of her evil laughs, it made her body collapse all the more. The floorboards of the Inner Sanctum drew closer.
After all that.
It's illness that kills me, after all?
—You should never have been born—
—Poor thing—
Poor thing, who should never have been born.
That's me.
I should have died, I shouldn't be alive.
Honestly.
I wish someone had killed me—
Doesn't matter who, but well, if I could choose—
"Sis!"
Just as Nanami Yasuri began to close her eyes—her brother, Shichika Yasuri, made a run at her, aiming between her body and the floorboards.
He made it—*barely.*
—Shichika.
My—kid brother.
Finally—killing me.
"Last Fatal Orchid of the Kyotoryu—Shichika Hachiretsu Redux!"
Without hesitation.
Shichika unleashed his Last Fatal Orchid on Nanami.
"..."
By now the vessels of her brain had probably burst.
Nanami's grip on consciousness was slipping,[48] and her head had filled with fog.
And yet—her body had maintained its reflexes.
Her genius shone impeccably.
Even though the more it shone—the more her body fell apart.
Fielding Fatal Orchid Four, Ryuryoku Kako.
Dodging Fatal Orchid One, Kyoka Suigetsu.
Blocking Fatal Orchid Five, Hika Rakuyo.
Evading Fatal Orchid Seven, Rakka Rozeki.
Avoiding Fatal Orchid Three, Hyakka Ryoran.
Seeing through Fatal Orchid Six, Kinjo Tenka.
And catching Fatal Orchid Two, Kacho Fugetsu.
Defending herself.
Wracking her body with a pain more savage than if she had suffered the attack—she defended herself anyway.

[48] 朦朧　MŌRŌ　woozy

As if it were simply good etiquette.[49]
But Shichika—would not let up.[50]
He refused to let up on Nanami.
After finishing Fatal Orchid Two, Kacho Fugetsu, he seized the collar of her monkish robes and stabbed her with her spear hand.
—*I won't make it.*
Not in time.
With her unraveling body, she couldn't defend herself in time—but in truth, not even his spear hand should have been capable of injuring her.
Her body was collapsing, unable to stand up to her own strength.
But she could still stand up—to anything from Shichika.
He came nowhere close to her.
Except.
The blade of his hand was aimed at Nanami's bosom—her bosom.
The place where she had carried Akuto the Eel.
The gap yawning—from the middle of her chest.
Eyes on the hole—he drove his hand inside.
Ah, I see, Nanami thought to herself.
That's what a sword gets—for trying to use another sword.
The swordsmen of the Kyotoryu did not refuse to use swords.
They were unable to use swords.
When it came to wielding swords, they possessed absolutely no ability.
—*Oh, Dad.*
I guess I'm part of the Kyotoryu, after all.
"Kyotoryu—Tampopo!"
The highest cliff can crumble from a single cavity—
Or so the saying[51] goes.
Shichika plunged his spear hand deep—deep into Nanami's breast.
That move.
Oddly enough—was perhaps Nanami's favorite part of the Kyotoryu.
"..."
Lifted up forcibly, Nanami, who'd been about to collapse onto the floor—found herself leaning against Shichika's giant body.
"Shichika."
She had almost nothing left.
Giving it everything she had, and destroying herself in the process—she whispered in her brother's ear.
"Shichika, y-you..."
You really killed me.
Is what she meant to say.
To praise her little brother for proving he could beat his older sister.

[49] 礼儀　REIGI　manners; the proper thing to do
[50] 諦める　AKIRAMERU　cease (an action); abandon (hope)
[51] 故事　KOJI　legend; tradition

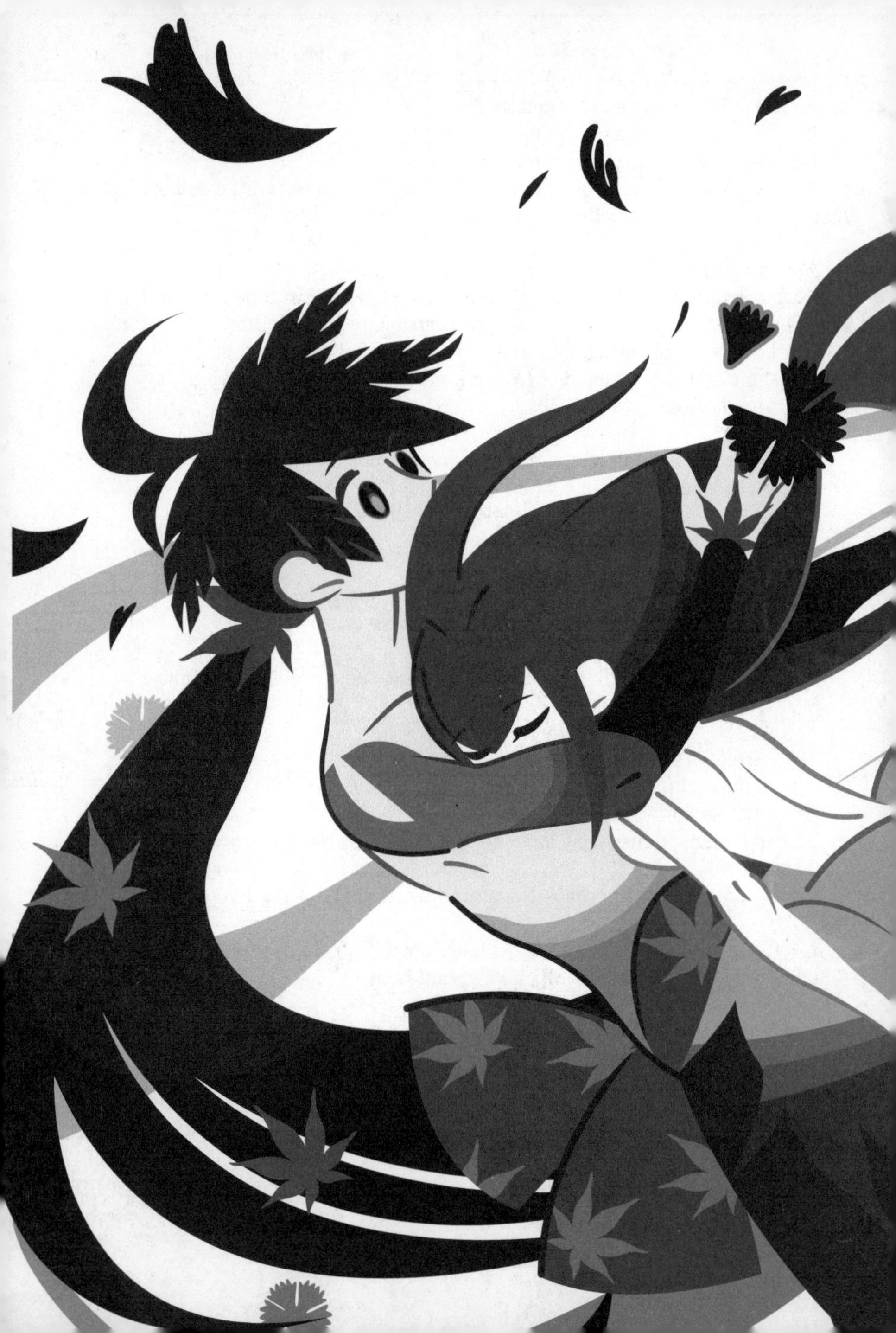

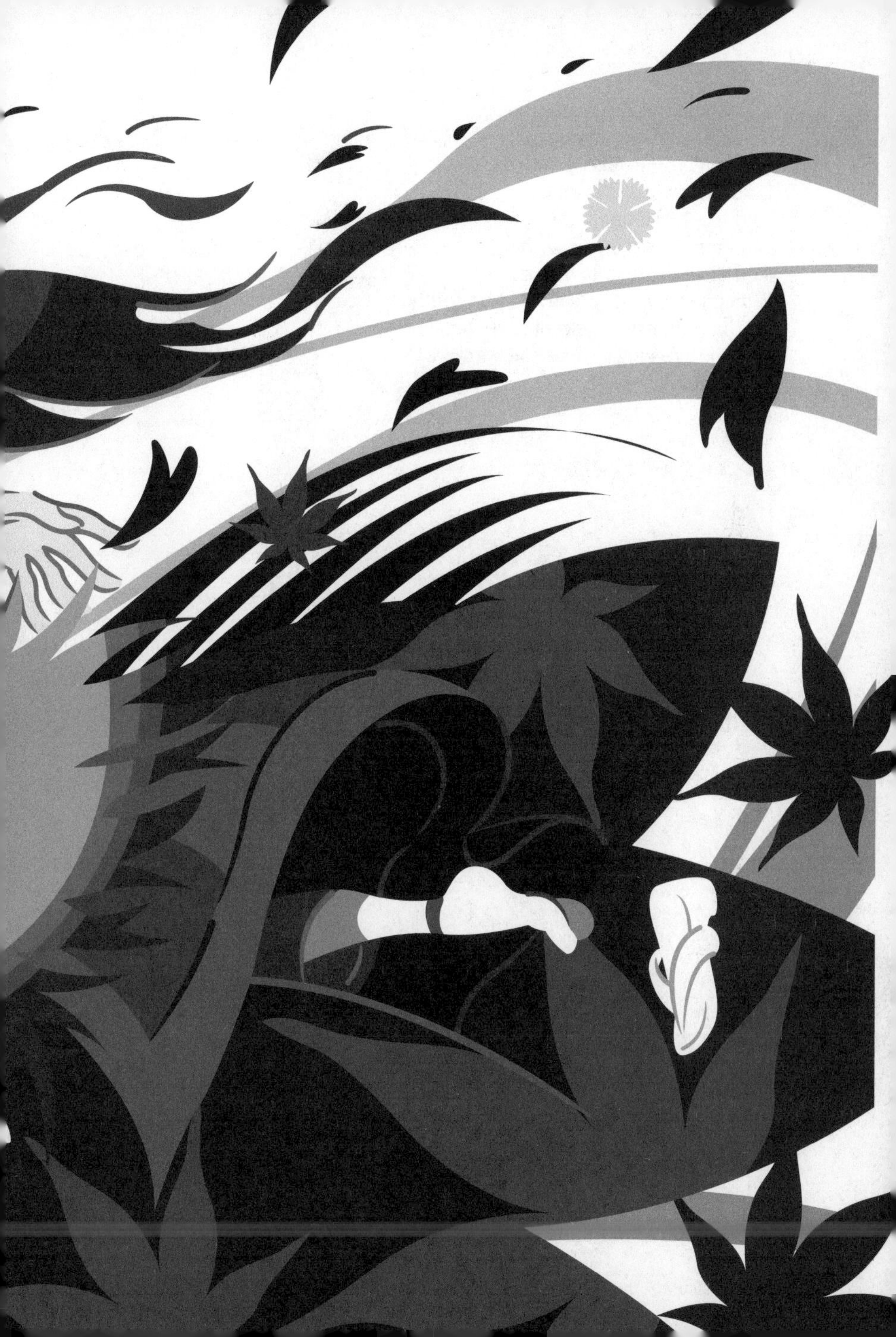

She would not die from illness.
Or by dint of her own genius.
She could die—like a swordsman.
Like the sword she was.
And like a human being.
A member of the Kyotoryu.
And of the House of Yasuri.
Which is why—she wanted him to know.
To thank her dear, sweet little brother—
For killing her, just like she wanted.
"You'd really[52] kill me."
...
Oops.
Did she—mangle that?

---

[52] よくも YOKUMO "how dare you" vs. the earlier よくぞ "good on you"/"well done"

EPILOGUE

■ ■

"Nanami—wanted to be killed, didn't she," Togame said.

Three days had passed.

Togame the Schemer and Shichika Yasuri, Seventh Master of the Kyotoryu, were back at the same harbor where they landed when they arrived in Shikoku. After the showdown with Nanami at the Inner Sanctum of Seiryoin Gokenji Temple, they'd gone back up the road they'd come in on.

The albeit brief appearance of Nanami Yasuri—a monster of a swordswoman, or swordswoman of a monster—at that holy site for swordsmen could only amplify the reputation of the temple. The fight between Nanami and Shichika would doubtlessly go down in history[1] alongside the famous duel, between a man bearing a greatsword and another bearing two, on Ganryu Island, that other holy site. But putting aside a matter for scholars of a later era, the near prospects of Gokenji Temple, its monks obliterated by their so-called guest of honor, were dire. Luckily for Togame, the cleanup did not fall under her purview.

It looked like a job for the Magistrate of Shrines and Temples.

She couldn't help but feel a little sorry for that particular directorate—but Togame made a point of staying out of everything that was not specifically her job.

And what was her job?

But of course—the Sword Hunt.

Now—waiting by the harbor for the boat to take them to Owari, Togame held a dagger.

Akuto the Eel.

One of the Twelve Possessed, the masterworks of Kiki Shikizaki.

Each of which was worth an inordinate sum, enough to buy a country, but since no passerby would ever dream this thing[2] would command such a price, Togame had no issue with examining its features like that—out in the open.

Besides, Akuto the Eel didn't look like a katana.

Charged with lightning—same as ever.

What on earth was it made of?

Thus far, whenever they had landed a katana on the Sword Hunt, Togame had it posted[3] to Owari, but they were heading to Owari too—had no choice but to do so. Since Akuto the Eel was such a manageable[4] sword (small enough for even Togame to hold), nothing like Zokuto the Armor or Soto the Twin, she'd decided to appoint herself its courier.

"I couldn't understand why she was throwing herself into a silly battle, and

[1] 語り継がれる　KATARI TSUGARERU　told from one generation to the next
[2] 代物　SHIROMONO　article; stuff
[3] 別便　BETSUBIN　"mail separately"
[4] 手ごろ　TEGORO　handy

forcing you into it to boot—but that was it. Which isn't the same as wanting to die. Her body was too weak for her to want such a thing—to Nanami, dying was a fact of life."

Togame twirled her hair, which she apparently was fond of cut this short.

"And I'm sure she thought nothing of being killed, either—but hoped for it nonetheless."

Pain and suffering were old friends for Nanami.

And likewise—death was an old friend, too.

For Nanami Yasuri—

Death and killing, and being killed, for that matter.

It was nothing special.

And yet, for the first time—

She had hoped to be killed.

"Facing off against the Bug Unit back on Haphazard Island—must have been the trigger.[5] I suppose the Maniwa were no match for someone as strong as her...but in the end, she couldn't hold up against her own strength."

"It's not just her," said Shichika.

He was sitting right across from Togame—but his vacant gaze was set upon the sky.

As if something—was on his mind.

Out of character.

"No body could ever hold up to that kind of strength. Even I can see that. Dad used to say her sickliness was a sign of the wrath of the gods, but it was simpler than that. It's like when you blow too much air into a balloon—that's why she was frail."

"Too much genius for a single human being to bear. Whereby—she set her sights upon the strength of others, always weaker by comparison. Like when you splash cold water in a boiling pot to cool it down—that's why she always watched and learned."

"I never realized that till now—"

In that case, thought Togame.

Mutsue's refusal to share even a single aspect of the Kyotoryu with Nanami takes on an entirely new dimension.

Nanami Yasuri was too strong to be taken under anybody's wing.

What if her genius had not followed apace with her alien strength?

If she had never learned to watch and learn—what would have become of Nanami?

As soon as he realized that she had such an ability.

Mutsue tried to kill her—in cold blood.

And soon after—got murdered by his son.

A man suspected of murdering his own wife.

—Not to mention.

My own dad.

[5] 契機 KEIKI opportunity, impetus

"Nanami's throwdown with the Bug Unit was her first taste of battle. And she won—with flying colors, hands down.[6] And yet—all of that exertion must have taken a huge toll on her body... She must have realized she was not long for this world. I'm sure she felt her battle with the Bug Unit—taking countless years off of her life."

"Sis was the best," Shichika said, "but she was too strong for her own good—too strong to fight."

"..."

"Her genius made up for her frail body—but you could also blame her frailty on her genius. I think so, anyway."

"That's why she left the island—right? She knew the air over on the mainland was too rich for her, she came anyway. Warning you about the weakness of your Last Fatal Orchid was a convenient excuse. All she wanted—was for you to kill her off."

She wanted somebody to kill her.

And not just anybody.

It had to be her brother—Shichika.

"That's why she went to all the trouble of hunting down one of the swords—to give you a good reason to face off. Hmph. That explains everything—"

"Wanted somebody—to kill her."

"I can't pretend to understand what that must feel like, but I have a hunch that you can do a better job."

She didn't want to die from illness.

Or by dint of her own genius.

She wanted to die a normal death, like a human being.

She hadn't chosen her life, but had chosen how to die.

"Makes me wonder."

Shichika spoke gazing off into the sky.

"Did Nanami also want Dad to kill her?"

"Remember what she told you, Shichika. She wouldn't have minded. But acceptance and hope are two very different things. Still—just as you still love your father," Togame said, "I'm sure Nanami loved him too, in her own twisted way."

When it came to fathers, Togame had her own mix of feelings.

In that respect, she understood exactly where Nanami came from.

They both—carried the burdens of their fathers.

That was the deal.

"I dunno, Togame."

Shichika turned his gaze from the sky—to her.

"Sis may have wanted me to kill her," he muttered, as if to himself, "but that doesn't mean—that I wanted to do it."

In fact, Shichika looked like he was about to cry.

This caught Togame by surprise.

She recalled Nanami's words.

[6] 楽勝 圧勝 RAKUSHŌ ASSHŌ easy victory sweeping victory

—Since you want to treat him as a human—
—Just take good care of him—
Maybe things would have been different half a year ago.

He wouldn't have thought twice about killing his own sister—as a sword, he wouldn't have thought anything at all.

No hesitation—

Like when he cut down Meisai Tsuruga—or any of his adversaries thus far.

Or his own father, Mutsue Yasuri.

He would have cut Nanami down.

Unencumbered by emotion—a sword doing what it was made to do.

He would have murdered his own sister.

But that was then.

After six months traveling alongside Togame—

Shichika had stopped behaving like a sword.

And started acting—like a human being.

Hence him being on the verge of tears.

"..."

The sadness that she saw in Shichika was her own fault.

He had not failed her, as a sword.

But he had failed to keep it together [7]—through no fault but her own.

—Did I...

Did I make a mistake?

Had Nanami been correct—that it was wrong to treat swords as people?

To be sure, the Hero of the Rebellion, Mutsue Yasuri—had not served the House of Tetsubi like any human being.

He had been treated—like the sword he was.

And hence became Hero of the Rebellion.

"Either way, her time was up. If you hadn't been the one to kill her, her illness would have killed her. Think of it that way, Shichika."

"If I hadn't taken Akuto the Eel from her...would sis still be alive?"

"You're mistaken."

Togame raised the dagger in her hand for him to see—as if to warn[8] him.

"Nanami was killed by Akuto the Eel. It's just like you said before. Swords can't handle other swords. This thing isn't called the Eel for show—it sucked the life right out of her."

"I guess Mt. Shirei, where she found the sword—was known as a hangout for monsters."

"Not monsters, so much as ghosts. I'm not saying I believe in all that hocus-pocus...but this sword was the only thing keeping that moribund mountain alive. It was bound to die. You can't force nature."

"So you're saying that Mt. Shirei's ruined too... I dunno about this Sword

---

[7] 心を折られた KOKORO WO ORARETA his heart got broken, snapped in half
preceding sentence also uses verb 折る ORU to fold (as in 折り紙 ORIGAMI); "to snap" if object is hard
[8] 諭す SATOSU admonish

Hunt... It seems like everywhere we go winds up turning into wasteland."

"There is no path for us to follow, nor do any remain in our wake? Well, I suppose it's not quite that gruesome."

Gekoku Castle fell.

Triad Shrine in Izumo no longer was a fortress.

Suo saw the strongest in Japan replaced.

The Armored Pirates of Satsuma lost their namesake.

And the holy land of Seiryoin Gokenji Temple—would be short-staffed[9] for the foreseeable future.

"Is it wearing on you, Shichika?" Togame gently prodded. "Are you sick of pushing people—to give up their swords?"

"..."

"I'm ready to make anything or anybody step aside in the name of carrying out my mission. It means more to me than life itself, but it's only mine in the end. Have you had enough this time around? Then fine—just say so."

"No," answered Shichika.

Without hesitation.

The same way that he always answered Togame—straight up.

"I've already decided I'd fight for you. That works best for the both of us. You're the most important thing to me—that hasn't changed one bit. I want to be of use to you."

"..."

"That's—that's my purpose."

Purpose.[10]

By having his heart broken by his sister—

Shichika had gained, in exchange, a sense of purpose.

Perhaps he had actually failed Togame as a sword.

But Togame, for her part, found this Shichika all the more reliable.

Who knows whether she had been right or wrong.

They'd find out soon enough—but in any case, regrets seemed unnecessary.

"Oh, that reminds me, Shichika. Now that my hair is shorter, are you sure that you can tell the difference between me and other people?"

She hassled him to bury her embarrassment.

"What the heck are you talking about—"

Shichika laughed.

Not a lively laugh, but a laugh all the same.

"I liked your hair when it was long—but it looks really good short, too. Man, sis was really good at cutting hair."

"I was about to say the same thing. I won't need a trim for quite some time."

"Can I touch it?"

"Do as you please. I know how much my hair excites you."

With her permission, Shichika touched her hair.

---

[9] 人手不足 HITODE BUSOKU "not enough hands"
[10] 覚悟 KAKUGO resolve has also been rendered as "agenda" "cause" "mission"

Stroking the tresses—trimmed to her shoulders.

Her hair symbolized her anger—it was her grudge made manifest, the emblem of her vengeance.

"Ahhh."

Shichika—let out a deep sigh.

Running his hands through her hair.

Perhaps sighing didn't suit him like his sister.

But he exhaled—as if he were lamenting.

"This makes me a lone wolf just like you, Togame. I never thought that it'd be so lonely—to be on your own."

"On your own?"

Togame frowned at his choice of words.

Sheesh.

This guy really has no clue.

"Quit spewing nonsense, Shichika. What are you talking about? I'm not a lone wolf."

"Huh?"

"Because I have you."

Do I really have to spell everything[11] out for you?

"And that means you have me."

∎ ∎

Thus our two travelers finally returned to Owari, the seat of the Yanari Shogunate. Togame the Schemer would soon have her delayed[12] reunion with the Inspector General of the Yanari Shogunate, Princess Negative—but the news[13] about the Twelve Possessed of Kiki Shikizaki vouchsafed by Princess Negative at their meeting would have major implications for the future of the Sword Hunt.

Five swords were waiting to be found.

Little by little, Togame and Shichika—were nearing the conclusion of their journey.

Akuto the Eel: Check
End of Book Seven
To Be Continued

---

[11] いちいち　ICHI ICHI　"one by one"　point by point
[12] 久方振り　HISAKATA BURI　for the first time in ages
[13] 新事実　SHINJIJITSU　"new fact"

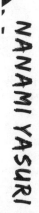

CHARACTER INDEX 7 - NANAMI YASURI

AGE	Twenty-seven
OCCUPATION	None
AFFILIATION	Kyotoryu
STATUS	Head of the House
POSSESSED	Akuto the Eel
HEIGHT	4' 11"
WEIGHT	69 lbs.
HOBBY	Weeding

LIST OF SPECIAL MOVES

OMINAESHI	⇦⇦⇨⇨ THRUST
HINAGESHI	⇩ SLASH
TAMPOPO	⇨ SLASH ⇦ THRUST
JINCHOGE	⇦ (HOLD) ⇨ SLASH + THRUST + KICK
SHICHIKA HACHIRETSU	⇦⇨⇧⇩⇦⇨ SLASH + THRUST + KICK
WATCH AND LEARN	USE ANY OF OPPONENT'S MOVES
NANAMI THE HEEL	⇦⇦⇦ THRUST THRUST THRUST

AFTER(S)WORD

Once you start down the path with this sort of thinking, you never stop, so it's best to never pay it any mind at all, but for the record, let me say that nothing is more upsetting than when someone shows you just how big the gap between your skill and theirs really is. This has absolutely nothing to do with them being more dedicated or diligent, more focused or gung-ho, and everything to do with them being leagues ahead of you—stronger, plain and simple. While I'm the first to be suspicious whenever anybody mentions genius, some things can only be explained as gifts (or curses?) from the gods, and bizarrely, these things seem to pop up fairly often. Most people want to think they're special, on account of which they often wind up feeling frustrated, but when you get right down to it, thinking that you're special is just a way of wishing like a madman you were special, when you know you're really not. There's nothing special about being special, if you are, which probably makes the really special people overlook what makes them that way, focusing instead on whatever seems special in their eyes, which sends them down the same slippery slope as normal folks. This is the sort of thing that's funny if you have an audience, but unfortunately, in the real world, we perform for no one but ourselves. I'm not saying genius is a casualty—I'm just saying that while things could always be worse than they are, there's a cap on how good things can get. Know what I'm saying? Since people are never happy with the status quo, some special people probably wind up wondering what good being special ever did for them. But if you go down that rabbit hole, soon you'll be saying that you're special just the way you are, so who needs talent anyway, let other people have it, sounding like a person who has given up for good, and you know what? Maybe it takes a normal person to appreciate the workings of a beautiful mind. Otherwise, how could we ever stand in awe of anything?

That's all for Book Seven of *Sword Tale*. Now that we've plunged into the second half of the twelve books, things are heating up, for better or for worse, but the crux of the story was the showdown between Shichika and Nanami Yasuri, brother and sister. I set the scene in Tosa, in Shikoku, a part of Japan close to my heart. I hate to say goodbye, and can't help feeling that I haven't fully captured the atmosphere of Shikoku, but I think that my depiction of the family showdown speaks to the power of the place. I hope that you'll agree.

The ending of Togame the Schemer's hunt for all the Mutant Blades of Legendary Swordsmith Kiki Shikizaki is finally in sight. At first, I had no clue where this series was going to take me, but at this point in the writing I can safely say I'm having more fun than anyone else. I only hope I can keep producing good fodder for our illustrator *take*. That's all, folks, for *Katanagatari Book Seven: Akuto the Eel*.

Five books to go!

NISIOISIN

BOOK EIGHT

**BITO
THE SUNDIAL**

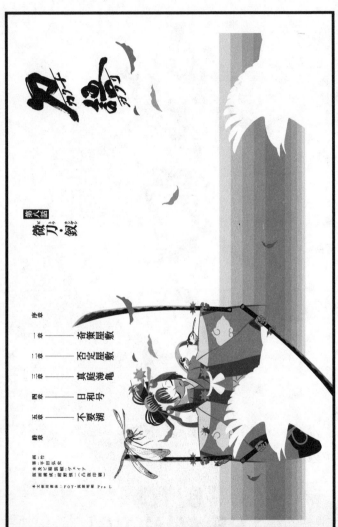

刀語

第八話 微刀・釵

- 序章
- 一章 ── 奇策屋敷
- 二章 ── 否定屋敷
- 三章 ── 真庭海亀
- 四章 ── 日和号参
- 五章 ── 不要湖
- 終章

本文挿画：竹
表紙画：竹
表紙画色と扉絵：西屋弘史
本文組版と装幀：紺野慎一（ハイト）
本文使用書体：FOT-筑紫明朝 Pro L

The original Book Eight Table of contents spread

PROLOGUE

■ ■

But before long, they were only fifty.
    Times changed with the generations.
    And yet their ranks diminished without hope.
    From fifty down to twenty-five.
    From twenty-five to thirteen.
    From thirteen to seven.
    From seven to four.
    Then four to two.
    Until finally—the two had been reduced to one.
    Only one of them remained.
    It took a hundred and seventy years—but all of them was dead but one.
    It took a hundred and seventy years—but all of them was gone, save one.
    You didn't need a crystal ball to see[1] that one would soon be zero, a fact of which the last one standing was painfully aware.
    Everything they had inherited.
    Everything they had succeeded.
    Everything they had been tasked with.
    Everything they had been saddled with.
    Everything would soon be lost.
    His generation—would be the last.
    He knew this—understood this more than anyone.
    Nevertheless, he had to stand his guard—even if it was the death of him.
    He was the last one standing.
    Which made it his responsibility—to stand guard until the bitter end.
    In practice, this meant doing nothing—but as the sole survivor, it was the best that he could do.
    Call him lazy or embarrassing.
    But he called this his life.
    Living on—to see tomorrow.
    He saw this as his obligation and his mission.
    No other motivation.
    No interest in revenge.
    Simply—living.
    Simply—waiting to die.
    For someone disappointed with himself and disenchanted with the world, this way of life was torture—and yet he chose this life without a moment's hesitation.

---

[1] 簡単に予測　KANTAN NI YOSOKU　easily predict

He would let the wind and rain destroy him.[2]
Letting the snow and summer sun devour him—that was the sort of person he'd be.
And yet—
"Unacceptable!" the woman told him. "Unacceptable—I cannot accept this way of life. I reject your choice to live this way. I reject it as disgusting, disgraceful, and deplorable. Diffident, despondent, and delinquent. What, you think it's cool?[3] How's that working out for you? You make me laugh."
Uninhibited, unending.
Like a runaway rapid—the woman deluged her subject with contempt and ridicule.
"Know what you are? A textbook lazy bum—I could watch you, like a specimen, all day. What a horrible waste of life. Seriously, nice job wasting your life away. Don't you think it's time you died already? Acting like some kind of mighty guardian. Well guess what—no one cares!"
She let this one sink in.
"I sure don't. I reject your whole existence—I cannot accept a single thing about you. Zero. Zilch. Nada.[4] People like you are the worst—the embodiment[5] of complacency and narcissism.[6] The very sight of you pisses me off."
She continued:
"But that's all well and good. Because you're *not without* your usefulness."
There it was—
The double negative.
"I grant you the prefix NON."[7]

■　■

In the first moon.
On Haphazard Island in Tango—
They dispossessed[8] Komori Maniwa of Zetto the Leveler.
In the second moon.
Inside Gekoku Castle in Inaba.
They dispossessed Ginkaku Uneri of Zanto the Razor.
In the third moon.
At Triad Shrine in Izumo.

---

[2] 雨にも負けて、風にも負けて　AME NI MO MAKETE, KAZE NI MO MAKETE　losing to rain, losing to wind
　　this and the next line parody a famous poem by Kenji Miyazawa about *not* ever succumbing
[3] いきがってる　IKIGATTERU　show off feigning nonchalant elegance, i.e.　粋 IKI
[4] 一切合財わずかたりとも　ISSAI GASSAI WAZUKA TARITOMO　not even the minutest aspect
[5] 権化　GONGE　avatar
[6] 自己満足 自己陶酔　JIKOMANZOKU JIKOTŌSUI　self-satisfaction self-intoxication
[7] 『不』の一文字　"FU" NO HITOMOJI　the single letter (kanji character) "non"
[8] 蒐集終了　SHŪSHŪ SHŪRYŌ　"collection complete"　phonic repetition of original is conspicuous

They dispossessed Meisai Tsuruga of Sento the Legion.
In the fourth moon.
On Ganryu Island in Suo.
They dispossessed Hakuhei Sabi of Hakuto the Whisper.
In the fifth moon.
By Dakuon Harbor in Satsuma.
They dispossessed Kanara Azekura of Zokuto the Armor.
In the sixth moon.
Atop Mt. Odori in Ezo.
They dispossessed Konayuki Itezora of Soto the Twin.
In the seventh moon.
Within Gokenji Temple in Tosa.
They dispossessed Nanami Yasuri of Akuto the Eel.
Out of the Twelve Possessed, those masterworks of legendary swordsmith Kiki Shikizaki, who effectively reigned over the Age of Warring States—the twelve Mutant Blades not even the Old Shogun, who had managed to unite the nation, had been able to collect, despite exerting every effort—Togame the Schemer had now managed to round up seven.

Five swords remained!
Bito the Sundial!
Oto the Cured!
Seito the Garland!
Dokuto the Basilisk!
Ento the Bead!
Saving these targets for later, the Schemer finally made her return to Owari—but before she had a chance to rest was thrust into the fray!
That sums up just about everything thus far!
Let's unroll the remainder of this scroll of swords!
Are you rip-roaring and ready to go?
Sword Tale, Book Eight, long past the point of no return ♪

CHAPTER ONE

SCHEMER MANSION

Lake Fuyo in Edo.

Like Mt. Odori in Ezo and Mt. Shirei in Mutsu, Lake Fuyo had been designated a Level One Disaster Area by the bakufu—but a few noteworthy things set it apart from the other two.

Being a lake, and not a mountain.

At least—it *used to be* a lake.

Furthermore, however sparsely populated, the other two maintained some semblance of human life, with the Itezoras on Mt. Odori and the Sacred Guardians on Mt. Shirei—whereas not a single human being called Lake Fuyo their home.

Though classified alongside those two mountains as a Level One Disaster Area, this sometime lake was more akin to Inaba Desert—at least in terms of its sheer barrenness.

And yet the first place named a Level One Disaster Area by the Yanari Shogunate—was Lake Fuyo, in the hinterlands[1] of Edo.

■ ■

Three people walked along the craggy highway, under the brutal summer sun.

A man wearing a coat and trousers took the lead—a mask covering his face. He was a thin[2] man, and wore a pair of swords—one big, one small. The word "NON-NINJA" scrawled across his mask. He walked along in silence, bearing himself in such a way that made his feelings difficult to read—and aloof to the two others behind him.

None other than—Lieutenant Emonzaemon Soda.

A safe distance behind him was a man stripped to the waist, with tousled hair—by far the tallest of the trio, this man was plainly dressed but no less eye-catching than Emonzaemon, who walked before him in his frippery and mask. From the restless way the tall man scanned the scenery, you could tell that he was out of his depth.

None other than—Shichika Yasuri.

Then, taking up the rear, but more conspicuous than the dandily bemasked Emonzaemon or the lanky and half-naked Shichika—we see a whitehaired woman, adorned in brash and brilliant finery. Trimmed to her shoulders and lustrous in the sun—that white hair was her oriflamme,[3] the ensign of her

[1] 奥地 OKUCHI deep in the interior
[2] すらり SURARI (onomatopoeic) slender
[3] 日光に映える NIKKŌ NI HAERU shining in the sun

mission. Walking in seta, and wearing a perturbed expression—she kept half a step behind Shichika, but always within reach.

As goes without saying.

She was none other than—Togame the Schemer.

Emonzaemon was too far ahead of Shichika and Togame to fairly call these three a trio—the distances between them spoke volumes of their interrelationships.

Lieutenant Emonzaemon Soda—Counselor[4] to the Inspector General of the Yanari Shogunate.

Togame the Schemer—Grand Commander of Arms of the Yanari Shogunate Military Directorate, Owari Bakufu.

And Shichika Yasuri—Seventh Master of the Kyotoryu and trusty blade of Togame the Schemer.

"Well then."

It had been quite some time since any of them had spoken—but Togame finally broke the silence. She could have endured it longer, no doubt, but her voice was as perturbed as her expression.

She was addressing Emonzaemon, up ahead of them.

"It would appear the Princess is as rough as ever with her staff—I pity you, Lieutenant Emonzaemon. Running errands for her up and down the country—"

"*No need.*"

Though Emonzaemon deigned to answer Togame's sarcastic comment, he declined to turn around.

"Don't worry about me—Madame Schemer. While I can't pretend to speak on your behalf, this kind of a journey is no trouble[5] for me."

"Right—after all, you are a former ninja. You're used to being on the road." Togame took no pains to hide her bitterness. "Besides, who knows how long you've already been on our tail—I'm sure we have no reason to worry whatsoever. But what about your other obligations? If you're out here showing us the way, doesn't that mean the Princess is all on her lonesome back in Owari? As both her counselor and bodyguard, have you not made her vulnerable by making yourself scarce?"

"*No need*—to be concerned."

Emonzaemon was undaunted by this provocative remark.

"Unlike you, Madame Schemer, the Princess has no sworn[6] enemies—in fact, she has *but one enemy* in all Owari. And since that *single enemy of hers* is all the way out here—her safety is as good as guaranteed. As long as I have you in my sight, Madame Schemer, my duties as her bodyguard are more than adequately fulfilled."

"..."

Caught between them, Shichika listened tamely to this repartee. Togame

---

[4] 補佐　HOSA　aide　e.g.　首席補佐官　SHUSEKI HOSAKAN　chief of staff
[5] 苦にもならん　KU NI MO NARAN　not even a hardship; dukkha, the Buddhist term for suffering
[6] 表だった　OMOTE DATTA　"on the surface"　out in the open

openly regarded Emonzaemon as her adversary, and however gracious the lieutenant may have been, the content of his speech made it quite clear that he did not view the Schemer fondly[7]—but none of them was more aware of three being a crowd than Shichika Yasuri.

He and Togame had been adventuring all year.

For most of the Sword Hunt, they had walked alone, embarking from Haphazard Island, the desert island that had been Shichika's home most of his life, and moving onward to Inaba, Izumo, Suo, Satsuma, and Ezo, until reaching Tosa—

But since then, they had been graced with the presence of this man in pantaloons—Emonzaemon Soda.

In Tosa, he had been responsible for leading them up Mt. Sayabashiri to Seiryoin Gokenji Temple, the holy site for swordsmen whose grounds encompass the Katana Buddha, known throughout the land for being cast from the metal of one hundred thousand swords—and this month, he had been tasked with guiding them to Edo's Level One Disaster Area, Lake Fuyo.

And yet.

As far as Shichika was concerned, his contribution as their guide was at best superficial.

Thus far on the journey, Shichika and Togame had been all kinds of places—and dangerous ones at that. They leapt into the fray after the Twelve Possessed, venturing to locales like Inaba Desert and Mt. Odori in Ezo, which you would have to be insane to brave without a properly outfitted party—but they had done it on their own.

It didn't matter what kind of a place Lake Fuyo was. As long as they could find it on a map, they wouldn't need a guide to get there. Not with the Schemer behind this Sword Hunt.

But there he was.

In which case—he had to be watching them.

Monitoring their progress—tasked not with leading them or guiding them, but watching them, at the request of his superior—*the Princess.*

That's how Shichika saw it, anyway.

Which is what made the man's presence so unpleasant.

And how could any trip be otherwise, when you're being watched every step of the way?

Make no mistake, it was absolutely, positively not Emonzaemon's shameless intrusion on the privacy of their Sword Hunt that disagreed with Shichika.

Done prodding at each other for the time being, Togame and Emonzaemon settled down (an inevitable result, for such a barren[8] conversation), and silence once more reigned over the scene.

Which is why—actually, for no good reason.

"Hey, Emonzaemon—"

---

[7] 快く KOKOROYOKU pleasantly　from こころ KOKORO heart　よく YOKU well, goodly
[8] 不毛 FUMŌ "hairless" sterile

Shichika spoke up.

"What kind of a place is Lake Fuyo anyway? I forgot to ask—"

"*Not necessary*," Emonzaemon replied bluntly, as if he had been waiting for the question just so he could say this. "And not merely because it's called Lake Fuyo[9]—the place is self-explanatory. You'll have to see it for yourself,[10] Shichika Yasuri. Once you set eyes on it, you'll understand. Isn't that right, Madame Schemer."

"Don't ask me for approval," Togame told him off. "Still, Shichika," she continued, "the place is sort of difficult to explain—words somehow fail to capture the big picture. It's quicker to see for yourself."

"Hmm...it's a Level One Disaster Area, right? Like Mt. Odori, where we met Konayuki—"

"That's true," Togame nodded, "but in terms of mortal danger, it falls short of the forbidding clime[11] of that mountain—at least in my opinion."

"Only because you can't take the cold, Madame Schemer," Emonzaemon retorted.

Without looking back, the same as ever.

"I wasn't talking to you," Togame said defensively; but indeed her weakness to the cold had gotten them in serious trouble up on Mt. Odori, and Shichika felt he could detect a certain falter in her tone.

"Lake Fuyo is no place—for human beings to live," remarked Emonzaemon. "It is unfit for any form of life—I have zero interest in religion, but when people talk about the netherworld, they mean a place like that."

"Netherworld?"[12]

The word choice struck Shichika as odd.

Even if it was unfit for human life—calling it the netherworld was silly[13]—to him.

After all, he had grown up on a desert island—did that make Haphazard Island a netherworld as well?

When he said as much, Emonzaemon quickly backed down. "Fair enough. But it would be best to call it otherworldly,[14] if not the netherworld. As a matter of fact, this trip will be my first as well."

"You don't say."

"Unlike Mt. Odori and Mt. Shirei or Inaba Desert—Lake Fuyo falls outside the jurisdiction of the bakufu. Every time they've tried to take control of it, they've failed—as a result of which no one can claim to understand its current state."

"They can't control it?"

"No, but even if they could it would be pointless."

---

[9] 不要湖　FUYŌKO　"Unnecessary Lake"
[10] 百聞は一見に如かず　HYAKUBUN WA IKKEN NI SHIKAZU　"one look is worth a hundred tales"
[11] 極寒　GOKKAN　extreme low temperatures
[12] 魔界　MAKAI　"demon realm"
[13] 大袈裟　ŌGESA　exaggerated
[14] 異界　IKAI　"other/strange realm"

Shichika had been asking Emonzaemon, but it was Togame who had answered, butting in before the lieutenant had a chance to get a word in edgewise.

"Were you listening, Shichika? Mt. Odori had the Itezoras, and Mt. Shirei had the Sacred Guardians—but no one lives at Lake Fuyo. It's unfit for human life—like the man said."

"Hmm."

"And another thing," Togame said. "Don't talk to him unless it's absolutely necessary."

"..."

She'd waded into the conversation to say that?

Shichika was blown away by how much she despised the guy.

But only because she despised his superior—

The Princess.

"Ha."

Emonzaemon—laughed it off.

Like it was nothing.

Togame pounced. "What's so funny?"

Shichika felt she could have easily let this one go—but she was so emotional around Emonzaemon.

Reminiscent of her bearing toward the Maniwa.

Like when she met Komori—or had her rendezvous with Hohoh.

Or the way she comported herself around Kyoken and Kawauso.

Togame lost her cool so thoroughly it would be fair to say she lost her mind.

It was perhaps too tall an order to expect someone in her position to stay cool in the face of "traitors" like the Maniwa—but things were different with the Princess. Togame may have seen her as an enemy, but the Princess hadn't actually betrayed her. It was difficult to understand what made her so impassioned.

Indeed, in terms of her standing—the Princess was comparable to the former owners of the Twelve Possessed, like Ginkaku Uneri, Meisai Tsuruga, and Kanara Azekura.

Togame had taken her on countless times, and each time knocked her down—

Except the Princess had rebounded.

Every single time.

This obstinacy reminded Shichika of Togame.

Having met the Princess in Owari—his hunch was now a certainty.

This was a case of hating someone else for what you hate about yourself.[15]

At the root of their antagonism was a fundamental incompatibility.

As people—

"..."

But Shichika—was a katana.

A living, breathing sword.

Brought up in this fashion by his father, on a desert island.

---

[15] 同族嫌悪 DŌZOKU KEN'O "disdain within the tribe"

Trained—to see the world in such a way.

Hence Shichika felt the *lifeforce* of the Twelve Possessed, those masterworks of Kiki Shikizaki—as if through a sixth sense.

And now, as a katana.

He had pledged his heart and soul to Togame the Schemer.

Shichika Yasuri—trusty blade of Togame the Schemer.

But this guy?

Counselor to the Inspector General of the Yanari Shogunate—"The Non-Ninja," no longer ninja Emonzaemon Soda.

Dressed in his trousers, coat and mask—he was the trusty blade of Princess Negative.

In which case—if you took the expression[16] at face value.

—He's just like me.

Both a human—and a weapon.

And yet, despite Togame's loathing for the Princess, for whatever reason Shichika could not bring himself to loathe Emonzaemon.

As unwelcome as this guy's intrusion on their private Sword Hunt was (whoops, spilled the beans),[17] his dedicated service to the Princess, as her sword—made sense to Shichika.

Shichika sympathized—not as a sword.

But as a person.

And felt that lifeforce.[18]

—If the Princess is Togame's enemy.

Considering Togame's final goal...

Someday.

Before too long—would he have to fight Emonzaemon?

Most probably.

Which made this the perfect opportunity to watch him—to figure out what kind of man he was, to gauge the "strength" of this "Non-Ninja"...

"Kyotoryu."

While Shichika was thus engaged in thought—

Emonzaemon spun around.

Turning towards him, so that he was walking backwards, he addressed Shichika.

"You've had your chance. Now it's my turn to ask the questions. There's something that I'd like for you to tell me—to make sure I've got it straight."

"Huh? What is it."

"Hey, Emonzaemon. Quit bothering my sword. I don't recall giving you permission," Togame butted in before Emonzaemon had a chance to pop his question. She was being such a stickler[19] about this, but her intransigence must

---

[16] i.e. 懐刀 FUTOKORO GATANA confidant 懐 FUTOKORO "close to bosom" 刀 KATANA sword

[17] あ、言っちゃった A, ICCHATTA ah, (I) said it

[18] 共感覚を憶える KYŌKANKAKU WO OBOERU experience synesthesia
vs. "sympathized" above: 共感を覚える KYŌKAN WO OBOERU "have feelings in common"

[19] 徹底して TETTEI SHITE be thorough

have amused Emonzaemon, because he smirked under his mask.

"Jealousy doesn't suit you, Madame Schemer. Are you really that upset that your sword took his eyes off you?"

Togame immediately lost her temper.

"I said nothing of the sort!"

Shichika had to wonder. Wasn't a tactician supposed to be calm and cool, collected and unflappable, no matter what the circumstances? But Togame was no mere tactician: she was the Schemer.

Perhaps getting fired up like this was one of the quirks that set her apart.

"Alright, let's get on with it. I can't believe you'd think that I was jealous of you. Shichika, tell the man anything he wants to know."

"Anything..."

A dangerous request.

By now Shichika was worldly enough not to take her words literally. Back in the second month, say, of their journey, he would have surely blurted out something he never should have said—

Emotional or otherwise, Togame was herself.

She had factored in all of this.

No matter how dangerous the bridge, she was prepared to cross.

Without testing its structural integrity.[20]

"Kyotoryu," Emonzaemon started over, still walking backwards. "Out of all the owners of the Twelve Possessed you've fought so far—Komori Maniwa, one of the Maniwa Bosses, Ginkaku Uneri, the Lord of Gekoku Castle, Meisai Tsuruga, the Mistress of Triad Shrine, Hakuhei Sabi, the strongest swordsman in Japan, Kanara Azekura, the Captain of the Armored Pirates, Konayuki Itezora, of the Itezoras, and your older sister—Nanami Yasuri. Of those seven...who was the strongest?"

"...?"

What a weird question.

What made it necessary to ask about that now? Shichika hadn't the foggiest idea.

"Granted," Emonzaemon continued, "I can make an educated guess, based on Madame Schemer's official[21] reports—though I'm afraid that they amount to little more than an opinion. I'd like to hear what you think, Kyotoryu, since you're the one who goes into the fray and clashes[22] with the Mutant Blades."

"Oh...I see."

"I mean, obviously Nanami Yasuri was number one, right? Making number two Hakuhei Sabi—I'm wondering how you'd rank the rest of them."

"Is this the Princess asking?" queried Togame.

Evidently she was not okay with sitting back and letting Emonzaemon ask questions after all. She had a problem with Shichika and Emonzaemon

---

20 石橋を叩かず　ISHIBASHI WO TATAKAZU　not tapping a stone bridge
　　　　　a common expression meaning "taking extra precautions," appearing here in the negative
21 提出された　TEISHUTSU SARETA　submitted (for review)
22 切り結びあった　KIRIMUSUBI ATTA　"cut and tied each other" tangled with

conversing on their own. Not like she was really jealous...

"*No doubt*—I don't mind if you think of it that way. After all, every move I make and every step I take is for the Princess. It would be pointless to search for any deeper meaning in my work."

"How about it, Shichika?" asked Togame. "Now that he mentions it, I'm not without a certain curiosity myself. Don't worry about who was harder to beat. Just who was stronger. All he wants is your personal opinion. Think subjectively."

"Thinking is kinda hard for me..." said Shichika.

And yet he tried to think it over.

Who was the strongest—in terms of pure strength?

Like Emonzaemon said, Nanami topped the ranking without question, and after her came Hakuhei Sabi—but frankly, the rest of them were more or less tied.[23] All of them were hard to beat, as far as that went.

But if he had to pick—

"I guess number three would be—Komori the Maniwac."

"Maniwac?"

Emonzaemon was puzzled by this term.

Indeed, this must have been the first time Shichika had used it on him.

"'Maniwa Ninja Clan' is way too long, so we gave them a nickname."

"Ah...good one." Emonzaemon sounded oddly satisfied.

He did use to be a ninja.

Was it possible he had some kind of connection to the Maniwa? Judging from his tone, it didn't seem as if he used to be one of the Maniwa himself...

"So, Komori Maniwa, one of the Twelve Bosses of the Maniwa Clan, comes right after Hakuhei Sabi—may I ask why? Wasn't he the first person you ever fought? He may have put up a good fight, but I dare say that was only because you had no experience."

"Other way around. I only beat Komori because I lacked experience. I'm not sure what you read in the report."

In fact.

There was a high chance that Togame bent the truth in her report for her own convenience. Even if she hadn't written any outright lies, she had probably glossed over plenty of facts.

He had to be careful about what he said—but this seemed safe enough. Besides, if he started blurting out something classified, Togame would jump on him before he had the chance.

"If I had to fight Komori again—I'm honestly not sure how it would go. I've dealt with most of the Twelve Bosses, but ninjutsu is totally insane. It's basically unstoppable," said Shichika. "At least for me. Sis could have beat him, though."

Whumping three of the bosses in a row—Nanami Yasuri was off the charts. Number one, without a doubt.

"Hmm. And number four?"

"Meisai Tsuruga," answered Shichika. "Her Sentoryu was such a pain. I

---

[23] 団子状態 DANGO JŌTAI "balled up," like a mass of dough

know her moves depended on Sento the Legion and everything—but the real pain was the Togame-style[24] strategies she used on me. I have a hard time with backhanded[25] approaches."

"Fair enough," Togame agreed. "Except, if it was me, I'd rank Meisai number three."

"So, number five is gonna be...uhh, I guess Ginkaku Uneri."

The master of iainuki.

Lord of Gekoku Castle—the hermit swordsman of Inaba Desert.

Ginkaku Uneri.

"Talk about cutting it close. I know he was only my second opponent, and my first fight after we set off on the Sword Hunt—but his iainuki and that Zerosen are still enough to make me tremble. And let's not forget the Danger Zone."

"Certainly," said Togame, "if Ginkaku Uneri hadn't had the Danger Zone, it would have been far less of an ordeal. Hmm...so Shichika—I suppose number six is Konayuki Itezora, and number seven is Kanara Azekura?"

"Yep," assented Shichika.

Togame was spot on.

She knew it all.[26]

"Not to make a huge generalization, but their styles were so basic. Azekura, he was the kind of guy who'd even make things harder for himself and accept disadvantageous terms. At the end of the day, I'd say they were about equal—apart from the fact that Konayuki beat me the first time around."

"Let it go already," Togame groaned. "I've warned you about wallowing in your losses."

Therefore—in summary:
#1 Nanami Yasuri
#2 Hakuhei Sabi
#3 Komori Maniwa
#4 Meisai Tsuruga
#5 Ginkaku Uneri
#6 Konayuki Itezora
#7 Kanara Azekura

That was how Shichika would rank his battles so far.

No more than his personal opinion—but still.

"I see, thanks for clarifying," Emonzaemon said when he was finished. "Everything is clear now—the exceptional cases of Nanami Yasuri and Hakuhei Sabi aside, you have a low tolerance for people playing tricks[27] on you."

"...!"

Shichika was taken aback.

He was right—the ranking made this all too clear.

---

[24] とがめばり TOGAME BARI Togame-esque declension of 張る HARU (here) vie with
[25] 搦め手 KARAMETE rear entrance; weak point
[26] お見通し OMITŌSHI "seeing through" turned into a quality and distinction
[27] 策を弄する SAKU WO RŌ SURU engage in schemes

In terms of raw power and sheer ability,[28] Komori Maniwa and Meisai Tsuruga didn't hold a candle to Konayuki Itezora or Kanara Azekura—but fighting Komori and Meisai had been much more of a struggle.

And why? Because they *didn't simply fight him*.

They wove confounding webs.[29]

Played—tricks.

And the same could be said—of Ginkaku Uneri and his Danger Zone.

"These two who, as you put it, *were too basic*—do you realize how strange that is? Everybody has a strategy, as Madame Schemer demonstrated so strikingly in your bouts against Hakuhei Sabi and Nanami Yasuri."

"Hey," Togame said, hearing her name. "No reason to get all proud for making such an observation. You think I didn't notice all of this?"

"..."

Shichika was about to tell her not to bother lying, but reconsidered, since maybe she had noticed after all.

"I'm sure you did. Which goes to say—why Kyotoryu is nothing without you, Madame Schemer. Just as I would be nothing without the Princess..."

With that.

Emonzaemon spun around again, facing the road ahead.

Shichika racked his brains to understand the meaning of his question—and soon thought up one possibility.

So long as Togame and the Princess were rivals.

There would come a day—when Shichika would fight Emonzaemon.

Which is why Shichika had been availing himself of the opportunity to observe every little thing about Emonzaemon—who had to be doing the same thing with him.

Trying to spot the weaknesses of Shichika Yasuri, Seventh Master of the Kyotoryu.

If that's what he was up to, he had done a marvelous job of it.

—But that's okay.

He was still okay.

Like Emonzaemon said, as long as he had Togame, she would more than make up for his weaknesses—

"*No good*," said Emonzaemon, as if peering into Shichika's soul. "Worrying[30] will get you nowhere, Kyotoryu—even if I learn all of your weaknesses, I'm no match for a swordsman of your caliber, who beat the likes of Nanami Yasuri and Hakuhei Sabi. You can trust that I'll do all I can to avoid a tussle with you. Isn't that right, Madame Schemer."

Togame glared at Emonzaemon, making it clear that she was not entirely convinced.

"In that case, why not tell your precious princess to stop meddling in my

---

[28] 実力地力 JITSURYOKU JIRIKI "true strength" "ground strength (baseline competency)"
[29] 複雑怪奇 FUKUZATSU KAIKI complex and mystifying
[30] 不安になる FUAN NI NARU become anxious 不安 FUAN no peace/security

affairs—I'd rather not collaborate with her."

"Quite right, except the Princess would never take my advice—believe me, Kyotoryu. You have bigger things to worry about."

"Bigger things?"

"Alright, we're here."

After heading straight for some time.

They took a turn—and Emonzaemon cut off their conversation.

"This is it—Lake Fuyo."

Edo's Lake Fuyo, a Level One Disaster Area.

There was—

Nothing but rubbish[31] as far as the eye could see.

■   ■

The week prior.

At Seiryoin Gokenji Temple, that holy site for swordsmen, on Mt. Sayabashiri in Tosa, Shichika Yasuri had battled his own sister, Nanami Yasuri, once the strongest in Japan and bane of the Maniwa Bug Unit, every last Itezora save Konayuki, and the Sacred Guardians of Mt. Shirei—annihilating, devastating, and eradicating[32] all of them...and unanimously[33] proclaimed a monster by whosoever heard the tale. But after his miraculous victory, which collected Akuto the Eel, their seventh Mutant Blade—Shichika found himself at the end of his rope.

Togame the Schemer had launched her Sword Hunt armed only with a knowledge of the whereabouts and owners of six of the Shikizaki masterworks.

All six of which—the Leveler, the Razor, the Legion, the Whisper, the Armor, and the Twin—were now in their possession.

True, they had gleaned bits of information on the remaining six swords along the way. By forging an alliance with Hohoh Maniwa, effectively the head of the entire ninja clan (reluctant as Togame was to partner up with them, after they stabbed her in the back), they learned two Mutant Blades awaited them in Edo and in Tendo, respectively—although taking information from a ninja at face value was perhaps unwise. While Hohoh was the one who filled them in on what Nanami had been up to, he had surely only done so because telling them was beneficial to the Maniwa.

When it came to vanquishing that monster, Nanami Yasuri, there was no one better suited for the job than her own brother, Shichika Yasuri.

In fact—

If he hadn't been her brother—Shichika would likely not have won against

---

[31] がらくた GARAKUTA junk
[32] 全滅・壊滅・絶滅 ZENMETSU/KAIMETSU/ZETSUMETSU "totally/breakingly/extremely ruin"
[33] 異口同音 IKU DŌ'ON "different mouths, same sound"

Nanami.
And thus, Shichika and Togame returned briefly, or rather, finally to Owari.
Owari—the seat of the Yanari Shogunate.
They had hoped to return after capturing Sento the Legion at Triad Shrine, but then they had the duel with Hakuhei Sabi, and were duped by Kanara Azekura, and had to fend off Nanami Yasuri, of all people, postponing[34] their return indefinitely—
But at last.
The two of them had made it back.
Shichika's first impression was how severe[35] the city was.
To be sure, it lacked the glitziness and gaiety[36] of the Capital, the first place they had visited after crossing over from Haphazard Island to the mainland—but it was not without an air of dignity, most likely the result of being under the administration of the bakufu.
And also—it was huge.
Everything about the town was big.
The streets—were wide.
"This is what planned cities look like," explained Togame. "It's laid out to prepare for earthquakes. See how there's space between the buildings? It's been predicted that this area is due for a big earthquake at some point, so the city is designed to maintain order during that kind of a disaster."
"Wow—kind of incredible that the Yanari Bakufu decided to base itself in such an area."
"I think that we can rest assured the big one isn't going to hit while we're alive. Besides, I don't put faith in prophecies."
"I bet not. It's up to each of us to shape our fate—and all that?"
"Not quite," Togame laughed. "It's up to each of us to chalk it up[37] to fate."
If you chalk your successes up to fate, you can avoid sounding smug; and if you chalk your failures up to fate, you just don't feel as bitter—
In her opinion.
Shichika could see the truth in that.
As they loped into the residential area, they found themselves surrounded by the homes of all the bakufu higher-ups, where the streets were all the more stark and stately. Even Shichika, the eternal optimist,[38] caught himself tensing up—the place gave off a different vibe than any other place they'd visited. Owari Castle loomed beyond the rooflines of the homes—a league above Gekoku Castle.
Is that—
Is that where Togame—works?

[34] 延び延び NOBI NOBI "stretched and stretched"
[35] 厳格 GENKAKU strict; austere
[36] きらびやかさ KIRABIYAKASA glitter, flamboyance
[37] 言い張る IIHARU insist, assert, claim (often stubbornly, despite evidence to the contrary)
[38] 能天気 NŌTENKI blissfully ignorant 能 NŌ ability (cognate: 脳 NŌ brain)
 　　天気 TENKI (fair) weather the nuance: "sunshine of the spotless mind"

Is that—her enemy?

The thought made Shichika even more tense.

For Togame, this was her hometown and her home base—but also the heart of enemy territory. She'd spent a couple of decades of her life here.

How she felt about that defies imagination.

To Shichika, raised on a desert island—it was incomprehensible.

Which stopped him from shooting the breeze with Togame, who was now slightly ahead of him.

Before long, he saw a house that stood out from the local color, or lack thereof, and felt his anxiety slip away.

He couldn't resist pointing it out to Togame.

"Hey, check out that crazy mansion—the one painted like a toy and decked out with enough ornaments for the entire neighborhood. Man, get a load of those bright golden fish things[39] at the corners of the roof... Not like I'm one to talk, but I guess you can find obtuse[40] people anywhere you go... So tasteless. Looks like someone is desperate to be the center of attention."

"This is my house."

Amidst this exchange.

After eight long months away—Togame the Schemer was finally home.

Evidently, she had hired somebody to keep the house in order—to come by once a week and keep it looking clean. Since today was not the scheduled day, Togame's house, known commonly as Schemer Mansion, was empty.

The space was far less brash and brilliant than you might expect from its exterior—Togame explained that she had done her absolute best to clear things out before embarking on the Sword Hunt. She must have understood she wasn't coming home for quite some time. Either that, or she was putting on a show[41] for her neighbors in Owari, making it clear that she was serious about her venture.

"I'd love to fix you some tea, but I'm afraid I need to head straight to the castle. I'm sorry, Shichika, but you'll have to wait here until I'm done."

Having taken a quick breather, Togame was in the midst of changing for her visit with the shogun. She couldn't simply show up in her travel clothes (not that double a dozen layers of kimono made any sense for someone on the move). As usual, Shichika had started helping her get dressed before she had the chance to ask. He was getting pretty good at it, too.

"Wait here?" Shichika asked. "I thought you were gonna introduce me to the people at the castle..."

"That was the initial plan[42]—but things have changed. After the resurgence of that nasty woman, I'm afraid that bringing you inside the castle—is too risky."

"Risky...for me?"

---

[39] しゃちほこ SHACHIHOKO mythical creatures with the heads of a tiger and the body of a fish; often featured in roofline decorations on Japanese temples and castles
[40] 空気の読めない奴 KŪKI NO YOMENAI YATSU someone who can't read the air (i.e. the mood/room)
[41] 示威行動 JI'I KŌDŌ conspicuous demonstration
[42] 手筈 TEHAZU scheduled arrangement

"No. For me," Togame said. "I'll stow my sword for this trip to the castle. And honestly, I think that's for the best—especially with Emonzaemon around... Hey, quit looking so glum. So far, the Sword Hunt has been flawless—in order to gather all the information that we'll need to capture the remaining swords, we may need to reside in Owari for a while. Which means that you'll be living here, for the time being."

"Here in this mansion?"

"Yes. In this tasteless mansion."

She was bruised.[43]

Black and blue.

"The sooner you get used to it the better—I've gotten rid of almost all my things, so we'll have to do some shopping. And hire some new help... Oh dear. Life's so much easier when you're traveling."

And with that.

Togame—headed off in the direction of Owari Castle.

Leaving Shichika idle.

He did his best to get used to the place, wandering up and down the halls, but in no time he had seen it all. Schemer Mansion was a grand affair, befitting someone of Togame's social standing, but not so vast that you could lose your way.[44] He thought about taking a nap, but snoring away[45] while Togame was off at the castle, hard at work, felt wrong to him.

Not sure of how else to spend his time, he stepped out into the garden (which looked so trim and tidy that it must have been included in the weekly property maintenance) and tried practicing his moves, but found it hard to focus.

About half an hour later.

When Shichika was gazing at Owari Castle, in the distance beyond the garden walls, and wondering when Togame would be coming home—

"No see, long time."

Shichika heard a voice—behind him.

Startled, he spun around—(how on earth had he snuck up on him?)—and saw Emonzaemon Soda.

Shichika had seen this face before, at the harborside in Tosa—though since Emonzaemon wore a mask, he couldn't rightfully say that he had actually seen his face—

"It's been a while—no, not that long a while, Kyotoryu," spake Emonzaemon. "I gather that you vanquished Nanami Yasuri. It sounds to me as if your sibling rivalry[46] had become spliced together with the Sword Hunt—but anyway, as a fellow warrior, I salute you."

"How the heck did you get in here?" asked Shichika.

"I walked right in," the lieutenant answered blandly. "When I came through

---

[43] 根に持っていた　NE NI MOTTE ITA　"held at the root" bore a grudge
[44] 迷子になる　MAIGO NI NARU　"become a lost child"
[45] 惰眠をむさぼる　DAMIN WO MUSABORU　"gorge on lazy sleep"
[46] 姉弟喧嘩　KYŌDAI GENKA　quarrel between older sister and younger brother　兄弟　KYŌDAI if bros.

the gate, I spotted you out back—it seemed like you were busy practicing, so I refrained from interrupting you. And here we are."

"Don't sneak up on people like that."

"Please forgive me," Emonzaemon said unapologetically. "Sneaking is my strong suit."

Forget *how* he'd gotten in here—*why* was he here at all?

"Togame...isn't home right now," Shichika did his best to read between the lines. "She's over at the castle."

"Yeah, I know—that's why I'm here."

"That's why? You mean that you were sent by Princess...what's her name?"

"Princess Negative," Emonzaemon answered brusquely. "Don't call her Princess What's-Her-Name—ever again."

His voice was quiet and relaxed—but Shichika had hit a nerve.[47]

—*This guy is loyal.*

But that made sense to Shichika.

To be sure, if Emonzaemon had called Togame "What's-Her-Facer," Shichika would have been equally upset.

"As servant to the Princess, I'd only be here if she sent me—I act only upon orders from Her Highness."

"Alright, so did something happen—at the castle?"

Shichika was concerned.

And Emonzaemon could sense it.

"No need to be alarmed. It's *not like that*."

Not like that—what was it then?

Shichika steeled himself[48]—but Emonzaemon didn't care.

"In no time, Madame Schemer collected seven of the Twelve Possessed not even the Old Shogun could obtain. Her superiors showered her with praise and encouraged her enthusiastically to proceed in her quest. Madame Schemer has made quite the splash—and yet she didn't even smile, which is either commendable, or just stuck up."[49]

"...And?"

"Your Sword Hunt is far from over—and the Princess," Emonzaemon lowered his voice to a whisper, "*has information—on the remaining swords.*"

"..."

"Because the Princess is eager to share this information with Madame Schemer, *she has invited her to visit her estate*—asking her to stop by on her way home from the castle. But since in practice, Kyotoryu, you're the one who physically collects the swords, it wouldn't do for you to not be present—hence why I've come to pick you up."

So that's why he's here—now Shichika understood.

Togame had been reluctant to reveal Shichika, her sword, to Princess

---

[47] 気分を害した KIBUN WO GAISHITA offended his feelings
[48] 警戒 KEIKAI exercise caution
[49] 可愛げがない KAWAIGE GA NAI un-cute

Negative, her nemesis—but the way things were playing out, she had no choice.

The Sword Hunt was their everything.

If someone had a lead on the Twelve Possessed—like it or not, they had no say[50] in the matter. Transparent as her interlocutor's agenda may have been, Togame was in no position to keep her personal sword a secret.

Meeting not at the castle, but at home—was a smart way of finding common ground.

The Princess appeared ready to compromise.

So long as the terms were favorable to her.[51]

"So is Togame—already at the Princess's house?"

"Yeah—by the way, Kyotoryu. Madame Schemer knows the Princess sent someone to fetch you—but not that the person happens to be me."

"..."

If she had known, Shichika mused, she wouldn't have agreed.

He realized this entire story could be some kind of trap laid by the Princess—at this point, however, it made little sense for her to lay one trap on top of the other. But say she did. Shichika was not about to drive himself crazy second-guessing a woman who saw herself as comparable to the Schemer. He decided not to think about it.

Shichika only cared about one thing.

And that was the extent to which they could rely on *information on the Possessed*—when it was coming from Princess Negative.

It was possible the whole thing was codswallop, a hoax[52]—merely a pretext for luring in Togame and Shichika.

But it was hard to say... Would someone of the Princess's standing really tell them such a boldfaced lie? If she blew things out of proportion, and sabotaged the state-mandated[53] Sword Hunt, she was sure to lose face[54] in the process.

Even Shichika could understand that.

This made him doubt it was a total lie.

Of course, this only mattered—*if the Princess was concerned with losing face...*

Shichika tried pushing back a little, just to see what happened.

"But Togame asked me to watch her house."

"Why watch a house if nobody is home?" rejoindered Emonzaemon. "Correct me if I'm wrong, but isn't it your job to protect Madame Schemer?"

"I guess—you're right."

"Well then, it seems you have no choice but to come with me. I'm the second biggest threat to Madame Schemer—as long as she is in this place we call Owari."

"..."

50 否応もなく　IYAŌ MO NAKU　"without no or yes"
51 妥協という名の狡猾さ　DAKYŌ TO IU NA NO KŌKATSUSA　a cunningness called compromise
52 まったくの嘘、でたらめ　MATTAKU NO USO, DETARAME　a complete lie, nonsense
53 勅命　CHOKUMEI　imperial/royal order
54 失点　SHITTEN　score given up (in sports); demerit

"*No mistake*—it's not in your best interest[55] *to leave me to my own devices.* Shall we?"

Emonzaemon had really talked him into it.

Shichika had no stomach for this kind of repartee—raised on a desert island, he never learned to hold his own in a debate. Somehow, despite being raised in the same circumstances, Nanami Yasuri had something of a way with words, but rhetoric was not among Shichika's talents.

It may well be his best bet was to stand his ground and watch the house, following orders from Togame—still.

Something told him Emonzaemon meant what he said.

As somebody devoted to his master, just like Shichika.

In the end—after some more deliberation—he left Schemer Mansion with Emonzaemon.

Heading for Mansion Negative.

Located in a patch of forest[56] on the other side of the castle, this was a home fit for a samurai—stark and stately as can be, the polar opposite of the tasteless Schemer Mansion. In fact, Mansion Negative was perhaps the sternest residence in the entire residential area.

The power of its habitant was palpable.

They found Togame waiting by the gate, refusing to go further until Shichika arrived. The Schemer was not about to access the estate without her sword—that much was clear. When she saw him arriving with Emonzaemon, she froze with panic, but immediately caught herself.

"What the hell!" she said. "Why'd you have to come along with him? If you'd stayed home, I could've used that as an excuse not to see that nasty woman."

"Oh, sorry, I just—"

"It's fine. Now that she's hinted[57] at this info on the Twelve Possessed—I would've had to meet with her at some point anyway."

Togame's words did little to conceal her foul mood.

According to Emonzaemon, her superiors had showered her with praise—but perhaps that victory withered in the shadow of a tête-à-tête with Princess Negative.

"To think that I just came back to Owari! She got one over[58] on me."

Princess Negative.

Archnemesis[59] of Togame the Schemer—

"There'll be time to talk about that later," said Emonzaemon. "You'll keep the Princess waiting. Head inside."

---

[55] 得策　TOKUSAKU　"gainful plan"
[56] 雑木林　ZŌKIBAYASHI　mix of trees
[57] ちらつかされれば　CHIRATSUKA SAREREBA　dangled; shown just a peek
[58] 一本取られた　IPPON TORARETA　give up one full point (in kendo, etc.)
[59] 天敵　TENTEKI　natural enemy

CHAPTER TWO

MANSION NEGATIVE

■ ■

This may be a new chapter—but the time frame[1] is still the week before.
At Mansion Negative.
In one of its many chambers—
Togame the Schemer and Shichika Yasuri.
Took audience—with Princess Negative.
"Hmh..."
Thus.
Following a period of silence—
"Heh, heheh...hah, haha ha!"
Princess Negative—laughed.
At first, she seemed to stifle herself, but there was no stifling this laughter—the whole room filled with her uproarious guffaws.
"Looks—looks great on you."
"..."
It would seem—she was referring to Togame's haircut.
Up until last month, Togame the Schemer had let her white hair grow so long it almost interfered with her mobility, but now it was cropped short at the shoulders. She suffered this dear loss[2] at Gokenji Temple in Tosa, in the leadup to the fight against Nanami Yasuri; it would appear her hair had never been this short since entering the bakufu, as Princess Negative was quite enthused by how girlish it made her look.
Understandable.
It suited her absurdly well.
Just after it was snipped off, Shichika had felt a little weird about the way it looked, but the white bob matched her face so perfectly it made it hard for him to remember what she looked like with long hair.
Though he knew better not to say as much.
Princess Negative, however, had come right out and said it.
—*Princess Negative.*
Togame had done her best to conceal Shichika from Princess Negative—but just as Princess Negative had insisted that Shichika join her, so that she could size him up, Shichika was dying to learn more about the Princess, his owner's mortal enemy—
He studied the woman who was pompously occupying the seat of honor[3] and holding her stomach and cracking up.
—*I can't just watch and learn like sis.*

[1] 時系列 JIKEIRETSU chronological order
[2] 尊き犠牲 TŌTOKI GISEI noble sacrifice
[3] 上座 KAMIZA "high seat" taken by whoever is deemed worthier, often the guest

But he watched nevertheless—for information.
Focused.
On her eye-catching appearance.
Eye-catching—yet her clothing was not overly embellished like the brash and brilliant finery of Togame, or bespoke like the suit of Emonzaemon Soda. The fact is her kimono, though fine enough for someone of her class and status, was a little on the plain side.
What caught the eye was not her clothing—but herself.
Long hair of gold.
Blue eyes.
Clear, white skin—
"..."
She was—not Japanese.[4]
Shichika had seen a person like this only once, when they were down in Kyushu fixing to capture Zokuto the Armor—someone from a foreign land, across the sea.
Princess Negative.
Blond hair and dazzling blue eyes.
What made her striking was her presence in Japan, whose isolationist policy all but banned relations with the outside world. If she returned to where she came from, she would have disappeared into the crowd.
In that sense, perhaps there was no cause for alarm—but one thing was for sure. In all that Shichika had learned about the world in his eight months away from home, the idea of a foreigner being installed so close to the heart of the bakufu made no sense.
—*Don't foreigners speak other languages?*
But the Princess spoke Japanese—impeccably.[5]
Full of questions, Shichika shot a look at Togame, seated beside him—but she would not look at him. Her eyes were locked on Princess Negative, and her face was flushed red with shame at being laughed at.
Eventually it seemed the Princess had laughed as much as she could laugh.[6]
"First and foremost," Togame began. "You must have known that the word 'Cheerio'—comes from another language."
Yikes, that's foremost?
Shichika was appalled. Togame had spoken with the utmost seriousness, which made it all the more absurd.
The Princess must have felt the same, and had herself another laugh.
"What, cat's out of the bag?"[7]
So—she had known.
"..."
Speechless—Togame stood.

[4] 外国人 GAIKOKUJIN foreigner
[5] 流暢 RYŪCHŌ fluently
[6] 途切れ途切れ TOGIRE TOGIRE tapering off
[7] 気付いちゃったの KIZUICHATTA NO "so you've realized (at last)"

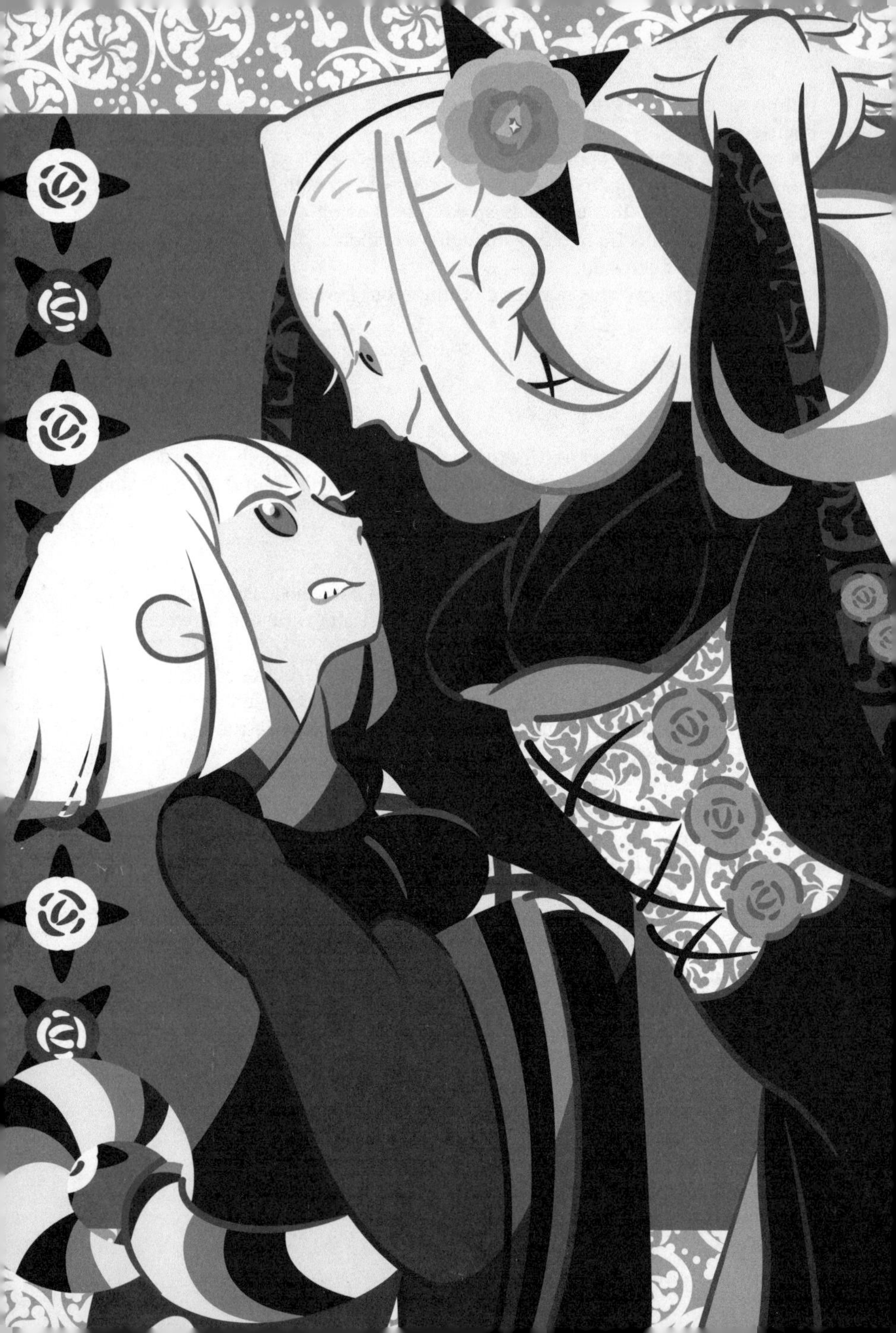

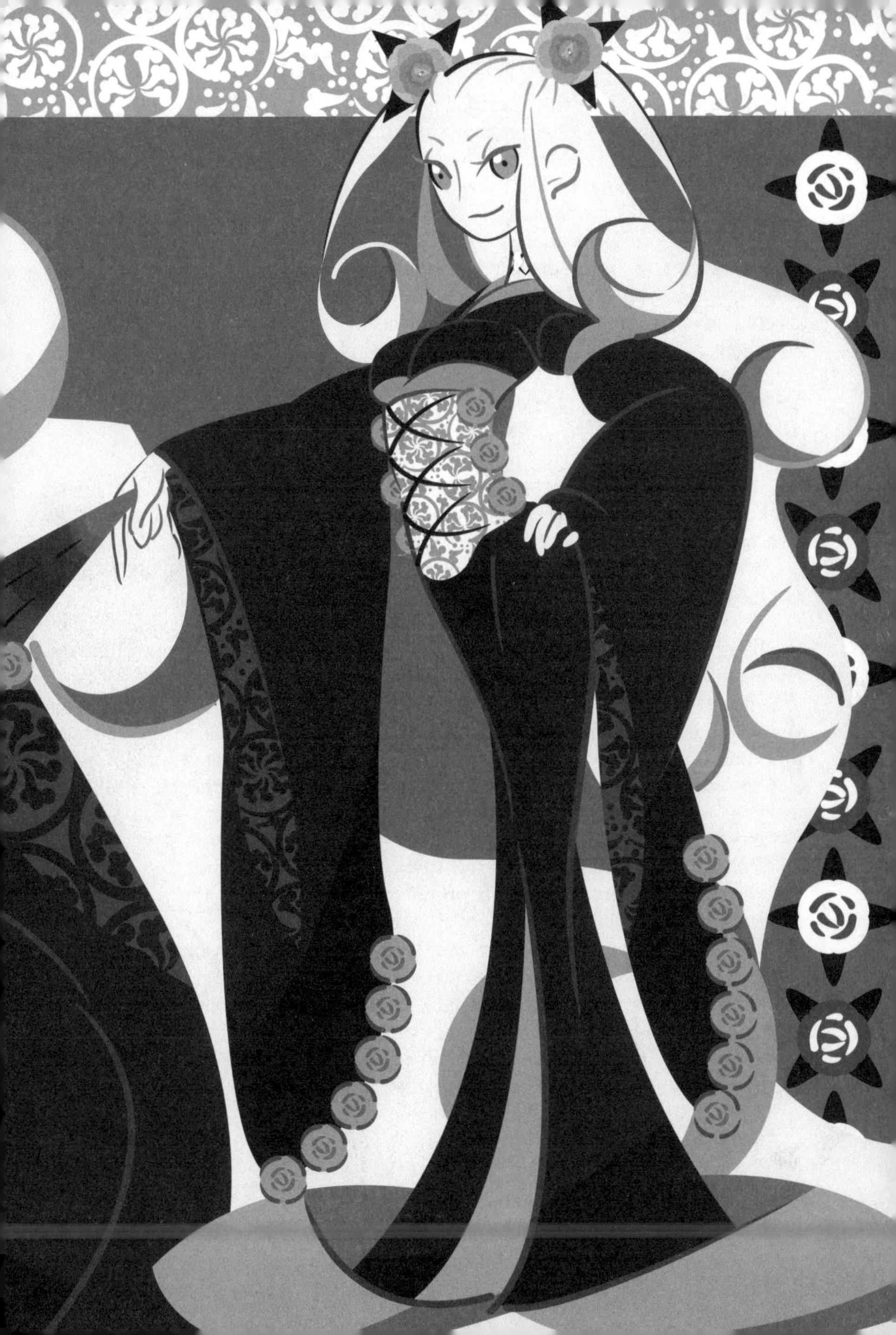

Following suit, the Princess stood as well.

In a succession of footsteps, they closed the distance between them.

Before Shichika was able to exhibit a reaction, the two of them were in the center of the chamber, on the verge of colliding—staring each other down.

Their faces all but smooshed together.

In sooth, their noses rubbed.

In contrast to the petite Togame, Princess Negative was quite tall (—*At least as tall as Meisai Tsuruga, probably taller*). This meant that Togame was glaring up at her, and Princess Negative was glaring down.

Togame with her arms crossed—Princess Negative with her hands clasped behind her head.

Practically shooting sparks.

Inapproachable.

Yikes.[8]

Shichika was genuinely terrified.

That the both of them—the two of them were smiling, at least outwardly, was scariest of all.

"I thought I'd crushed you for good—your stubbornness is absolutely stupefying. Why can't you go and die already?"

"How many times do I have to tell you? I'm not so weak[9] as to be killed off by the likes of you—I'll keep coming back to life until I've spilled[10] your guts and found out every deep, dark secret that they harbor."

"Just go ahead and try. The abyss inside of me is far too deep and dark for you to handle. You'll just keep coming back into the same scenario, until one day I'll crush you once and for all—but why not end things now, once and for all?"

"Unacceptable—I refuse. I'd wager that you've lost your chance to take me down—I wager the tables have turned, so that it's me who crushes you. Without a trace—unlike some people, I don't make mistakes."

"Be my guest—I'll gladly put you in your place."

"Please, allow me. Once you're in hell, you can hatch all the schemes and rotten eggs[11] you want."

"Quit running your mouth. It's over. Give it up, you nasty woman."

"Ditto that. I've got you where I want you. Nasty, nasty woman."

Princess Negative produced a metal fan[12] from her kimono—and snapped it open.

Almost involuntarily, Togame backed up and took her seat by Shichika, while the Princess returned to her place of honor.

"Well then, shall we talk business?"

"Sure, why not."

...

---

[8] 怖い。 KOWAI "Scary."
[9] やわ YAWA fragile
[10] 暴く ABAKU expose; plunder
[11] うどん粉 UDONKO udon flour the original verb is 練る NERU knead; work over
[12] 鉄扇 TESSEN robust folding fan carried by samurai for self-defense

Huh? Was that their way of saying hello?

Shichika looked back and forth between Togame and the Princess, who to his astonishment were carrying on like nothing happened—talking business.

Business.

In other words, about the Mutant Blades of Kiki Shikizaki—

"First off—I have to say you've done a fabulous job. Truly. No wonder they call you the Schemer. In seven short months, you've captured seven of the Twelve Possessed. Astonishing."

"I started the Sword Hunt a little before I got the first one, so it's seven months only if you start counting from the first moon—"

"Or from the point where Mr. Kyotoryu became your sword," the Princess brought Shichika into the conversation.

She closed her fan and pointed at him with its tip.

"Hello, Shichika—I'm Princess Negative."

"Howdy."

He bowed perfunctorily.

"Shichika!" Togame's angry voice rang out beside him. "Don't bow to scum like her."

So strict.

"Heheheh," Princess Negative couldn't help but laugh seeing this.

He was so different—from what she had imagined.

She hadn't thought the sword would be so affable.

Then again, the Princess got her mental picture secondhand from Emonzaemon Soda, so it was bound to be a little biased—

"By the way, where did that guy go?" Shichika asked the Princess.

Not fearful in the least.

Thanks to his sheltered upbringing.

"Emonzaemon—the Lieutenant. Isn't he your confidant[13] or something?"

"Oh, him. He's in the ceiling." Using her fan, the Princess pointed upwards. "He has an awfully dismal mug on him. Just looking at him is enough to get you down—so when I need him, I have him stay behind the ceiling, and not show himself."

"..."

Poor guy...

Shichika took pity on him earnestly.

"That mask," explained the Princess, "is there for his own good, but he's so hopelessly gloomy[14] that no mask can conceal it."

"..."

That's enough...[15]

"Bah." Togame puffed out her chest exultantly. "I've never forced Shichika to do something so silly."

[13] 側近 SOKKIN close aide
[14] 根暗 NEKURA "dark at the root" slang from the 80's
originally also had nuance of "being outwardly sociable, but dank at heart"
[15] 聞きたくない KIKITAKU NAI "I don't want to hear it"

"..."

Except for when you forced me to use that silly catchphrase, Shichika mused—but he kept his mouth shut.

He wouldn't want to make his owner look bad.

No use having a spitting contest about that sort of thing.

Anyway—it would appear that Emonzaemon was hiding in the ceiling. And unclear as his thoughts were on this exchange between Togame and the Princess—they could assume that he was listening, and Shichika needed to keep that in mind. For Togame, this was no less than an unspoken premise of the meeting, no doubt—

"So there. I just felt like lending you a helping hand. I couldn't sit back and watch when you were doing your damned best to round up those swords, not after everything we've been through—hence sending Emonzaemon to find you."

"Quit putting me on—I know you're just trying to do away with me."

"Perhaps. But remember, I am Inspector General of the Yanari Shogunate. In my position, I can't let a character[16] like you run rampant."

"Character? Try looking in the mirror, Princess."

"Me? I'm no such thing. But we digress—I caught wind of something interesting that you should know. I've been waiting."

"Waiting, huh. That's just your style," Togame took the Princess's remark in stride. "Go on, I'm all ears. You happen to have caught us at a standstill—for now, I'm learning everything I can. If you have some valuable information, I'd be absolutely thrilled to hear it."

"Sounds like you're not expecting much."

"'Course not. From you I expect nothing. But let me warn you, out of kindness: If whatever you're about to tell me turns out to be bogus,[17] even if you think it's true—I'll use it as an excuse to crush you."

"Scary stuff—but you don't need to remind me. I remember just the other day—the last time you pulled that one on me and crushed me. Splat!"

The Princess cackled.

She sure laughed a lot.

Even laughing off being beaten—Shichika thought, dumbfounded.

"Make no mistake, this tip is solid[18]—trust me, I'd be upset if something disrupted your Sword Hunt."

"Upset? How come?" Togame sounded genuinely perplexed. "You belong to an entirely separate branch of government. What do you care whether the Sword Hunt is a success?"

"Because your work portends all kinds of political implications for me—or not so much implications, but complications.[19] I hope to capitalize on your success, think of it that way. That must be clear to you, now that you've returned to the castle. The lords of the keep are paying close attention to your progress—

[16] 怪しい人間　AYASHII NINGEN suspicious human being
[17] がせ　GASE fake (news)
[18] 信憑性のある情報　SHINPYŌSEI NO ARU JŌHŌ credible information
[19] からみ しがらみ　KARAMI SHIGARAMI entanglements tethers

at this point, no portion of the bakufu is truly separate from your quest to track down all the Mutant Blades of Kiki Shikizaki."

"..."

In other words, they had tasked Togame with the Sword Hunt—though for the record, it had been her own idea—without actually believing it was realistic.

No way she'll succeed.

That had been their thinking.

But now that she had landed more than half the swords, possessing seven of the twelve—the scheme was a reality.

No longer merely a fancy—they could practically taste it.[20]

It was happening.

"I had been waiting for you to gain traction—I'll admit that the appearance of that monster Nanami Yasuri was more than I had bargained for, but once you started heading for the eighth sword, the mood inside the bakufu changed entirely. I knew that I was free to make a move. Able to step up and assist you."

"I don't recall requesting your assistance. Are you trying to take credit for my work?"

"I can't reject that idea entirely. I'd have no chance in the Sword Hunt with Emonzaemon—but I'm sincere about lending you a hand."

"Are you about to tell me where I might find the five remaining swords, and who owns them?"

"Sadly, no," said Princess Negative—shaking her head.

Negating Togame's expectations.

"Oh. You aren't?" Togame did not sound even slightly disappointed. "No offense, Princess, but I could care less about your info if it's not—"

"Not even if it concerns *Kiki Shikizaki himself?*"

These words—were unexpected.

Togame had been interrupted in the middle of her sentence, but let it go.

The Princess giggled.

"Lake Fuyo in Edo. You know the place?"

"Yeah—of course I do," Togame answered carefully, trying to feel out her rival's motive. "The Level One Disaster Area, like Mt. Odori in Ezo and Mt. Shirei in Mutsu—right?"

"Exactly," said the Princess. "But were you aware that Lake Fuyo—is the place Kiki Shikizaki kept his *workshop*?"[21]

"Wha...?!"

Togame leaned forward, stupefied.

"That's where he had—his workshop?"

"Correct. In that uninhabitable terrain, the only of the three Level One Disaster Areas devoid of human life, the legendary swordsmith built his base of operations. Although," the Princess corrected herself glibly,[22] "I suppose Mt.

---

[20] 外連味　現実味　KERENMI GENJITSUMI　"outré flavor" "reality flavor"
[21] 工房　KŌBŌ　"crafting chamber"
[22] わざとらしく　WAZATO RASHIKU　"like on purpose" deliberately, affectedly

Odori and Mt. Shirei are devoid of life by now as well."

Workshop—the word set Shichika thinking.

Did it mean that Lake Fuyo—was where Kiki Shikizaki made his swords?

"Of course, there were exceptions, like Soto the Twin. It isn't where he made all of the Twelve Possessed. But evidently, he crafted the *majority* of the thousand Mutant Blades at Lake Fuyo in Edo."

The forge where Kiki Shikizaki made his swords.

Locating the workshop of swordsmith Kiki Shikizaki, who despite being so legendary, or perhaps due to his legendary status, was essentially an enigma—would be most valuable indeed. If they perused his forge, surely they would find some information on the five remaining swords.

Hearing this made Shichika remember something.

The same thing that Togame recalled at the mention of Lake Fuyo: when Hohoh Maniwa proposed his alliance with Togame back in Satsuma, he had dropped[23] some information.

A sword at Mt. Shirei in Mutsu—which Nanami Yasuri had captured.

A sword in Tendo, in Dewa—whose presence they had yet to verify.

And another sword—at Lake Fuyo in Edo.

"Apparently this, evidently that...not at all what I would call reliable information."

"That's just my way of speaking. The leads are solid. Although I can't tell you who tipped me off."

"But you said so yourself, Princess...that place is uninhabitable."

"Which makes it the perfect setting for producing the secret and elusive Mutant Blades! But remember, Kiki Shikizaki made his magic swords hundreds of years ago, during the Age of Warring States. Needless to say, Lake Fuyo had not as yet received its designation as a Level One Disaster Area, since the Owari Bakufu who came up with that designation didn't exist either. That's how long ago we're talking. I suppose that means Lake Fuyo was far better off than it is now. You'd think so, anyway."

"But—Skytron *is still there*."

"Well, it probably wasn't before Shikizaki—it can't have existed since prehistoric times."

Skytron?[24]

Naturally, Shichika was flummoxed by the appearance of this strange word in Togame's conversation with the Princess—but the ladies made it sound like the most natural thing and carried on before he had a chance to get a word in.

"Chew on this, Miss Schemer. Remember when the Onmitsu got laughed at for their wacky intel[25] on Lake Fuyo? You know, the Onmitsu you took your anger out on when the Maniwa betrayed you."

"That wasn't my intention. Bad luck for them."

---

[23] 流して NAGASHITE provided (hints) liquid overtones, as when water is sent through pipes
[24] 日和号 BIYORIGŌ "favorable weather" plus a suffix for boats and other machines
[25] 変な結論 HEN NA KETSURON bizarre conclusion

"Was it? You certainly did nothing to save them."
"Because I owed them nothing."
"Hahaha."
"Well, what was this intel of theirs? I can't seem to recall."
"My dear, your memory is full of holes. They came back saying Skytron had been installed at Lake Fuyo *to protect something*—ring any bells?"
"Ah, I remember that."
Togame slapped her knee.
Like a cliché[26] of a person recollecting something.
"In that case, I was probably laughing with the rest of them. There's nothing to protect out by Lake Fuyo—"
"But what if it's protecting *Kiki Shikizaki's workshop*?"
"..."
This time, Togame was left speechless.
It took the words right out of her mouth.
"Hundreds of years after Kiki Shikizaki reigned over the Age of Warring States, I dare say Skytron is still out there, protecting the old workshop."

■ ■

Level One Disaster Area—Lake Fuyo.
Though called a lake on maps, it hadn't been one for at least a thousand years—from a time dizzyingly far into the past, it was what you might call a garbage dump.
A place, as the name would suggest, for disposing[27] of unnecessary things—nay, the word *dispose* suggests waste management, which is far from applicable—since people simply tossed their rubbish in the water.
Over the years, discarded rubbish sank into the bottom of the lake, then piled ever higher through its depths—until finally the lake was filled.[28]
Overfilled.[29]
A lake filled in with unnecessary rubbish.
A badland made from scraps of wood and metal.
This is how Lake Fuyo looked today.
As it turned out, Shichika and Togame barely had a chance to catch their breath in Owari. Wasting no time, they took leave of Mansion Negative, packed up their things, and headed straightaway for Edo—which brings us at long last back to the present moment, with Togame the Schemer and the Seventh Master of the Kyotoryu, Shichika Yasuri, newly arrived at Lake Fuyo.
Emonzaemon Soda, who had led the way, had just made himself scarce—

[26] わかりやすい　WAKARI YASUI　(too) easy to understand
[27] 処分　SHOBUN　throw away; deal with　can also mean "punish"
[28] 埋めた　UMETA　buried
[29] 埋め尽くした　UMETSUKUSHITA　buried consummately

announcing that his work was done, he bid the two of them good day. Shichika was slightly miffed, since after leading them to Tosa the lieutenant had stayed on to make sure they got their bearings, but Emonzaemon insisted that he had another order from the Princess to fulfill.

He declined to mention what this order was, but being from the Princess, it was bound to be a tall[30] one.

Shichika had plenty of sympathy for Emonzaemon.

It was almost like he was sympathizing with himself, in a way.

They were in the same proverbial boat.[31]

In any case, after about a week, Shichika finally had Togame to himself again—although as luck would have it, not for long.

Crossing the field of rubbish, at this point only nominally a lake, they took great care in choosing where to step (sharp pieces of metal threatening to slice their feet), and a little ways ahead—*this thing* came into view.

"..."

At first—he thought it was a person.

Another human being.

Or at the very least, something designed to resemble one—but upon closer examination, it became all too apparent that this thing was not a person.

For starters—it was made of metal.

It had four arms, two on each side of its body.

Its head was complete with a face, eyes, and a nose; and hair, or something like it, had been planted in its scalp. It even wore a tattered kimono—but it was clearly not a human.

Because it was—

"A robot."[32]

A life-size—mechanical doll.

On their journey, he had seen a doll that served you tea[33]—was this like a deluxe[34] version of that?

"That's it," Togame said. *"That thing is Skytron."*

Why had the bakufu made Lake Fuyo a Level One Disaster Area?

In part, of course, because it was extremely hazardous, filled to the brim with rubbish no one wanted—but the main reason? Lake Fuyo was *inhabited by Skytron.*

Which is the same reason that nobody lived here, unlike Mt. Odori and Mt. Shirei.

Because of Skytron.

Indiscriminately and automatically felling anyone who so much as neared Lake Fuyo—

[30] 理不尽　RIFUJIN　unreasonable, unjust　理 RI reason　不 FU non　尽 JIN "to the last"
[31] 同病相哀れむ　DŌBYŌ AI'AWAREMU　mutual pity for (suffering) the same illness
[32] からくり人形　KARAKURI NINGYŌ　"gimmick person form"　animatronics; automaton
[33] 茶運びの人形　CHAHAKOBI NO NINGYŌ　茶 CHA tea　運ぶ HAKOBU transport
　　　Edo-period windup doll that rolls ahead carrying a cup of tea and stops when the teacup is removed
[34] 高性能版　KŌSEINŌ BAN　high-performance version

Skytron.
Each of its four arms—held a sword.
Like the Katana Buddha they had seen in Tosa—
"Are we okay?"
"We're safe back here," Togame said. "I'm pretty sure as long as we stay far enough away, it can't pick up on us. I know it looks like it's a person, but those eyes are merely decorative. It uses some kind of a sensor[35] to make sense of its surroundings."
"So, if we go closer—it'll make a run at us?"
"Yep."
"Uh, well, what's next? From this far back—*I can't tell.*"
"That's fine, stick with the plan," Togame said. "Okay, Shichika? Let's go through this again—we're just scoping things out. We're not trying to finish anything today, right here, right now."
"I get it."
"I'll admit I had my doubts, but I think that Princess Negative's intelligence is sound—at this juncture, giving me false information would endanger her far more than me. In which case, the workshop of Kiki Shikizaki was somewhere in this lake bloated[36] with rubbish, and the continuation of our Sword Hunt is dependent on pinpointing exactly where. To do so, we must get rid of Skytron, essentially the guardian of Lake Fuyo—but before we do, there are some things I must investigate."
"I said I got it, Togame."
"Alright," she nodded. "Go have a look."
Before she finished speaking, he sped off.
Though not straight for the machine—Skytron. Taking advantage of its inability to notice him, so long as he maintained the proper distance, Shichika made a grand circuit around Skytron as it marauded the field of trash on its four legs, until he caught it from behind—and pounced.
As soon as he did.
Skytron's head—spun 180 degrees.
Turning to Shichika.
From this distance he could tell.
Skytron had been made—in the likeness of *a young woman.*
"HUMAN DETECTED"
Its mouth worked as the words came out.
"EXTERMINATE NOW"
Its four arms, wielding four swords—turned on Shichika.
In that instant, Shichika understood.
This verified what Togame had suspected.
The hunch she had, on top of what the Princess told them—Shichika was confident that Skytron was not simply here to guard Kiki Shikizaki's workshop.

[35] 感覚器　KANKAKUKI　sensory apparatus
[36] だらけ　DARAKE　rife

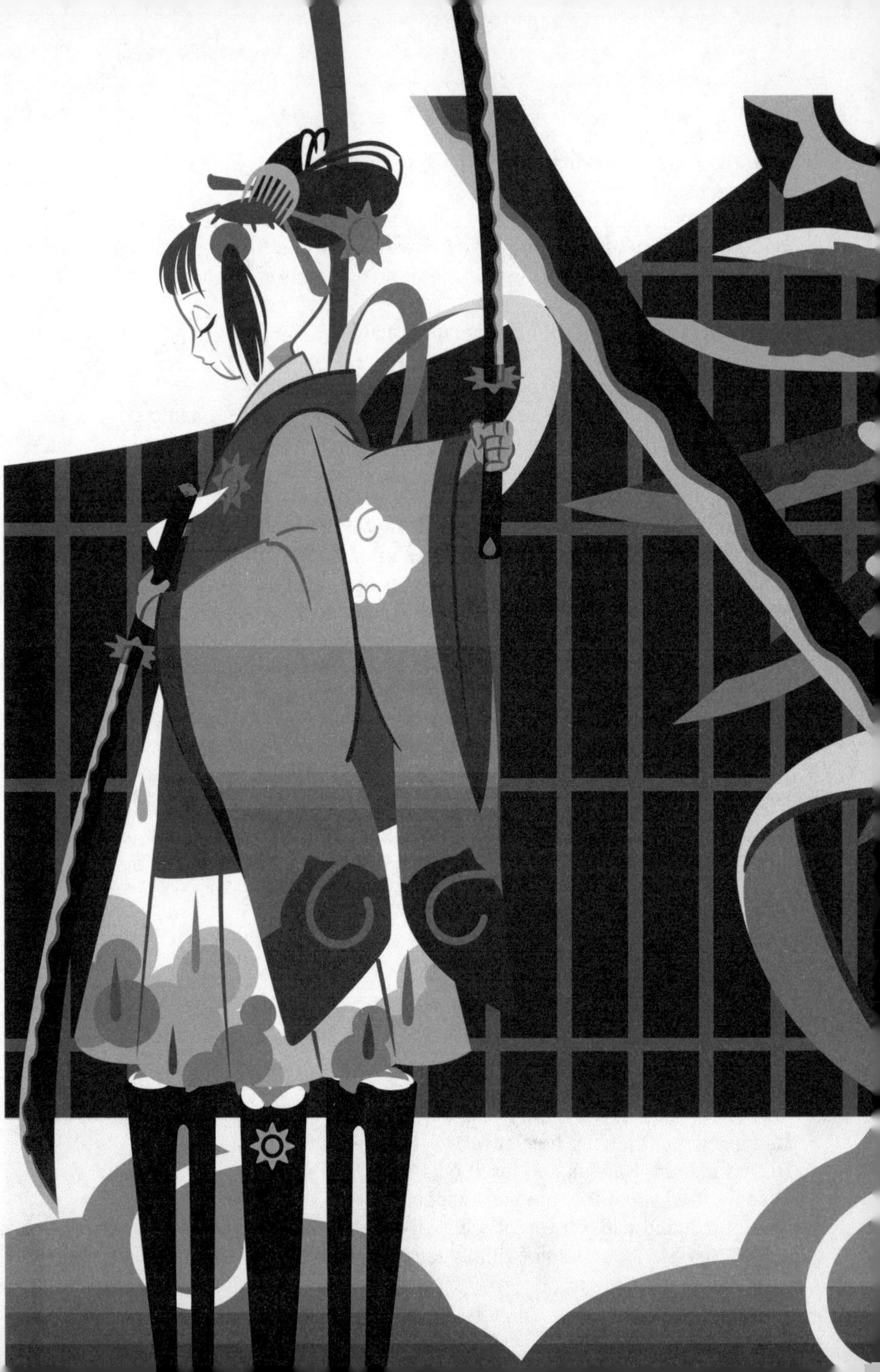

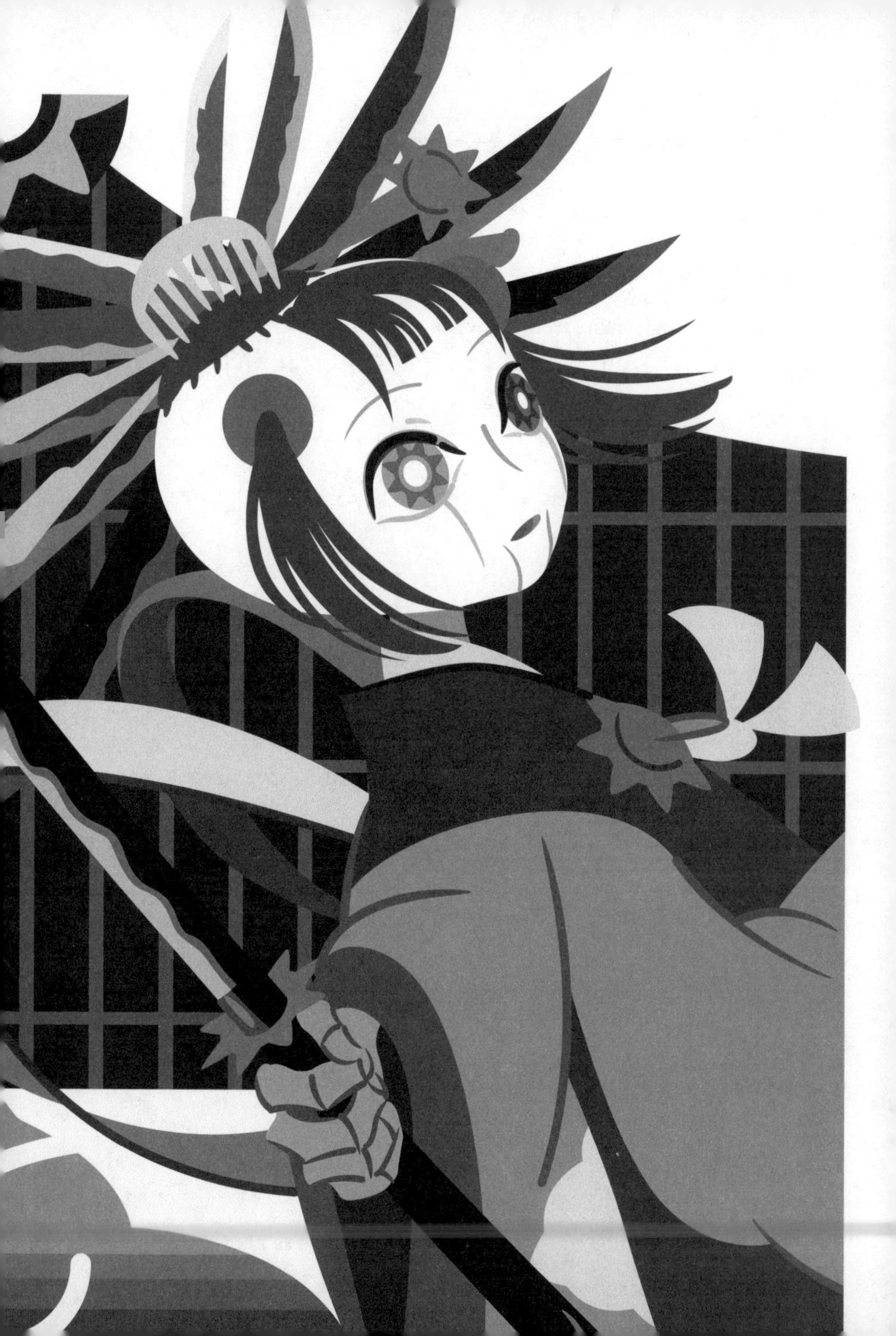

He felt the lifeforce.
That strange sensation Shichika experienced in the presence of a Mutant Blade—from this distance, he could feel it.
Coming from the four swords held by Skytron? Nay.
Coming from Skytron.
"...nkk."
As Togame had predicted,[37] this contraption was—
"BITO SUNDIAL"[38]
The words had come from[39] Skytron.

---

[37] 読んだ通り　YONDA TŌRI　as (she) read　読む　YOMU　read (a book etc.); fathom
[38] 微刀・釵　BITŌ KANZASHI　"The Subtle Sword: Hairpin"
[39] 発音　HATSUON　to pronounce

CHAPTER THREE

UMIGAME MANIWA

Skytron the Robo-Sword.

Marauding[1] the terrain of Lake Fuyo, she was the epitome of the unwanted trash abandoned all around her, the manifestation[2] of refuse discarded well before its time has come.

The Queen of Rubbish.

That was Skytron's sobriquet.[3]

An inanimate object with a vendetta against humanity.

An inhuman, mechanical swordsman.

Puppet[4] sword, robotic[5] sword.

True, neither Togame the Schemer, the realist, nor Princess Negative, the negativist, had believed the urban legends word for word—but Skytron could indeed be found at Lake Fuyo.

In that case, what was it doing there?

What reason did it have to be there?

If it was one of the Twelve Possessed of Kiki Shikizaki—that fact alone was plenty.

This is how Togame the Schemer saw things now.

She felt for certain Princess Negative had admitted this possibility, although she never said as much. The idea of Skytron being there to protect Kiki Shikizaki's workshop led naturally toward such a conclusion.

The conjecture hadn't been off the mark.

In truth, however, Princess Negative had no need to weigh the possibilities—*not when she knew every detail of the story.*

"Hey, Princess, one more thing," Togame had turned around and asked her.

On their way out of Mansion Negative—

"What was that in the alcove? The pair of lumpy metal things."

"Those? Oh, they're just a decoration," she'd brushed off the question.

"It doesn't seem to fit your taste. Lemme guess, a crappy present? We're heading to Lake Fuyo, after all. I'll toss it for you."

"Thanks so much," the Princess had laughed, "but I'm afraid that won't be necessary."

---

[1] 徘徊 HAIKAI prowl
[2] 化身 KESHIN incarnate
[3] 異名 IMYŌ nickname
[4] 傀儡 KAIRAI dummy
[5] 自動 JIDŌ automated

■ ■

His features were young—and he walked like he had all the time in the world. The leisurely[6] look on his face said it all.

While looking nothing like a warrior, the man did wear a sword—though there was something odd about its shape.

Compared with your average katana, the blade was inordinately narrow.

Even the scabbard was little over an inch wide.

Almost like—a rapier.[7]

Moreover, much like the strange sword at his hip, the clothing worn by this leisurely man was somewhat strange—like ninja garb, but sleeveless.

Chains wrapped around his body.

Indeed—

"You must be one of the Twelve Bosses of the Maniwa Clan—unless my eyes deceive me, Captain of the Fish Unit, Umigame Maniwa."

The man—Umigame Maniwa turned around.

Whereupon he saw another man who was oddly attired—in a coat and trousers, clothing that was uncommon, or rather exceedingly rare, in that era. The top part of his face was covered by a mask emblazoned with the word "NON-NINJA." Though they were plain compared to the one worn by Umigame, he wore a pair of swords: one big, one small.

"Hm—who the heck are you? How'd you know I'm Umigame Maniwa, the coolest, snazziest, strongest, handsomest, and richest of them all?"

Giving weight, leisurely yet confidently, to every word he uttered, the ninja pressed the strange man.

"You're correct in guessing that I'm Umigame Maniwa, the coolest, snazziest, strongest, handsomest, and richest of them all—but I've never seen the likes of you before, you clown.[8] I don't believe we've met."

"My name is Emonzaemon Soda." Getting the hint, the man in the mask and trousers introduced himself. "*Not off*—I'm glad I found the right man. Since they call you the Immortal Turtle, I'd been expecting I would find an elderly gentleman, but now that we finally meet, I'm surprised to see how young you are. Frankly, I thought I must've had the wrong guy—but I'm glad that's not the case."

"Yeah? One look and anyone can see that I'm the coolest, snazziest, strongest, handsomest, and richest of them all, but if you know my alias,[9] then you must really mean business... You said your name is Emonzaemon Soda? Not sure I've heard of you—that's a pretty goofy name. An obvious pseudonym[10] if I've ever heard one."

---

[6] のんびり NONBIRI (onomatopoeic) unhurried
[7] 刺突剣 SHITOTSUKEN "pierce-thrust sword"
[8] 頓珍漢 TONCHINKAN off-base; a fool cacophony of a smith's apprentice striking off-rhythm
[9] 二つ名 FUTATSUNA "second name"
[10] 偽名 GIMEI fake name

"It's not a pseudonym."

The man in mask and trousers, Emonzaemon Soda, shook his head.

"It's my real name—or it is now."

"Whatever floats your boat," said Umigame.

He gauged the distance between them.

His interlocutor stood a good number of paces away—as if he, too, were wary.

"Well? You're the one who called to me. What do you want? I'm on a journey—kind of in a rush, in fact. So please, don't hold me up, if you don't mind."

"You sure know how to stroll about for someone in a rush."

"I'm the turtle. I take my time. If you ask me, most people need to chill."

"Unfortunately," said Emonzaemon, "holding you up is exactly what I'm here to do."

"..."

Sure, muttered Umigame.

The man in mask and trousers—had been hostile from the first.

Not even concealing it, he seemed downright bloodthirsty.

"I'm not exactly confident in my memory, so I'll ask you just in case—have we met?"

"No, this is the first time—and the last."

"Salty,"[11] admitted Umigame. "Makes me wish I said it first."

Aiming at Emonzaemon's shod feet, he flung a shuriken that he had extracted, stealthily, from his ninja garb.

With the utmost efficiency, the lieutenant stepped back, dodging the missile.

Umigame had not been expecting that the shuriken, his way of saying howdy-doo,[12] would hit its target—but the way that Emonzaemon moved perplexed him.

—Hm.

That air.

"This can't be anything personal? I don't peddle in the sort of shoddy work that wins you enemies[13]—that Schemer girl is about the only person who has it in for me. Wait, don't tell me that she sent you. According to Hohoh, we've supposedly forged some kind of an alliance—"

"*Not involved,*" Emonzaemon quietly negated.

Negated.

"I have no relations with Madame Schemer—but I do know that she's at Lake Fuyo in Edo, trying to capture Bito the Sundial. I'm curious to see how the Kyotoryu stands up against that deranged contraption—curious indeed."

"..."

Not sent for by the Schemer—

And yet this man knew who she was.

---

[11] 渋い SHIBUI bitter can be used as a compliment for quiet elegance, mature taste
[12] 挨拶代わり AISATSU GAWARI by way of greeting
[13] 恨みを買う URAMI WO KAU "buy a grudge"

And knew about the Kyotoryu, her chosen weapon on the Sword Hunt.
Above all—he knew about the Sword Hunt.
Though looking calm as ever—on the inside Umigame felt his steady nature curdle.[14]
Lake Fuyo in Edo.
Where, according to the tip they had received from Hohoh Maniwa, his brother in arms, they could expect to find another of the swords. Hohoh said he didn't know what kind of katana they would find—but evidently it was Bito the Sundial.
And yet...
"Am I correct," Emonzaemon continued, twisting the knife,[15] "to assume that you, too, Umigame Maniwa, are here in Shinano in search of yet another of the Twelve Possessed?"
"Please, are you serious?"
Umigame tried to play dumb, but what was the point?
The man sounded like he knew exactly what was up.
As if to prove it, Emonzaemon dropped some additional information on Umigame, which was news to him.
"It's true that *once upon a time*—Ento the Bead could be found in this land. Assuming that's what brings you here?"
Ento the Bead.[16]
That name.
Umigame had no idea *what it was* the sword entailed—but Emonzaemon said its name like it was an old friend.
He made it clear, however—that the sword was there no more.
When this sank in, Umigame shed the last traces of his smile. That carefree air was gone entirely. His mien shifted, turning treacherous,[17] as if he had donned a different mask—to glare at Emonzaemon.
"Who the hell are you?" asked Umigame—taking one step closer. "Why are you here?"
"I told you, I'm here to hold you up. Though for the most part, we'll let you Maniwa Bosses do your thing—on account of this alliance with Madame Schemer, I'm not about to mess things up for you... You're free to go about the Sword Hunt as you please. That said, I don't claim to understand what Hohoh Maniwa has in mind..."
"How do you know Hohoh?"
Though Umigame had casually mentioned him earlier, Emonzaemon had spoken as if that wasn't the first time he'd heard about the Divine Phoenix.
His delivery suggested he and Hohoh knew of one another.
But in answer to Umigame's question—
"*No reply*," he said. "It's none of your business whether he and I are old ac-

[14] 変貌　HENBŌ　"change face"　metamorphose
[15] 畳み掛ける　TATAMI KAKERU　pile/press on　畳む　TATAMU fold multiple times　畳　TATAMI tatami mat
[16] 炎刀『銃』　ENTŌ JŪ　"The Flame Sword: Gun"
[17] 剣呑　KEN'NON　"sword swallowing"　hazardous

quaintances or strangers... As a general rule, we'd like to leave you to your own devices. *As long as you don't try and snatch Ento the Bead—*"

"...?"

"Go ahead and claim any of the other Mutant Blades, but the Bead is off-limits. If you delve any deeper—you just might arrive at the Princess."

The Princess?

That word—gave Umigame pause.

Right—he *remembered*.

There were two she-devils[18] at the center of the bakufu—

Two women whose true origins and real names were unknown.

The first being the Whitehaired Schemer—needless to say.

The Grand Commander of Arms, with whom the Maniwa had dealt extensively.

And the second—

"Princess Negative..." muttered Umigame—stepping back just as he had stepped forward.

Princess Negative.

Inspector General of the Yanari Shogunate.

"Do you work for—Princess Negative?"

It made sense. From the way he called Togame "Madame Schemer" and spoke about her circumstances, one could be forgiven for assuming he not only knew about her, but knew her personally, in which case...

—*Princess Negative.*

According to Hohoh—she had made a comeback just a few months prior.

He recalled the twinge of dread he had experienced when he heard—and why? Because she had been toppled by none other than the Maniwa.

In a maneuver led by Togame the Schemer.

Well, that would explain how this man knew Hohoh. And Umigame's alias—

"Is this some kind of a retaliation?"[19] Umigame let out a little breath and asked Emonzaemon. "Is the Princess seeking vengeance[20]—on what happened to her last?"

"Please. Princess Negative *rejects* such nonsense—she wouldn't waste her time retaliating. She's given up on you entirely. Hence—the choice to let you do your thing. As long as you steer clear of the Bead."

"What's so special about that one sword? Wait a second, *are you saying that the Princess has Ento the Bead in her possession? And keeping it a secret from the bakufu?*"

"Well done. Leave it to a ninja."

Umigame had not asked him with the utmost confidence—he could have seen it either way.

Yet *unfortunately*—his guess had been correct.

---

[18] 鬼女　KIJO "demon woman"
[19] 意趣返し　ISHUGAESHI "returning the malice"　意趣 ISHU intention, grudge
[20] 仕返し　SHIKAESHI "returning the deed"　仕返す SHIKAESU can also mean "do over"

Not good.

Without realizing—he had waltzed into the lion's mouth.[21] If he had known it would be this way, he would have partnered up, like Pengin had with Hohoh. He had never meant to pick a fight with Princess Negative.

But then again, the fact that Oshidori wasn't with him was a blessing, really. Perhaps Hohoh and Pengin—but Oshidori would have made it hard to extricate themselves from this situation.

This man would not have been tasked with an errand of this magnitude if he were merely working under Princess Negative—he had to be a close aide.

Which meant he was no pushover.

"I'm afraid," said Emonzaemon, "you're in over your head."

"..."

"If you're a ninja, be a ninja—and if you're a pushover, play the part. You had the chance to shy away from the limelight of history, but you had to outrun all the others and *almost* reach the core. You got so close—if Madame Schemer and the Kyotoryu had suffered even one more unexpected interference, I doubt that I'd have caught you, and you would have been the first to arrive at the historical truth. A close call."

"History? Historical? What are you saying? I don't understand."

"No need to understand—when you're about to die. You almost made it. Just a little further—good luck in your next history."

Stepping over the shuriken lodged at his feet, Emonzaemon approached Umigame and slowly drew his sword from its scabbard.

"Hey, wait a second. Wait!"

Umigame—

Threw both hands in the air.

"S-So I touched something untouchable, or I've been messing where I shouldn't have been? Fine, fine, I apologize. It really was an accident—"

"..."

"I give up, okay? I never wanted any part of this Sword Hunt in the first place. Since everyone else was onboard, I got the sense it wasn't the right time to stick my neck out and figured I had no choice but to join them. Or at least pretend to join them, see? I mean, I'm only here in Shinano to see the sights—I love this place, Shinano. Great spot."

"Even if all that were true, I've told you too much. As far as I'm concerned, you have no right to live another day."

"Quit sounding so scary—oh, right, I've got a great idea. How's about you and me buddy up? I'm getting pretty sick of being in the Maniwa. Too many wise guys[22] running around—unlike the old days. See, I may look this way, but it's all just cosmetic,[23] and I'm actually pretty old. About as old as you, I'd reckon. And yet, that Kawauso insists on making fun of me. Ah, but I guess he's no longer

---

[21] 虎穴　KOKETSU　tiger's den
[22] 生意気　NAMA'IKI　"raw spirited"　smart-alecky
[23] 若作り　WAKAZUKURI　making oneself look young through makeup, clothing, etc.

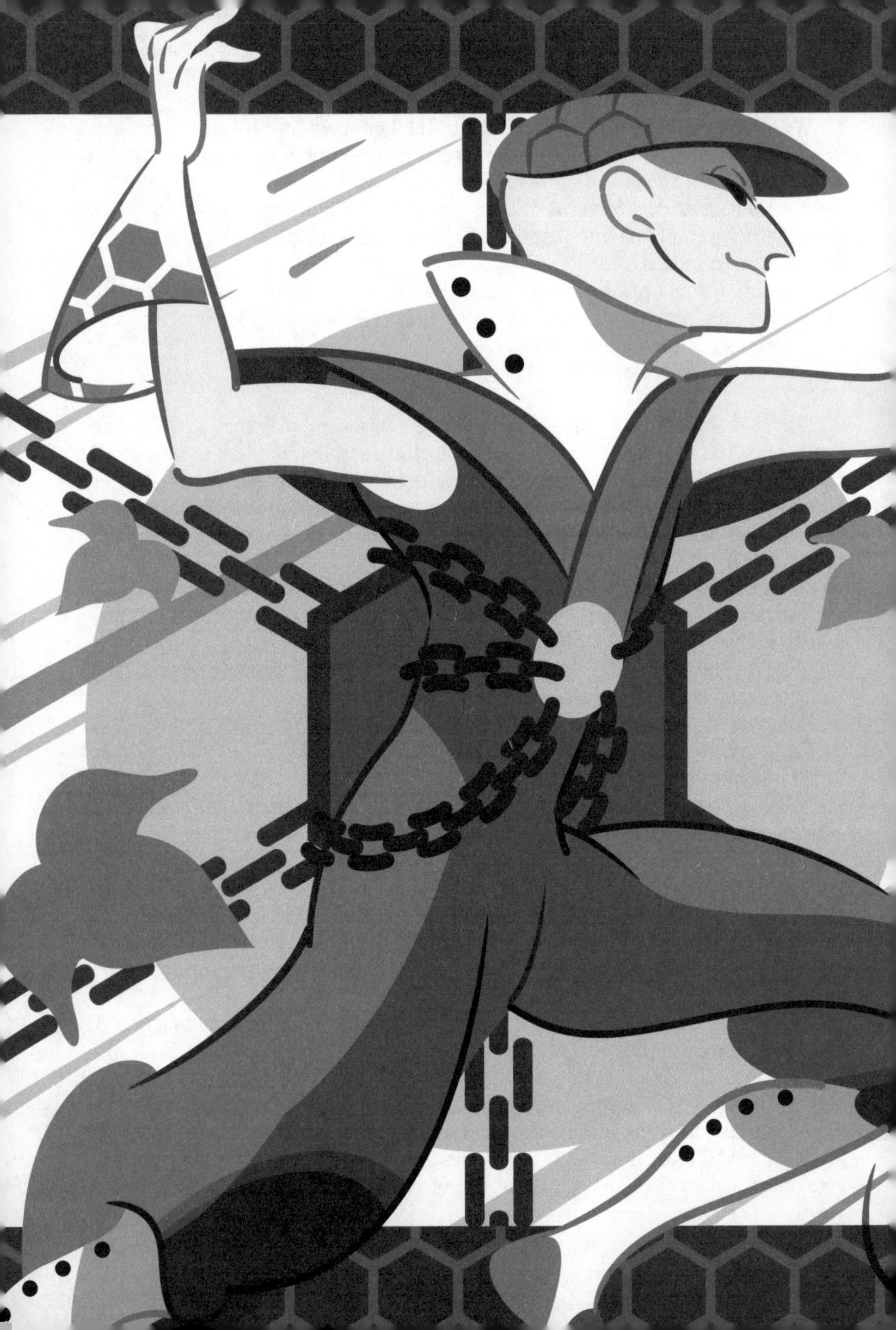

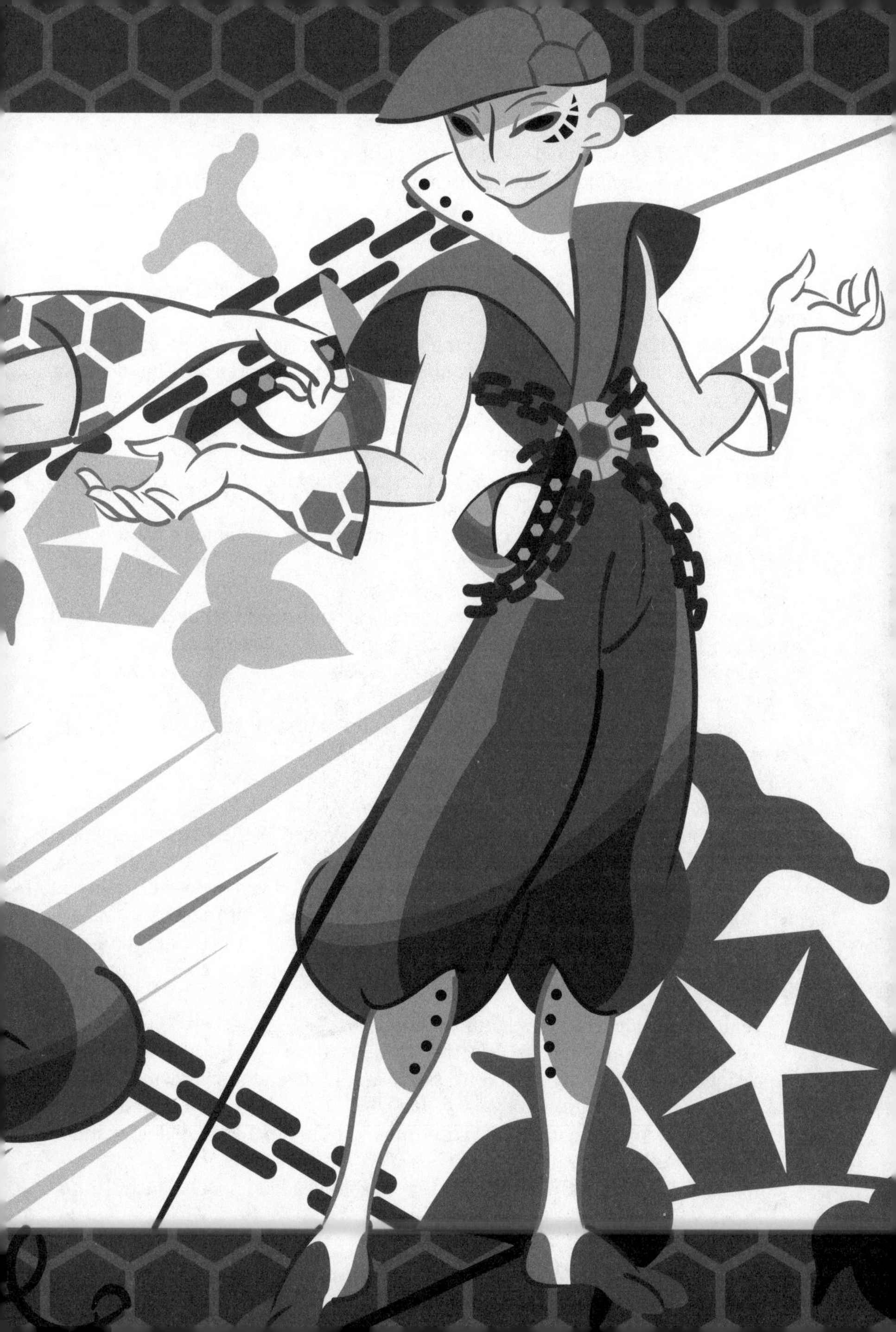

with us, is he—"

Then.

Once he had said as much—Umigame sprang to action.

The hands he had been holding high dropped—to bare his sword.

Emonzaemon had continued coming closer, undeterred by Umigame's speech, until the man was almost within range.

Umigame was a ninja.

Dirty deeds were how he made a living—begging for his life, however insincerely, was fine by him.

Besides, it had given him a chance to gauge the length of Emonzaemon's longsword—and his own rapier was slightly longer! If he reached his arm out all the way—

"...nkk!"

Shaken—Emonzaemon shrank back.

With the breadth[24] of his sword, he parried Umigame, who had been aiming for his heart—but that was all it took.

That was enough—to send a fracture[25] through Emonzaemon's katana.

"Heeheehee."

Step.

Planting one foot far ahead of the other, Umigame sank into his knees—and aimed the tip of the rapier, firm in his left hand, at Emonzaemon.

Nobody was around.

Free—to his heart's content.

But even if there were people around, he'd simply kill them off—*hey now, who am I, Kuizame?*

No good, no good.

I need to behave like an adult here, no matter what—

"I am Umigame Maniwa, one of the Twelve Bosses of the Maniwa—people call me the Immortal Turtle. Prepare to die."

"You're a swordfighter...a swordsman?" asked Emonzaemon—glancing at his longsword, which in just one clash had been turned into rubbish. "What's more, your sword is from the western lands...how ironic. Here I am, in a coat and trousers, wielding a katana, while you, clad in ninja garb, come at me with a rapier—"

"Yeah—an ironic situation. Your fate included."

"No, you're the one whose fate the irony includes—to be honest, I hadn't entertained the possibility that you'd be both a ninja and a swordsman. *If you had managed to lay hands on one of the Twelve Possessed*—you would have been a menace. With a name like 'The Immortal Turtle,' I assumed your ninpo let you live forever.

"*So I was taking it easy, thinking,*" Emonzaemon added nonchalantly, "*if he's*

---

[24] 腹 HARA "belly" the curved middle of the blade of a katana
[25] 亀裂 KIRETSU "turtle tears" from an old Chinese custom known as plastromancy, where turtle shells were baked to augur the future based on how the cracks formed

some kind of immortal ninja, I've killed five of those already."

Umigame didn't think he was bluffing.

But that confidence—would be the death of this man.

"Hahaha. I'm probably the worst[26] ninja that you'll ever meet—most ninpo is totally beyond me. Best I can do is fling a couple shuriken. Ninpo that helps you live forever? Who needs that. *If you want to live a long life, all you have to do is be the stronger one.*"

"..."

"The strong prey upon the weak! Simple as that. *As for immortal ninja—I've killed fifteen myself.* Where swordplay is concerned, I'll hold my own against the Kyotoryu or Hakuhei Sabi any day. Up against me and my rapier, no one stands a chance. Unlike you, sitting pretty in your cushy little office in the bakufu, I've lived through more carnage[27] than you'll ever know!"

Therein lay the reason why Chocho Maniwa and Umigame Maniwa were the only two out of the entire crew of bosses who knew about the Kyotoryu before this whole story began.

Chocho had studied the way of the fist.

Umigame studied the way of the sword.

Thus they had known of the Kyotoryu—the swordless form of swordplay.

"I'll teach[28] you—that the Sea Turtle is the strongest creature in all of Mother Ocean!"

This was not actually true.

But Umigame Maniwa was not above grandstanding.

Looking on, Emonzaemon, whose sword was still drawn, slipped it back into its sheath and dropped the sheath onto the ground beside him. There was no use lugging around the longsword as they fought, now that it had been rendered unusable.

In turn, he cast away the short sword, too, despite its good condition.

Brave man,[29] thought Umigame.

Most people cling to their weapons for dear life, broken or otherwise...

"Just in case I've missed something, that pair of swords wasn't Ento the Bead, was it?"

"Don't be foolish. The Bead is on display at Mansion Negative."

"Glad to hear it."

"How so? When it amounts to yet another reason you must perish."

"Hey—are you ninja?" Umigame took a verbal stab[30]—without breaking his form. "If I'm actually a swordsman, and you're actually a ninja, things are topsy-turvier[31] than I thought, but that has to be the case. From the way you

---

[26] 落ちこぼれ OCHIKOBORE "fall behind" dropout
[27] 修羅場 SHURABA scene reminiscent of the battle between Asura and Indra
[28] 教育 KYŌIKU educate 教える OSHIERU teach 育てる SODATERU nurture, raise
[29] いい判断 II HANDAN good judgment
[30] 言葉で切り込んだ KOTOBA DE KIRIKONDA cut into (charged in, struck) with words
[31] あべこべ ABE KOBE originally written as 彼方此辺 "that side (becoming) this side"

dodged the shuriken to how you parried just now, you couldn't be a normal[32] person. You carry a familiar reek unique to ninjadom—what's your clan? It doesn't seem like you're from the Onmitsu... I've learned a little bit about them way back when from that Schemer lady, but she didn't mention the likes of you."

"Incorrect," Emonzaemon said in a stern tone.

And pointed at his mask.

At the word "Non-Ninja."

"As you see, a ninja I am not. And haven't been—for ages."

"Okay, you're a former ninja—but all of us in the Maniwa are not so different today—and? What clan were you a part of? We ninjas have our code of conduct.[33] Depending on your clan—I mean, your former clan, we may be able to settle this without a fight... I'm not begging for dear life, you understand, I'm saying this for your sake. I know we'd betrayed the Schemer girl, but now we've entered an alliance, which in a sense links us to Princess Negative."

"...The Aioi[34] Clan," Emonzaemon—saw fit to respond.

To the question dropped by Umigame Maniwa.

The former ninja could not have been interested in a pact with Umigame—who, in turn, must have simply been curious, since he had the upper hand now, his foe having lost his weapon—

"Aye, oi? The Aye-Oi Clan..."

Umigame scanned his memory but came up short.

He had never heard this name in all his life.

"Who the hell are they? I haven't a clue. I figured any ninja fit to work for Princess Negative would belong to one of the famous villages."

"Ah. You haven't a clue."

The temperature dropped by a few degrees around Emonzaemon.

Or perhaps—it rose.

At any rate, he had a different air about him.

"I'll tell you, then. The Aioi Clan—"

Emptyhanded.

Taking no pains to rearm himself—Emonzaemon Soda started to close the distance between himself and Umigame.

"—*were wiped out by the Maniwa! One hundred and seventy years ago!*"

■ ■

Ages ago.

Long before even the Age of Warring States—there was a ninja village that had been founded around the same time as the Maniwa.

---

[32] 表の OMOTE NO of the surface/front vs. the underworld
[33] 義理道理 GIRI DŌRI duties/obligations & reasons/rationales
[34] 相生 AI'OI area in present-day Hyogo not known for ninja historically

The Aioi Ninja Clan.
The Maniwa and the Aioi were enemies.
Mortal enemies—who had been embroiled in conflict for centuries.
Which surely served to hone their skills and bolster their ninjutsu—but at the conclusion of the Age of Warring States, around the time today's Owari Bakufu took shape, the two clans had a fatal showdown.
The Maniwa were victorious.
You could say their victory came thanks to strategy—as this was when the Maniwa established their cooperative, governed not by a single boss but twelve. At first, it was believed the change would cause the structure of authority to collapse, turning their clan into a wild mob—but the result was anything but chaos.
This was when the Maniwa were liberated—from the core belief that ninjas must operate in concert.
The first iteration of the Twelve Bosses.
Boss Komori the First. Boss Kawauso the First. Boss Kyoken the First.
Boss Shirasagi the First. Boss Oshidori the First. Boss Hohoh the First.
Boss Kuizame the First. Boss Pengin the First. Boss Umigame the First.
Boss Mitsubachi the First. Boss Chocho the First. Boss Kamakiri the First.
Among them, only Kyoken Maniwa had *persisted*[35] up until the present day— but one hundred and seventy years later, the others remained the standard, as the strongest crew of ninjas to call the village home.
And those Twelve Bosses—bore through Aioi Village.
Thus—the village met its ruin.
Although their clan was not without survivors.
At first, they were a hundred strong.
But before long, they were only fifty.
Times changed with the generations.
And yet their ranks diminished without hope.
From fifty down to twenty-five.
From twenty-five to thirteen.
From thirteen to seven.
From seven to four.
Then four to two.
Until finally—the two had been reduced to one.
Only one of them remained.
It took a hundred and seventy years—but all of them was dead but one.
It took a hundred and seventy years—but all of them was gone, save one.
The Maniwa had forged ahead through history, until so much time[36] *had passed their former peers had been entirely forgotten—*
Only one remained. And that one—was Emonzaemon Soda.
"M-Maniwa Kenpo!"

---

[35] 共通している　KYŌTSŪ SHITE IRU　to be in common, the same
[36] 月日　TSUKIHI　"months and days"

That moment.
Umigame lunged.
Moving not only with his arms, but his whole body, legs and all, thrusting that rapier relentlessly—at Emonzaemon's heart.
There were things he could have learned.
And yet—he had decided that there wasn't time for that.
Umigame was now certain—he had touched upon something untouchable.
This was the first he heard about the Aioi Ninjas—but Umigame's intuition was far keener than the average person.
Indeed—it was ironic.
How Umigame could have such keen intuition, and saunter into a situation stickier than anyone!
Before any of the Twelve Bosses.
And before Togame the Schemer.
He had stepped into this steaming pile of taboo[37]—
"...Huh?"
His fulsome[38] thrust—cut through the air.
Emonzaemon Soda had vanished before his eyes.
"I know your kind," a voice said, *from behind*. "The ninjas of your clan know more than ninpo, dabbling in swordsmanship and the martial arts—but you are not alone. The ninjas of the Aioi Clan practiced their fair share of both kinds of kenpo."
"—Khh!"
Umigame spun around—but Emonzaemon Soda was not there.
He heard the voice, behind him once again.
"Here's a taste of Aioi Kenpo—*Shadow Fist*."[39]
"Urrrr—you, you—"
He spun around, but nobody was there.
It was simply that he sensed something behind him.
An uninhibited and powerful—fury.[40]
"Okay, Umigame. Perhaps I've seen less carnage than you—but hear this," said Emonzaemon.
Again from behind.
"The carnages that we have seen—are too different in kind to bear comparison."
He spoke like he was dispensing an obvious truth.
Essentially, talking down to him.
"C-Come on—who the hell do you think you're talking to? I-I'm one of the Twelve Bosses of the Maniwa!"
"What of it? You think that title makes you any stronger?"
Umigame could spin around in circles—but would never spot Emonzaemon.

[37] 禁忌 KINKI "forbidden odiousness"
[38] 渾身の KONSHIN NO using the whole body; with all one's might
[39] 背弄拳 HAIRŌKEN "fist playing tricks from the back"
[40] 殺気 SAKKI "murderous *ki*"

He was a sight alright, like watching a puppy chasing his own tail. It felt like somebody was breathing down his neck—but he was unable to catch[41] it.

He could spin and spin all day.

Around and around—and never find his adversary.

Aioi Ninpo, Shadow Fist.

The principle was simple.

It's hard to attack somebody behind you—and Umigame's rapier was perhaps one of the worst weapons on the planet for attacking someone coming from the rear.

Regardless of how deftly Umigame thrust a sword—or whether he was tough enough to hold his own against the Kyotoryu or Hakuhei Sabi, he would have no chance to demonstrate his abilities.

Thanks to this kenpo—Shadow Fist.

His enemy would always be behind him.

And though he could not see his adversary—he was staring squarely back at him.

A terror if there ever was one.

"Thrust all you want, but no one is in front of you," Emonzaemon remarked frigidly. "But with the Shadow Fist—*I always have the enemy in front of me.*"

"Shit...I'd never even heard...about the Aioi! Much less about a move like this. You call it kenpo, but a move like that clearly draws on ninjutsu!"

"Our moves were different in the Age of Warring States—the Maniwa today can't hold a candle...*except for maybe Hohoh*," Emonzaemon noted suggestively.

Did this guy—know Hohoh?

"I may be the last descendent[42] of the ninja village that your brethren swept off of the map—but I'm not acting on a grudge. I lost my cool earlier, but at least on that account you were spot on. It's all for the best."

"Th-The best?"

"The best in my opinion, anyway. Oh, since you mentioned begging for your life, this is a good a time as any—"

"Nghh..."

It may have been his turn to speak—but Umigame was all out of words.

No use trying to buy time.

This ninja—was a cut above. He was too good.

It made no sense to huff and puff or put up a front with him.

If his enemy was just a swordsman or a warrior, Umigame could have possibly outwitted him—but as one ninja to another, or at least against a "NON-NINJA," such trickery[43] would get him nowhere fast.

Which left him wrestling[44] with the question of how he wound up in this predicament. Where had he gone wrong? If he had acted more adeptly—the Maniwa could be in the lead now on the Sword Hunt.

[41] 視認　SHININ　"visually recognize"　identify
[42] 末裔　MATSU'EI　remaining descendant
[43] 小細工　KOZAIKU　"small artifice"　cheap moves
[44] 抱く　IDAKU　hug, embrace; harbor

I was closer to the truth.
Than anyone.
Which is why—
"Suit yourself. You are a Maniwa ninja, after all. You've tasted our kenpo, but let me now give you a proper demonstration of Aioi Ninpo. Although if you can't see me, what good is a demonstration...and besides, this next move, like the first, is too bizarre to be called ninpo—"
That voice.
Speaking behind him.
Umigame Maniwa did not try to escape.
He thought only of his remaining comrades—
Hohoh Maniwa, Pengin Maniwa, Oshidori Maniwa.
How might he warn them of *this situation*?
Even in the end.
Umigame—fought for his village.
"NON-NINPO—Endlessly Unsparing."[45]
Despite its name—
The move was indeed *not sparing*—but ended the enemy.
The Immortal Turtle—died young after all.

■   ■

Back at Owari, in Mansion Negative.
Princess Negative was standing stiffly, biding her time in the middle of her room, when she heard a voice above her.
"I have returned. All has gone as planned—I left Togame the Schemer and the Kyotoryu at Lake Fuyo, then put an end to Umigame Maniwa—Captain of the Fish Unit, the boss who had his sights set on Ento the Bead."
"Late again."
Although he had accomplished quite a lot in a short while, Princess Negative was set on negging Emonzaemon—declining to voice her thanks.
"But like you said, we must not underestimate the Maniwa—I reject myself for what I said a month ago. I sorely underestimated them...but you caught him before things got out of hand... You must feel better, no? Paying off the grudge borne by your ancestors."
"A one-hundred-and-seventy-year-old grudge cannot be paid off by the descendants of its perpetrators, one hundred and seventy years later. As I told Umigame Maniwa. I wasn't acting on a personal grudge. I would never follow out an order from Your Highness bearing such ulterior[46] motives."

---

[45] 不生不殺 IKASAZU KOROSAZU "neither keeping alive nor killing" the usual reading would be FUSHŌ FUSATSU, but the author's phonetic gloss makes it sound more colloquial
[46] 私情 SHIJŌ personal feelings

"Lieutenant, quit being so painfully formal. It aggravates me ... Though yes, I agree, it makes no sense to hunt down age-old[47] enemies. Well? What about that nasty woman?"

"It's been a few days now. At this point—they must have found Skytron. Or maybe—things have already been settled."

"Think they've figured out that Skytron is Bito the Sundial?"

"Easily. The Kyotoryu can feel the Mutant Blades' lifeforce."

"Can we be sure?"

Princess Negative—glanced toward the alcove.

At the *pair of lumpy metal things* on display.

"He didn't seem to pick up on *those two over there*—it would seem his sixth sense isn't so reliable. Just think how funny it would be if Shichika destroyed Skytron without realizing what it was—if he broke a sword, the whole Sword Hunt would be a wash.[48] That nasty woman would end up with her head cut off, unless she cut her stomach first."

"You sure play cat-and-mouse."[49]

"It's fine. It's been a little slow around here. I had to have some fun with them."

The Princess laughed hysterically.

Emonzaemon had nothing to say.

For the record.

While Emonzaemon apprised the Princess, at her mansion in Owari, of his detour in Shinano on the return trip from Edo—things had been settled indeed at Lake Fuyo.

Shichika versus Skytron.

And the victor—

---

[47] 大昔の　ŌMUKASHI NO　of the distant past
[48] 台無し　DAINASHI　totally wasted
[49] 意地の悪い仕掛け　IJI NO WARUI SHIKAKE　mean-spirited trick

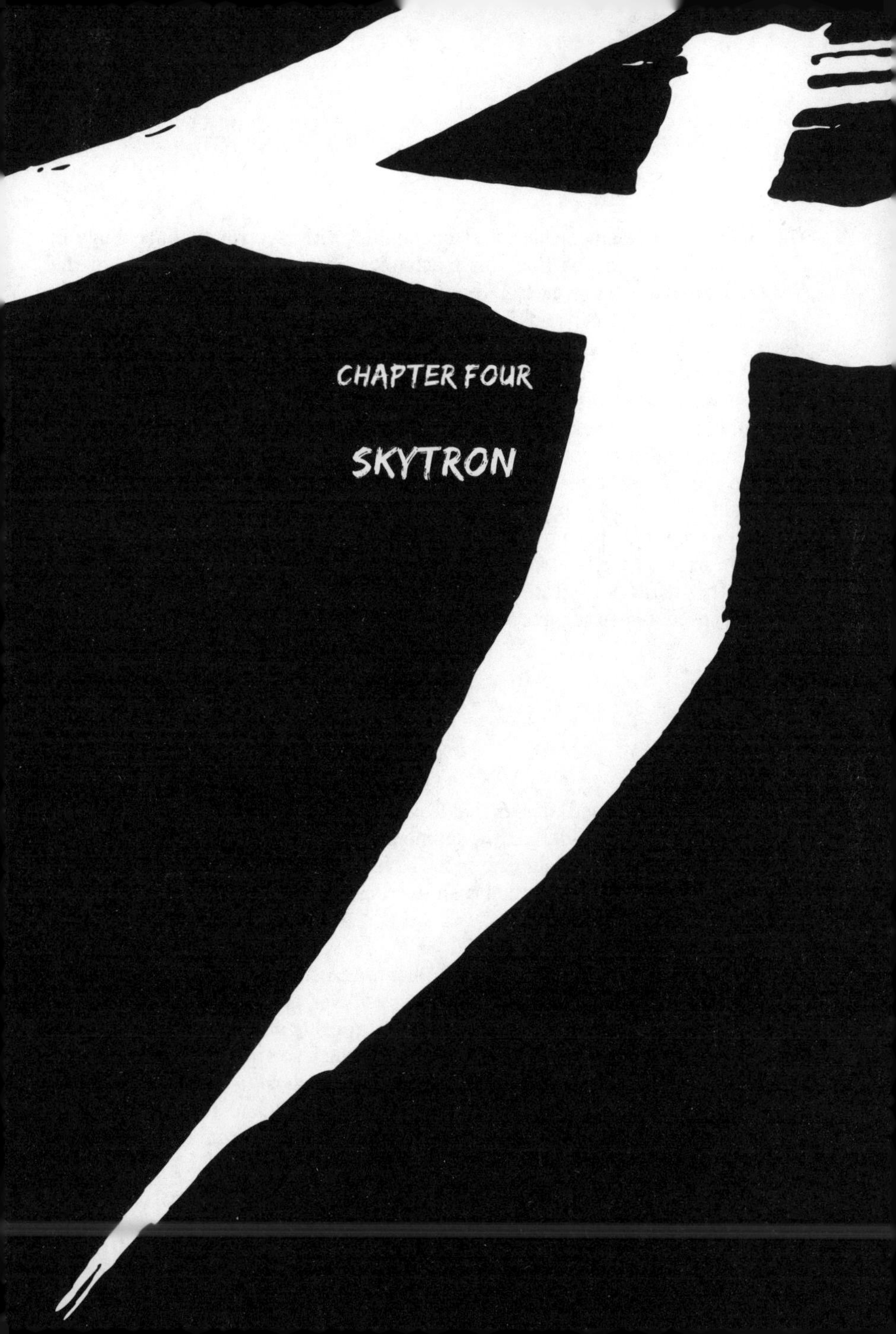

CHAPTER FOUR

SKYTRON

■ ■

On the fourth day since their first encounter[1] with Skytron at Lake Fuyo in Edo—when they learned that this mechanical menace was in fact one of the Twelve Possessed, those masterworks of Kiki Shikizaki...

Togame the Schemer and Shichika Yasuri, Seventh Master of the Kyotoryu, were sojourning at the closest inn to Lake Fuyo—incognito,[2] of course. And since Lake Fuyo was a Level One Disaster Area, *closest* was a relative term. The inn was a good distance from the nominal lake, and the facility itself, on account of its remoteness, was a melancholic affair; but after over half a year of slumbering in all kinds of different places, it struck the both of them as half-decent, no reason to complain.

In fact, the lack of people was ideal.

That gave them space to hatch their plan without concern for lookers-on.

Their strategy for Skytron—Bito the Sundial.

Together with their strategy for Princess Negative.

Both posed a heap of puzzles—

■ ■

"...Hmm."

You may be surprised to hear that Togame the Schemer wrote in a gorgeous hand and had an artsy side.[3] At the moment, she was sitting at a desk, composing something with a brush. She must have known what to say, because her hand proceeded effortlessly, the brush flowing across the page.

"Hnn...mm...ah."

Occasionally taking a brief pause.

A little bit more ink[4] and she was on her way again.

Sitting still, Shichika Yasuri glanced down over her head—he had no idea what she was writing, but he figured it was probably another one of those reports she sent to her superiors. Her accounts, which seemed to take all kinds of liberties[5] with the facts, apparently had quite *the readership* inside the bakufu...

Either way, he thought it best to let her do her thing and keep to himself.[6]

Keeping to himself—though as you may have guessed from the description

---

[1] 接触　SESSHOKU　contact
[2] 身分素性を偽って　MIBUN SUJŌ WO ITSUWATTE　falsifying one's name and background
[3] 絵心　EGOKORO　"picture heart"　a turn for drawing
[4] 墨を磨った　SUMI WO SUTTA　ground an inkstone in water to produce ink
[5] 捏造されている　NETUZŌ SARETE IRU　fabricated
[6] 大人しくしていた　OTONASHIKU SHITE ITA　"acted like an adult"　behaved, staying quiet

of him sitting still and glancing down over Togame's head while she wrote fervently at her desk, the two of them were not exactly sitting in a way that made them look like they were keeping to themselves.

To put it plainly, Togame was sitting in his lap.

Using Shichika, cross-legged behind her, for a chair, she was leaning back on his chest as she ran her brush across the page. Shichika, in typical Shichika fashion, had drawn his arms around Togame's skinny waist and idly stroked her sides. To say the least, the scene was not fit to be witnessed by young children.

So perplexing... Like the bridal carry on the staircase up the mountain or the piggyback ride in the blizzard, there was no need for them to be combined so shamelessly, but this was just their way. Neither of them had proposed to sit like this. It happened naturally.

With Emonzaemon gone, they were free to be as physical as they wanted.

Now, if we were to be generous, Shichika was just trying to fill the void left after losing Nanami, his only sister, at Gokenji Temple in Tosa, by hanging onto Togame more than before. For her part, Togame the Schemer showed a special tenderness toward Shichika, feeling no small sense of responsibility, aware that if she hadn't taken Shichika away from home Nanami would never have died, or at least not died that way—but all in all, they were their usual selves, comfortable and hopelessly inseparable.

If Princess Negative could only see them now—she'd have laughed hysterically.

"Here's the thing, Shichika."

Still in that embarrassing posture, Togame made a serious face and addressed her human chair.

"This time around, your special sense was absolutely indispensable. Without it, we never would have ascertained that Skytron was in fact one of the Twelve Possessed."

"I hate to feel entirely responsible—besides, we only know for sure that it's Bito the Sundial because it said so, right?"

"For this sword, we're working under the aegis[7] of that nasty woman, Princess Negative, which makes me doubt there's a mistake."

"Yeah, but all the Princess said was that Kiki Shikizaki built his workshop at Lake Fuyo, and that Skytron was probably left there to protect it. You're not saying that she actually knew that Skytron was one of the Twelve Possessed, are you?"

"I am. I think she did—or at the very least she guessed as much."

"Then why didn't she say so?"

"Probably because she thought it would be funny if we destroyed Skytron without realizing what it was."

Correct.

Equally evil-minded,[8] the Princess and Togame could surmise each other's

---

[7] 仕切り SHIKIRI partition, screen; guidance, direction
[8] 腹黒 HARAGURO "black-gutted"

motives with extreme precision.

The two she-devils of the bakufu—

The first with hair of white.

The other with hair of gold.

The Schemer—and the Princess.

"Still, though, I'm kinda lost... Why play games with us like that, Togame, if she's supposedly cooperating with you on the Sword Hunt?"

"Supposedly being the keyword... I'm not positive, but she could be planning to take credit for our efforts...or perhaps she's simply waiting for me to fumble. Though I suppose I'm not so different in my schemes."

"That makes me curious about what kind of an *order* Emonzaemon is fulfilling for the Princess. Where'd he go? What's that guy up to?"

"Who knows. It's good to have him out of our hair."

Togame had of course been referencing his interference in the Sword Hunt, but as she spoke, she nuzzled her little head into Shichika's shoulder blade, making the phrase sound quite suggestive, although she didn't seem to notice.

"Skytron," mumbled Shichika.

His thoughts returning to the machine.

Four arms, four legs.

A robot—capable of spinning its head 180 degrees.

"Finding out that armor was a sword was weird enough. At this point I give up. I'll never understand the Twelve Possessed."

"Don't talk like that."

"Hold on, let me finish. The whole katana thing is totally arbitrary.[9] What about Konayuki's sword, Soto the Twin? How is that thing a katana if it doesn't even have a blade? And Akuto the Eel? That thing is obviously a kunai. Different weapon altogether."

"Hmm. I guess they're all katana because he made them in Japan?"

The word meant everything and nothing.[10]

The rest aside, thought Shichika, *a robot sword is going way too far.*

Things had clearly crossed a line.

"I hear you, but think of it this way, Shichika—you're both sword and human, right?"

"Yeah, of course. I think that's well established. That's the definition of the Kyotoryu. Swords that have lives of our own—and you're looking at one, Shichika Yasuri."

"Right. So, along those lines," explained Togame, "Skytron is *both sword and robot*—if that makes sense."

Both sword and human—Kyotoryu.

Both sword and robot—Skytron.

"People don't use swords—swords make them who they are. If that was Kiki Shikizaki's basic premise," theorized Togame, "then Skytron, *by design*, is the

---

[9] 匙加減　SAJIKAGEN　"teaspoon adjustment"　discretionary
[10] 滅茶苦茶　MECHA KUCHA　gobbledygook; shitshow

most mutated of all the Mutant Blades."
"You said it."
Shichika was done.
At this point, why bother being snide.
"So then, that sword's characteristic must be its..."
Just as the first sword, Zetto the Leveler, boasted hardness.
And the second sword, Zanto the Razor, boasted sharpness.
And the third sword, Sento the Legion, boasted numerousness.
And the fourth sword, Hakuto the Whisper, boasted fragility.
And the fifth sword, Zokuto the Armor, boasted armor class.
And the sixth sword, Soto the Twin, boasted heaviness.
And the seventh sword, Akuto the Eel, boasted vitality.
The eighth sword, Bito the Sundial, boasted—
"Humanity," Togame finished his sentence.
Shichika did not appreciate her word choice.
"You call that humanity? I sure as hell don't think so—that thing is programmed to fire at you, whoever you are,[11] the second you come into range. Automatically, whoever you are. That thing is a total—"
Total.
Oh, wait—thought Shichika.
When Shichika Yasuri first left behind Haphazard Island to join Togame the Schemer on her journey—was he not guilty of the same behavior?
Search and destroy.
Follow orders.
Like a total—machine.
No agenda—
"Ah, makes sense."
"I mean...we can't honestly claim that killing people is inhuman, sad to say. Not when our history as a nation is essentially a list of who killed who and when."
"I guess this is a pretty dangerous place... Are countries overseas this bad?"
"Not sure. I couldn't tell you. But I dare say it must be pretty much the same."
"Oh, right. I'd been meaning to ask you. I couldn't earlier with Emonzaemon breathing down our necks[12]... Princess Negative, is she a foreigner?"
"Well, well. Looks like you've learned to be subtle—but if you were curious, you could have asked her pointblank. Honestly, who knows. As I believe I mentioned, her past is shrouded in obscurity, like mine. They say that in rare cases Japanese can have that color hair and eyes..."
"Hmm...really."
Past shrouded in obscurity, like Togame.
That said, Shichika knew all about Togame's past.

---

[11] 問答無用　MONDŌ MUYŌ　"no need for debate"　unquestioningly, on sight
[12] ぴったり　PITTARI　onomatopoeia for "close fit"　here, never letting them out of sight

She was the daughter—of Takahito Hida.

Once Kaoyaku of Oshu—but known today exclusively as Mastermind of the Rebellion.

The man behind the only major conflict to take place under the Yanari Shogunate, in these times of peace and order—but his Rebellion had ended in failure.

Takahito Hida had died in battle.

And his entire family—was massacred.

They killed them all—the sole survivor being a young girl who'd come to be known as Togame the Schemer.

The girl saw everything.

Saw her father's head lopped off his neck.

Saw Mutsue Yasuri—Sixth Master of the Kyotoryu, beheading Takahito Hida with the blade of his hand.

The sight of which—had made her lose the color of her hair.

Nay.

She had abandoned it.

Abandoning color.

As she had abandoned everything else, apart from her revenge.

Togame was not about to apprise Shichika of what she went through after that—but it wasn't difficult to imagine she had lived through hell on earth.[13] Even after scheming her way into the bakufu by hook or by crook,[14] she could not possibly have had an easy time. Especially not with an Inspector General like Princess Negative.

"..."

Yes—Princess Negative.

How had that woman climbed the ranks so high at her young age? Seeing that she hadn't ceded the seat of honor at her home, it would seem in terms of status she ranked even higher than Togame.

Togame said that she had finished her off multiple times.

Which could only mean that she had made multiple comebacks.

Even Shichika was well aware that climbing up the ladder after a fall from grace was much easier said than done—

Now obviously, Princess Negative was not imaginary.

She was real.

And as long as she existed, she had a past, just like Togame had a past.

—*What about Emonzaemon?*

Does he know about her past, just like I know about Togame's?

Shichika had to wonder.

"Why all this talk of Princess Negative? What makes her so interesting... W-Wait! Have you had a change of heart?! Don't tell me you've fallen for her, of all people!"

---

[13] 途炭の苦しみ TOTAN NO KURUSHIMI suffering mud water and charcoal (fire)
[14] 手練手管で TEREN TEKUDA DE willy-nilly

"Togame, stop worrying so much..."
Was she actually that insecure?[15]
If you keep worrying like crazy, I'll start worrying myself you don't believe in me.
"She's your sworn enemy. That's why I'm interested in her."
"Oh. In that case, fine."
"Just like I'm interested in what the Maniwacs are up to—although I guess they're honoring[16] the alliance. They didn't show when we were down in Tosa, and like Hohoh told us when we met him in Satsuma, one of the Twelve Possessed was at Lake Fuyo in Edo."
"Well...in any case, don't let down your guard. Come what may, you can never really trust a ninja."
"I wonder what they're doing, as we speak."
"Hard to say. But wherever they are, they're still the pushovers of this tale."
Correct again.
Although in terms of time frame, that's a little down the road.
"The Maniwacs aren't really complicated as enemies go," Shichika said. "All we gotta do is watch our back—Princess Negative, on the other hand, seems hard to handle, Togame, what with her working in the bakufu with you and all. Isn't that tough?"[17]
"It sure is. But there's no use getting all worked up about her. She'll just have an easier time pulling the rug right out from under you. But this is something altogether different from the Maniwa and Princess Negative—the situation at hand, I mean."
"At hand?"
"I'm talking about Skytron. Who cares about the thing being both sword and robot. I'm not surprised. There's something odd about the word *Sundial*, though."
"Huh? What makes you say that?"
"Out of all the Twelve Possessed, Sundial is the only name consisting of two words."
"Two words?"[18]
"Leveler, Razor, Legion, Whisper, Armor, Twin, Eel, SUN-DIAL...then Cured, Garland, Basilisk, Bead."
"Oh...I get it," nodded Shichika. "Hadn't notice that before. Two words, huh."
"The only one of the Twelve Possessed. Stuff like this is used for secret codes all of the time. I figured something about the Sundial must set it apart from all the other swords."
"Hmm..."
This was not exactly an epiphany—but the fact of the matter was that Sky-

---

[15] 自信がない　JISHIN GA NAI　lacking in confidence
[16] 守る　MAMORU　protect; observe
[17] やりにくい　YARINIKUI　hard to do
[18] 三文字　SANMOJI　three letters　　in the original, this is about　びとう BITŌ being written with just three characters in hiragana, while all the other sword names require four

tron was odd, so in that sense Togame's reading was spot-on.

"Since it's called the Sundial," reasoned Shichika, "I thought that it would actually be a sundial, the way Zokuto the Armor was literally a suit of armor."

"Rehashing[19] stuff wouldn't be fun."

"...You're talking about Kiki Shikizaki, right?"

A tricky exchange.

In any case.

"Alright, I'm done." Togame lay her brush down on her inkstone—and holding the corners of the paper raised it high, to make it easier for Shichika to read. "That should work. What do you think?"

"Think? I can't even read it—"

"Idiot. It's not a letter. It's a map."

"A map? You were drawing a map?"

"Indeed." Togame rested the piece of paper on the desk. "It's a map of Lake Fuyo."

"Huh..."

Now that she mentioned it, if he looked closely—he could see it.

Following their encounter with Skytron, the two of them had spent three days exploring Lake Fuyo (obviously, taking care not to fall into Skytron's range of fire), during which time they got a sense of its entirety.

The fruit of their labor—being this map.

"Wow, so that's what it looks like from above... How can you see this in your head? It's not like you've ever seen it from above, in real life. Is it to scale?"

"Though I'm sure it has its flaws,[20] aren't you impressed at my superb artistry? I'm quite proud of my spatial orientation skills.[21] Without them, we would never have a chance of finishing this Sword Hunt."

"Huh..."

When she put it that way, while traveling with Togame over the course of the last eight months, Shichika had almost never felt them stray off the trail. Even in Inaba Desert, where there was no trail to speak of. The only time they didn't make it to their destination was on Mt. Odori in Ezo, and that was as good as inevitable.[22] Apart from the Itezoras, only a handful of people could go up and down that mountain as they pleased. It would take a ninja like the Maniwa, or a Nanami Yasuri.

It went beyond—not needing a guide.

Because she never got lost, her competence had gone unnoticed, but at this point it was evident that Togame had a special knack for reading maps—and by extension, she excelled at creating maps from the landscapes she beheld—apparently.

"Yeah...this thing is great. Makes me glad I carried you on my shoulders."

"Yep," Togame nodded, showing her satisfaction.

[19] 同工異曲　DŌKŌ IKYOKU　"same make, different song"　practically identical
[20] 誤差　GOSA　margin of error
[21] 三次元の空間把握能力　SANJIGEN NO KŪKAN HA'AKU NŌRYOKU　"3D space grasping ability"
[22] 不可抗力　FUKA KŌRYOKU　"not possible to fight back"　force majeure

In the third moon, when they climbed the thousand steps to Triad Shrine, Togame had been appalled by the idea of doing something so indecent as riding on Shichika's shoulders, but that detail had been conveniently forgotten.

"No offense to your cool map...I mean, I get this border marks the general shape of Lake Fuyo, but what's up with this skinny line—wiggling through the lake itself?"

"Can't you tell? It's Skytron's orbit."

"Its—orbit?"

"The path it makes across the terrain," Togame restated.

Shichika was stunned—how had she locked that down in just three days?

"Orbit... Are you saying that it follows some kind of rule? I figured it just bumped around until—"

"It only looks that way because its stops and starts are so aggressive. In actuality, its movements are incredibly precise, so exact that I might even call them stubborn[23]—in other words, it follows a fixed path."

"Yeah. Just when it's acting like this busy bee, wandering all around, it stops and sits still for a minute, like it's basking in the sun. That totally confused me."

"So, Shichika. Looking over this map, does anything stand out?"

"I guess—actually, no."

"Sometimes you're so incredibly slow I feel like I can't take you anywhere... Lose the yokel[24] act before I get upset. See this?"

Togame pointed at the map.

The ink seemed dry by now, but Shichika worried unnecessarily that if it wasn't, it would make Togame's finger black.

But as it turns out, his worry truly was unnecessary.

Togame was pointing at a portion of the map where she had never touched the brush.

"If you consider Skytron's orbit as a whole—you'll find that it essentially revolves around *this zone*."

"Are you sure? What about this part of the—"

"Like I said, essentially. With all that rubbish piled up, it's no surprise it can't move in a perfect circle."

"Ah, right."

That made sense.

Taking another look—Shichika recognized that Skytron's movements did indeed follow a clear pattern. Like Togame said—it revolved around that zone, in a roughly circular path.

"Have I made myself adequately clear?"

"Uh, I'm not sure what you're driving at..."

"Shichika, once we round up Bito the Sundial, let's do a little studying. I'll teach you."

So it had finally come to this.

---

[23] 融通が利かない　YŪZŪ GA KIKANAI　inflexible; unable to play things by ear
[24] 世間知らず　SEKEN SHIRAZU　being ignorant of the world; naive

But why try? It was over his head, and he wasn't getting any taller.

"Get this—if Kiki Shikizaki's workshop was in Lake Fuyo, and Skytron a.k.a. Bito the Sundial is its guardian, I would deduce that *this zone here* is where the workshop used to be. Any questions?"

"Uh, no, thank you."

So polite.

For whatever reason, Togame thought it was uncool to spell out every single detail. She liked to leave things unsaid—but expecting Shichika to catch on?

Coolness was not his forte.

"Wow...I'd thought that it would be next to impossible to figure out where in that sea of trash the Kiki Shikizaki workshop was, but this makes so much sense—now that you've mapped out Skytron's movements. The Schemer strikes again."

"I'm not exactly thrilled to get a compliment from you. Besides, this has nothing to do with schemes. It's just an inference."

"An inference[25]..." Shichika echoed Togame. "And how reliable is this inference?"

"I'd say eighty percent. Of course, only if Kiki Shikizaki's workshop was in fact in Lake Fuyo, and if Skytron is in fact Bito the Sundial, one of the Twelve Possessed."

"But this area...it's hard for me to tell, just looking at the map, but have we *seen* this zone already?"

"From afar."

"Okay, but I don't remember seeing anything that could have been[26] a workshop—"

"It's centuries-old. I'm sure the workshop must be buried under rubbish."

"Ah...right. Sure."

Of course.

Shichika really should have seen this on his own.

"So—I guess we'll have to dig?"

"Seems that way."

"Wish we had some help."

"I'd rather not rely on outside parties. Someone might spill the beans."

"..."

In other words, since they could hardly expect Togame to engage in manual labor, Shichika would have to excavate the workshop on his own...

Not a nice surprise.

"Still—even though we have a high chance of finding valuable information upon excavating the workshop...nothing is guaranteed. All our work may end in vain. Nevertheless, we can't pass up the chance to plumb the depths of that elusive swordsmith Kiki Shikizaki—"

"Yeah, but this whole excavating thing...can't be treated lightly, not with Sky-

---

[25] 推理 SUIRI deductive reasoning 推理小説 SUIRI SHŌSETSU mystery fiction
[26] らしき RASHIKI resembling

tron on the move. Halfway down, I might get chopped to bits by its four arms."

"I see. In that case, even if we know exactly where the workshop was, before we commence digging, we must defeat[27] Skytron."

"Yeah," agreed Shichika.

Whether by inference or scheming, it would seem this ludicrously difficult conversation was finally over—to be honest, his head hurt.

But now the rest was up to Shichika.

In the ensuing battle—

"Last time, I was just trying to identify Skytron, so I couldn't go all out[28]—but this time, I'm gonna give her everything I've got."

"Whoa, everything?"

"Yeah, everything."

"And what does everything entail?"

"I'm gonna totally dest—"

"Cheerio!"

Crying out, Togame pinched at Shichika's inner thigh.

For such a spirited cry, it was a fairly bland[29] attack.

"Is your brain unable to retain things? If Skytron is Bito the Sundial, you can't simply destroy her! I'm sure even that nasty woman doesn't actually expect us to destroy Skytron!"

"Ah, um...okay."

He forgot.

They had only just discussed the matter, but transitioning to his field of expertise had made him feel a little too relaxed.

"Right...this time, unlike all the times before, *the sword and owner are the same*. So weird...but I guess it's not far off from when I fought Kanara Azekura for the Armor."

Zokuto the Armor.

A katana shaped like armor, and unparalleled in armor class.

Facing that seamless panoply, cast in the western style—he felt like he was fighting another sword. But in the end, Shichika capitalized[30] on Kanara Azekura, bearer of the Armor, being a human being after all—and thereby proved victorious.

But this was different.

Skytron—was a sword in and of itself, and at the same time.

It was a robot.

It was—not human.

"Also," Togame noted, "the fact that the Sundial is in all likelihood less durable than the Armor will function as a disadvantage. The Armor could withstand the majority—no, any kind of attack, but the Sundial must be treated differently."

[27] 打倒　DATŌ　"hit and cause to fall"　overthrow
[28] 不完全燃焼　FUKANZEN NENSHŌ　"incomplete combustion"
[29] 地味　JIMI　"ground taste"　plain
[30] 突破口に　TOPPAKŌ NI　use as a breakthrough; (exploit) a breach

"I think I get the picture."
Protect the swords—right.

The first rule that Togame set forth at the beginning of the Sword Hunt.

But what was he supposed to do, now that the enemy and sword were one? Togame said that she wasn't surprised, but surely this was more than she'd bargained for.

"Hold up, Togame... If you ask me, all of that aside, this fight is gonna be really tough."

"Tough? Come on, you weakling."

"Weakling—I mean, that's not what I was saying, but then again I'm not sure that I can disagree. Weakling or not, I'm whining,[31] but just listen to me for a second—there's almost no place out there where I can find a proper footing."

"..."

Lake Fuyo, Level One Disaster Area.

A lake no more—filled in with rubbish.

"Those scraps of wood and metal are the *product of civilization*. For a *wild boy*[32] like me, it's probably the toughest battlefield on earth."

"I hadn't—thought of that." Togame nodded, acknowledging her oversight. "I see...I took for granted that you'd have an easy time as long as we fought out of doors, but come to think of it, a garbage dump sounds like a difficult place for you to fight..."

"Give me a desert or a mountain any day[33]—but I almost hurt myself just walking around on that field of rubbish. It'll be challenging."

"Meanwhile, Skytron has it made. I mean, that thing has four legs. It's quadrupedal.[34] No one could ever be that stable on their feet."

"Right. Exactly. And the only thing worse than the fact that it has four legs," Shichika continued, "is that it has four arms. Four legs, four arms."

"That's easy enough to see."

"I'm not an idiot—or maybe I am, but I'm well aware of my responsibilities, and since I first approached—or first encountered[35] Skytron, I've been obsessing over what I'd do when it came time for us to fight."

"You mean obsessing over your strategy for destroying Skytron..."

"Yeah, sure—but seriously, those extra arms and legs are really making my life miserable... Just think about the Sumire, the Kyotoryu throw move I used on Konayuki—the whole idea is kicking their legs out, which isn't gonna happen if they have four legs."

"Oh..."

"Also, it has four arms, and each of them has a katana. I can tackle a dual wield, but in all the Kyotoryu there isn't any move for the quadruple wield.[36]

---

[31] 弱音　YOWANE　"weak sound"　(making) feeble noises
[32] 野生児　YASEIJI　"feral child"　usually hyperbole for being outdoorsy, rambunctious
[33] お手のもの　OTE NO MONO　"something one is handy with"　specialty
[34] 四脚　YONKYAKU　four legs vs. 三脚　SANKYAKU　tripod　二足歩行　NISOKU HOKŌ bipedal locomotion
[35] 接近 接敵　SEKKIN SETTEKI　close in　make contact with an enemy
[36] 四刀流対策　YONTŌRYŪ TAISAKU　"four sword-style countermeasure"

Even if I could take on four guys with their own swords, fighting one person swinging four swords—is something that I never thought I'd have to do."

"Of course—why would you."

"Plus, if I try coming at it from behind, its head does a one-eighty. This thing is not built like a human being—but the Kyotoryu is made for fighting humans. I never thought I'd have to fight a robot."

"Hmm..."

He had a point—even Nanami Yasuri, whose genius eyes and limitless capacity to watch and learn, acquiring any kind of move, regardless of the enemy—would likely be unable to acquire moves from Skytron, whose physicality was simply too unlike her own.

"I mean, if this thing isn't seeing with its eyes, I'm not sure that I understand what made it spin its head around."

"It was expressing the humanity bestowed upon it by its maker, Kiki Shikizaki."

"Is that what people looked like in the eyes of Kiki Shikizaki? The guy was broken."

"Sure was," Togame agreed. "I'm not sure what *Bito* signifies, or what makes this thing a *Sundial*—but Shichika, I understand why you're concerned."

"It's not exactly that I'm concerned."

"Sounds like we'll be relying on my schemes, as usual. Well then. Allow me to drop some knowledge on that stupid[37] noggin of yours, Shichika. If you need help, just ask me instead of beating around the bush, you silly boy."[38]

"Um..."

Shichika shook his head; Togame was preening even as she chewed him out.

"About the schemes. This time, well, I guess maybe I'm concerned after all. This thing—is a machine. A robot. A mechanical doll."

"Uh huh."

"Well—that means it has no will, no feelings, no thoughts...none of that stuff."

"Spit it out, Shichika."

"I noticed this the first time we made contact. I know we were just scoping things out, but when I see a sword, I don't take any chances. So I made some feints as usual, on my way in," Shichika said, recalling the details of the fight. "But—*Skytron showed no reaction whatsoever* to my feints."

"She didn't—react? What exactly do you mean?"

"This wasn't like my fight with sis, where she saw through all of my feints—the thing didn't even seem to notice[39] them. Which makes sense—since Skytron is a robot or a doll, that means it *doesn't think*. There's no use feinting, *trying to make it jump or catch it by surprise.*"

No reaction to his feints.

Responding *solely to his last attack*.

---

[37] 愚昧　GUMAI　slow-witted
[38] 可愛い奴　KAWAII YATSU　cute fellow
[39] 気を取られない　KI WO TORARENAI　not be distracted by

As if it didn't see his movements.

The polar opposite of his sister's Watch and Learn—but yielding an identical scenario.

It may have been a robot—but it acted like a total monster.

"Hmm...I see. In that case, the element of surprise afforded by your school's obscurity means nothing against Skytron. Your moves can be standards or oddities, in your face or out of nowhere. To Skytron, it makes no difference—"

"Right," Shichika nodded. "And another thing. If we can't catch it by surprise, I wonder if your schemes won't get through either."

"..."

Shichika had done his best to sound as casual as possible, but what he said still made Togame grow quiet. He instantly regretted it, certain that he'd made a gaffe[40] or said something he shouldn't have, but it was too late now. Before Shichika could try and clear things up, Togame made a sound.

"Heh heh heh."

She was laughing—in a really creepy way.

"Heh heh heh heh heh."

"Uh, Togame?"

"Mwa ha ha ha ha—you take me for a fool? Even if there were an enemy who my schemes didn't work on, you think I need you worrying about me? No longer the silent one, are you."

"Y-Yeah, but...this enemy is different. It's a robot. It doesn't think."

"So what?" Togame said.

She had stopped laughing.

"Human or robot—regardless of what the circumstances do or don't entail—my schemes have gotten me this far. Faced with adversity and hardship,[41] I see a normal day. Alright—to make sure these off-base concerns are gone for good, we're going to stop everything and have a little lesson."

Togame took up her brush.

"Since you can't read hiragana—how about I draw a simple picture."

"Anything that I can do to help?"

Knowing he was already in too deep, Shichika declined to utter most of the things that came to mind, opting instead for this diffident[42] offer.

"Yeah, actually," Togame answered, turning slightly back toward Shichika. "Just sit right there and hold me while I work."

---

[40] 失言　SHITSUGEN　inappropriate remark
[41] 逆境も苦境も　GYAKKYŌ MO KUKYŌ MO　"antagonistic border or painful border"
[42] 遠慮がち　ENRYO GACHI　shy; standing on ceremony

CHAPTER FIVE

LAKE FUYO

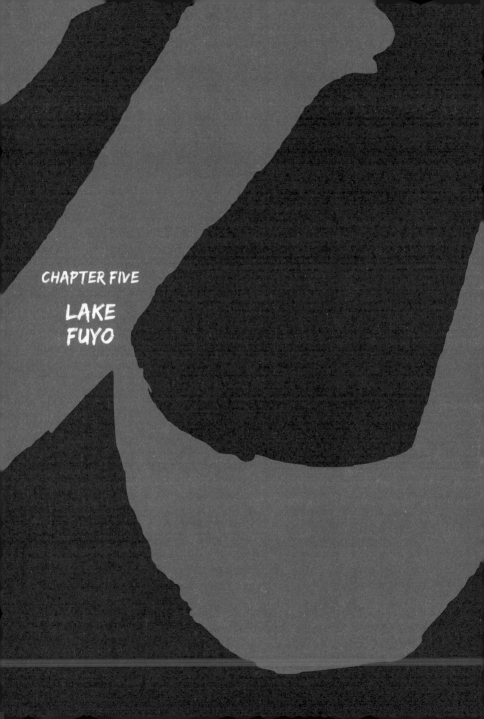

■ ■

Time to review the victory conditions.

The ensuing showdown at Lake Fuyo would by necessity take on a different form than all the others thus far on the Sword Hunt—as different as the various opponents were, two things were constant: all Shichika had to do was take them down, without harming the swords.

This time, however, the opponent and the sword were one and the same.

There was no way he could take his enemy down without harming the sword, yet harming the sword was intrinsic to taking down the enemy.

While Togame and Shichika had originally ventured to Lake Fuyo to investigate the workshop of the legendary swordsmith Kiki Shikizaki, lest we forget: Togame had been tasked with rounding up the Twelve Possessed.

As such, damaging Skytron was not an option.

Things were troublesome enough for Shichika already, faced with a four-armed, four-legged enemy whose body functioned nothing like that of a human being—(not to mention the fact his feints had zero effect on her)—but these rules of battle made it impossible for him to bare the blades of his hands or his feet.

What scheme could get them through this?

A few days passed before they left the inn behind and returned to Lake Fuyo. The sky was full of clouds, as if it might rain any second.

The same day that one of the Twelve Bosses of the Maniwa Ninja Clan played the part of a pushover the way it should be played—

■ ■

"Kyotoryu—Bara!"

Come to think of it.

Not counting the battle on Haphazard Island against Komori Maniwa, which was more like being ambushed, all the fights thus far on the Sword Hunt, with the exception of the first, against Ginkaku Uneri, had been to some extent, to varying degrees, *civilized*[1] affairs.

Meisai Tsuruga at Triad Shrine.

Hakuhei Sabi on Ganryu Island.

Kanara Azekura by Dakuon Harbor.

Konayuki Itezora atop Mt. Odori.

Nanami Yasuri within Gokenji Temple.

[1] 行儀の正しい GYŌGI NO TADASHII having good manners; obeying proper etiquette

All five of these battles, without exception, had a *referee*.
Who gave the signal to begin—*Fight!*

These were formal duels in their own way, and fitting for an age of peace and order (although in most cases the referee was Togame, Shichika's boss, which gave him what may be called a gross advantage)—but this time would be different.

As a robot, Skytron had no will.

The fight would not have no formal start or end.

If anything—the battle would begin the second Shichika entered Skytron's range of fire.

Shichika leapt at Skytron from Form Seven, the Kakitsubata—and into the Kyotoryu's front kick, the Bara.

By the way, that whole issue about not finding a proper footing was resolved by switching his straw sandals for a pair of geta. This painfully obvious solution coming courtesy of not Shichika, of course, but Togame the Schemer.

The heaps of rubbish were as prone to crumbling and unreliable as ever—but at least wearing the geta he could stop worrying about impaling his foot on a scrap of metal.

As much as he would have enjoyed doffing his arm guards and fighting barefoot, as long as they were at Lake Fuyo, Shichika would have to compromise, like in the snows of Mt. Odori.

"Kyotoryu—Yuri!"

The Bara had been blocked by Skytron's four arms.

Unfazed, Shichika unleashed his backspin spinning kick, the Yuri—but this too was blocked by the arms.

"HUMAN DETECTED"

Skytron said.

Or, more accurately—pronounced.

"EXTERMINATE NOW"

"...nkk!"

Indeed—amazing blocking skills.

Just like Togame said.

"Exterminate me? I'd like to see you try—" yelled Shichika, *"once you're torn to smithereens!"*

This time around, the catchphrase Togame had assigned him felt all wrong.

For one thing, how could he tear a machine to pieces?

"Alright...Kyotoryu—Sagigusa!"[2]

Another kick move—only this time his foot rained down from above, aiming to slash across[3] the robot's body. Yet Skytron blocked this too, using its arms.

The advantage of having four arms.

Each could focus on a smaller range—allowing for increased efficiency.

Of course, the same went for its legs.

---

[2] 鷺草 SAGIGUSA "The White Egret Flower" a fringed orchid, often read SAGISŌ
[3] 袈裟懸けに KESAGAKE NI "like the robe of a priest" diagonally down from the shoulder

In fact, its extra legs provided an even greater advantage than the arms—using one leg for defense, it kept the other three rooted in the earth.

No one could ever be that stable.

"Kyotoryu Combo—from Zakuro to Ayame!"[4]

As soon as he landed, Shichika planted his feet and launched into a rapid-fire display of hand techniques—after trying linked attacks like this against his sister at Gokenji Temple, the moves flowed with smooth precision.

Skytron blocked with ease, until the Ayame—at which point Shichika finally discerned an opening among the arms.

A space through which—he may have hit its torso.

"...Hup!"

Nevertheless—he gritted his teeth and *reeled in* the Ayame. This sent him staggering, whereupon he came dangerously close to falling on his face—but somehow Shichika regained his footing.

Easy now—easy now.

He took a deep breath, filling his lungs.

Prior to his fight with Skytron.

Togame the Schemer had given Shichika a couple of precautions.

Above all—he was to only use strike moves.

Shichika could get behind this. He'd said so himself—there was no way he could use a throw move on a four-armed, four-legged robot, and grappling moves would fare even worse. If he got Skytron in a deadlock,[5] he was going to be the dead one.

This is not to say, however, that strike moves would get the job done. As indicated moments earlier, Skytron blocked every strike, rebuffing Shichika so consistently it made his own head spin.[6] In his fight against Kanara Azekura, he had confronted the unparalleled armor class of Zokuto the Armor, but its defensive properties were just a matter of materials—

"Interesting."

At a safe distance away, well out of Skytron's range of fire.

Togame the Schemer muttered to herself—watching Shichika fight.

"I'd say that's a good sign—after all, we must not harm the swords. Let Skytron do its thing *and protect itself on its own*—"

Togame had given Shichika one more precaution.

So long as he stuck to the strike moves, he could wallop Skytron to his heart's content.

Except—*he must not hit its head or torso.*

Meaning—he had to let Skytron *block* every single move he made.

Using its four arms—and four legs!

"Hmm."

Shichika brought his furious[7] attack to a halt and moved away from Sky-

[4] 石榴 菖蒲 ZAKURO AYAME "The Pomegranate" "The Siberian Iris"
[5] がっぷりよつ GAPPURI YOTSU in sumo, both wrestlers gripping each other's *mawashi* with both hands
[6] 舌を巻く SHITA WO MAKU roll one's tongue to marvel (no wordplay here in the original)
[7] 怒濤の DOTŌ NO like angry waves

tron.
Yeah—not a bad idea.
They were on the right track.
"Togame sure knows how to think—though I can't harm the katana, she comes up with the idea of *forcing Skytron to defend itself*... That allows me to attack it without pulling all my punches—she has some devilish ideas, taking advantage of a doll that can't think for itself."
"Hello!" Togame yelled to him across the field. "I can hear you."
He must have been talking to himself quite loudly.
Not like it really mattered—he could talk to himself all he wanted, and Skytron's robot brain would never understand him.
Which also meant diplomacy was off the table.
"Crap, I almost hit it in the torso with the Ayame—"
Strikes to the head and torso—were off limits.
Which meant he was unable to use Fatal Orchid Four, Ryuryoku Kako, despite it involving a strike move.
Here is how Togame had explained it.
Because Skytron was a robot.
Extremities like arms and legs—were mere *appendages*.[8]
Parts that were replaceable.
The mechanisms that allowed Skytron its Skytronic activity were housed exclusively inside its head and torso, while the arms and legs remained apart, operating as directed—an inhuman advantage known only to robots.
A human being who injures an arm or leg cannot simply sub out *the damaged part* for a replacement arm or leg—but a robot can.
Whereby.
Its arms and legs—were fair game.
They were replaceable.
They were removable.
Which made the situation—salvageable.
The Sword Hunt for the Twelve Possessed of Kiki Shikizaki—staying on track!
"Still, though—my feints not working is such a pain. At this point, it's second nature.[9] Even though I know it isn't helping, they come out of me at those moments."
These idle moments were dangerous indeed.
But perhaps it was fine.
Because the goal was *to have Skytron block his attacks*.
"COUNTERSTRIKE NOW"
Suddenly.
Skytron strayed from its strict pattern of defense—and made a run on Shichika.

---

[8] 外装 GAISŌ "outside adornments"
[9] 身体が覚えちゃてる KARADA GA OBOECHATTERU "the body remembers"

"ROBOSLAY[10]—TORNADO"

Swinging four swords simultaneously—from four different directions.

While these four swords were not the work of Kiki Shikizaki—which made them replaceable appendages as well—the Kyotoryu was without any moves for taking on a four-armed foe barehanded, not to mention destroying four swords at once.

All Shichika could do was dodge the attack.

"ROBOSLAY—WHIRLWIND"

All four swords swung at once—but Shichika dodged this, too.

"ROBOSLAY—VERNAL BLAST"[11]

This time it leaned back, raising its front legs together for a dropkick—although since dropkicks involve jumping, and Skytron's robotic mechanisms meant it didn't have to jump, the term sounds contradictory—

Shichika leapt into the air to dodge this *jump-free dropkick.*

Just then.

"ROBOSLAY—BLUSTER"[12]

As it pronounced these words—a pointy[13] sword shot like a tongue out of the same mouth.

"Wh-Whoaaa!"

Using Skytron's legs for a springboard, Shichika shifted position in midair and got away. His hands touched down first, followed acrobatically by his feet.

The sword slipped back inside of Skytron's body—much to Shichika's amazement. He had never dreamt of such a trick.

A blade flying from the robot's mouth—was not part of the plan.

But.

"*Almost everything else has gone exactly as predicted*—right?"

This time he wasn't talking to himself, but checking with Togame.

"Why wouldn't it," she said, yet the Schemer was also sticking her chest out with evident pride. "While I may not be as observant as your sister...I've got a decent set of eyes. From the way something is built on the outside, *I can envision* how it's going to move, or what moves it is capable of making."

Except if it's a person, Togame admitted in a little voice.

"Machines are simple, that way. They move exactly how you think they'll move."

The picture Togame drew Shichika back at the inn—had been a diagram of Skytron.

Demonstrating with a figure.

How Skytron made its movements.

How far its arms could bend. How far it could raise its legs. How its head could spin 180 degrees, but probably not its torso. How far its mouth could open. How far its swords would reach—illustrating him all of the things that she

[10] 人形殺法　NINGYŌ SAPPŌ　"Doll('s) Killing Method"
[11] 春一番　HARU ICHIBAN　the first strong wind in springtime
[12] 突風　TOPPŪ　"thrusting wind"　sharp gust
[13] 槍のような　YARI NO YŌ NA　spear-like

could tell from its exterior.

Showing—her artsy side.

She had not been observing Skytron on the move for three days straight for fun.

For Togame, who could draw a map with ease, albeit cutting a few corners—schematizing[14] Skytron was a cinch.

Of course, all sorts of things could not be gleaned from mere appearances—concealed within the body, the gadgetry of "ROBOSLAY—BLUSTER" fell beyond her scope. In any case, even if she were clued in on this surprise, she herself could never have evaded it.

It was through her katana, Shichika Yasuri, that her "set of eyes" truly came alive.

"I had hoped the drawing cleared things up for you, but I guess you needed a few days to digest it... That's fine, though."

This was about—form.

Much as questions of form, or lack thereof, had figured prominently up against Konayuki Itezora—here, too, they posed the central obstacle to victory. For although the Kyotoryu lacked forms for handling a four-armed, four-legged adversary, to Skytron, having four arms and four legs was only natural, its very *form*. What could be more annoying?

While far less difficult, and not really a fair comparison, to use a simple metaphor, it was sort of like a right-handed person fighting a left-handed person. Quite disorienting.

The gap between the known and the unknown—

And since Skytron was a robot, the difference exceeded that gap.

Yet.

Togame the Schemer had turned this all around.

Thought of a way to turn it all around.

For a fighter[15] such as Shichika to dispose of feinting altogether was frustrating indeed—but on the flipside, they knew that Skytron would never feint at them.

Robots don't try to make you jump or catch you by surprise.

Of course, things were not necessarily so simple, since Skytron was capable of some complex moves—but even these were simply *commands*[16] built into it.

Therefore—*as long as he understood them as such*, Shichika and Skytron were on equal footing, at least in that regard.

If Skytron never feinted.

They could begin to anticipate—its form.

Once they did, the rest was up to Shichika. It had taken them some time—but it was worth all the time it took.

Because he was holding his own against Skytron, an inhuman robot sword!

---

[14] 分析 BUNSEKI analyze
[15] 格闘者 KAKUTŌSHA (melee, if not unarmed) combatant, a scrapper
[16] 命令 MEIREI orders

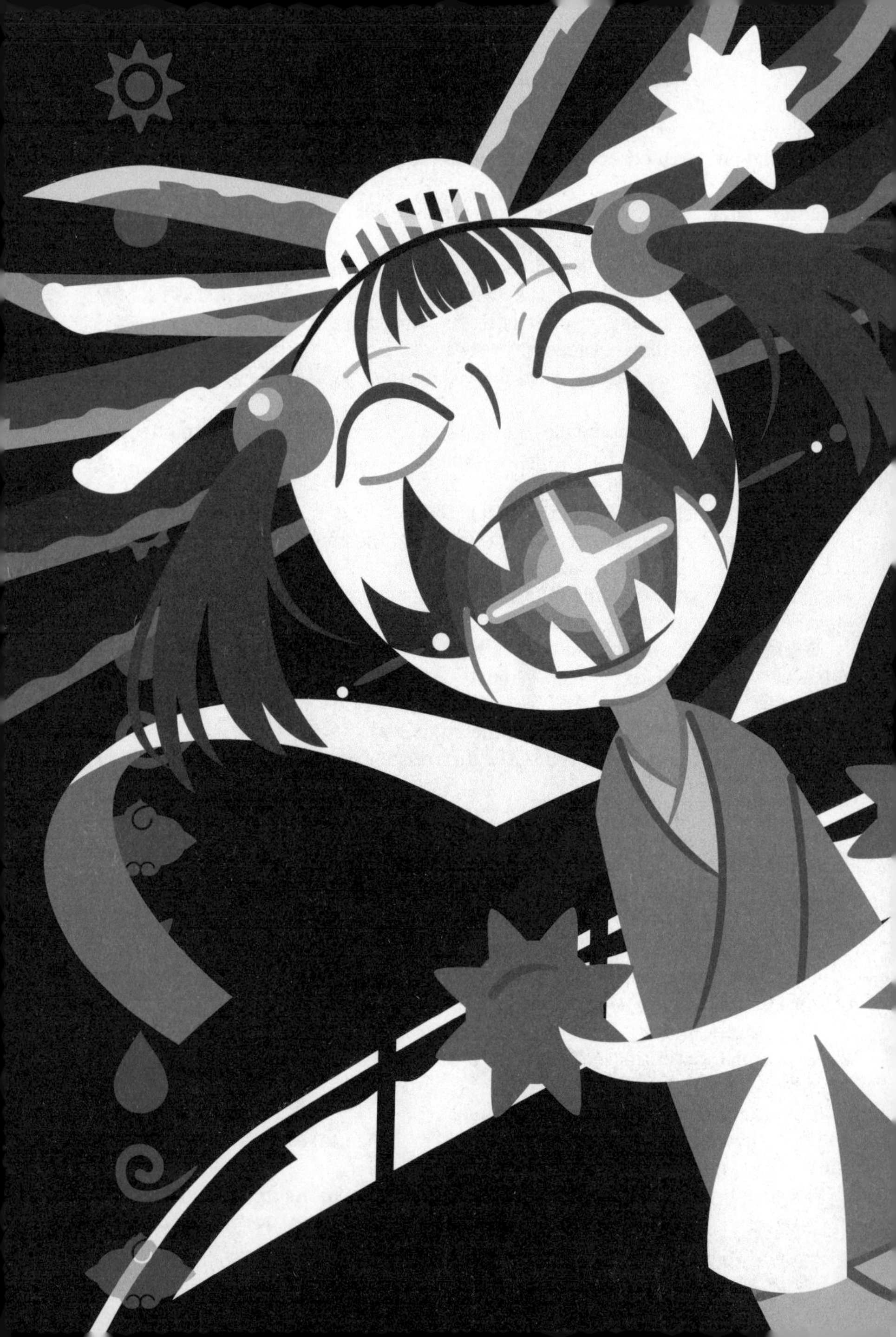

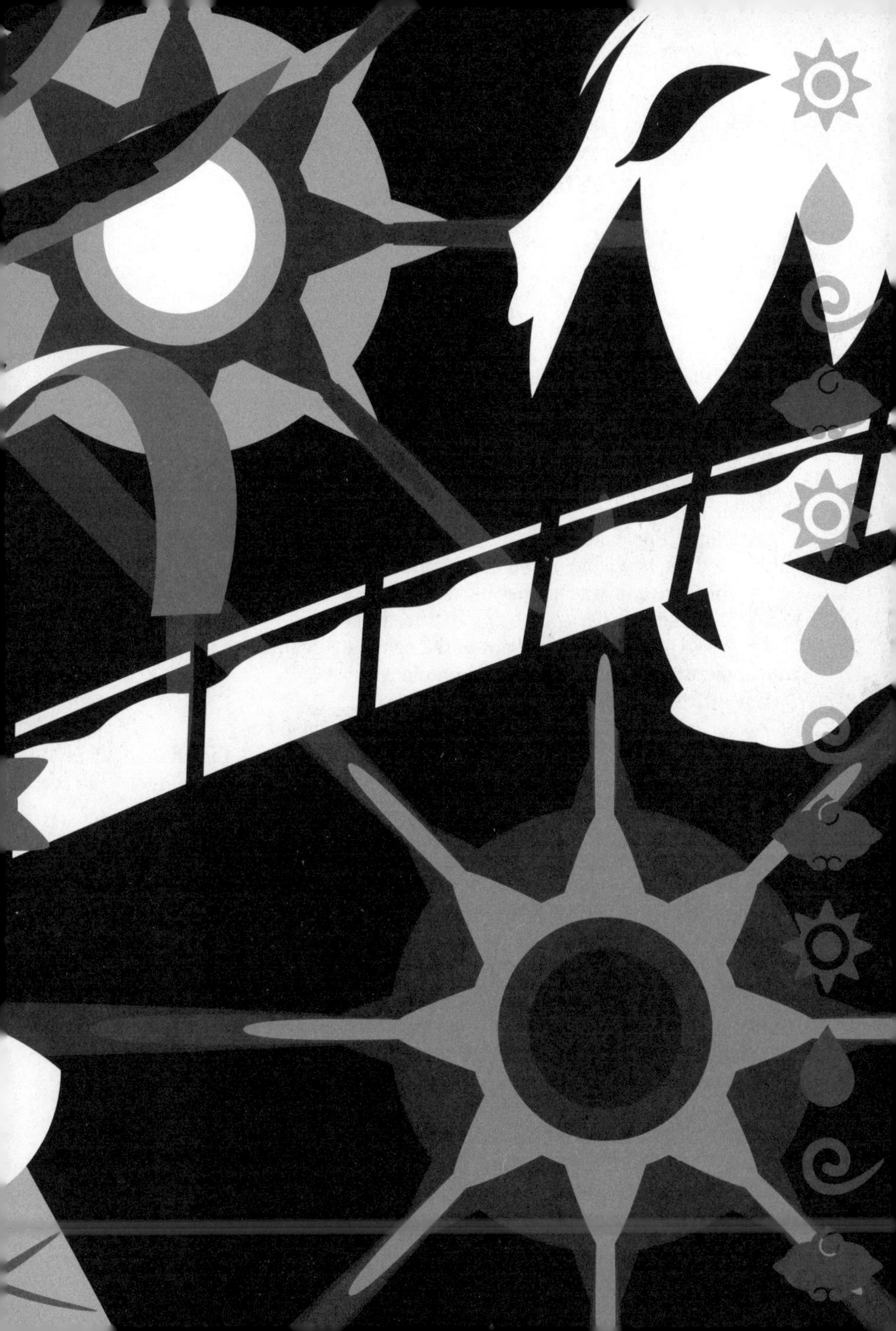

"Kyotoryu—Mokuren!"[17]
"ROBOSLAY—TEMPEST"
"Kyotoryu—Oto!"[18]
"ROBOSLAY—SANDSTORM"
"Kyotoryu—Noichigo!"[19]
"ROBOSLAY—TYPHOON"

...
...
...

Yes.

After making some adjustments to the rules—they were finally square.

There was nothing they could do to make them squarer—since while Skytron had no handicaps, Shichika had an enormous one, having been forbidden to strike the robot on the head or torso *under any circumstances.*

If it seemed a strike might land outside of the appendages, he must do everything within his power to abort.

As long as they continued this way for a while, no matter how much Shichika anticipated its *form*, one of the robot's moves would get past him.

In which case, it was almost like a slow-paced suicide—as square as it may seem, Shichika was basically being tortured to death.

Even so, this was no blind spot in the scheme Togame had in mind—she had a vivid picture of how things would unfold.

But for them to make it there—

It was essential that Shichika Yasuri's stamina held out.

Perhaps Nanami Yasuri could have seen that far, but not Togame the Schemer—they were entering treacherous terrain.

Unlike Nanami Yasuri.

Togame was unable to see everything or see beyond things.

All she could do was believe in Shichika Yasuri and keep her eyes on him[20]—

■ ■

It's almost been too long to call it requisite—but time for another reminiscence.

Shichika Yasuri, Seventh Master of the Kyotoryu, looked back on life.

To a time before he embarked on the Sword Hunt.

To when his father—Mutsue Yasuri, was still among the living.

Before he had taken on the title Seventh Master.

Back when all he did was train, day in day out, a sword on a desert island—

"Remember, Shichika."

[17] 木蓮　MOKUREN　"The Magnolia"
[18] 桜桃　ŌTŌ　"The Cherry"
[19] 野苺　NOICHIGO　"The Wild Strawberry"
[20] 見守る　MIMAMORU　watch over

Trained by the Sixth Master of the Kyotoryu—Mutsue Yasuri.

"I am—a katana."

He was always saying that.

"Just as you—are a katana."

Shichika, who looked up to[21] his father—listened quietly.

For nineteen years.

He had heard Mutsue say these words.

"If a sword cannot kill, it has no point—consider that the fundamental truth.[22] Everything else is trivial. Take my word for it—as a sword, you're only good as long as you stay sharp."

Now he understood.

What his father had meant was—*Don't feel.*

It meant—*Don't think.*

Don't think—and don't feel.

A katana has nothing like a will to speak of.

Perhaps Mutsue was unable to train Shichika to his satisfaction—leaving this world before he had a chance to convey fully what it was to be the Kyotoryu.

All the same, to say the least—Shichika was the Kyotoryu.

He was a katana.

But when Shichika came to blows with Skytron...

Bito the Sundial, eighth of the Twelve Possessed.

The mechanical doll who had no will—

It all made sense to him—*Hey, this was me until a little while ago.*

No agenda.

No resolve.

Relinquishing nothing—it knew no law or justice,[23] no ambition or scorn.[24]

Like Shichika Yasuri on that portion of the Sword Hunt when he did what he was told to do—rounding up the swords without entertaining doubt.

A lack of hesitation so profound it jarred Togame, although she was the one calling the shots.

What he truly lacked was not hesitation—but will.

As goes without saying, swords have no need for will.

Swords may choose their owner, but they do not choose who to kill.

At first—Shichika saw nothing strange in that.

What could be strange—however.

This state of being came with strengths and weaknesses alike.

If I was only a katana—there's no way that I would've beaten sis last month. Right?

Dad and I may both be swords—but we're entirely different people.

"ROBOSLAY—WIND FANG"[25]

---

[21] 尊敬　SONKEI　respect
[22] 第一に　DAI'ICHINI　as number one
[23] 正義 定義　SEIGI TEIGI　righteousness (legal) definitions　order reversed in main text
[24] 野心 復讐心　YASHIN FUKUSHŪSHIN　(often sinister) goals　desire for revenge
[25] 鎌鼬　KAMA ITACHI　"sickle weasel"　a flesh wound caused by contact with an atmospheric vacuum, such as that created by a whirlwind, thus named for its resemblance to the bite of a vermin

Skytron attacked.

No will or aim—simply following the commands built into it centuries ago.

Evading[26] the attack—Shichika realized.

Wow.

This was me—I used to be like this.

Does that mean—what on earth have I done?

Komori Maniwa. Ginkaku Uneri. Meisai Tsuruga. Hakuhei Sabi.

All four of them fought me when I was like this.

It must have been no fun at all to fight me when I was acting like a robot—but hold on.

When Skytron first sensed Shichika, it voiced the words "HUMAN DETECTED"—

Ah.

When I see you all I see is another sword.

But you'd call me human?

"Kyotoryu—Kyoka Suigetsu!"

Shichika unleashed the fastest of the Fatal Orchids, though not full force—and when Skytron blocked this too, he jumped away, toward safety.

He was short on breath already—practically hyperventilating.[27]

Drenched in sweat.

Of course he was. He had been fighting Skytron now for almost fifteen minutes straight—back and forth,[28] jumping from one move to the next without a break.

Endlessly energetic as Shichika may be, it's not like he never felt fatigue.

Skytron, on the other hand, neither breathed heavily nor sweat.

Obviously.

Skytron never breathed at all, and had no sweat glands anywhere on its body.

Humans and robots.

Different beasts.

And yet.

Resting now was—out of the question.

He had his orders from Togame—*Keep going back and forth with Skytron for as long as physically possible,* is how she put it.

A month or two before, he would have done what he was told unthinkingly.

Followed orders, like a sword.

Whereby everything that transpired, all responsibility, would fall on Togame.

But things were different now.

Now Shichika operated as an individual—he trusted Togame, and followed orders consciously.

The same way that Togame believes in me—I believe in Togame.

---

[26] 捌きながら　SABAKI NAGARA　fielding, handling
[27] 過呼吸　KAKOKYŪ　"excess breathing"
[28] 攻防　KŌBŌ　offense and defense

Even if I break in two—I'll assume full responsibility!
"Hm?"

Full of conviction and resolve, Shichika charged straight for Skytron—but then he noticed something strange about the ground around it.

Skytron had dropped all four of its swords.

The four swords—that it held in its four arms.

Tossing them like trash into the field of trash.

"...? What are you up to?" Shichika asked Skytron.

Knowing full well it was pointless, since Skytron only looked human, and not even convincingly—pointless indeed, it registered no reaction to his voice.

Though for a second there, he thought it had.

Skytron looked like it was bowing[29]—but not in answer to what Shichika had asked.

Although she did effectively answer his question.

Now that it had dropped the swords and freed its hands, Skytron pressed them to the earth—and raised its lower body into a handstand.

Using its arms for legs, changing its stature.

Its head and eyes were quite low to the ground, but it stared up at Shichika.

No—those eyes saw nothing.

"BITO SUNDIAL"

Skytron.

Voice like cold steel.

"ROBOSLAY—PAIN RAIN"[30]

Suddenly—its four legs began to *spin.*

Not 180 degrees—but 360, 720, 1440 degrees—around and around and around it went.

Slow at first—but gradually faster—taking on speed—whirling.

"...nkk!"

Naturally, Shichika leapt back.

Forced to do so by the fierce wind pressure generated by the revolutions—that tells you just how fast Skytron's four legs were spinning.

Next—Skytron, standing on its four hands, bent its elbows—

And then *shot up.*

High into air, as if it had a powerful spring hidden inside its body—*and hovered.*

Harlequin Buttery, the move his sister Nanami Yasuri had acquired from Chocho Maniwa, late of the Twelve Bosses, reportedly involved making the body weightless—but this didn't go that far. No way this robot could do ninpo, too.

What was Skytron up to—but flying of its own accord.

Creating lift by spinning its four legs at furious speed—staying so high off the ground that Shichika would not have even grazed it with his fingertips if he leapt with all his might.

[29] お辞儀 OJIGI leaning forward to show respect or say hello
[30] 微風刀風 BIFŪ TŌFŪ "subtle breeze, sword breeze"

Floating—like a bamboo dragonfly.[31]
Bito the Sundial's secret move—Pain Rain.
There was no spring. What it had been hiding—was its wings.
Using its legs as rotators,[32] Skytron gained air supremacy[33] over the battlefield. Just as with Rakka Rozeki, one of the Fatal Orchids of the Kyotoryu, attacks like this from overhead are brutally effective—
This would explain it casting off the four swords.
Those spinning wings could serve as blades and slice a foe in two.
Skytron had pulled out all the stops.[34]
As commanded centuries before.
To put a full stop on this run-on sentence[35] of a battle—
"Hey! Hey! You serious?" asked Shichika, face pale.
Looking up into the sky—up toward the floating mechanical doll.
Then turned toward Togame and spoke.
"Just like you said! I can't believe it does this too," Shichika confessed. *"I never thought—that it could actually fly."*
"I've got good eyes. Besides, machines are simple. Unlike people—"
But the very moment that she uttered this with feeling—something strange happened to Skytron, floating overhead.
No, not just strange—extraordinary.[36]
Without warning, all four of its legs stopped spinning. Not gradually coming to a halt the way they took on speed—but all at once, as though an instant had been captured pictorially.
Since Skytron had been floating on the lift that it created with its spinning legs, it promptly fell down from the sky—without flailing, writhing, or wailing.
Falling like a brick.
"Cripes. That took forever," Togame said.
Checking the display on the clock inside her head.
"Finally—*out of fuel.*"

■　■

No heavy breath or sweat.
　　Skytron—the robot that never felt fatigue.
　　But fatigue is one thing, and exhaustion[37] is another—all tricks and gadgetry aside, Bito the Sundial, a.k.a. Skytron, was a robot, and that meant that it

---

[31] 竹蜻蛉　TAKE TONBO　flying toys that zip up when spun from the hands
[32] 回転翼　KAITEN YOKU　"spinning wings"　rotor blades
[33] 制空権　SEIKŪKEN　"sky control authority"　also anachronistic in original
[34] 最後の手段に出た　SAIGO NO SHUDAN NI DETA　turned to last resort
[35] 膠着状態に終止符　KŌCHAKU JŌTAI NI SHŪSHIFU　period to the stalemate
[36] 異変　異常　IHEN IJŌ　"different & weird" anomaly; "different from usual" abnormality
[37] 消耗はする　SHŌMŌ WA SURU　does expend　消耗戦　SHŌMŌSEN　war of attrition

depended on a power source.

A robot that *continued to protect* Lake Fuyo across hundreds of years.

What kind of power source was this?

Togame had been pondering this question since before she set off on the Sword Hunt—since she first heard that a strange mechanical doll wandered the badlands of Lake Fuyo, the Level One Disaster Area.

Pondered in vain.

There was no way it was winding itself up—if this thing had the power to cut down any human being that crossed its path, it had to have a serious source of power, but Togame hadn't the foggiest idea what it might be.

However, since Skytron was one of the Mutant Blades of Kiki Shikizaki—one hypothesis[38] did come to mind.

She gleaned a hint the month before, when observing the Shikizaki blade wielded by Nanami Yasuri, Akuto the Eel. It was able to revitalize and replenish its owner because it had been charged with lightning—so.

What if Skytron, too, had some way of harnessing a natural form of energy? Specifically—that's right, the sun.

Prowling the badlands of Lake Fuyo—Skytron would often pause. As a result, it had taken extra time to ascertain the method to the madness of its orbit.

Shichika had said these pauses made it look like Skytron was—

Basking in the sun.

Could Skytron be converting sunlight into energy?

If so, the scheme could be absurdly simple—fight on a cloudy day.

One option was to provoke Skytron after the sun went down, but since Shichika was human, and unlike Skytron needed proper visibility to fight, a nighttime battle would be rough on him. As a concession, Togame settled for cloudy skies. It was a compromise, but it would do.

While they were waiting for a day like this, when it might rain any second, Togame schooled[39] Shichika on the mechanics of Skytron, pointing to the pictures that she drew.

Before long—the day came they were waiting for.

Today.

Under these circumstances, they could expect that Skytron would be unable to recharge—even if it could, it would never be enough. *If they ran Skytron ragged*—it would eventually run out of fuel.

Which is why Togame had told Shichika to assault Skytron relentlessly.

To never give Skytron a chance to rest.

Togame had surmised that it would use its legs for rotators quite early in her prognostications, leading her to conclude that *getting it to fly would be best*.

If they got it to fly—it would expend itself all the more quickly.

And soon run out of fuel.

Shichika might run out of stamina before Skytron burned through all its

---

[38] 仮説 KASETSU "provisional theory"
[39] 理解させた RIKAI SASETA made him understand

fuel, so the fight was a contest of endurance—but now.

Skytron was theirs.

Another of the Twelve Possessed was theirs. Without a scratch.

The Mutant Blade, unscathed.

"Hey...now that it's stopped fighting..."

Hugging the stalled body of Skytron—Shichika peered into its face.

"She's actually pretty cute. I guess this must be Kiki Shikizaki's type—"

When Skytron ran out of steam and fell from such great heights, Shichika followed through on his responsibilities and caught her—things had been a little dicey, but now the sword was safe in his embrace. And incredibly light. You never would have known from her appearance—but this made a world of sense, since Skytron had been made to fly. The robot must have been designed to be as light as possible.

Or perhaps.

Over the centuries—her parts had thinned from wear and tear.

"So if we left her in the sun, she'd start hacking away again?"

"I believe so. In any case, it isn't broken. In ROBOSLAY terms, I guess you might call this one LULL."[40]

Once she was certain that the battle was over, Togame came closer to examine Skytron's features and answered Shichika's question.

"This would be a good time to remove its starting system[41]...although I'm not sure where to find it. In the meantime, let's take off its arms and legs, just to be safe."

"Its arms and legs? I kinda feel bad."

"You dummy. Don't project emotions on[42] a robot. It may have a human face, but this thing is one of the Twelve Possessed, Bito the Sundial."

Though giving Shichika a few choice words, Togame betrayed her embarrassment, fiddling with the white hair cropped around her shoulders.

"But who am I to say not to project your feelings on a sword."

"Huh?"

"Plum flowers open on the easterly breeze—but when I'm gone, forget me not."

Brushing her hand on Skytron's cheek, Togame recited a tanka[43] from the *Collection of Gleanings*.[44]

"Bereft of its maker, alone without a master, left to protect Lake Fuyo over the centuries. I think this thing deserves a word of gratitude."

With that.

Togame closed Skytron's artificial eyes.

"Bravo,[45] Sundial."

---

[40] 凪 NAGI calm air and skies incorporates parts from 風 KAZE wind 止む YAMU cease
[41] 起動装置 KIDŌ SŌCHI "raise-move apparatus" another deliberate anachronism
[42] 感情移入 KANJŌ INYŪ "transfuse feelings" identify with
[43] 短歌 TANKA "short song" thirty-one (5-7-5-7-7) syllable poem evoking a tableau
[44] 拾遺和歌集 SHŪI WAKASHŪ third imperial poetry anthology of the Heian period
[45] 敵ながらあっぱれ TEKI NAGARA APPARE "albeit an enemy, admirable"

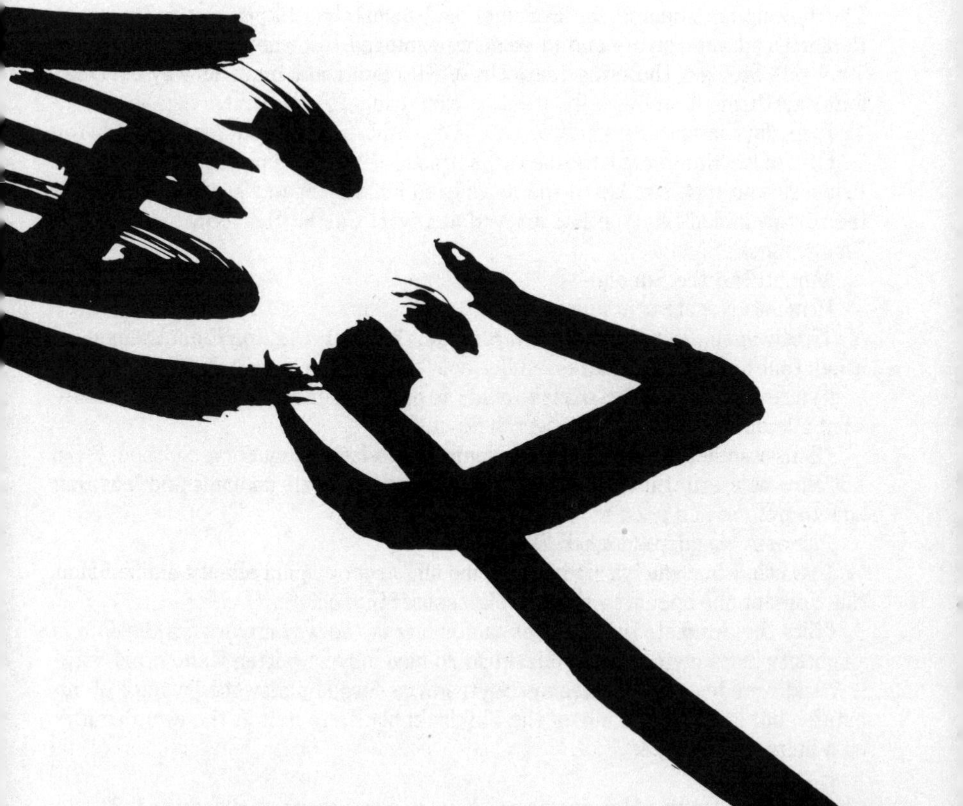

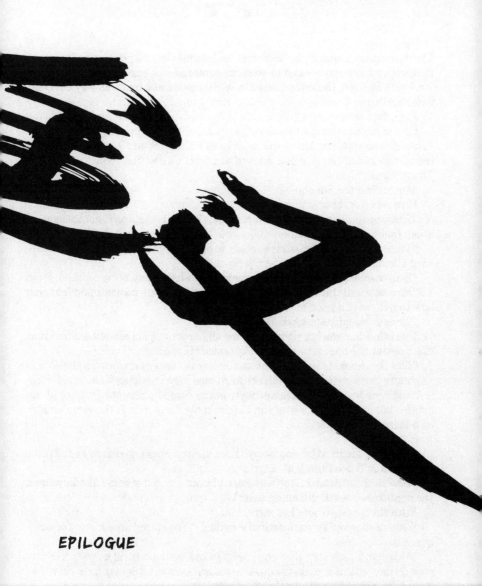

EPILOGUE

■ ■

The news that Togame the Schemer had dispatched Skytron, the Queen of Rubbish, at Lake Fuyo—and in so doing captured Bito the Sundial, one of the Twelve Possessed, those masterworks of Kiki Shikizaki, made its way to Owari four days later.

Four days later.

Of course this meant the news had made it to Mansion Negative and the Princess—in fact, she heard the news even before Togame's latest report and the disassembled Skytron had arrived at Owari Castle. Heard it, that is, from Emonzaemon Soda.

"About Bito the Sundial—"

Princess Negative.

Threw open her metal fan—*snap!*—and then (after telling Emonzaemon, as usual, that he was late) addressed her counselor, in his nook behind the ceiling.

"They say that Kiki Shikizaki made it in the likeness of his sweetheart—what a laugh."

"Is that something," asked Emonzaemon, "to laugh about?"

"How now, are you rejecting what I say? Not bad at all, you're finally learning how to put me in a good mood."

Princess Negative laughed like crazy.

In truth, when she wasn't in the mood she never even cracked a smile, but at the moment she appeared to be in high spirits indeed.

"Bito the Sundial...the *Sundial* part points at the way it works, while *Bito* is a subtlety in its own right. Shikizaki could have never written it the other way,[1] it would have been embarrassing. Skytron was forged under the premise of humanity, but it's also the only of the Shikizaki blades to hint at the swordsmith's own humanity—*ta-da!*"[2]

"..."

"Come on, laugh. Why so gloomy? You sure you aren't darkness itself?"

"Um...I still don't think it's anything to laugh at—"

"Why not? Otherwise, it's just gross.[3] Making a doll version of the woman you're obsessed with? Who does that?"

Princess Negative shut her metal fan.

Without so much as glancing at the ceiling—she stared ahead, into the empty room.

"Although I must say, that nasty woman has outdone herself again, cleverly recognizing what made Skytron tick[4]—while Akuto the Eel may have served as

[1] 美刀 BITŌ "beautiful sword" vs. 微刀 BITŌ "subtle sword"
[2] ちゃんちゃん CHAN CHAN onomatopoeic expression mimicking a coda, connotating a neat finish
[3] 気持ち悪い KIMOCHI WARUI "feels bad (icky)" creepy
[4] 仕組みに気付く SHIKUMI NI KIZUKU noticing the mechanism

a precedent, she sure pulled that one out of the blue, *considering solar batteries[5] haven't been invented yet.* Even if the name *Skytron* is a bit of a giveaway. Well? What did that nasty woman do next? After sending it home with her report—do they have any plans to come back here?"

"No, it would seem they're moving on to the next sword," said Emonzaemon, "in Tendo—in Dewa."

"Ah yes, may as well, when they're nearly there. I'm assuming that they found Kiki Shikizaki's workshop at Lake Fuyo?"

"Yes. Kyotoryu excavated it with his own two hands."

"That woman is rough with her staff! She could learn a thing or two from me."

"...They must have found—some information. Though unless it concerns Ento the Bead, we needn't get excited—hence why they won't be coming home. They did head straight for Tendo. When they forged their alliance with Hohoh Maniwa, or 'The Divine Phoenix'—one of the Twelve Bosses and effectively the head of the entire ninja clan, they learned the whereabouts of three of the swords...one on Mt. Shirei, another at Lake Fuyo...and the last of them in Tendo. At first, they had been hesitant to act on any claim from Hohoh alone."

"Tendo, huh." The Princess nodded. "Which one was that? I can't remember."

"Oto the Cured. If Skytron was a queen, then this sword, in sooth—is king."

"Quit trying to sound all cool for me, Emonzaemon. It's aggravating—but Oto the Cured. While it may put them through the wringer, I'm sure that they'll retrieve it in the end. As long as nothing unexpected happens. Hmm..."

Princess Negative closed her eyes, slipping into a reverie.

"Your Highness?" prodded Emonzaemon, puzzled by her sudden silence, but to no avail—she remained silent for some time.

Then suddenly she opened her eyes.

"What a nuisance."

"Nuisance? Have I wronged you?"

"At this point your being a nuisance is hardly noteworthy. I was referring to the Maniwa—this alliance between them and the Schemer. It's made it very difficult for me to guess what happens next."

"But I thought—your fundamental stance was that the Maniwa posed no threat?"

"I may have said that earlier—but I say we reject the Princess Negative of the past. I think I underestimated[6] them, and your killing of Umigame Maniwa has piqued my interest. We must take pains to prevent the unexpected. How many of the Maniwa are left now, three? Well then," continued the Princess, "I think I'll lend a helping hand to that nasty woman, from the shadows."

"Really..."

"I've thought of something perfectly negative."

With that, the Princess gave an order to Emonzaemon—behind the ceiling

---

[5] 太陽電池　TAIYŌ DENCHI　"sun electric pool"
[6] なめ過ぎ　NAMESUGI　"lick too much"　make light of

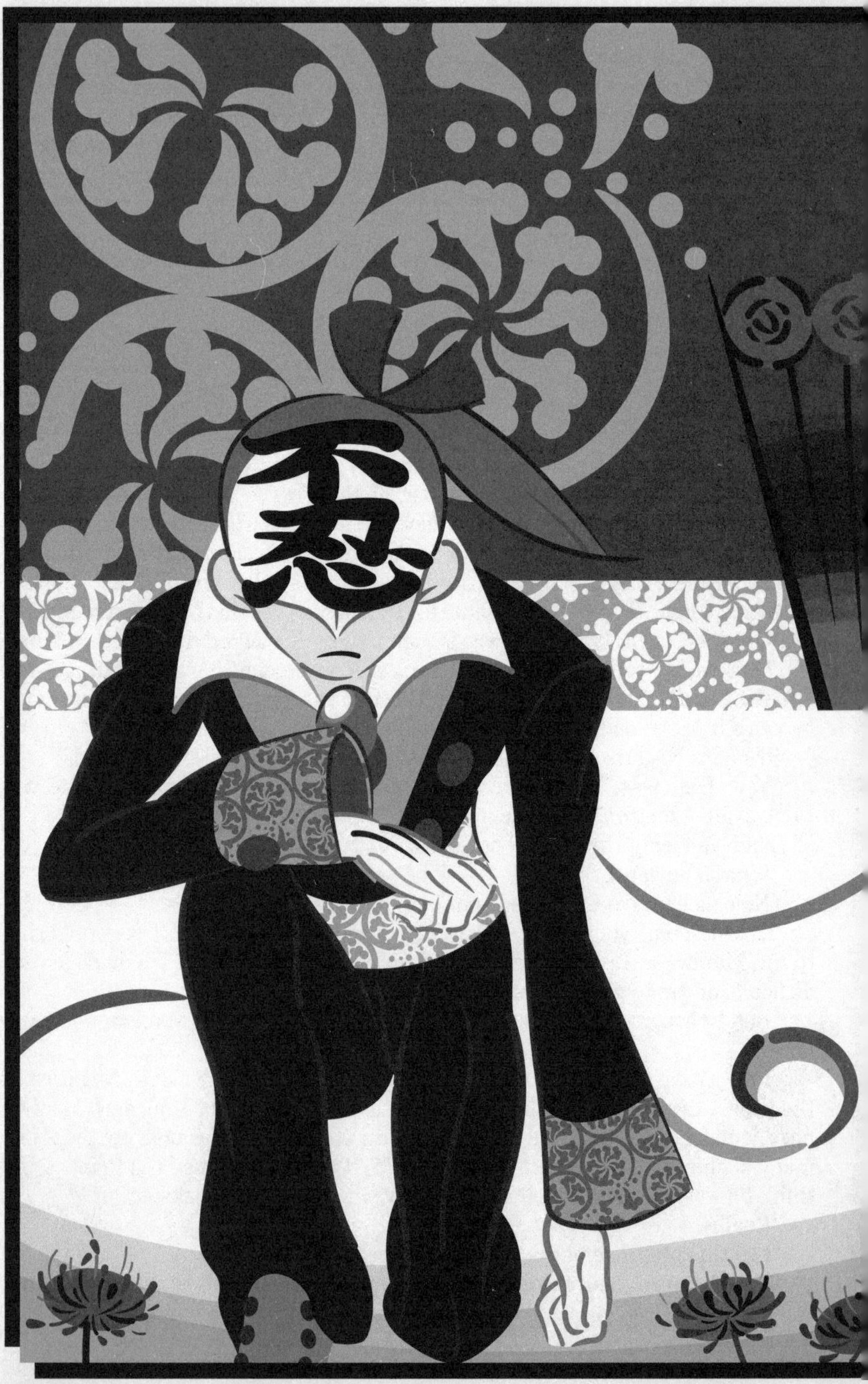
忍

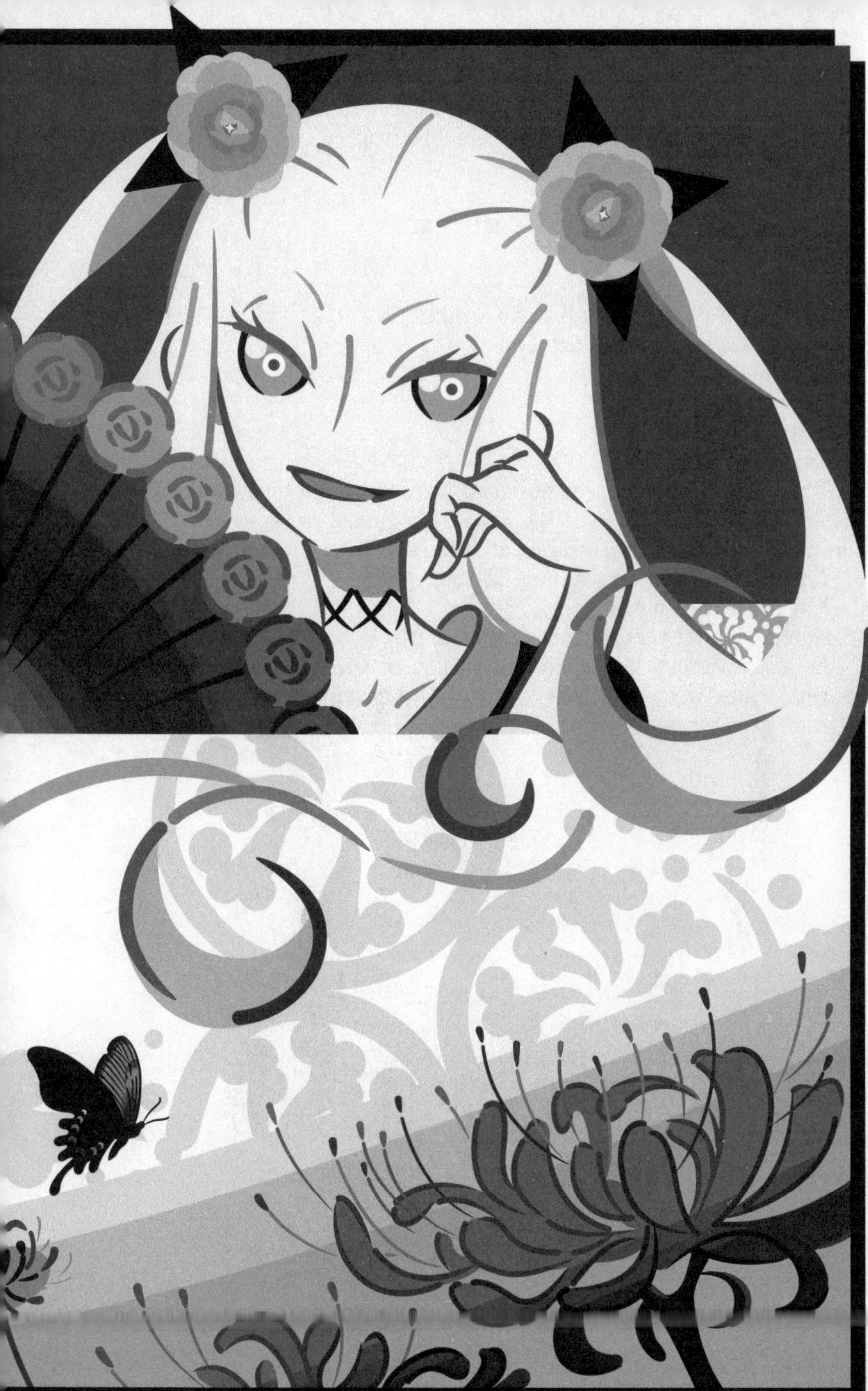

Casually, like she was asking him to run over to the store for her. "While you're out, assassinate Hohoh Maniwa."

■   ■

Of the Twelve Possessed of Kiki Shikizaki.
　There now remained—just four.
　Oto the Cured.
　Seito the Garland.
　Dokuto the Basilisk.
　Ento the Bead.
　Togame the Schemer, who designed[7] to round up all thousand of the Mutant Blades under the auspices of the Yanari Shogunate of the Owari Bakufu, was coming ever closer to her goal—but in the shadows, another battle had begun.
　The Maniwa Clan versus the Aioi Clan.
　Ninja versus ex-ninja.
　Hohoh Maniwa versus Emonzaemon Soda—
　As goes without saying, the conclusion of this one-hundred-and-seventy-year-old feud—would engender very negative developments.

Bito the Sundial: Check
End of Book Eight
To Be Continued

---

[7] 企み　TAKURAMI　plot, intrigue

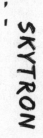

CHARACTER INDEX 8 - SKYTRON

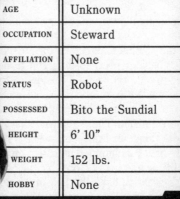

AGE	Unknown
OCCUPATION	Steward
AFFILIATION	None
STATUS	Robot
POSSESSED	Bito the Sundial
HEIGHT	6' 10"
WEIGHT	152 lbs.
HOBBY	None

LIST OF SPECIAL MOVES

TORNADO	⇦ (HOLD) ⇨ SLASH
WHIRLWIND	⇩⇘⇨ SLASH
VERNAL BLAST	⇦ (HOLD) ⇨ KICK
BLUSTER	⇦ (HOLD) ⇨ THRUST
TEMPEST	⇧⇗⇨ SLASH
SANDSTORM	⇧⇗⇨ SLASH + THRUST
TYPHOON	⇦⇘⇧⇗⇨ SLASH + THRUST
WIND FANG	⇩ (HOLD) ⇧ THRUST
PAIN RAIN	⇧ (HOLD) ⇩ SLASH + THRUST + KICK

AFTER(S)WORD

I'm not sure how to put this into words, since it's a little hard to grasp, so I'll just say what's on my mind, no matter how it sounds, but sometimes a command ceases to be relevant. Whether this happens to you personally or you see it happening from the sidelines makes no difference, it's a bummer. To give you an example, let's consider prerecording things off of the television. Say you set your recorder to tape the same TV show every week and walk away; even after the show has made it to the final episode and through its grand finale, the following week your recorder will diligently start taping a completely unrelated show in the same time slot. Thanks but no thanks, right, nice as it was to go ahead and tape the thing. Or how about when a baseball game goes into extra innings, and your show gets bumped up thirty minutes, but the recording starts at the designated time and cuts before the episode reaches its climax? Thanks but no thanks, it's great to have the episode, but not so much when you were hoping for the whole thing. I'm aware that this comparison to taping television dramas may strike some as idyllic, but this question of commands ceasing to be relevant runs quite deep: I'm not exaggerating when I say it influences every aspect of our world. Thanks to misunderstandings like these, no small number of people have been killed in countless wars. While the central powers may have come to an agreement, somehow word fails to travel fast enough, and the results are tragic. It's really sad. Along these lines, it's easy to say, "As cool as machines are, it's way cooler when people make their own decisions," but that view is overly simplistic. It's not uncommon for people to think they're deciding on their own, when in fact they're following some directive burnt into their memory. I guess we call it instinct? I'm not saying we should fight our instincts, though, since probably we couldn't if we tried. Our only option is to do the best we can, to the extent that we can, which is probably the closest thing we have to an expression of our freedom.

Thus ends Book Eight of *Sword Tale*. Since there are twelve books in total, we are now transitioning from the middle stages to the final stages of the story. I tried to make this Edo episode a little different from the ones before it. To be honest, when I wrote Book One, I didn't really think that I would make it this far, but here we go—and I intend to keep it up to the end. We're on the homestretch, but I only made it this far, and with enough energy to finish, thanks to the one and only *take*'s powerful illustrations. It makes me want to make full use of my time for each of the remaining swords.

Four books left!

NISIOISIN

BOOK NINE

OTO
THE CURED

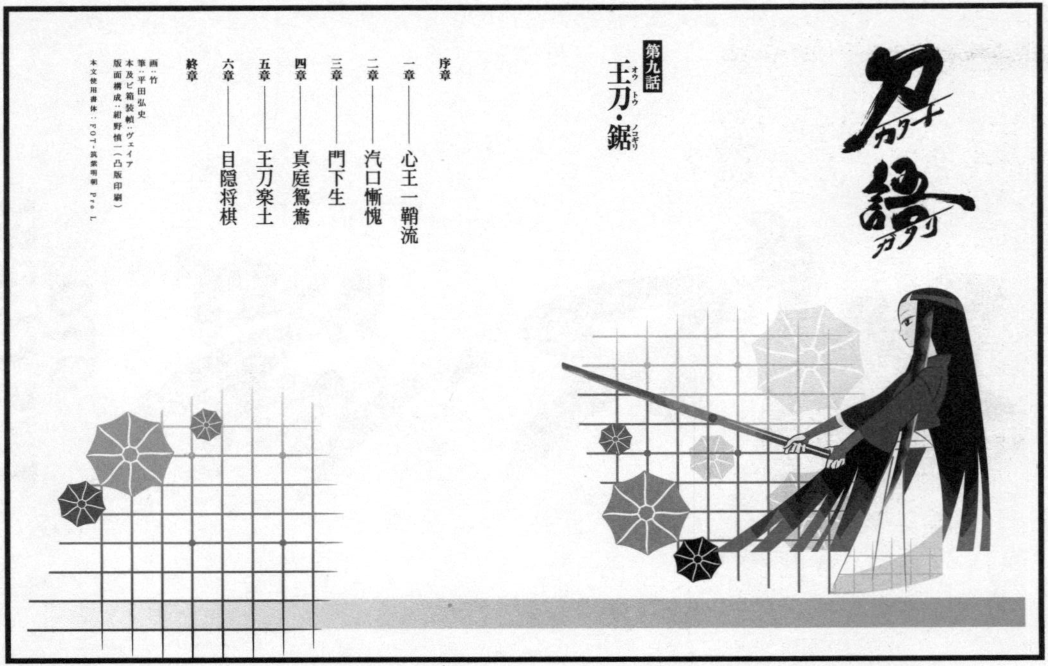

刀語 カタナガタリ

第九話
王刀・鋸（オウトウ・ノコギリ）

画：竹
筆：平田弘史
本及ビ箱装幀：ヴェイア
版面構成：紺野慎一（凸版印刷）
本文使用書体：FOT-筑紫明朝 Pro L

The original Book Nine Table of Contents spread

PROLOGUE

■ ■

In Owari Town—at Mansion Negative, residence of Princess Negative, Inspector General of the Yanari Shogunate, whose true origins and real name were unknown.

Lord of the Manor, Princess Negative presided[1] over her chamber.
No candles lit.
Not sitting, but standing.
Presided.
Expressionless.

The blond-haired blue-eyed Princess was unconventional[2] among the people of this country, an oddity among those in the employ of the Owari Bakufu—but her kimono, however Japanese, suited her well.

Nobody wore a kimono quite like her.
Suddenly.
Princess Negative opened her metal fan, gesturing toward the ceiling.
"That nasty woman—may be powerful, but her power is affirmative. But wait, have we spoken of this before?"
Speaking fluent Japanese.
She uttered each syllable clearly.
"My power, of course, being the negative variety—my feud with that nasty woman, and hence our animosity,[3] is an unfriendly blend of positive and negative energies. If I am Princess Negative, then I suppose that makes her Princess Positive. Hah!"
Princess Negative giggled.
"She validates everything, having the power to cast all things in a positive light, from her own weakness to the ugliness of life. What could be more horrific? Especially for me. Hence why I have rejected her. Rejecting her with all I have, body and soul. I've always had a feeling she was up to something fishy."[4]
True to her name.
Princess Negative—negged the Schemer.
"While I can't prove it, I know it when I smell it. But so far—at least in terms of outcomes, that woman has squashed me like a bug. Thanks to her schemes, I've been demoted more times than I would care to count—and you haven't gone unscathed yourself. Is this not your fight, too?" she asked the ceiling.
But there was no reply.
Unbothered, she continued. "Whereas, for my part, I've failed to do her any serious damage—sure, we've gotten in the way and meddled in her affairs, but

[1] 佇んで TATAZUNDE upright with the feet set
[2] 異端 ITAN heterodox
[3] せめぎあい SEMEGI'AI antagonism, friction
[4] 怪しい AYASHII suspicious; unreliable

she's shaken us off every time. And hit back hard."

Princess Negative.

Rejecting—the results of her own campaign.

"Though I suppose that my ability to reinstate myself repeatedly shows just how wonderful I really am..."

When this attempt at humor elicited no reaction from the ceiling, Princess Negative closed her metal fan and slipped it into her obi.

"Conversely, that woman is a little on the sloppy side—she sees herself as being so committed to her plan, but as far as I can see it's full of holes. Thanks to which she's given me the benefit of the doubt. But if this, too," added the Princess, "is a product of her positivity, that makes the holes essential, and in that sense unintentional—"

One thing was for sure.

This analysis—had no holes whatsoever.

"Like me, she is a woman with a murky past... Her early life must hold the secret to the way that she is now. I can—relate. That said, I have no way of dredging up the details of her early life. No use thinking it over..."

Princess Negative paused for a time.

But after indulging in this pensive moment, she hummed and nodded, like she had thought of something good.

"This just occurred to me—but maybe that woman's power isn't purely positive after all. Indeed—positive and negative are not evenly matched. Negativity tends to have the upper hand."

Human beings negate.

We assert our own existence by rejecting that of others.

Which is why.

The very reason why—she *had made herself* Princess Negative.

"That led me to assume I was more powerful than her—but it appears that nasty woman is operating on another plane entirely. I had been certain that I enjoyed an advantage in our fight—but apparently she sees me from a different vantage point. Hmm...very interesting. That explains a lot."

Princess Negative took a breath.

Then uttered softly, "Right. Coincidentally, last time you and I discussed this, you said as much yourself—I believe you said that 'Oftentimes, the Schemer has no scheme at all. She has a way of going with the flow, of going in without a plan.' While I cannot deny this being an assertion of her positivity...I think it's something much more fundamental."

That is why, she muttered.

"By dint of being the Schemer, she can only scheme—and lacks a strategy. She is a warrior who has no need for armaments, advancing through the ranks through intellect alone, all of which suggests a consummate thinker—but just as she has this genius for thinking, *perhaps she also has an equal measure of genius for not thinking.*"

The Princess drew her metal fan.

This time opening it slowly, over her face—so that it hid her mouth.

"There are times when it's no use thinking things over, but most of us can't help it—we just keep thinking anyway. *But an ability to turn off certain thoughts*—would be extremely handy for a person working out a scheme, wouldn't you say? If that's her ace in the hole, she's done a fabulous job of playing innocent—I had thought she was simply a ditz,[5] but perhaps I undersold her."

Right, of course, Princess Negative nodded solemnly to herself.

Her face looking like a host of problems had been solved.

After nodding for a minute, she closed the fan and pointed it toward the ceiling.

"Emonzaemon—in any case, the Sword Hunt for the Twelve Possessed of Kiki Shikizaki launched by Togame the Schemer, Grand Commander of Arms of the Yanari Shogunate Military Directorate, Owari Bakufu, is my hunting ground—one way or another, our longstanding rivalry will soon be settled. At first I thought there was a high chance she would be her own undoing—but now that she has eight of the twelve swords, her chances of capturing the three others, and making her way to the last—are about *fifty-fifty*."

Princess Negative gave each word extra weight.

This was a declaration.[6]

"If all goes well, you and I can partake in the spoils without toiling.[7] We will be credited with rounding up the Twelve Possessed, those masterworks of legendary swordsmith Kiki Shikizaki—and will disclose the true nature of the Schemer in the process... I never would have thought Hakuhei Sabi a tergiversator, but as that debacle helped me regain power, I'd say that things worked out alright. Sabi was more genius than I could handle, anyway. Heheh—one thing's for sure, though, if this means the ruin of those pesky Maniwa Ninjas, that Schemer's Sword Hunt hasn't been the worst thing in the world—I know you said you don't care about ancestral grudges, but you must feel some kind of a relief[8] seeing the Maniwa wiped out. Right—Emonzaemon?"

Her tone was nettling—

But there was no reaction from the ceiling.

It took her a second.

"Oh yeah," the Princess said as if she had just remembered something. "I forgot...he's out."

■　■

This opening sequence, like those of Book Five and Book Eight, has been brought to you by Princess Negative!

[5] どじっ娘　DOJIKKO　daft girl
[6] 宣言　SENGEN　proclamation e.g. 独立宣言　DOKURITSU SENGEN declaration of independence
[7] 漁夫の利　GYOFU NO RI　windfall from the distraction of two other warring parties
[8] 溜飲くらいは下がる　RYŪIN KURAI WA SAGARU　"at least your bile will descend"

Whose right-hand man, Emonzaemon Soda, was currently a long way from Owari, having been tasked with assassinating "The Divine Phoenix," Hohoh Maniwa!

Meanwhile, our favorite duo has arrived in Tendo, seeking the ninth sword!

Another month, another battle!

Like a scrolling tome, with no direction home!

Tangled up in this intangible period piece!

Tale of the Sword, Book Nine ♪

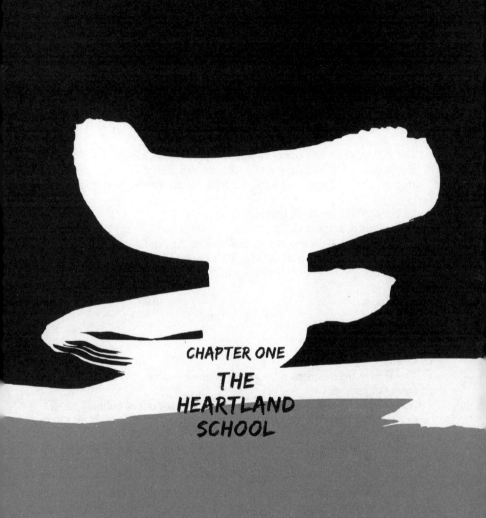

CHAPTER ONE
THE HEARTLAND SCHOOL

■ ■

"Thank you for the explanation."

The Twelfth Master of the Heartland[1] School of swordplay—Zanki Kiguchi,[2] hearing them out, said these words quietly.

She entertained her visitors in her spacious dojo.

Dressed in her gi and seated on her heels.

Her two guests, facing her, were sitting the same way.

The first a petite whitehaired woman in flamboyant robes.

The second a tall half-naked man with tousled hair.

Togame the Schemer—and the Seventh Master of the Kyotoryu, Shichika Yasuri.

"Still," Zanki Kiguchi continued.

Stoic in mien.

Eyes resting on the wooden sword placed on the tatami mats between them.

"As Master of the Heartland School—I regret to inform you that I will not relinquish Oto the Cured[3] for any reason."

■ ■

To recap.

The Whitehaired Schemer known as Togame—whose actual name and origins were unknown.

Was born the daughter of Takahito Hida, the Kaoyaku of Oshu.

But the Rebellion, an attempt to overthrow the Yanari Bakufu, is where it all began.

As the only conflict in what one might call a centuries-long Pax Japonica—this missile, flung by Takahito Hida, shook the very bedrock of Japan.

A revolution on the national scale.

It was the product of careful planning and deliberate execution—not to mention a laxened attitude toward crisis management brought on by domestic tranquility. The war spiraled out of proportion, and before long, the bakufu was cornered, by no exaggeration on the verge of being overthrown—a fate only prevented by dumb luck.

Or perhaps.

It was all thanks to the Sixth Master of the Kyotoryu—Mutsue Yasuri.

---

[1] 心王一鞘　SHIN'Ō ISSŌ　"the mind itself a scabbard"　nuance of being grounded, centered
[2] 汽口慚愧　KIGUCHI ZANKI　"shame for spouting steam"　sounds modest
[3] 王刀『鋸』　ŌTŌ NOKOGIRI　"The King Sword: Saw"

Retainer of the House of Tetsubi, one of the six daimyos of the Age of Warring States.

The Swordless Swordsman.

Though tempting to depict him as part of a select force, Mutsue simply joined a ragtag group of warriors in their besiegement of Oshu, whereupon he took down Takahito Hida.

Taking the head of Takahito Hida—with the blade of his own hand.

Having lost their mastermind, the rebel army was soon ravaged by a merciless counterstrike, leading to its rapid dissolution.

With no one to take over after Takahito Hida, it was all over without Takahito Hida.

Hence—the Rebellion ended, the war over.

Domestic tranquility.

Peace and order—had returned.

Callooh. Callay.[4]

Or so was the opinion of the members of the bakufu, and too the modest country folk who had no interest in the wars with which the reigning elite[5] amused themselves—but on the side of the Rebellion, especially those close to Takahito Hida, the result was far from peaceful.

Not for the war dead.

Nor those who lived—only to lose their heads.

Nor those who fled but strayed into the fire.

While the Owari Bakufu had created a peaceful body politic, its political body was far from peaceful—as plainly demonstrated by the iron fist it hammered on the rebels.

No room for human kindness—crushing them like ants.

And the family of Takahito Hida, as goes without saying.

All terminated—every single one of them.

No callooing or callaying here.

And yet, somehow there was a sole survivor.

In the girl who would be schemer—Togame the Schemer.

She had watched them.

Watched as Mutsue battered her own father.

Her corvine hair, praised by those who knew her for its deep black color, like raven feathers slick with rain[6]—lost all pigmentation.

By then, the girl had already pledged—her revenge.

To take revenge upon the bakufu.

Swore on that hair of white—to avenge the murder of her father.

She was still young enough to call a child—but after witnessing the tables turn, their numbers decimated, then obliterated, each rebel killed before they could so much as raise their hands in protest, the girl was first and foremost—a

---

[4] めでたしめでたし　MEDETASHI MEDETASHI　Happily Ever After
[5] 雲の上　KUMO NO UE　"above the clouds"
[6] 烏の濡れ羽　KARASU NO NUREBA　wet crow's feather cf. setting of the author's debut novel

survivor.

Surviving not because she was a child—but through an ingenuity well beyond her years. Not giving a damn about the consequences,[7] she flung away her pride and all the rest—in order to survive.

Not that she wanted to live.

Or that she was scared to die.

Her survival was indispensable—to her revenge.

Her ability to outstrip the cleanup efforts of the bakufu—being but one small glimpse of the agile, tactful way she led her life.

Of course.

Were she to have escaped, they never would have ceased to chase her—so she dressed[8] another body as a scapegoat,[9] which she left for those rats to find. Once they identified the corpse as being the daughter of Takahito Hida, she got away scot-free,[10] becoming a girl without a name, without a past.

Since then much time had passed, during which she had not let up for a second, making moves, though blundering some, but making more moves anyway—eventually slipping her way into the Owari Bakufu.

She strode into the all-boys club[11] that was the government, caparisoned in all her brash and brilliant finery. The cautious[12] style of working out a plan in secret, and taking care that no one noticed—was simply not her way.

On the contrary.

After accessing the inner circle of the bakufu, despite being a woman, she proudly took the brazen name of Togame the Schemer—crushing all those who would crush her and standing on their heads to climb the ranks.

Princess Negative—being one.

That their feud had benefitted the ascent of Togame the Schemer was a fact that could not be negated.

Still—it was also a fact that Princess Negative, popping up each time she pushed her down, had perpetually frustrated Togame the Schemer. The fact that the Princess held the office of Inspector General of the Yanari Shogunate helped Togame none—but regardless.

In this way, she shouldered her way up, vying for power, pushing as high as possible and higher still. Nothing was sacred.

Her efforts paid off, for she attained the rank of Grand Commander of Arms of the Yanari Shogunate Military Directorate.

By then, she had built herself a firm foundation[13] slight disturbances could never shake. On the one hand she was making great strides toward her sole goal of taking vengeance on the Owari Bakufu—but on the other hand, this

---

[7] 恥も外聞もなく HAJI MO GAIBUN MO NAKU neither ashamed nor mindful of one's reputation
[8] 用意 YŌI prepped
[9] 身代わり MIGAWARI "substitute body"
[10] 晴れて HARETE "blue skies" in the clear
[11] 完全な男社会 KANZEN NA OTOKO SHAKAI a total men's society/world
[12] まどろっこしい MADOROKKOSHII irritatingly roundabout
[13] 牙城 GAJŌ "fang castle" stronghold

complicated things.

With her high status, no one would be quick to call her out.

A firm foundation slight disturbances could never shake—

The one exception being Princess Negative, ever her sworn enemy, dedicated to their feud—but this relationship was not simply about goals or careers: it was a clash of personalities, a rivalry ordained by heaven.

That the Princess was Inspector General did not help. In fact, taking her on conferred no benefit.

In the end, Togame would be rubbed out.

Worn down—to nothing.

Hence why she had enlisted the cooperation of the Maniwa, tasking them with crushing Princess Negative (—which they had, except she popped back up again—) before devising what would be her last resort.

The Sword Hunt for the Twelve Possessed of legendary swordsmith Kiki Shikizaki.

This warrants a brief explanation of who Kiki Shikizaki was.

It happened before the Owari Bakufu had formed a body politic of peace and order, when Japan was caught in what was called the Age of Warring States—a rumor began to spread among the swordsmen on the fields of war.

The rumor involving swords.

The gist was that by wielding a katana fashioned by this crazy swordsmith, a lone wolf who belonged to no tradition, you would be invested with the power to take on a whole army—while on the flipside, were you to face a swordsman bearing a katana made by the same swordsmith, you would have no hope of winning and be forced to flee—

These swords were called the Mutant Blades.

And the swordsmith was named Kiki Shikizaki.

He made exactly one thousand Mutant Blades.

In the battles between states, the number of Mutant Blades held by a power is said to have been the deciding factor—and in practice, this was true.

The clashes between the twenty-five states of the period were all biased by the number of Mutant Blades.

The Great Unifier[14]—known today as the Old Shogun, came out of the war with five hundred and seven Mutant Blades.

His appetite for these swords was insatiable.

With that many, it would have been stranger had he failed to rule the land—perhaps.

From his base in Tosa, in Shikoku—he ruled over the nation.

Although by now, his heart had already been poisoned.

Poisoned.

By the venom of the Shikizaki blades.

Although the land had been returned to order, he showed no sign of stopping—nay, he was unable to stop. Now that he possessed just over half the

---

[14]. 戦国の覇者 SENGOKU NO HASHA conqueror of the warring states

Mutant Blades, he absolutely had to have them all.

To this end, he exhausted his resources.

This should have been a time of nation building.

But disregarding all the varied chores of reconstruction, he gave the quest for swords his undivided attention.

Already well along in years[15]—he had no time to spare.

No room for scrupulosity.

The most notorious example of his rampage being the Great Sword Hunt, the most ignoble act of legislation in the history of the nation.

Whereby he hunted swordsmen.

This fearsome law took pains to funnel all the swords and all the swordsmen in Japan into Shikoku—dressing it up, of course, in the appealing notion of erecting the Katana Buddha, installed at Seiryoin Gokenji Temple, to commemorate the ending of the war—although his true motive was not even to cull swordsmen, but to amass the Mutant Blades of Kiki Shikizaki.

And this unselfconscious lust for swords bore fruit.[16]

From across Japan, four hundred and eighty-one more swords were brought to him—for a total of nine hundred and eighty-eight.

Twelve remained.

But these twelve—were perverse.

Absurd perversions all—

Of all the Mutant Blades of Kiki Shikizaki, these twelve swords were the most precious—his masterworks, known as the Twelve Possessed.

Zetto the Leveler.

Zanto the Razor.

Sento the Legion.

Hakuto the Whisper.

Zokuto the Armor.

Soto the Twin.

Akuto the Eel.

Bito the Sundial.

Oto the Cured.

Seito the Garland.

Dokuto the Basilisk.

Ento the Bead.

These twelve swords had evaded his every effort.

Worse still, in failing to attain these precious twelve, he fell from power, tumbling so far down that in the end, this man who had once unified the nation maintained a fiefdom worth no more than fifty thousand koku of rice.

Because he had no heir, his family line died out—leaving the current Yanari Shogunate to reap the benefits of his accomplishments and legacy.[17]

---

[15] 高齢　KŌREI　"high age"　old
[16] 実る　MINORU　ripen　実　MI　fruit, nut; substance
[17] 功績 足跡　KŌSEKI ASHIATO　accumulated honor; credit　footprints

The adage about food only feeling hot until it passes down the throat[18] is perhaps a little quaint—but it is human nature for us to forget the stench of blood in steady periods of peace.

Or perhaps not to forget, so much as give ourselves permission to forget.

Before long, the name of Kiki Shikizaki, who in his day had been a legend, slipped from memory, together with the Mutant Blades that ruled over the Age of Warring States.

The nine hundred and eighty-eight Mutant Blades that were collected— whiled the centuries away in idleness, treated not as swords but relics, locked in a chamber of Owari Castle.

Until.

Togame the Schemer—set her sights on the rest of them.

The swords not even the Old Shogun had been able to collect.

If she could complete the Sword Hunt—great honors would await her.

In these sleepy times when there was little opportunity for daring feats of valor, this quest would give her career definite traction.[19] It may even bring—

The neck of the shogun within her reach.

With honor—would come vengeance.

Hence the scheme Togame conjured from the precipice of her success—her scheme to hunt down all the Mutant Blades of Kiki Shikizaki. Of course, she had not launched the scheme herself, but left enough hints here and there so that her immediate superior proposed the idea on his own—and while the higher-ups reacted unenthusiastically at first, eventually they gave the greenlight.

Trouble is, her schemes had a way of varying in quality, ranging from merry success to abysmal failure. Since the outset of the Sword Hunt, Togame had experienced two massive upsets.

The first of which being the betrayal of the Maniwa, whose cooperation she had elicited in suppressing Princess Negative.

And the second being the betrayal of the party she selected to replace the Maniwa, one Hakuhei Sabi—the strongest swordsman in Japan, already in the employ of the bakufu.

Learning from the errors of the Old Shogun, she had captured two swords, only to watch them slip out of her hands when each betrayed her.

Far from a boost to her career—these efforts were a bust.[20]

Although the foundation of her position was firm as ever, her chosen methods had been dubious. The number of enemies she had within the bakufu remained significant, and only less manifest than at first.

So different from Princess Negative, who despite being a woman, and concealing her real name and actual origins, just like Togame, had no trouble getting along within the bakufu.

If Togame fell from grace—she may be unable to climb her way back up

[18] 喉もと過ぎれば熱さを忘れる　NODOMOTO SUGIREBA ATSUSA WO WASURERU
the notion that danger, once impalpable, is easy to dismiss
[19] 足がかり　ASHIGAKARI "foot grip"
[20] 没落の危機　BOTSURAKU NO KIKI "sinking-and-falling crisis"

again.

But as the Sword Hunt was well underway—

She had no choice but to hatch another scheme.

And while this may have been her last resort, it was a painful, agonizing plan of action.

She resolved to call upon the man who killed her father, Takahito Hida—and ask this murderer to join her on the Sword Hunt.

The Hero of the Rebellion—

Now banished to a desert island.

The Master of the Kyotoryu would need to be released into the wider world.

Unaffected by the venom of the Mutant Blades, and not enticed by the allure of lucre, this swordsman would be an asset to her quest, as much as she had mixed feelings about the venture—being perhaps her craziest scheme to date.

Indeed.

Hiring the man who had decapitated her own dad, in the name of taking her revenge—was far from an ideal arrangement, and among the toughest choices she would ever make.

From Tango, she sailed across the waters stretching from the Cliffs of Shinso to a nameless desert island out on the horizon.

No, since Mutsue Yasuri had been banished with his children to the island twenty years earlier, it could no longer be rightly called deserted—and was referred to by some as Haphazard Island.

But that is all beside the point.

The man whom Togame had hoped to hire, Mutsue Yasuri, the Sixth Master of the Kyotoryu, the man who killed her father—had been killed himself.

She was about a year too late.

This is when Togame the Schemer made the acquaintance of Shichika Yasuri.

The Seventh Master of the Kyotoryu—

Who twenty years earlier.

At age four, had been sculled over[21] to Haphazard Island with his father, Mutsue Yasuri—and for nineteen years had been reared to function like a living, breathing sword.

She saw something—of a resemblance.

The memory was ancient, but Togame had held onto the image of Mutsue.

How could she forget the visage of Mutsue—when he took the head of Takahito Hida? It seemed to her that Shichika was even taller than his father.

In short time—

"Shichika Yasuri. Go ahead and fall for me."

She chose Shichika—

To be her sword.

And, in turn, Shichika Yasuri—

"I'm going ahead and falling for you."

[21] 流され NAGASARE streamed, drifted e.g. 流刑 RUKEI sentence of exile

Chose to be her katana.

Shichika Yasuri and Togame the Schemer—thus embarked on their Sword Hunt.

Before leaving Haphazard Island, they vanquished Komori Maniwa, one of the Twelve Bosses of the Maniwa Ninja Clan, and reclaimed Zetto the Leveler, a sword of superlative hardness that could never bend or break.

Next, in Inaba Desert, they seized Zanto the Razor, a sword boasting a fearsome edge, from Ginkaku Uneri, the Lord of Gekoku Castle.

After which, in Izumo, they received Sento the Legion, a thousand swords in one, from Meisai Tsuruga, the Mistress of Triad Shrine.

Moving on to Ganryu Island, they repossessed Hakuto the Whisper, a sword delicate as glasswork, from Hakuhei Sabi, who like the Maniwa had stabbed Togame in the back.

Thereafter, in Satsuma, they forced Kanara Azekura, Captain of the Armored Pirates, to surrender Zokuto the Armor, a sword unparalleled in armor class.

Whereupon, in Ezo, they accepted Soto the Twin, the heaviest sword in existence, from Konayuki Itezora, the sole survivor of the Itezora Clan.

Following which, in Tosa, they prized Akuto the Eel, the most sinister of all the Mutant Blades of Kiki Shikizaki, from Nanami Yasuri, the older sister of Shichika Yasuri.

And finally, in Edo, they bested Skytron, the robot who patrolled Lake Fuyo, and in so doing corralled Skytron, who was also Bito the Sundial, at once a robot and a sword.

Eight swords in total!

The Sword Hunt launched by Togame the Schemer had pushed through to its final stages—but there was something special about Bito the Sundial, the sword they captured last month at Lake Fuyo in Edo.

Designated a Level One Disaster Area, Lake Fuyo had once been home to the forge where Kiki Shikizaki made his swords—the site of which Skytron had been tasked with watching over and protecting.

Having destroyed Skytron—although since Skytron was both sword and robot, a frustrating combination, they could not actually *destroy* her—they set about finding the ruins of the workshop.

It was just like Kiki Shikizaki to set his workshop up among the rubbish—all the scraps of wood, metal, and rubble burying Lake Fuyo, but if they could locate where it was, perhaps they would learn something essential about the four remaining swords—Oto the Cured, Seito the Garland, Dokuto the Basilisk, and Ento the Bead.

In which case.

Togame the Schemer would be one step closer to exacting her revenge—which just about catches us up.

Except—

"...No luck," Shichika said when they had probed most of the lake.

Endlessly energetic as he was, his years of constant training had not prepared him for spending a whole day digging, on his own, through mountains of rubbish. One look and you could tell he was depleted.[22]

Besides, he had only just finished his battle against Skytron.

"Huh. Okay."

Togame sounded unsatisfied.

Supervising the excavation from the sidelines.

For the record, she had not so much as offered her assistance.

"It looks like..." observed Shichika, "people used to live here, at least once upon a time, so I don't think the Princess lied to us about Lake Fuyo being where Kiki Shikizaki had his workshop...but I'm not finding anything that seems like it would help us figure out who owns the four remaining swords, or where they are."

"Well, we did our best."

Togame looked off to the side toward Skytron—Bito the Sundial, which they had partially disassembled and bundled up.

"No use digging any further," Togame said. "I know there's still a few spots left, but let's get out of here."

"Is it okay to leave a mess like this?"

"You mean the heaps of rubbish? What difference would it make to move the piles around? Granted, now that you've taken care of Skytron, it's possible this place will lose its status as a Level One Disaster Area—but Lake Fuyo is still the mess it's always been."

"Right. So, are we going back to Owari?"

"Nope," Togame shook her head. "From here we'll head for Tendo."

"T-Tendo?"

This was not the response Shichika had been expecting.

"Wh-Where the heck—is Tendo?"

"With you it's always in one ear and out the other. Don't you remember what Hohoh Maniwa told us? He told us where we could find three more of the Mutant Blades—on Mt. Shirei in Mutsu, at Lake Fuyo in Edo, and in Tendo, in Dewa."

"Ahhh, I remember now."

Nanami Yasuri had beaten them to the punch with Akuto the Eel, the sword that had been waiting atop Mt. Shirei in Mutsu—but there had been a sword there, like the ninja said. And here, too, at Lake Fuyo, this time in Bito the Sundial, at once a robot and a sword, known otherwise as Skytron.

True to his word.

---

[22] 疲弊の色は隠せなかった HIHEI NO IRO WA KAKUSENAKATTA unable to conceal the hue of fatigue

That being said, it was perhaps too optimistic[23] to take for granted that another of the Shikizaki blades was waiting for them in Tendo, in Dewa.

Hohoh Maniwa was a ninja, after all. He made a living out of dirty deeds.

He wouldn't think twice about bundling[24] two facts and a lie. On the contrary, this was just the sort of trap they should expect from a band of expert assassins like the Maniwa. And the stakes were high enough that if they fell for it—the fall might be too far for them to save themselves.

Forget the alliance, the Maniwa were ultimately vying for the Twelve Possessed themselves—and there was no telling the lengths they would go to.

"I only asked because you said that we were gonna lay low in Owari for a while, so you could gather information... We ended up spending our whole time at Lake Fuyo dealing with Bito the Sundial, but wasn't this supposed to be a search for info too?"

"It sure was—and it bothers me a great deal that there was no information to be found. Especially, if like you said before, the Princess wasn't lying. In that case, I would have to assume full responsibility for our failure to discover anything of value."

"What? Don't say that—couldn't it just mean that Kiki Shikizaki destroyed anything that could have tipped somebody off about his Mutant Blades?"

"That would certainly make sense. But try explaining that to my superiors. The higher-ups have gotten onboard with the Sword Hunt in a big way—I can't just show up emptyhanded now. I'd hate to spoil my winning streak."[25]

"Why you gotta make things so political?"

Shichika was losing patience.

Dedicated as he was—these intricacies left a bad taste in his mouth.[26]

"Unfortunately, this is a political situation," Togame said dismissively.

This had been a difficult[27] decision for her.

In the interest of the Sword Hunt, it made sense to head back to Owari and return to her research—but we must remember that her quest to amass all the Mutant Blades of Kiki Shikizaki was a means and not an end.

A distinction not to be ignored.

"As a result, we'll have to tell the bakufu—we found something that *wasn't there*."

"I knew the day would come when you'd start putting straight-up lies in your reports..."

"Honestly, I probably should have given them a mix of truth and fiction all along."

"Uh, isn't that what you've been doing all along?"

"No. I made sure to draw a line. But now I need to cross it—since these people are actually reading my reports, I should assume the Princess has been

---

[23] 楽観的 RAKKANTEKI "view pleasantly" vs. 悲観的 HIKANTEKI pessimistic 悲しい KANASHII sad
[24] 抱き合わせ DAKIAWASE packaging together; forced purchase
[25] 追い風 OIKAZE "chasing wind" tailwind
[26] 苦手 NIGATE "bitter (eschewed) hand (opponent)" not one's favorite
[27] 微妙 BIMYŌ dicey; sensitive shares first character with 微刀 BITO

reading every word I write. If like a fool I wrote things down exactly as they happened, she would have everything she need to pull the rug right out from under me."

"We can't have that—things are finally going well for us. We can't get waylaid[28] now."

"Yeah, but it seems the Princess has been observing our Sword Hunt from a different vantage point than all the others... She's more than just curious, she must be up to something... How foolish of me. I can't believe I failed to consider that Princess Negative would be among the readers of those first reports."

"Too late now. I guess you weren't expecting her to pop back up again?"

"Guess not. Still, this way of seeing things raises a lot of questions about what Emonzaemon has been up to..."

"Hmm...you know, I've been wondering about him too. But hey, I think I get it now. I've figured it out, Togame. The whole political thing aside, you're basically making a feint against the bakufu, right?"

"That's the idea. What can I say, attracting attention isn't always a good thing. I suppose that discouraging the wrong kind of attention has allowed me to enact my schemes however I please thus far—but things have changed. Operating with a disregard for others will no longer do. And I'm not only talking about Princess Negative."

Come again?

This wasn't intricate—it was plain complicated.[29]

That said, there was no way that Togame was going to ask for Shichika to help her out with any of this, so there would likely be no problem if he left it up to her.

This was a division of labor.[30]

It would be best for Shichika—to tackle only simple topics.

The simplest and most approachable of conversations.

"So, you're gonna tell them we found *something* in Lake Fuyo at the former site of Kiki Shikizaki's workshop? Well—what are you gonna say we found?"

"That's why we're going to Tendo. To figure things out. At this point, we have no choice but to use Hohoh's information as a starting point."

"Even though it might be a trap?"

Information from that old fox[31] of a ninja.

Hohoh Maniwa—head of a ninja clan that perpetrated one betrayal after another.

The chances of this all being some kind of trap—

"Who cares if it's a trap," said Togame. "Sounds like fun.[32] And if it's not a trap, all the better—I wouldn't say we stand to lose that much."

Hearing her voice, Shichika thought she sounded pretty confident. At the

---

[28] 横槍を入れられ　YOKOYARI WO IRERARE　"speared from the side"
[29] 小難しい　難しい　KOMUZUKASHII MUZUKASHII　"small-difficult" fastidious　difficult
[30] 役割分担　YAKUWARI BUNTAN　splitting up roles vs. 分業 BUNGYŌ (economic) division of labor
[31] 海千山千　UMISEN YAMASEN　"thousand seas, thousand mountains"　versed in the way of the world
[32] 一興　IKKYŌ　"point/moment of interest"　an amusement

very least, he was convinced this course of action was a choice, and not simply the last option[33] that they had.

"Do you have any leads there?"

"I'm not so sure I'd call it that—but what I will say is in Tendo, there's a dojo where we're bound to find our footing."

"Dojo?"

"Yup," Togame nodded resolutely.

And briefed him on the plan for what came next.

"In Tendo, in Dewa—we're going to pay a visit to Shogi Village, and the dojo of the Heartland School."

■ ■

The following month.

In the ninth moon.

Where the tale began, they got an answer from Zanki Kiguchi.

"As Master of the Heartland School—I regret to inform you that I will not relinquish Oto the Cured for any reason."

---

[33] 消去法　SHŌKYOHŌ　process of elimination

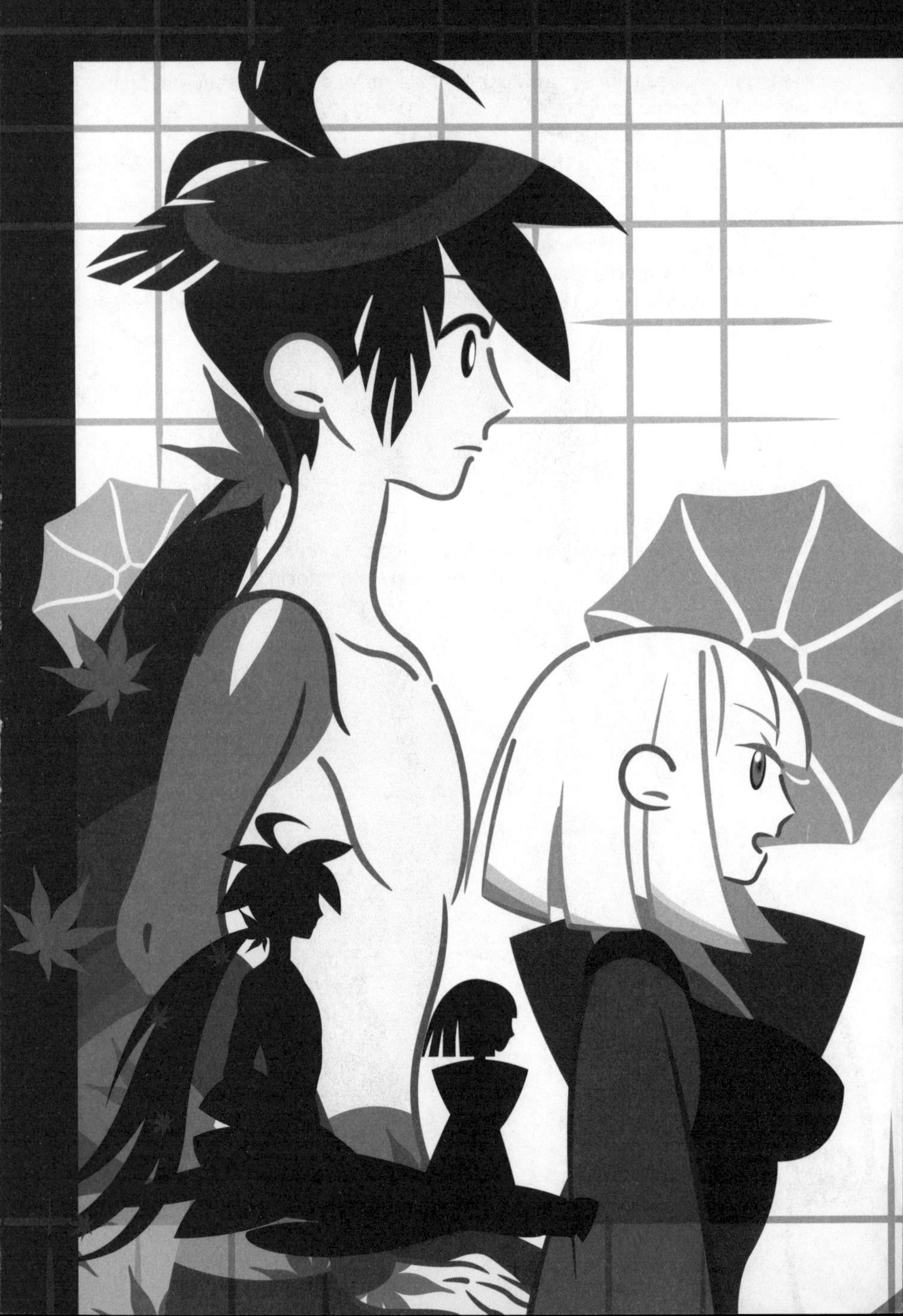

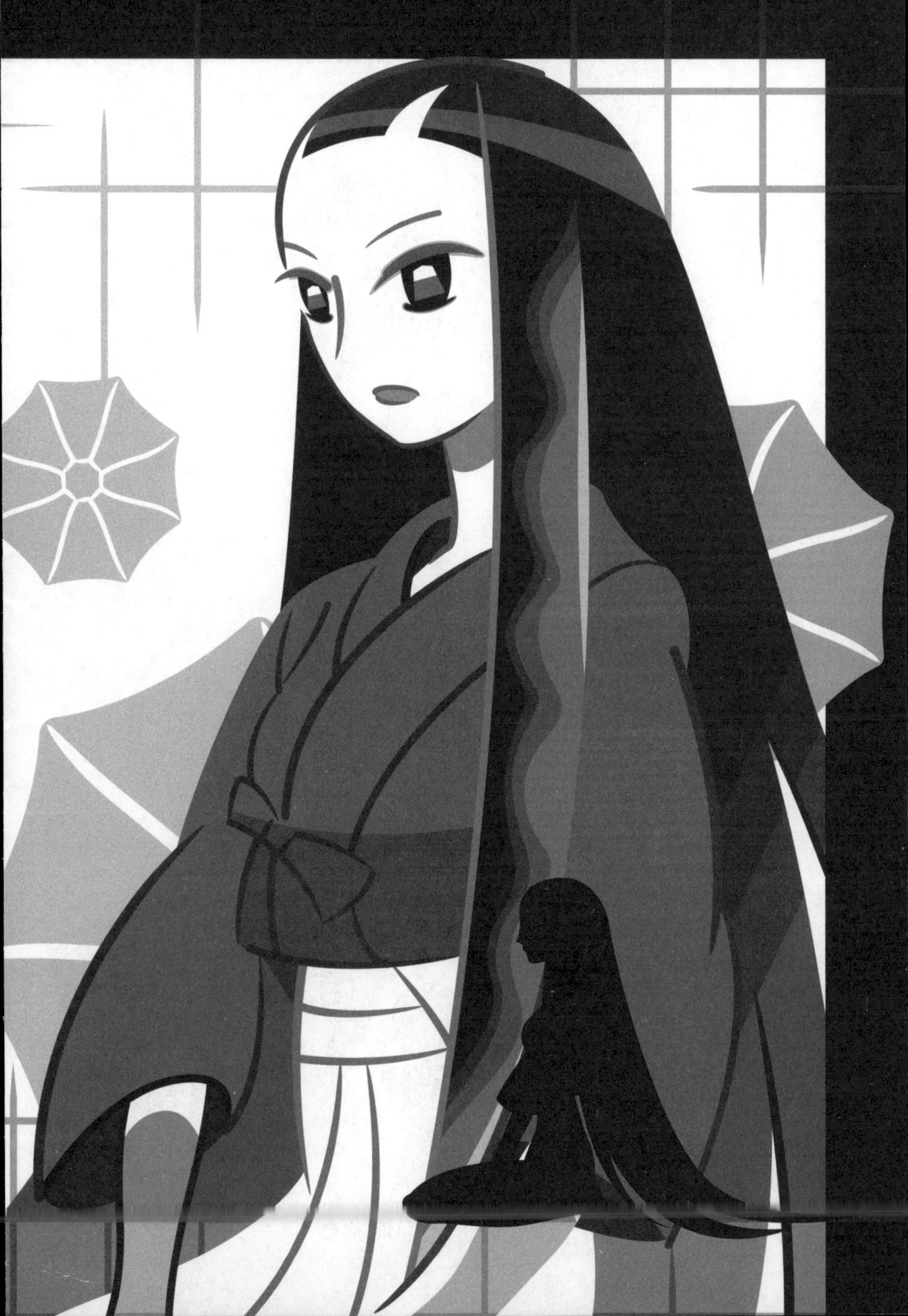

CHAPTER TWO

ZANKI KIGUCHI

■ ■

If Ganryu Island in Suo, where once upon a time a man bearing a greatsword fought another bearing two, and Seiryoin Gokenji Temple on Mt. Sayabashiri in Tosa, encompassing the Katana Buddha, are the Two Great Holy Sites for swordsmen, then Shogi Village in Tendo, in Dewa, is the holy land of shogi players.

Shogi[1] has its origins in India.

By the Heian period, the game had made it to Japan.

In the era of our story, where the Owari Bakufu has unified the land, ushering in an age of peace and order, during which no large-scale wars broke out besides the late rebellion, tacticians used the shogi board as a mock battlefield, competing over games to gauge each other's fitness in the art of war—in other words, at this point in Japanese history, shogi was much more than a parlor game.

Although Togame the Schemer dealt exclusively in schemes, by definition she was certainly a tactician, and knew her way around the shogi board—which is why, thus far in her career, she had visited Shogi Village in Tendo on multiple occasions.

Which is why.

She had long known there was a dojo there for swordplay—and about the Heartland School.

■ ■

"Guess the master—was a new generation."

The next day.

Taking refuge in a local inn, under a pseudonym as always, our two travelers had enjoyed a good night's sleep, to soothe the aches of travel, and were breaking their fast.

Holy sites are also tourist destinations. They had their pick of all the inns (as luck would have it, they had evidently shown up in the off-season, when the village was not overrun with tourists), and the breakfast brought directly to their room was passable.[2]

"New generation, huh?"

Setting down his chopsticks after eating, Shichika thought back to the day before.

[1] 将棋　SHŌGI　a Japanese board game using pieces and moves much like those of chess
[2] それなりのもの　SORENARI NO MONO　adequate; as one might expect

Thinking about that stately dojo, situated in the middle of the village—and the master of the dojo, Zanki Kiguchi.

Tall for a woman—though on closer examination, not as conspicuously tall as Meisai Tsuruga, from a few months back. It must have been her fabulous posture. That makes people look bigger than they really are.

Long tresses[3] of black hair—probably as long as Togame's was until quite recently.

As for her physique, she was quite thin.

She didn't come across as someone who had honed her body.

Yet Shichika could not ignore the aura[4] that pervaded her and almost filled the room.

It made him hesitant to approach her.

Gracious as she may be.

Kiguchi—had the poise of a drawn katana.

"She seems to be—about your age," Togame said.

"So, like twenty-four or something? Hmm...I'm not saying she looks younger, but I have a hard time guessing how old women are."

"Hah. You would, I guess."

"I mean, it's obvious you're way younger than me, Togame."

"Cheerio!"

Slugged him one.

It had been a long time since she slugged him good.

As you'll recall, Togame was the older one—a fact of which Shichika was well aware, which made it clear to her this was some kind of joke.

They were just playing around.

"Who're you calling a waif[5] here, who?"

"Nah, I didn't say anything like that..."

"Thanks to this haircut from your sister, I'll admit that I look more childlike than before."

"Nobody's asking for you to admit anything..."

Shichika shook his head, at a loss.

"Funny, though." He would just as soon move on to something else. "I mean, doesn't it sort of feel like we're back in the early days of the Sword Hunt? Until now, it's been one off-kilter[6] encounter after the other—"

"Yeah, for at least the last three months."

Konayuki Itezora—Soto the Twin.

Nanami Yasuri—Akuto the Eel.

Skytron—Bito the Sundial.

Each of which had something about them that outshined the Sword Hunt as it were.

Of course, nothing had changed about their dedication to the Sword Hunt—

[3] 直手 CHOKUMŌ "straight hair"
[4] 気迫 KIHAKU spirit
[5] 童子属性 DŌJI ZOKUSEI "young-child attributes" Lolita-like
[6] 変則的 HENSOKUTEKI "odd/changed rules" irregular, atypical

it had simply been a long while since they confronted one of the owners of the Twelve Possessed on such proper terms.

"I guess we're lucky that Oto the Cured was passed down by the Masters of Heartland Dojo like you predicted?"

"Hmm, hard to say. I don't know."

Wearing a face of consternation, Togame folded her arms.

"It's hard to say?"

"Yeah. This is not the situation I foresaw. All I said was that by visiting the hallowed dojo of the Heartland School, we had a decent chance of gleaning some more information on the Twelve Possessed."

Finishing her breakfast after Shichika, Togame rested her chopsticks on the table.

"We're lucky to have come in contact with Oto the Cured comparatively easily, sure, but I wouldn't call it good luck that the sword is being guarded[7] by *that woman, in that space.*"

"Why?"

"Because we aren't here simply on a journey to discover swords. We've come to bring them home. I'm thinking that we're in for another bumpy ride. That woman—Zanki Kiguchi is the Twelfth Master of her school."

"Hmph."

Shichika had to agree.

From the little they had spoken, he could tell. Zanki Kiguchi was *unlike any of the other owners* they had met thus far—she was a different breed of human being entirely.

Unlike Komori Maniwa, or Ginkaku Uneri, or Meisai Tsuruga, or Hakuhei Sabi, or Kanara Azekura, or Konayuki Itezora, or Nanami Yasuri, or Skytron—

She was quite simply—an honest citizen.[8]

"Unlike all the other owners, she has no glaring character flaw—either that's a product of a robust will, or it's what makes Oto the Cured so special—"

"The Cured, huh."

Kiguchi.

Making it clear she was not giving up the sword—she had encouraged Shichika and Togame to take a closer look at Oto the Cured, one of the Twelve Possessed of Kiki Shikizaki.

This sword—was made of wood.

Less than three feet long, including the handle.

Being wooden, it lacked both sheath and tsuba.

And nothing like a temper line across its blade.

Only the natural woodgrain—nothing more.

It had the feeling of a bygone era—but somehow made you feel like it had been carved only hours earlier, thus puzzling whosoever looked upon it.

This could only mean it had been properly maintained.

---

[7] 保有　HOYŪ　possess
[8] 真人間　MANINGEN　true (good) human being　often, who has reformed

Just one look, and it was easy to imagine—the care with which the Zanki Kiguchis of yesteryear had passed Oto the Cured down through the generations.

Which is precisely why.

Interrupting the tradition would be challenging—

"At first, I almost missed this, but how can this thing be a katana if it's made of wood? Who's being cured here? Is it just gonna snap in two? After all those wacky swords not even shaped like swords, I barely stopped to wonder."

"Shichika, don't raise these questions. It'll only get tiresome."

Togame slowly shook her head.

Resigned.[9]

"I will say this. The fact that the Cured turned out to be a wooden sword just proves how little we knew going in—among the Twelve Possessed, this one was especially mysterious. As curious as I am to learn the premise under which the Cured was crafted, and what the sword is all about in general, our chief concern is with its owner, Zanki Kiguchi. If she's already this uncooperative, not even entertaining our request, it seems there's little room for practicing diplomacy."

"Yeah, the fact that she actually is so open to conversation at the same time is what makes this so hard. Oh well... And, Togame, you knew the previous Zanki Kiguchi? Like her father or whatever?"

"Not her father, but her grandfather. They say her father died quite young. There was some question of who would carry on the family line, but it evidently went to the former master's granddaughter—which means the Zanki Kiguchi that I knew is dead and gone."

"Maybe he just stepped down[10]—although it seems as if she's living in that dojo on her own. That would make sense...but Togame. What's up with her being the only person in that enormous dojo? That time of day, aren't dojos usually full of followers?"[11]

"Ah. Good question."

Looking a little stumped, Togame stalled a moment before attempting an explanation.

"The answer has much to do with the history of the village—but I'm afraid if I dig too deep, you'll just stop listening to me. Hm...I guess I'll just give you the highlights, to make things as simple for you as possible. Alright, Shichika. Once upon a time, this area was famous for its swordplay."

"Huh? Doesn't look that way at all."

The place seemed more concerned with culture than with war. Heartland Dojo may have been smack dab in the middle of the village, in what might well be called prime real estate,[12] but it felt absurdly out of place. Today, this was the only school for swordplay, or anything like it, in the village.

"Like I said—once upon a time. I'm speaking historically. Listen, Shichika. After the Age of Warring States, the Old Shogun's fall from power, and the rise

---

[9] 諦め顔 AKIRAME GAO "give-up face"
[10] 引退 INTAI retire
[11] 門下生 MONKASEI "students under the gate" pupils of a school of martial arts
[12] 一等地 ITTŌCHI "first-class land"

of the Owari Bakufu, there were far less opportunities for swordplay—and as times changed, people had to change their way of life. As a result, most of the schools went out of fashion."

"Out of fashion?"[13]

Her cut-and-dry wording unnerved Shichika—but Togame carried on, not wavering the slightest in the timbre of her speech.

"The schools went out of fashion. How else can I describe it? Unlike you with the Kyotoryu, or Ginkaku Uneri with the Uneriryu, or all the Maniwa Bosses and their ninpo—the swordsmen of this village were adaptive, not fixated upon adhering to a rigid code. Lucky for them, the village had a custom that easily took the place of swordplay."

"You mean—shogi?"

This was—the holy land of shogi players.

Raised on a desert island, Shichika had no idea how to play shogi, but after their first night staying in the village, he understood how much this game pervaded village life.

Tellingly, a shogi board had even been left on the table of their room.

It wouldn't have surprised him if a Shogi Buddha stood behind the dojo.

"So? You're saying all the swordsmen in the area gave up swordplay?"

"Not all of them. Just one, the last of them, didn't: Twelfth Master Zanki Kiguchi."

Twelfth Master of the Heartland School.

Her school was a known quantity in the bakufu.

But in spite of having such a reputation, it had no followers and no heir to the tradition—oh, how the mighty fall.

All that remained was a handsome dojo.

And inside—Oto the Cured.

"Makes sense why she wouldn't wanna hand over the sword. It's like the pride of her school. It symbolizes[14] the tradition."

"Yeah. Which makes diplomacy even harder."

"For the Kyotoryu it'd be like someone asking me to chop off one of my arms."

"Uh, I wouldn't go that far."

No, thought Shichika. *Not like giving up my arm—but giving up my heart.*

"When was that—oh, right. Just before I fought Ginkaku Uneri. Remember what you said, Togame? *What would you do if a good guy had one of these swords.* Is that what we're up against this time around?"

"Whether or not Zanki Kiguchi is honest remains to be seen—but that would appear to be the situation. Which wouldn't be a problem, if like Konayuki she was willing to negotiate—but it seems that's off the table."

"Yeah," Shichika nodded. "She doesn't seem like someone who would risk losing her sword to get a leg up, either. It seems like Oto the Cured is real

---

[13] 廃れた SUTARETA became obsolete, died out
[14] 証明 SHŌMEI proof

important to her, but I get the sense she doesn't care about the other Shikizaki blades. That's what sets her apart from Meisai Tsuruga—and unlike Kanara Azekura, she isn't asking for something unrelated to katana."

"Thanks for reminding me of that. Hmph. I must say, for a person such as myself, she is probably the most frustrating enemy imaginable—Kiguchi has no wants or vanity, but is nevertheless noble and proud. I still have no idea what to expect out of the Cured, but I'll say this much. That woman walks the path of righteousness."[15]

"Was the last Zanki Kiguchi like that too?"

"We never exactly made acquaintances.[16] As the Schemer, I take great pains not to stray into the line of fire[17]—though I've heard he was a great man. So great that even I, clear of the line of fire, know how great he was. It's possible the man himself[18] knew of the Kyotoryu as well—but Kiguchi, meaning the current master, is apparently too young for that."

"We've really become nobodies over the past twenty years."

Not like Shichika desired celebrity.[19]

But as the *current master* of his own school, he felt a touch of sadness.

"Such is life. Well, what next?—with the way things are, it almost makes me wish the Cured was not in Tendo, and still a mystery..."

Togame sighed, demonstrating her exasperation.

But something she had said got Shichika thinking.

"Okay. But since we did find one of the Twelve Possessed in Tendo—that means that all the information Hohoh has ever given us, every bit of it, was absolutely true. Including the resurgence of the Princess, and when he told us about sis on Mt. Odori—not a single lie."

The ninja—had been honest. And yet this only made his actions more suspicious.

Even Shichika was able to see that.

In other words.

He must be getting something out of this—*why else would the Maniwa give up such priceless information?*

"I'm pretty sure there's no trap waiting for us here, but I still think this alliance has a flip side—or perhaps Hohoh simply had total confidence."

"Total—confidence?"

"I'm saying he must have been confident that distracting us would give the Maniwa a chance to snag the three remaining swords—Seito the Garland, Dokuto the Basilisk, and Ento the Bead. Who knows what bizarre tricks the Maniwa have up their sleeves—or lack thereof.[20] Their ninpo is beyond me."

"Yeah, but that's a good thing, right? You said yourself that it'd be way easier

---

[15] 王道を歩む　ŌDŌ WO AYUMU　take the royal road
[16] 面識　MENSHIKI　"face knowledge"
[17] 武道方面　BUDŌ HŌMEN　"martial arts region"
[18] ご仁　GOJIN　a respectful way of referring to a third party
[19] 知名度　CHIMEIDO　degree to which a name is known　a modern term
[20] どのようなものがあるのか　DONOYŌNA MONO GA ARUNOKA　[the "sleeves" pun isn't in the original]

to let the Maniwa track down the other swords, so that we could have a showdown over everything that each side has, winner take all—"

"Well, that's one way of looking at it, but there's no guarantee that things would work out nicely—and I see little reason to be optimistic. Besides, even if we took that route," Togame the Schemer steered them back on topic, "if Hohoh's information is all true, we won't be getting anywhere unless we take Oto the Cured. We may need to dig our heels in. But what we really need to do is..."

As she spoke—Togame reached for the shogi board left for them on the table. Well, not for the board itself, but for the box of pieces that sat on top of it.

Opening the lid, she took out a random piece.

"Play the game—that might be our only way[21] in."

"You mean...play shogi?" Shichika was having a hard time understanding. "How would shogi give us a way in?"

"Because as luck would have it, in this town, all disputes are settled over shogi, as a matter of course."

The circumstances under which they had discovered Oto the Cured were far from good, even with the rosiest of glasses[22]—but Togame smiled anyway, bold as ever.

■ ■

Only the heart can slay what chokes the heart.[23]

Hence the name Zanki.

The next day, Shichika and Togame paid another visit to Heartland Dojo, home of Twelfth Master Zanki Kiguchi.

They called her from the gate, but no one answered—so they took it upon themselves to walk onto the grounds. Judging from the spirited cries echoing from within, it seemed Kiguchi was home alright—and sure enough, they found her in the middle of the dojo, swinging her sword alone.[24]

Alone.

Swinging a wooden sword—in the middle of the dojo.

Oto the Cured—Shichika could feel the lifeforce. He was certain. After all, if he had failed to sense the lifeforce emanated by all Mutant Blades when they were handling the Cured two days before, he could never have been certain that this was the Cured at all.

An official appraiser of the Twelve Possessed.

But Kiguchi really uses the Cured to practice?

---

[21] 取っ掛かり　TOKKAKARI　handhold
[22] お世辞にも　OSEJI NI MO　even as flattery
[23] 心の鬼を心で斬る。これをもって 慚愧　KOKORO NO ONI WO KOKORO DE KIRU. KORE WO MOTTE ZANKI
　　　cutting, with the heart, the demon in one's heart—thus *shame* (which combines the first four kanji)
[24] 素振り　SUBURI　"plain swings"　analogous to shadowboxing

He'd reckoned she would keep it somewhere safe most of the time.
"Hayah! Whah! Dah!"
Voice ringing loud, Kiguchi swung the wooden sword—Oto the Cured.

After training for who knows how many hours, her body was drenched in sweat. And yet her posture remained perfect, and Shichika could tell that it would stay that way. Throughout the sequences, she maintained perfect posture, from one moment to the next, no matter how she swung the wooden sword.

—Almost too perfect.

Of all the swordsmen Shichika had seen thus far, in training or in battle—Ginkaku Uneri and Hakuhei Sabi...the former swordsman Meisai Tsuruga...his father Mutsue Yasuri...the staggering genius Nanami Yasuri...and all the others he had met in dojos in the Capital or fought along the way—every one of them had something rough or loose[25] about their style, but he did not sense this coming from Zanki Kiguchi.

She went all out.

One hundred percent.

Pushing her body to the limit—swinging her sword to the brink of collapse. As if she wasn't one misstep away from splitting the precious sword in two—

This isn't going to be easy.

Shichika was sure of that.

She was a model owner of a Mutant Blade.

In that sense, perhaps using the Cured to practice revealed how deeply her dedication was ingrained.

Her ingrained dedication—to that sword of wood.

"..."

Zanki Kiguchi.

Her majestic, forthright fighting style convinced Shichika that she would be a painful adversary—and while the fact that she fought fairly offered some relief, he saw little reason to be optimistic either.

Thing is.

He would only get to fight her if Togame did some fancy footwork, in her diplomacy.

"Hayah! Whah! Dah!"

Continuing through her forms, Zanki Kiguchi almost acted like she hadn't noticed Togame and Shichika step into her dojo uninvited—in fact, perhaps she hadn't noticed after all.

As admirable as her concentration was, you had to call her somewhat careless for allowing them to do so.

Missing the opportunity to call her name again, they stood by idly and watched Zanki Kiguchi train—and went unnoticed, until after she had finished the prescribed number of rounds.

"...Huh?"

---

[25] 余裕、遊び　YOYŪ, ASOBI　wiggle room, or play

Mopping her forehead with a tenugui.
Kiguchi acted surprised.
"Weren't you two here—just yesterday?"
"We're back," declared Togame.
Swagger will only go so far in justifying a rude opener like that.
Shichika found himself bowing his head.
Meanwhile, Kiguchi—faced with these two intruders, because that is what they were—bowed to them from the waist.
Then raising her head with perfect posture, she said, "If you'll excuse me, I just need to freshen up."
"No, you're fine," Togame told her, "as you are."
By the way, Togame had identified herself the day before—as being Togame the Schemer, Grand Commander of Arms of the Yanari Shogunate Military Directorate, Owari Bakufu. Furthermore, she had insisted that this second coming of the Sword Hunt was being carried out "for the sake of the nation"—making her position clear.[26]
Given Kiguchi's personality, Togame had surmised that she would hand over Oto the Cured quite willingly, but this was wishful thinking.
Her answer was as stated above.
"Madame Togame."
Kiguchi's tone was gracious, but her answer had not changed.
"You are welcome anytime—but as the Master of the Heartland School, I will not relinquish Oto the Cured. This wooden sword is the pride of the Heartland School, and verifies that I am the school's master."
"Okay. I get the picture—I'm not trying to have the same conversation twice. But I hope that you can understand why we are disinclined to thank you and be on our way."
"If you must resort to violence—"
Zanki Kiguchi—raised her wooden sword.
Her reflexes were perfect.[27]
"I'll answer you in kind. Go on, I'm ready."
"Whoa, easy..."
This was too much even for Togame.
Kiguchi, though not quick-tempered—was quick to draw.[28]
Because this sword was made of wood, Togame was more hesitant to resort to violence than she had been for all the other Mutant Blades. Except perhaps for Hakuto the Whisper, it was surely far more delicate than steel. One false move, and Oto the Cured would be reduced to splinters.
And if the sword was broken, they would have nothing to collect—therefore, ideally.
They would reach a mutual agreement, before the tumult of the battle!

[26] 率直 SOCCHOKU frank
[27] 即応 SOKUŌ "instant reply"
[28] 短気 短絡的 TANKI TANRAKUTEKI "short spirit" easily perturbed "short circuit" simplistic

"If you give us a chance," said Togame, "I'm sure that we can work this thing out peaceably. It's poor form to send a visitor away."[29]

"..."

"As long as I can verify that you have the right caliber to be the owner of Oto the Cured, then my work here is done."

"Is that—it? But..."

Kiguchi sounded unconvinced—this was no favorable reaction. If you read into her gestures, it appeared that she was trying to find a way to rid herself of a couple of pesky visitors.

But Togame was relentless.

All she had to do was mix her up—and wriggle her way in.

"Madame Kiguchi, I would like for you to join me for a game of shogi—and providing that I come away victorious, I would then request for you and Shichika Yasuri, the Seventh Master of the Kyotoryu, to have a contest over who can keep Oto the Cured."

---

[29] 門前払い MONZEN BARAI "shoo from the gates" reject outright; not even give the time of day

CHAPTER THREE

THE FOLLOWER

■ ■

The outcome was deplorable.[1]

Though not because Togame the Schemer lost to Zanki Kiguchi in their game of shogi—on the contrary, she beat her host, which was exactly what she had planned to do.

All disputes were settled over shogi.

While this may have been something of an exaggeration, it was true enough to call a rule in Tendo—though even if this was the holy land of shogi players, there were surely people here and there who never played. If Zanki Kiguchi had fallen into this category,[2] the scheme would have gone nowhere, but the other day, when they first visited Heartland Dojo, the keen Schemer had not failed to espy a shogi board positioned in the alcove.

If the terms had simply been "Fight Shichika, and if he wins, we get to have Oto the Cured," Kiguchi would probably have refused—in which case Togame would be unable to receive consent, pushing them out of the realm of negotiation and into that of violence.

Considering the possibility that Kiguchi would sooner snap the Cured in half than let someone outside the Heartland School take it away, those terms would never do—so Togame introduced a buffer or two.

They would play a game of shogi.

But the game would not directly impact the result—if Togame won at shogi, Kiguchi would fight Shichika, creating a second opportunity for Togame to convince their adversary to cooperate.

For Kiguchi, beating Togame in their game of shogi[3] would yield the status quo,[4] but even if she lost against Togame, all she would have to do toward maintaining the status quo was defeat Shichika—thus safeguarding Oto the Cured. It would appear the stakes were fairly low.

The Heartland School was not designed for taking life, but giving life.

In turn, it forswore unnecessary conflict, being a discipline of swordplay for its own sake—although to witness Kiguchi practice in the Heartland Dojo was to know that she had no shortage of faith in her abilities.

There was no telling how skilled she would be at shogi, but by dint of living in this village, if she played at all then surely she had some degree of confidence.

As a pretext for getting rid of a liaison from the bakufu, going along with what Togame had proposed would likely be a tempting option for Kiguchi—but once they had her onboard, the circumstances would prove to be quite satisfac-

---

[1] 惨敗　ZANPAI　miserable defeat
[2] 類　TAGUI　variety, sort in biology, 類　RUI genus
[3] 対局　TAIKYOKU　a bout of the game go or shogi
[4] それで問題ない　SOREDE MONDAI NAI　would make it a non-problem

tory indeed for capturing Oto the Cured.

Togame had a knack for shogi.

Her skill was known throughout the bakufu.

Indeed, though her prior visits to the village had been predominantly as a military advisor, not missing the opportunity to have some fun in this holy land of shogi players, she had behaved like a proper tourist—which was rare for her. An unsurprising hobby for a tactician, one might say, yet she did display extraordinary ability.

When she faced off against Kiguchi, she found her host to be quite skilled in her own right—but Togame made light work[5] of her.

Without letting on that it was light work for her, naturally.

One hundred and seventy-eight moves.

It would only be unhelpful to run through every single move, so let us dispense with a play-by-play[6]—and just say that Togame pretended that they were evenly matched. In that sense, she'd played not against Kiguchi, but against the shogi board itself.

There is no greater headache than staging an entire game of shogi.

Yet it would never do to win so overwhelmingly that it upset Kiguchi. At the end of the day, this game of shogi was no more than a skirmish[7] before the actual battle for Oto the Cured.

To put it another way, Togame had seen little reason to go easy on Kiguchi—to say the least, the match had been a league above the games she played for fun back in Owari.

"I'm out. You got me."

Kiguchi apparently had no regrets about the outcome—and resigned the game with gusto. So much gusto, in fact, that Togame realized that playing for real may have been an option.

But she was not here to delight herself in games of shogi—she was here for what came next.

Or what she hoped was next.

And yet one could fairly say that things turned into a farce—completely fell apart, even—because Kiguchi was such an honest person.

"Alright then," Kiguchi said, standing from the shogi board.

Dressed in the same gi as earlier.

Oto the Cured had sat beside her the whole match—she barely parted with it, carrying it everywhere she went.

Which meant that she was always ready for action.

She showed no sign of shying from the fight with Shichika (who, oblivious to how shogi was played, seemed bored throughout the game).

She welcomed it—with gusto.

This is when Twelfth Master Zanki Kiguchi truly won Togame over.

---

[5] うまくあしらった UMAKU ASHIRATTA handled it/her well
[6] 棋譜 KIFU a breakdown of a game of go or shogi
[7] 前哨戦 ZENSHŌSEN preliminary match

Perhaps she simply had the peace of mind now to see Kiguchi as a person. As confident as Togame had been in her abilities, there had been no guarantee that Kiguchi would not defeat[8] her. In the world of shogi, there is no way that you can size a player up without seeing them play.

"You must be tired from the game," Togame ventured. "Feel free to take a break."

"That won't be necessary."

Kiguchi had yet to relax her expression.

"If I may, I come from warrior lineage—and a warrior never goes back on her word. I am prepared to risk Oto the Cured, the trademark[9] of the Heartland School, according to the terms we have agreed upon. Let us begin."

Kiguchi gave off the impression of a string pulled taut—no wonder she declined to take a break.

"Soooo..."

Worlds away from this high-strung demeanor, a happy-go-lucky Shichika sat himself up (he had been sprawled out on the floor) and doffed his armguards.

His sandals he had left outside the dojo.

Happy-go-lucky? Sure—but now Shichika was ready for action, too, just like Kiguchi.

"Okay, let's get started—you know, I don't think that I've fought against a wooden sword since we were in the Capital. Don't worry, your sword is real important to us too. We won't break it. It's gonna be fine. Nothing's gonna happen to the Cured—*not if you're torn to smithereens.*"

Togame winced at this premature deployment of his catchphrase—and with good reason, as she would find out presently.

"Understood. Now, Master Shichika—as it would appear that you have not brought your own gear, I would be happy to provide you with a wooden sword and pads."

Zanki Kiguchi made this offer sound absolutely natural.

"Huh?" Shichika was stunned. "W-Wooden sword—and pads?"

"Yes. Please, don't be shy—we have loads of equipment leftover from when the school had followers. It may be vintage, but not to worry, I've kept it all in good condition. Though most of the pads will probably be too small for you, I'm sure we'll find something that will fit."

"U-Um..." Shichika could not hide his befuddlement. "Er, how can I put this... I don't use swords or pads..."

"What?"

With that.

Kiguchi's gaze, already sharp, grew twice as sharp.

"Are you playing games with me? If you spar[10] me without pads on, what happens if you hurt yourself?"

---

[8] 上回らない　UWA MAWARA NAI　not come out on top
[9] 看板　KANBAN　(store) sign; emblem
[10] 実戦稽古　JISSEN KEIKO　"actual-battle training"

"H-Hurt myself?"
"And not using a sword! Quit pulling my leg."
"It's just, the Kyotoryu—"
—*Oh.*
She must not know.
"Using my body as a sword is what makes me the Kyotoryu—so, uh, I can fight without a sword."
"If you don't stop joking around, I'm going to get seriously angry."
Kiguchi gave no credence to what Shichika was saying.
Standoffish[11] to the extreme.
"Yeah, but—"
"How can a swordsman fight without a sword!"
Too late. Shichika had pushed her far enough.
Kiguchi was already seriously angry.
"Are you honestly asking me to let you fight me without pads or a sword? That would be a disgrace[12] to the Heartland School!"
"..."
"If you're adamant about not needing a weapon or protection, I'll have to ask you to leave—I have no interest in taking gross advantage of a helpless individual!"
Totally lost, Shichika shot a glance to Togame, who was still sitting by the shogi board—but the Schemer was as baffled as him by this turn of events.
Though Shichika had no weapons.
He was a lethal weapon in his own right.
While his form of swordplay hardly left him helpless, she could not deny that in the eyes of the world, it must have looked like he was emptyhanded, or practicing karate. That said, Togame had honestly never imagined this to be grounds for refusing to do battle.
Confronting an unarmed adversary, most enemies let their guard down, assuming they would have the upper hand—even those who knew about the Kyotoryu inevitably underestimated it on that account. True, here and there, someone like Meisai Tsuruga would take the nature of the Kyotoryu into consideration and snooker him with traps—
But Kiguchi was the opposite.
In fact.
She wanted Shichika to be armed, albeit with a wooden sword!
"Sh-Shichika."
"Y-Yeah."
"Sorry. I don't know what to say."
"...nkk!"
As this was to be a good, clean fight on principle—Shichika could not possibly refuse.

---

[11] 取り付く島もない TORITSUKU SHIMA MO NAI "not even an island to cling to" inaccessible
[12] 侮辱 BUJOKU insult

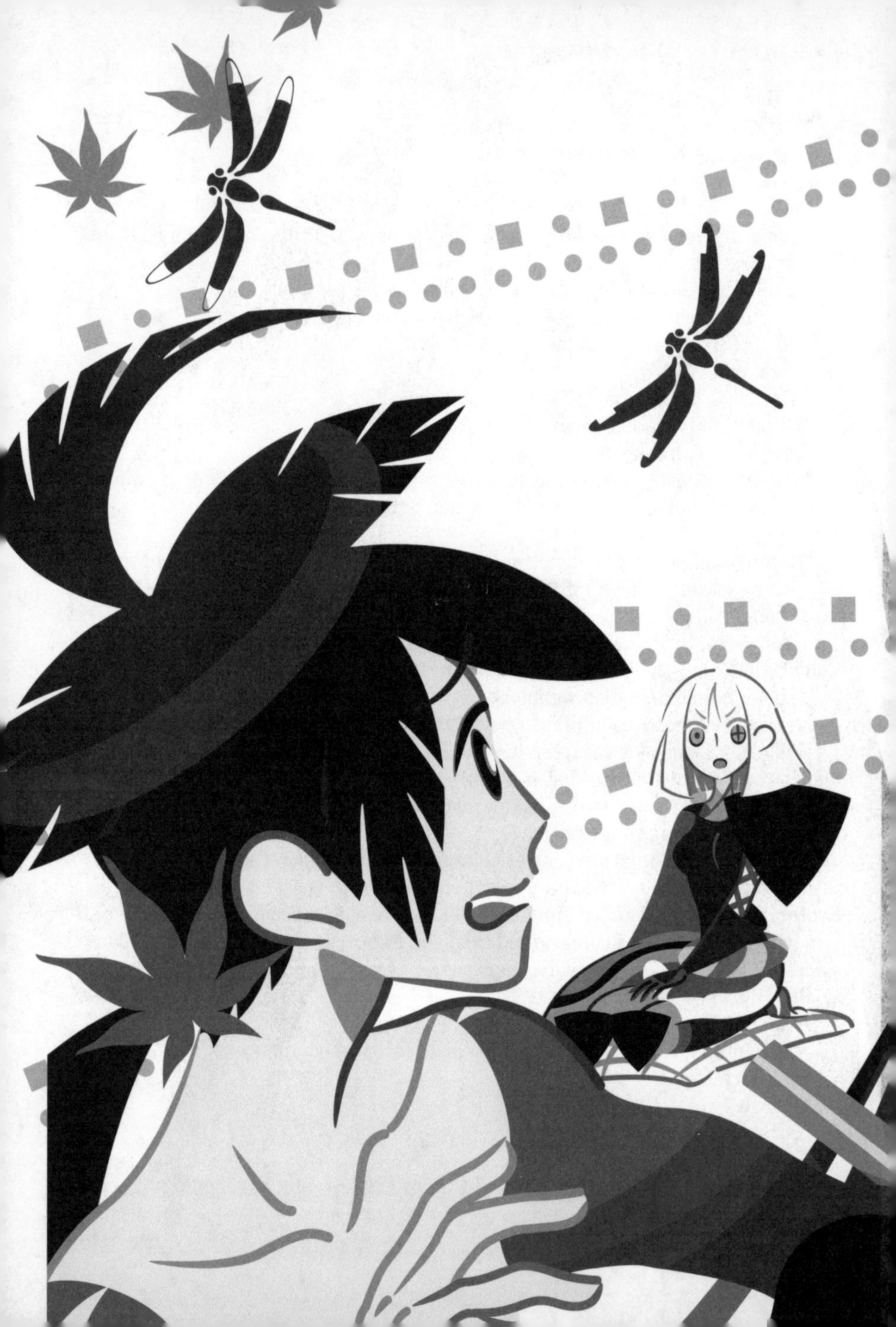

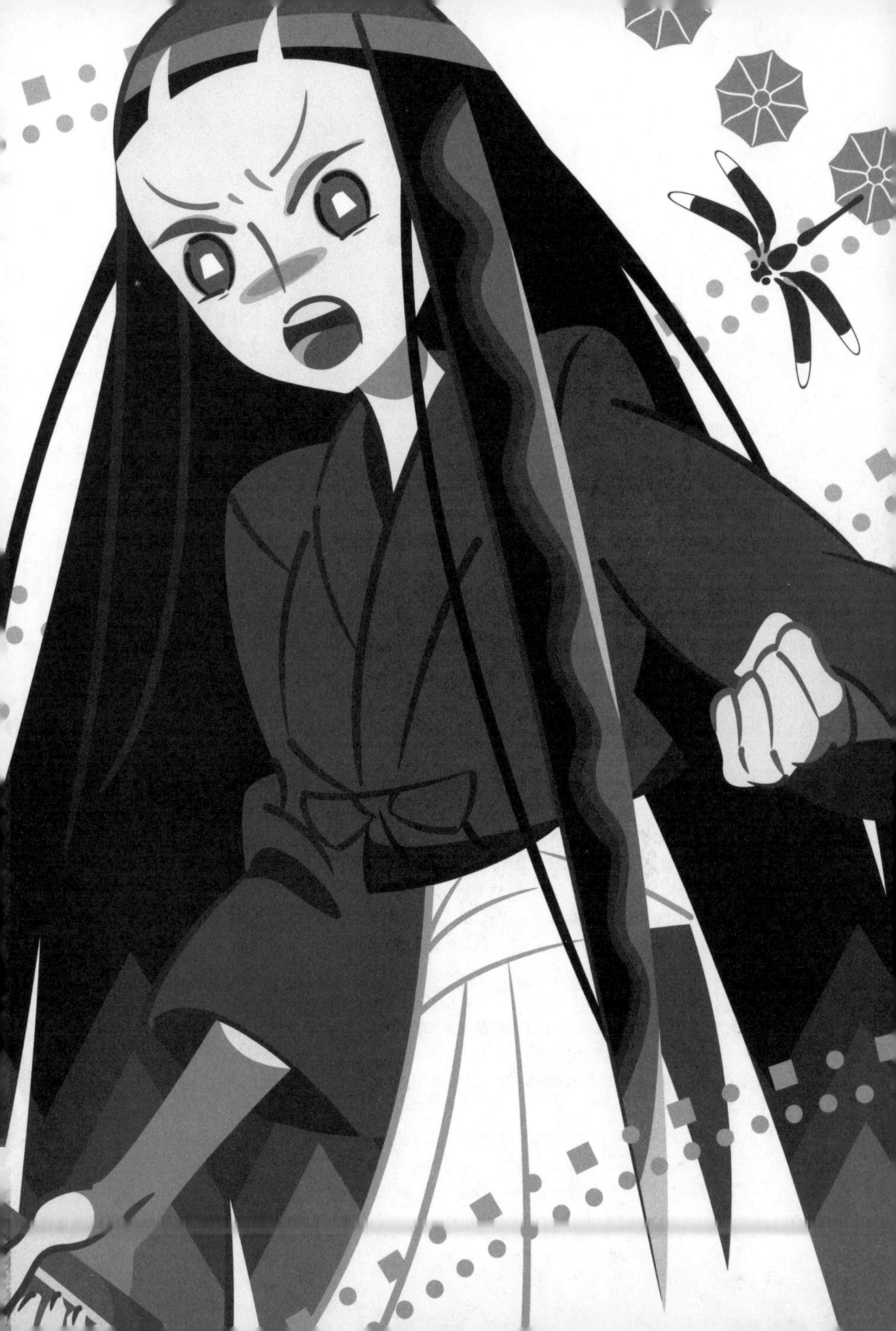

And thus Shichika Yasuri, the swordless swordsman.
Had no choice but to fight using a wooden sword—and sure enough.
The outcome was deplorable.

■ ■

Thus far on the Sword Hunt for the Twelve Possessed of Kiki Shikizaki, Shichika Yasuri had elsewhere been defeated twice—first, on Mt. Odori in Ezo, in his initial bout with Konayuki Itezora, and again at Gokenji Temple in Tosa, versus Nanami Yasuri. Since in both cases they ultimately captured the Mutant Blades they sought, Togame had insisted that they not count these as defeats (besides, in his fight against Nanami, if not against Konayuki, he had more than made up for the initial poor performance), but at the end of the day, a loss was a loss. Still, his failure against Zanki Kiguchi was altogether different from these two previous defeats—frankly, Shichika was having a hard time processing what happened.

It made no sense[13] to get depressed, but it was hard to shake it off.[14]

Following this upset, they took leave of the dojo and repaired to the village inn—but Shichika was unable to pull himself together.

His mood was placid compared to Togame's. Kiguchi had behaved in a completely unexpected manner, and the result had been the Schemer's undeniable failure as a tactician.

At least that was how she saw things.

Kiguchi, on the other hand, most likely saw things differently. *How could a swordsman be less competent by taking up a sword?*

The Kyotoryu.

Founded way back when, amid the chaos of the Age of Warring States.

Its founder, the First Master, being Kazune Yasuri—who had thought long and hard about the drawbacks of the katana, so long and heavy. Its length made it lethal, as did its weight—but the length of the katana, like its weight, made wielding it impractical.

Its pros and cons were two sides of the same coin.

Its perks and faults were two sides of the same coin.

Most people would take these paradoxes in passing[15]—but not Kazune Yasuri. Instead, he passed beyond them, taking the idea even further.

Get this.

If a katana could somehow be neither long nor heavy—

It would be the strongest weapon imaginable.

To truly be the strongest swordsman, perhaps the swordsman had to forsake

---

[13] おかしいし　OKASHII SHI　would be odd, funny
[14] 開き直る　HIRAKI NAORU　"open anew"　stand defiant
[15] 呑み込む　NOMIKOMU　swallow; accept

the sword.

And that is what he did.

Forsaking the sword, Kazune retreated to the mountains for ten years and transformed[16] himself into a katana.

Toning[17] his body until it shone like a katana.

He became a living, breathing sword.

And gave shape to a school—the Kyotoryu.

But this historical episode came with a caveat that had been unknown to Togame the Schemer until she heard it straight from Shichika, in that Kazune had tossed the sword aside out of necessity—*he couldn't swing a sword to save his life*.

The Kyotoryu—that school shrouded in darkness.

Had a skeleton in its closet.

What's more, this *complete and utter inability to wield a sword* turned out to be hereditary, passed down to all the scions of the House of Yasuri—not even that genius Nanami Yasuri, much less her father, Mutsue Yasuri, could shed the fetters of this spell.[18]

Which is to say—Shichika Yasuri was no better off.

And although, on one occasion, his ignorance of how to use a sword had actually saved his life, this time around things were essentially reversed.

To partake in battle, he was forced to use a wooden sword.

Saddled with this condition, even Shichika Yasuri, who thus far had slain numerous fearsome foes, battering Hakuhei Sabi and earning himself the title of the Strongest Swordsman in Japan, was as good as helpless.

Worse, the pads only got in the way.

Kiguchi had lent them to Shichika out of genuine concern, what one might even call goodwill,[19] but to him they were impediments[20] and nothing more.

As Shichika preferred to fight stripped to the waist and barefoot, they were an encumbrance, and one that he would sooner do without.

Thus armed and padded, Shichika was literally unable to bare his blade—but there was yet another reason for despair.

There would be rules.

The fight between Kiguchi and Shichika was bound[21] by many rules.

The rules of kendo.

All of his previous fights had essentially been free-for-alls—even the more formal duels were only regulated nominally, starting on the signal "Fight!" and ending on the word "Match!"

This time was different.

While Togame played the role of referee as usual, Kiguchi defined the start-

---

[16] 鍛え上げた　KITAE AGETA　forged (up)　　上 UE above　上げる AGERU raise
[17] 研ぎ上げた　TOGI AGETA　honed (up)
[18] 呪縛　JUBAKU　"enchained by a curse"
[19] 善意　ZEN'I　good intentions
[20] 枷　KASE　shackles
[21] がんじがらめ　GANJI GARAME　entangled

ing line and boundaries, and even indicated the appropriate stance.

Shichika did not know what it was to foul.

Because in a real fight, there was no such thing as going out of bounds.

And though he'd never deal in dirty deeds like those despicable Maniwacs, this time his ignorance was not an asset.

The Kyotoryu was meant for taking life.

Whereas the Heartland School was meant for giving life—the difference between which had been demonstrated vividly.

In a certain sense, Kiguchi wielded her sword for sport.

Hers was not a sword for killing.

Hers was a sword intent on cultivating the soul.

Though perhaps rooted in and aiming at the same goals—in essence it bore no relation to the Kyotoryu.

That being said, if mortal combat could not be avoided, the Heartland School allowed for her to take a lethal blade in hand—but such mortal combat had been ridden from the world amid these times of peace and order.

The one exception being the battle in which Mutsue Yasuri, Sixth Master of the Kyotoryu, had proved himself a hero, that is, the rebellion started by one Takahito Hida, Togame's father, but evidently the Heartland School had declined to join the fray.

Of course not.

The dojo was already without almost any followers.

Eleventh Master Zanki Kiguchi, who at the time headed the school, was far too old by then to head away to war—having retired as a swordsman.

Which meant—for ages, the Heartland School had fought exclusively with wooden swords.

The outcome had been clear from the beginning.

And things had gone exactly as they looked like they would go.

The rules dictated the fight and its results; and while raw ability prevented him from being beaten to a pulp,[22] Shichika handled the wooden sword so ineptly that Togame almost had to cover her eyes.

He was so bad that Togame wished that she was in there instead with the wooden sword.

From someone who took pride in being weak as shoji paper, who claimed that she would lose in a fight against a rabbit, this reaction was inconceivable.

"I know you told me, but still..."

Upon returning to the inn, the two of them had sat without exchanging words for quite some time, but at a certain point Togame got sick of the oppressive silence and cut to the chase.

She had considered starting with a different topic, but knew there was no way around it.

"You can't swing a sword...to save your life."

"Nope..."

[22] 滅多打ち METTA UCHI brutal thrashing

Shichika nodded dejectedly.[23]

"How is that possible?" asked Togame. "Forget the Mutant Blades. You're the sword shrouded in mystery today. Like the lady said, how can you be worse off with a weapon in your hands? No wonder she saw it as some excuse."

Togame conceded, however, that the pads would have slowed anybody down. Shichika looked distraught—she supposed he couldn't explain it himself. If he could tell her what was stopping him, then it would stand to reason that he could have told himself, as well, and overcome it.

To begin with—when Shichika held a katana, he lost sight of his duty as the Master of the Kyotoryu.

"Hold on, though. I've been meaning to ask you, how exactly did you train on Haphazard Island? Doesn't the Kyotryu have moves that you would need to practice on a sword to master?"

"Well yeah, I couldn't master them," replied Shichika. "The first sword that I ever saw was Zetto the Leveler, when that Maniwac Komori Maniwa whipped it out down on the beach. I told you, right? Blades were forbidden on the island. But hey, since I knew how the moves were done, I've managed to master a bunch of them since coming over to the mainland. I practice every time I'm in a fight."

"I see. So you're saying your skill sharpens every time you battle... You knew the basic premise of the moves, but you had yet to have a chance to try them out. And here I was thinking that you made up all of those moves on your own."

"Sis is different, though. Once she understands the premise, the move is hers."

"What a genius..."

That little mystery had been resolved, but it got them nowhere closer to the resolution of their actual dilemma.

"Well then, what to do," Togame said, doing her best to rid her voice of desperation, her eyes directed at the ceiling. "This situation is almost funny, like a cruel[24] joke or something—we're stuck, alright. I saw this coming. We couldn't just keep bumping along[25] like that. There had to be some kind of pitfall[26]—but no way was I expecting this. Since Kiguchi has no cruel intentions, we can't exactly just give her a taste of her own medicine."

"If she did this to us on purpose, then wow, I'm speechless," admitted Shichika. "She says she doesn't want to fight unless it's fair, and wants to make sure nobody gets hurt—what a pain in the butt. She must be immune to the Shikizaki venom."

"Maybe—she is."

Watching her in action, it was abundantly clear that Kiguchi was different from the other owners of the swords.

No madness or creepiness.[27]

---

[23] 力なく CHIKARA NAKU "no power" floppily
[24] 悪質な AKUSHITSU NA malicious
[25] とんとん拍子で話が進む TONTON BYŌSHI DE HANASHI GA SUSUMU story unfolding to a steady beat
[26] 落とし穴 OTOSHI ANA hole used as a booby trap
[27] 狂気も妖気も KYŌKI MO YŌKI MO neither deranged spirit nor enchanted air

The closest they had come to this was Konayuki Itezora, who was so innocent and naive; but when Shichika and Togame met her, she had only just become the owner of the Twin.

The venom of the Twin had needed more time to sink in.

But with Kiguchi—a considerable amount of time had surely passed since she inherited the Cured from her predecessor.[28]

"Perhaps that's what makes Oto the Cured special," Togame said.

"Huh? That? What do you mean?"

"This sword—is the only Shikizaki blade that has no Shikizaki venom. To put it plainly, the lack of poison is what makes the sword Oto the Cured."

"Uh, but wouldn't that disqualify it from being a Mutant Blade?"

"Maybe. Or maybe he was just testing his own limits. Judging from the other Mutant Blades, this crackpot swordsmith Kiki Shikizaki loved exceptions. Or who knows, maybe you were just unable to get her going enough to show us what the Cured can do."

"And where does that leave me?"[29] griped Shichika with a wry smile. "Still, I'm not bitter like I was after I lost to Konayuki or sis—if I had still won with a wooden sword and pads and all those teeny tiny rules, I wouldn't be the Master of the Kyotoryu."

"Fair point. But Shichika..."

Togame had decided to go ahead and ask him—not necessarily to get them anywhere, but more to get the question off her chest.

"Hypothetically, if you faced off against Kiguchi without pads or anything else, and didn't have to play by any of her rules—do you suppose you'd have been able to beat her?"

"...Could I kick her?"

"Kicks, elbows, headbutts, all fair game—" Togame hesitated before going on, but deeming it a way of speaking, she spat it out. "No need to hold back. You could even kill her, if you had to."

Shichika took this in.

"Hmm." For a moment it appeared that he was thinking—but his answer raised more questions. "I'm not sure. Like you said a little earlier, I couldn't get her going—so who knows how she'd fight back once I do."

"Make an educated guess."[30]

"I can't even do that. But, I mean, if I had to...I'd go by the way she acted when we saw her practicing, rather than when we sparred."

"Say more."

"Her form was impeccable. Like tight string."

Shichika spoke slowly, like he was picturing himself back in the dojo.

"She was so full of spirit. I could feel it radiating from her body. I've never seen a person so incredibly devoted to the way of the sword."

---

[28] 先代 SENDAI preceding generation
[29] 立つ瀬がねえ TATSU SE GA NEH "no shallows to stand on"
[30] 印象でよい INSHŌ DE YOI "an impression would be fine"

Togame—felt the same.

So far on their journey, Togame and Shichika had encountered a variety of swordsmen—but never had she seen somebody so absorbed[31] in her training. For all the others, the sword was but a means to an end. Even Hakuhei Sabi, nature's gift[32] to swords, was mostly interested in how his sword made him a saint than in the act of swordplay, in and of itself.

But not Kiguchi.

To her, the sword was everything—both endgame and end.[33]

For somebody like Shichika, who took things as they came, no personal goals, content to go through life doing whatever he was told, somebody so devoted to their cause was, well, frankly kind of scary.

For the record, the reason Shichika had fallen for Togame, who in her case lived only for revenge, had something fundamentally in common with what he saw as scary in Kiguchi—but at the moment, Togame failed to make the connection.

No need to go there.

"I mean—even if I fought her barehanded, in the way I usually fight, I'm pretty sure she'd make life hard[34] for me. She's nowhere near as good as Sabi or sis...but she's definitely up there, out of all the owners that I've fought so far."

"Right."

"We know sis is strongest, no contest,[35] and second place is definitely Hakuhei Sabi, but Kiguchi would come in somewhere between third and sixth—"

Shichika had a low tolerance for people playing tricks on him.

At least, that was how Emonzaemon Soda had sized him up—and while Kiguchi was by no means what you might call a trickster, she had left quite the impression on Shichika.

In fact, she gave him the chills.

"How are we supposed to have you beat this lady in a weakened state, armed with a wooden sword? I'm getting a headache."

This was not a turn of phrase. Togame actually had a headache.

Their dilemma had taxed her brain immensely.

"Can't you come up with a strategy, like you did with Sabi, or with sis, or Skytron?"

"Strategies I can do, but you know that I'm an outsider when it comes to battle. I'm afraid that if I go too far, things will just backfire... Remember what happened to us in Satsuma, when we were going after Zokuto the Armor. That armor-piercing move that I proposed was useless against Azekura."

"Huh. I guess I forgot about that."

"For the most part, the schemes that I devised when you fought Sabi, Nanami, and Skytron played off of your strength and expertise—but when it comes

---

[31] 入れ込む IREKOMU "go all in" to be committed
[32] 申し子 MŌSHIGO "the child one prayed for"
[33] 目的であり、目的地 MOKUTEKI DE ARI, MOKUTEKICHI the purpose, and the destination
[34] 苦戦 KUSEN "bitter battle"
[35] 不動 FUDŌ immovable

to having you fight in a weakened state, I have to admit, I'm fresh out of moves."

"Out of moves, huh?"

In other words—stuck.

While Togame had not intended to make a pun, her figure of speech got Shichika thinking about shogi.

"How good was she, anyway?" he asked. "At playing shogi."

"Half decent. If she devoted all the energy she puts into the Heartland School to playing shogi instead, she'd be a force to be reckoned with—I dare say out of my league."

"Wow. That good, huh?" Shichika sounded a little surprised. "So she's a poet warrior!"[36]

"Poet warrior... Yeah, I guess you could say that. Although they say that cultural pursuits and war are incompatible."

"With us, I'm obviously the warrior, and you're the cultured one. I'd say things have been going pretty well so far—but if I can't be the warrior, we're in trouble."

"Not just in trouble. Done for."

"But you're more cultured than Kiguchi, right?"

"I suppose. Although if she can play shogi like that while dedicating her entire life to swordsmanship, I have to give her credit."

"Think you could try it out again?" asked Shichika. It would seem that all the talk about Kiguchi's shogi skills was just buildup to the question that he really wanted to ask. "The whole thing where you beat her first, and she and I decide things over battle?"

"If I play my cards right, I think I can talk her into one more showdown..."

All disputes were settled over shogi.

In this town, that's the way things worked.

"But suppose I can. If you two fight under the same circumstances, there's still no way we're winning Oto the Cured."

"What if the circumstances changed? I don't care if she uses the Cured or body armor. If we can get her to let me fight barehanded—"

"Impossible. She would never go along with that, even if I gave myself a six-piece handicap. There's a chance I could convince her to do things the other way around, where she's without a weapon or protection. She'd put herself at a disadvantage, but won't put her opponent at a disadvantage. That's her way."

"..."

"There are people like her out there in the world—as hard as it is for somebody like me, only interested in plots and schemes, to comprehend."

"Honest, huh?"

"Though when you go that far, you start to seem inhuman. Sort of sheds some light on why the Heartland School has no more followers. Unless..."

Unless.

Togame stopped herself.

[36] 文武両道 BUNBU RYŌDŌ master of the pen and sword...or in this case, shogi board and sword

There was a sound outside their room, a sound of footsteps coming down the hall. It was too early for mealtime—and doubtful that an inn worker was bringing their dinner to them.

But in that case, who was it?

Togame ran through all sorts of possibilities, but before she could gather her thoughts, a voice addressed them from beyond the fusuma.

"Sorry to disturb you. Mind if I come in?"

That gracious way of speaking was a giveaway.

When Togame permitted her to enter, the fusuma slid open, and as expected—

It was Zanki Kiguchi.

Dressed in the same gi as earlier.

Although considering how drenched her gi was when they found her at the dojo—she had probably changed into a fresh gi before paying them a visit.

You can only do so much to dress a gi up.

Her closet must be full of these things. She would have looked pretty good in a kosode[37]—but Zanki Kiguchi was the picture of austerity and fortitude.

Hawkeyed, stoic in mien—

She looked down at Shichika and Togame, seated on the floor.

"Wh-What seems to be the trouble, Madame Kiguchi?"

Ever cautious, Togame offered Kiguchi a cushion, but she refused.

"No thank you. I can't stay very long."

She had told Kiguchi where it was that they were staying, and even mentioned that they checked in using fake names—which explains how she had found them at the inn—but why?

The fight was over. What could she want?

As it turns out, the fight was actually what Kiguchi wanted to discuss.

"Madame Togame. About the match."

"Y-Yes?"

"I'm afraid that the conditions were unfair."

This—is what she was here to say?

"After you and Master Shichika left, I thought things over, and, well, if Master Shichika is that weak, I don't think we can fairly call the game—I'm afraid it was unjust."

"..."

"And I want to make it right,"[38] Kiguchi said.

This was a declaration.

Loud and clear.

"I want Master Shichika to study under me. I will personally teach him everything I know. Then, once he is ready, we can have a rematch. What do you say?"

---

[37] 小袖　KOSODE　short-sleeved kimono
[38] 是正　ZESEI　straighten out, correct

CHAPTER FOUR

OSHIDORI MANIWA

. .

The Maniwa Ninja—that heterodox band of expert assassins.

Led collectively[1] by the Twelve Bosses.

"Komori the Hell-Made"—Komori Maniwa.

"Backwords Shirasagi"—Shirasagi Maniwa.

"Kuizame the Sand Trap"—Kuizame Maniwa.

"Kamakiri the Head Hunter"—Kamakiri Maniwa.

"Flying Butter Chocho"—Chocho Maniwa.

"Mitsubachi the Sharpshooter"—Mitsubachi Maniwa.

"The Divine Phoenix"—Hohoh Maniwa.

"The Feathered Reel"—Oshidori Maniwa.

"The Nosey Otter"—Kawauso Maniwa.

"The Immortal Turtle"—Umigame Maniwa.

"Pengin the Breeder"—Pengin Maniwa.

"The Dogged Scourge"—Kyoken Maniwa.

Of the Twelve Bosses, of late on close terms with the Owari Bakufu, but three survived.

Hohoh Maniwa, Oshidori Maniwa, and Pengin Maniwa.

Three alone.

Although this sampling of names suggests birds of a feather—it had been quite some time since these three ninjas had sat down for a proper chat.[2]

They convened on a hilltop in Izu, leagues from any human habitation.[3]

A far cry from Old Maniwa and New Maniwa both—the Twelve Bosses having long since made a pact not to return home until the Twelve Possessed of Kiki Shikizaki were theirs.

At their last summit, there were still six bosses left—but just as they had seen their ranks reduced from twelve to six, they saw them now reduced from six to three.

From their dwindling numbers, it would be fair to say that it was curtains for the Maniwa.

However.

"So this—is Dokuto the Basilisk..."

Oshidori Maniwa spoke—gazing in wonderment at the katana, standing before them like a veritable Excalibur.[4]

The sword was long, sheathed in a creepy, motley scabbard—and like Zetto the Leveler, which had been owned momentarily by the Maniwa, it lacked a handguard between blade and grip.

[1] 統べる SUBERU bring together
[2] 膝を突き合わせていた HIZA WO TSUKI AWASETE ITA "bumped knees"
[3] 人里離れた HITOZATO HANARETA removed from civilization
[4] 聖剣 SEIKEN "holy sword"

Even sheathed, it emanated venom, deterring even the slightest contact, a sword almost too painful to behold.

Though not a swordsman, Oshidori Maniwa felt its power.

Who knows how it would harness the attention of an advanced swordsman—she had to wonder.

If Umigame Maniwa was still with them.

What would he have felt?

"'Tis."

Hohoh Maniwa nodded.

"Without a doubt—I've checked it with the left arm of Kawauso. We found it waiting for us in a wind cave in the greenwood of Mt. Fuji. Pengin's intel was spot on, as usual."

Hearing his name evoked, Pengin Maniwa shivered beside Hohoh—less pleased by these words of praise than scared about what might be said about him next.

Pengin needs to get a grip, thought Oshidori.

"To think, left in a climate harsh as that—" Changing the topic away from Pengin, Oshidori voiced her genuine reaction to the sword, "it shows no sign of rust or degradation, perfectly preserved."

"Perhaps the climate was just right."

"What?"

"Perhaps it was not merely waiting, but sealed[5] within the cave—when we found it there, embedded in the wall, it was not spraying eerie energy the way that it is now. But I suppose that's par for the course with these Shikizaki blades. This should go without saying, Oshidori, but don't even think—of unsheathing this katana."

"..."

As if he had to warn her.

Even fitted in its scabbard, the sword was seething venom—what horrors it would unleash once exposed! It was beyond the scope of her imagination.

She felt nothing close to this when shown Zetto the Leveler. She surmised that not all of the Mutant Blades of Kiki Shikizaki bore this trait—perhaps even among the Twelve Possessed.

This sword alone.

A trait unique—to Dokuto the Basilisk.

"In the wind cave at Mt. Fuji, when first I touched the hand of Kawauso to the scabbard of this sword, I sensed a terrifying energy. Just as Zetto the Leveler could never bend or break or lose its edge, boasting uncanny hardness, Dokuto the Basilisk boasts uncanny toxicity, its venom stronger than all the other Mutant Blades..."

Hohoh—couldn't help but chuckle.

"Keheheh."

"Wh-Wh-Wh..."

---

[5] 封印　FŪIN　"closure mark"　nuance of being sealed *away*

His laugh made Pengin even more uneasy than before.

"What is it, Sir Hohoh?"

"Isn't that a riot? Look, if you see the Sword Hunt for the Twelve Possessed of Kiki Shikizaki as a competition, the Owari Bakufu versus the Maniwa, the score has been uneven as it gets. The Schemer and the Kyotoryu have seven swords for sure, and I wouldn't be surprised if they've already grabbed themselves an eighth by now. For us to rise out of the ashes of embarrassment and beat them to this sword, the most possessed of all the twelve, is the epitome of irony."

Dokuto the Basilisk—boasting uncanny toxicity.

His appraisal was correct.

Hohoh Maniwa employed his Life Line.

That fearsome ninpo which allowed him to chop off parts of someone else's body and attach them to his own, thereby assuming their abilities.

The left arm of Kawauso Maniwa, distinguished among the Twelve Bosses of the Maniwa for his Infovac, which allowed him access, upon contact, to the memory and history of inanimate objects—was now *grafted* onto Hohoh.

And with this arm—he delved into[6] this sword.

Just as that genius Nanami Yasuri had used her eyes to see through Akuto the Eel, upon finding it enshrined atop Mt. Shirei, thus learning what the sword could do and how it should be used—Hohoh Maniwa had done the same, in his own way, with Dokuto the Basilisk.

"Saying we're now tied—might be going too far, but this gives us a bargaining chip to use against the Schemer."

"Buh, but..." chirped Pengin.

Boyish as this ninja was, so timid and skittish, he spoke his mind, and did so readily. How else could someone with a personality like his become a ninja boss?

"N-Not all the news today is good news... It seems Sir Umigame...failed to capture his Shikizaki blade, and perished in the process..."

"Perished," Oshidori muttered—realizing what Pengin had said.

Her thoughts turned to Chocho Maniwa.

Who along with Kamakiri Maniwa and Mitsubachi Maniwa, his brethren in the Bug Unit, had ventured to Haphazard Island with a mind to abduct Nanami Yasuri, as a way of furthering their Sword Hunt—only for Nanami Yasuri to rub them out like pests.

Chocho and Oshidori—had been lovers.

Once this "last hurrah"[7] was over, bringing the Sword Hunt to a close, the two had promised to be wed[8]—but alas, these best laid plans of bird and bug had gone awry.

And now.

Umigame Maniwa—gone too.

[6] 読み解いた　YOMI TOITA　deciphered
[7] 最後の仕事　SAIGO NO SHIGOTO　final job
[8] 祝言をあげる　SHŪGEN WO AGERU　exchange vows before a crowd

"Or from another angle, Sir Umigame came dangerously close to capturing the Shikizaki blade, but something cracked his shell—I reckon."

"Right..." Oshidori nodded.

After the last special assembly, she had done her part in chasing down the Shikizaki blades. Hohoh and Pengin had gone off together, leaving Umigame and Oshidori to operate independently.

Hohoh and Pengin had arrived victorious, toting Dokuto the Basilisk.

Unfortunately, Oshidori had nothing to show for herself.

And Umigame—dead.

In which case, perhaps Oshidori had been lucky, rather than unfortunate, in not coming so dangerously close.

Perhaps that made her cowardly, but the thought was there.

"Sir Umigame was bound for Shinano—was he not?" asked Oshidori.

"Indeed he was," Hohoh nodded. "I believe we have you to thank, Pengin—for the information on the Mutant Blade in Shinano. Is there anything that you would like to add?"

"N-Not really...but regardless of the circumstances...if Umigame, maybe the ablest fighter among us, lost his life...something awful must have happened..."

"I bet. That warrants an investigation," Hohoh seconded Pengin. "Well now, I think that sums things up. We need a new plan going forward. With Umigame perished, I think it would be advisable[9] for us, from here on out, to stay together every minute of the day. The Twelve Bosses have already been quartered. We must not lose another ninja."

"N-Not one," Pengin agreed, but he had more to say. "Sir Hohoh, when you used Kawauso's left arm to delve into Dokuto the Basilisk, d-d-did it tell you anything about the other swords?"

"I would have to try again, *going in*[10] deeper this time. As the Infovac was not originally my ninpo, I still have much to learn about its workings—it may take practice."

It was unlike Hohoh to admit this, but on the other hand, he made it sound like it was only a matter of time. Once he had mastered the Infovac, he would doubtless wield it more adeptly than even its original practitioner, the late Kawauso.

Hohoh Maniwa was that kind of a ninja.

And while he let on[11] like his brethren treated him like their effective head because he had more common sense than all the other crackpots in the clan—that wasn't it.

Oshidori knew that wasn't it at all.

Hohoh Maniwa—was effectively the head of the clan because he was the only boss capable of inspiring confidence.

Belief.

---

[9] 無難　BUNAN　"no difficulties"　safe
[10] 潜る　MOGURU　dive
[11] 嘯いている　USOBUITE IRU　pretend, aver

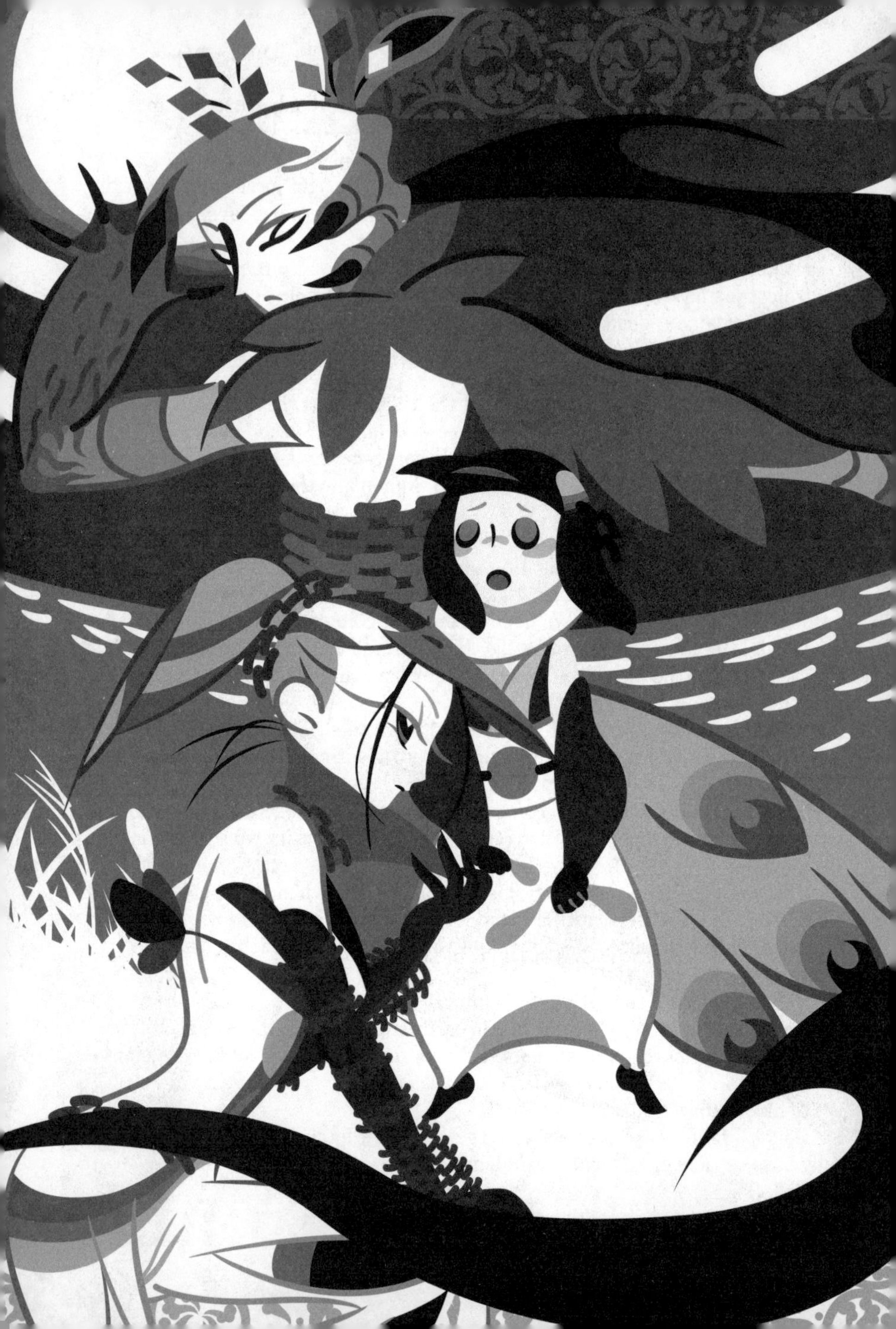

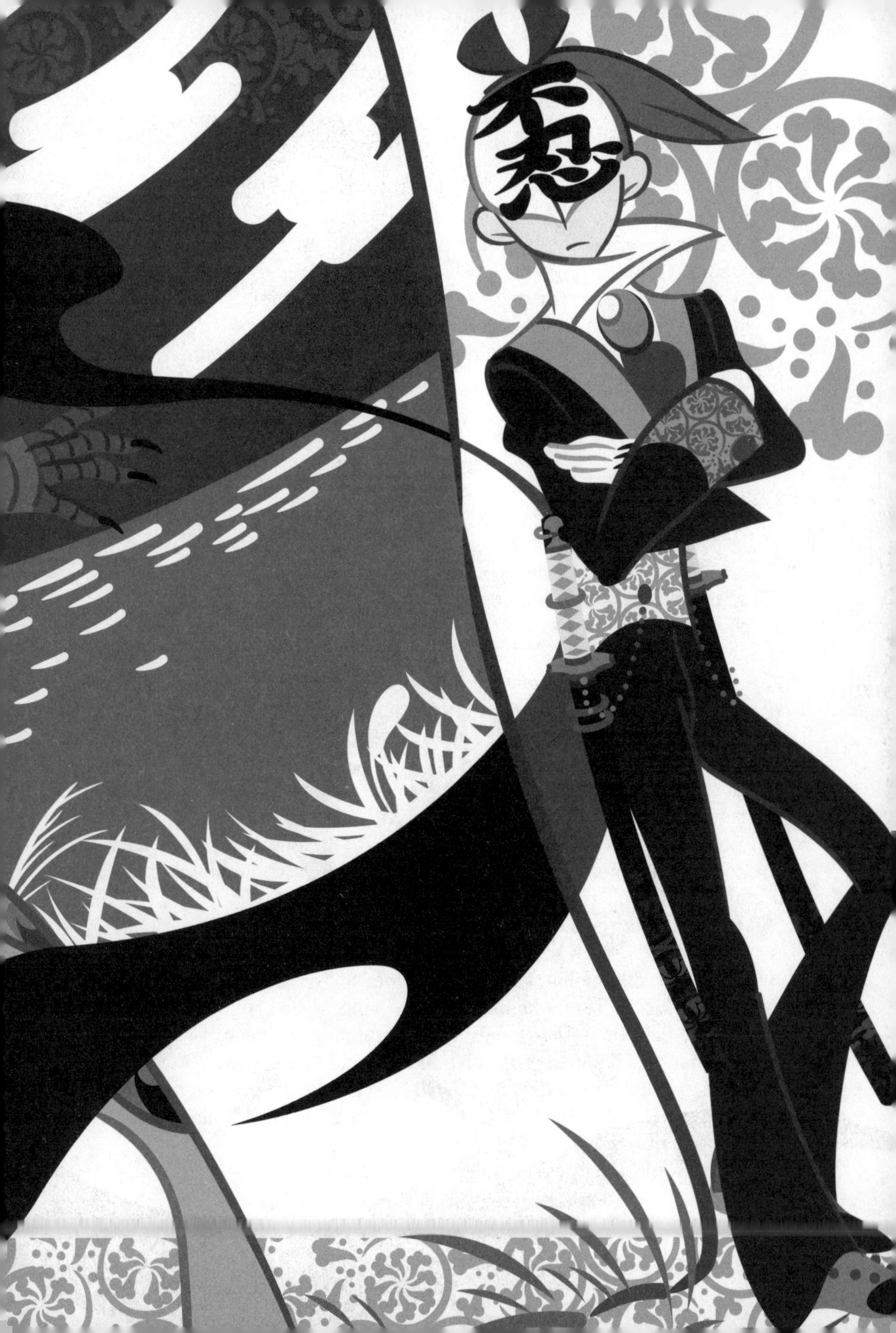

Reliability—
"Alright, let's head off toward Shinano, where Umigame fell—"
Thus.
Hohoh Maniwa led the way.
"Not permitted."
There had been no one but the three of them atop the hill—but now they had a visitor.
Coat and trousers, a pair of swords slung from his hips.
Wearing a mask, on which was scrawled the word "NON-NINJA"—
"There is no way I can permit that behavior—Maniwa Ninjas."
Lieutenant Emonzaemon Soda, Counselor to the Inspector General of the Yanari Shogunate—cometh.[12]

■ ■

Princess Negative, archnemesis of Togame the Schemer.
True name and origins unknown.
With blond hair and dazzling blue eyes[13] that gave her foreign blood away, she was in some ways even more of an anomaly within the bakufu than Togame—but given that she held the office of Inspector General, nobody would have an easy time of meddling with or harping on[14] about her anomalousness.
Hence—she was full of puzzles and mysteries.
Take the Sword Hunt.
What exactly did she think about this quest, proposed by Togame the Schemer, to round up the Twelve Possessed of Kiki Shikizaki, those Mutant Blades which not even the Old Shogun could obtain? The only two people who could speak to her innermost feelings were Princess Negative herself and her right-hand man, confidant, and trusty weapon Emonzaemon Soda.
As the Schemer guessed—the Princess was up to something.
However, she was not merely acting as the Inspector General.
Did she cherish ill will toward the Schemer for striking and defeating her so many times? Surely. The Schemer and the Princess had rubbed each other the wrong way[15] since their first meeting—even under the best of circumstances, their behavior was doomed to devolve into mutual opposition.
Though in that case, Princess Negative would have plotted against the Schemer even if the Sword Hunt never happened—her stance by no means limited to the situation at hand.
But how would she operate under the circumstances?

[12] 見参　KENZAN　audience (with a dignitary)　archaic word for announcing entry
[13] 金髪碧眼　KINPATSU HEKIGAN　gold hair and blue eyes
[14] 手出し口出し　TEDASHI KUCHIDASHI　"interfere with hand or mouth"
[15] 反りが合わなかった　SORI GA AWANAKATTA　"mismatched curves"　to be incompatible
reference to a sword not fitting in a scabbard because its arc is incorrect

And how would she take advantage of the situation?

At this point, Togame honestly hadn't the slightest idea—in which case, she may as well deal with her the same way that she always did.

And yet if Togame the Schemer were to agree with that assessment, one might be tempted to deem her negligent.

Princess Negative—felt differently than before.

As she said herself, the Sword Hunt was her hunting ground.

Princess Negative—Inspector General of the Yanari Shogunate, Owari Bakufu.

Only two souls knew the way she felt—but for the time being, since Togame the Schemer had succeeded in rounding up over half of the Twelve Possessed of Kiki Shikizaki, Princess Negative was her *ally*—in a certain sense.

At least for the time being.

Although as far as allies go, she was quite negative.

Still, this does explain why last month, Princess Negative gave Emonzaemon Soda, her right-hand man, confidant, and trusty weapon, an order to fulfill.

That order being: "While you're out, assassinate Hohoh Maniwa."

■ ■

Atop the hill—two souls remained.

The first was Emonzaemon Soda—armed with a pair of swords, dressed in a coat and trousers. Now the trusty weapon of Princess Negative, he was a former ninja—whose expression was impossible to comprehend, thanks to his mask, which labeled him "NON-NINJA."

The other was dressed in peculiar sleeveless ninja garb, chains wrapped around her body. She was voluptuous and had that special something—Oshidori Maniwa, one of the Twelve Bosses of the Maniwa Clan.

The other two who had been present, her fellow ninja bosses Hohoh Maniwa and Pengin Maniwa, had already disappeared—and Dokuto the Basilisk, which had been standing in the earth sheathed in its scabbard, had been absconded with as well.

Leaving these two.

Facing one another—for a time, without a word.

"*Not expected.*"

At length.

Emonzaemon was the one who broke the silence.[16]

"I show up ready to fight the three of you myself—and those two leave you in the lurch. I had not been expecting you to make a classic ninja move like that. Maniwa scum...you think you're just as good as any other ninja?"

"Ugh, I don't need this today." Oshidori spoke flippantly toward Emonzae-

[16] 口を開いた　KUCHI WO HIRAITA　opened his mouth

mon—nothing like the way she had toward Hohoh Maniwa, her senior, minutes earlier. "Nobody asked you for advice on our maneuvers, but for your information, I'm not taking one for the team.[17] I'm enough of a ninja to take care of you myself."

"Sound pretty confident," Emonzaemon took this in stride. "If you'll permit me to say so, I'm disappointed you're the one I'm forced to fight—since after all, I have been sent here to assassinate Hohoh Maniwa."

"Assassinate Hohoh?" Oshidori raised her eyebrows. "Who the hell are you?"

"*No reply*—why should I divulge that information?"

"You could at least introduce yourself."

"Emonzaemon Soda."

"*Ay-mon-za-ay-mon?*"

Has to be a joke, thought Oshidori, raising her eyebrows even higher—

"What kind of an alias is that?"

"Hah. You sound just like Umigame."

"*Umi—game?*"

"Oopsie," said Emonzaemon, touching his fingers to his lips. "Slip of the tongue[18]—but I have nothing to hide. Indeed, your brother Umigame Maniwa is dead—I killed him."

"...Oh."

This news—steeled Oshidori more than it stung. Partly because it settled a question that had weighed her down, and partly because it dictated her course of action against Emonzaemon.

"I must say, I'm surprised—to see the Maniwa obtained one of the Twelve Possessed of Kiki Shikizaki. Was that—Dokuto the Basilisk?"

"Huh? Wait, were you eavesdropping on us? You must have pretty good ears."

"I wasn't listening. I already knew."

"What?"

"It doesn't matter," said Emonzaemon. "You'll be dead soon."

This statement was so plain and direct, so firm and decisive—economical, no games, no tricks—that for a moment Oshidori froze, but quickly she rallied.

"Alright."

She stood on the ready—like the ninja that she was.

At first glance, it would seem she had no sword, or any kind of weapon for that matter—but in fact, her weapon was on display, for all to see.

If you looked closer at her peculiar ninja garb.

At those chains wrapped around her body—you would find her weapon, woven through the links of chain, encircling her every curve.

Oshidori Maniwa, one of the Twelve Bosses of the Maniwa.

Known to many as "The Feathered Reel."

Whose weapon of choice—was a pair of whips.

Not simple strips of leather, but ten far-reaching strands branching from

---

[17] 自己犠牲 JIKO GISEI self-sacrifice
[18] 口が滑った KUCHI GA SUBETTA "slip of the mouth"

each handgrip—the tips of which were dressed with tiny razors.

A pair of these atypical implements—one in each hand.[19]

Thus able to give twenty lashes at a time—with her two hands.

"Maniwa Ninpo—Thorough Thrashing."[20]

"..."

Challenged thusly—Emonzaemon drew both his swords at once, the short and the long, in a dual wield. The result was a bizarre scenario where both parties, Emonzaemon and Oshidori, faced off with both hands brandishing weapons.

"I am Oshidori Maniwa—coming to get you."

"And I am Emonzaemon Soda—not if I get you first."

True to his word, Emonzaemon made the first move—but Oshidori was the first[21] to make a hit.

Flicking her wrists.

That was enough—to rain the twenty razored tails on twenty different points of the lieutenant's body.

"...!"

Emonzaemon, who had been about to close in, backpedaled desperately—but was unable to dodge all twenty of her tails.

Those he failed to dodge—he caught with his sword.

Two tails with each.

And yet he was unable to cut through them—and the tails twirled around his swords like tentacles.[22]

"Guh..."

For a moment, Emonzaemon was stuck.

But only for a single moment—he let go of both swords, throwing them away, and retreated to safety.

This was the right move—if he had acted any slower, the remaining sixteen tails would have soon rained down once again.

"Hmph..."

Having robbed Emonzaemon of both his swords, Oshidori flailed her whips—with no more than another flick of the wrists—and flung his weapons far out of reach.

She could command the twenty tails of her two whips with total freedom.

Like they were her own limbs—nay, with greater freedom than her limbs!

Maniwa Ninpo—Thorough Thrashing.

One might think the sheer number of tails would be apt[23] to make this ninpo hard to handle—but in practice, this was not the case at all.

Like an extension of her nervous system, the twenty tails shot for their target with intelligence and speed—Oshidori was so instantaneously responsive that she could let her foe strike first and still have plenty of time to fend him

---

[19] 左右にふたつ SAYŪ NI FUTATSU "one on the left, one on the right"
[20] 永劫鞭 EIGŌBEN "eternal whip" vs. 永劫回帰 EIGŌ KAIKI the Eternal Return
[21] 早かった 速かった HAYAKATTA HAYAKATTA sooner vs. faster (both rendered as "the first")
[22] 軟体動物のごとく NANTAI DŌBUTSU NO GOTOKU in the manner of a mollusk
[23] ともすると TOMO SURUTO likely

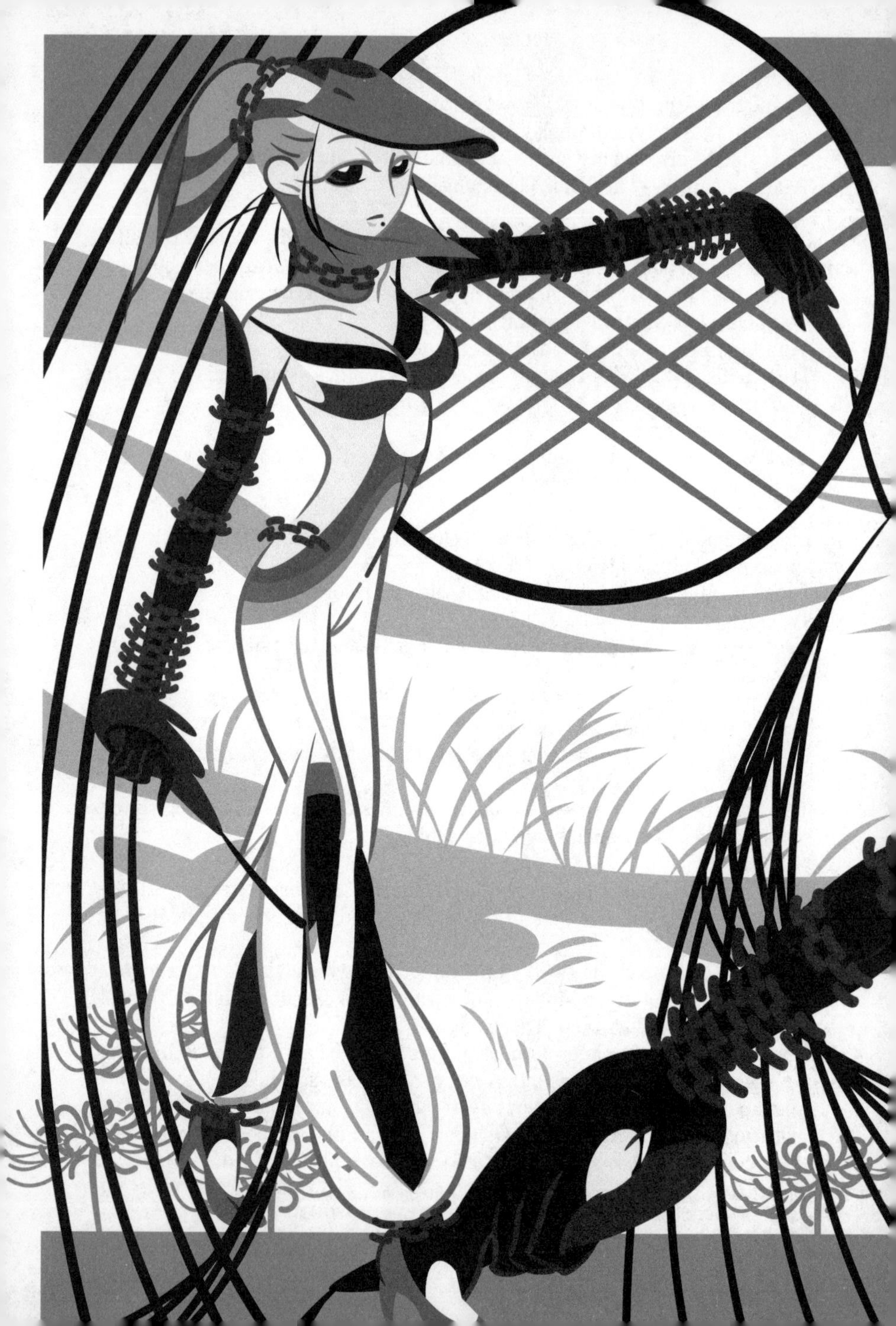

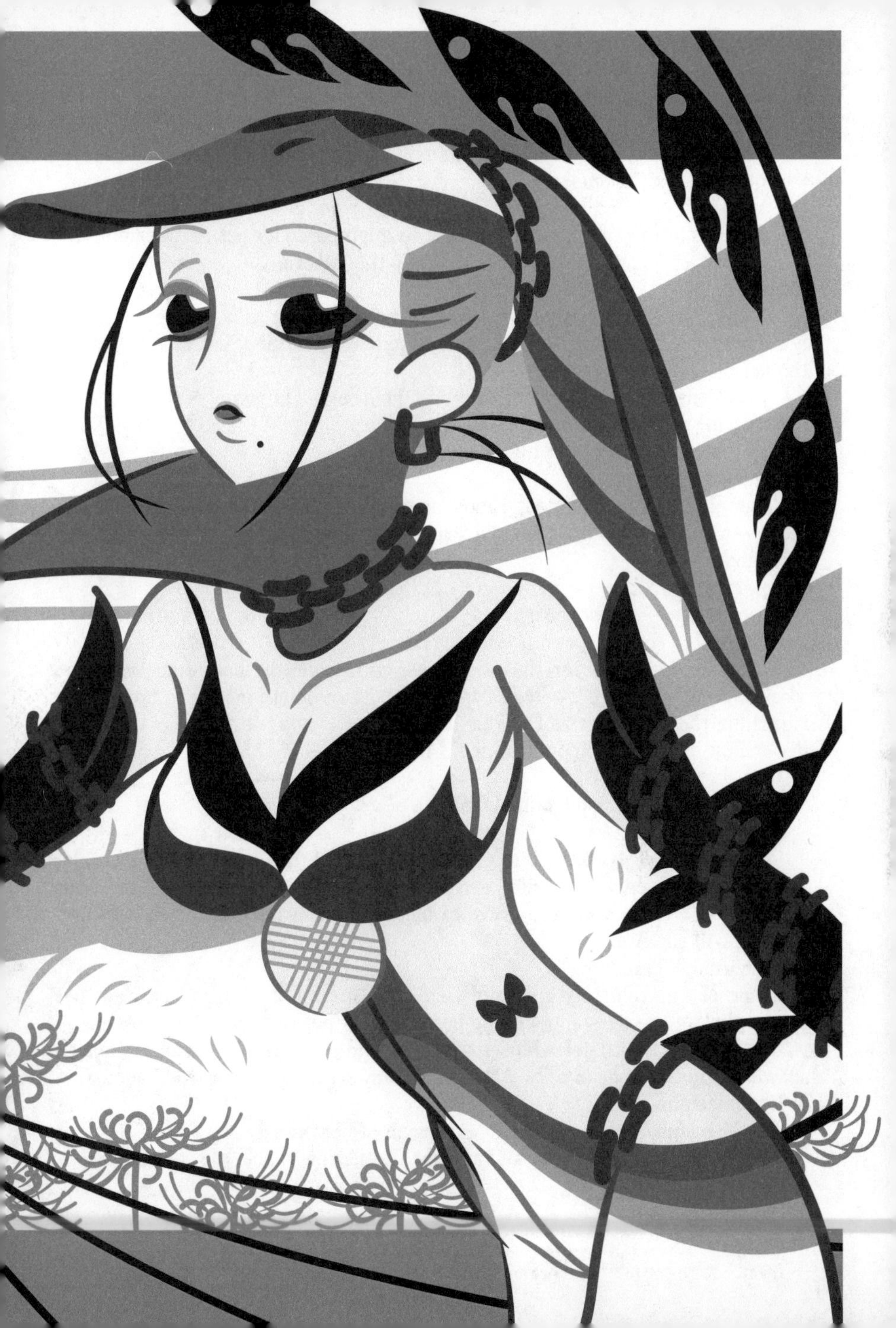

off. Lo, the essence of Oshidori Maniwa!

"Yet..."

This knowledge had cost Emonzaemon both his swords—but now that he was out of range, he spoke up.

"Your lashings aren't so powerful after all. From the way you stopped me before I could cut through them, they must be engineered for optimal flexibility."[24]

"What can I say. As long as you avoid the razors, you won't be mortally wounded."

Oshidori had voluntarily revealed what would appear to be the weakness of her Thorough Thrashing—but in actuality, it was nothing, not a weakness in the least.

"Does this get my *points* across?[25] My Thorough Thrashing is the ideal way of torturing an enemy to death."

"In that case, how about this?"

And so.

Though freshly disarmed, Emonzaemon transitioned fluidly to his next move—since he was not at heart a swordsman, losing his swords was no cause for alarm.

His next move?

"Aioi Kenpo—*Shadow Fist*."

Indeed.

Emonzaemon opted for the very move with which he had offed Umigame Maniwa, the last of the Twelve Bosses to perish, a month earlier in Shinano—launching the move just as Oshidori Maniwa was trying to figure out what he had meant by this strange utterance, *"Aioi Kenpo—Shadow Fist"*...and in that instant.

Emonzaemon slipped behind Oshidori.

Shadow Fist.

Remaining always behind the enemy, this kenpo had been all but lost, one hundred and seventy years ago, with the demise of the Aioi Ninja Clan—but here it was, from beyond the grave of history, a surprise kenpo freighted by[26] the ninpo of the Aioi—

"Thorough Thrashing."

None of this remotely bothered Oshidori Maniwa. This time she went beyond a flick of the wrists, twitching her elbows—but that was all it took.

All twenty tails of her whips sprayed behind her, firing at Emonzaemon—*without so much as looking back*, she was countering the rearward Shadow Fist of Emonzaemon.

Those whips of hers—were an extension of her being.

Without having to turn herself around, Oshidori was able to shoot her whips behind her.

---

[24] 柔らかさに重点　YAWARAKASA NI JŪTEN　emphasis on suppleness
[25] わかるかしら　WAKARU KASHIRA　"do you understand"
[26] 機軸にした　KIJIKU NI SHITA　using for an axis

Umigame Maniwa, in his fatal encounter with Emonzaemon Soda, had counted himself lucky Oshidori was not with him—but in actuality, as far as handling the Aioi Kenpo Shadow Fist was concerned, her Thorough Thrashing was far more appropriate than any Maniwa Ninpo Umigame could cook up with his rapier!

"*No way,*" Emonzaemon muttered to himself, just barely dodging the twenty tails—though with more leeway[27] than when they had traded blows facing each other. "I must say, I'm surprised. I had thought the Shadow Fist would work on anyone—except for Hohoh."

"Huh? Wait, how do you know Sir Hohoh?" inquired Oshidori.

Back facing him—not turning around.

"Umigame asked me the same thing—in his case, I gave no reply, but for you, I'll make an exception."

Emonzaemon—told her.

"We're more than acquaintances," he whispered, "but less than sworn enemies."

"...That doesn't answer my question."

Zipping[28] her twin whips through the air, Oshidori guarded her surroundings.

Whipping up a forcefield.[29]

From within which she responded to Emonzaemon.

"To begin with, Sir Hohoh didn't even flinch when you showed up."

"True. But remember—I am wearing a mask."

NON-NINJA.

Scrawled on the mask covering his face.

"Besides, Hohoh may have forgotten me by now."

"Sounds like you're not even acquaintances."

"Perhaps."

Smoothly—Emonzaemon slipped into his next move.

Being a ninja, Oshidori could sense her adversary all too keenly, without even having to turn around—but took no further action. Nothing more, that is, than continuing to flail her twenty whiptails in the air.

His Aioi Swordsmanship had failed.

She had blocked his Aioi Kenpo as well.

In addition to their obvious utility as weapons, the twenty tails of her Thorough Thrashing were a superb means of defense—thwarting every offense!

Thus—was Oshidori Maniwa's philosophy!

And yet.

"*No use,*" Emonzaemon muttered.

Whereupon—*he pulled the trigger.*[30]

---

[27] 抜け道　NUKEMICHI　"escape route"
[28] ひゅんひゅん　HYUN HYUN　onomatopoeia for fast motion slicing air
[29] 結界　KEKKAI　(mystical) barrier
[30] 引き金　HIKIGANE　"pull metal"　small lever that fires a gun

■ ■

Bang.
   Bang Bang Bang Bang Bang Bang.
   Just as she heard the repeated sounds, both strangely hollow and enormous, Oshidori Maniwa felt *something strange* riddle her body.
   Perforating her.
   She recognized her body being gored to bits.[31]
   "...Huh?"
   She hadn't let down the defenses of her Thorough Thrashing—for an instant.
   She hadn't even noticed any attack.
   Nevertheless—she felt as if she had been stabbed repeatedly in the back by Umigame's rapier—and her flesh burned, as if a fire had been lit inside of her.
   The thrashing ceased.
   Her hands could not feel to grip—both whips fell from her hands, and she followed after them, tumbling to the ground.
   Her senses stripped.
   She had been mortally wounded, several times over—of that much she was certain.
   But she had no idea—what had been done to her.
   She had made sure that Emonzaemon could not so much as step within her range—had he attacked her from outside her range?
   Using something like the Blunderbuzz of Mitsubachi Maniwa?
   But even a move like the Blunderbuzz, barring some unusual occurrence, would have been thwarted by the Thorough Thrashing—could this move have outpaced even Mitsubachi's?
   Too fast for even the Thorough Thrashing?
   Was it—a flintlock?
   Nay, no flintlock could be fired so *rapidly*—it was impossible! Besides, how could he have hidden its barrel?
   "...nkk!"
   Summoning her energy, she turned her head to where she thought she would find Emonzaemon.
   And in both hands.
   Emonzaemon held what looked like lumps of metal.
   He must have had them in his pockets, but *what were they?* Beginning to lose consciousness, Oshidori was unable to make sense of things. Though even if she had full mastery of her faculties, things would have made no sense.
   These things—these weapons should not, could not exist in this time or place.

[31] ずたずた   ZUTA ZUTA   onomatopoeia for being torn apart

But at first sight, *someone from our time* would have identified them precisely.

In his right hand he was holding a revolver.

And in his left hand he was holding an automatic.

Indeed.

No smoke and mirrors.[32]

Just one of the Twelve Possessed, those masterworks of legendary swordsmith Kiki Shikizaki—that pair of swords, Ento the Bead!

Weapons able to repeatedly launch bullets from a distance, far quicker than Oshidori could flick her wrists—

"*Not happy*," Emonzaemon said quietly. "When the Princess bid me to take this with me, I was sure that I would never use it—certainly not right away... Though I suppose if you show up to a battle armed like this, all kenpo, swordplay, and ninpo are in vain."[33]

Oshidori was too far gone—to hear this faint soliloquy.

"Besides, I let Hohoh Maniwa get away—the assassination was a failure. I've wasted too much time fending off this woman. I guess I won't be heading back to Owari. The way things turned out, perhaps I would have been better off not sticking to my guns[34]—or rather, if I stuck to them and used Ento the Bead from the outset... I hate to praise one of the Maniwa, but this woman—fulfilled her duty to her clan magnificently. Like a true ninja. With far more gusto than me, a former ninja."

But Oshidori Maniwa.

Contrary to this speech from Emonzaemon, which she would fail to hear— was thinking, until the very end, not of the ninja village, nor of the Twelve Possessed of Kiki Shikizaki, but of her lover, who had died ahead of her, five months before.

---

[32] 工夫も衒いもない　KUFŪ MO TERAI MO NAI　"no ingenuity or pretense"
[33] 形無し　KATANASHI　(become) formless　echoes 刀 KATANA
[34] 意地を張らずに　IJI WO HARAZU NI　not be stubborn [the "guns" pun isn't in the original]

CHAPTER FIVE

SHANGRI-OTO

Ten days had passed since Shichika Yasuri, the Seventh Master of the Kyotoryu, became a follower of the Heartland School.

All ten of which he had trained at the Heartland Dojo.

If she had wanted to, of course Togame the Schemer could have rejected[1] the offer from Twelfth Master Zanki Kiguchi, which depending on your stance was totally absurd, safe to dismiss as an impertinence—but reject it she did not, instead instructing Shichika to do whatever Kiguchi asked of him.

Clearly, toward the goal of capturing Oto the Cured.

In the wake of the match over the Cured, Togame figured it would benefit them to stay connected to Kiguchi—the intention, in typical Togame fashion, was to use the downtime this created to hatch a different scheme.

However, none of this sat well with Shichika, who was the one who had to become a follower of a different school. Carefree as he normally was, it vexed him terribly to think how he would ever face his father or his sister, but beyond that, being forced to relearn swordplay with a sword, the bane of his existence,[2] was such a pain.

Although.

In that sense, the experience was probably much more painful for Kiguchi, despite being the one who proposed the arrangement—at the very least, she must have been stunned to discover how little Shichika really knew about how to swing a sword.

Ten days in, they had yet to advance beyond the basics of the swing.

He couldn't even hold the sword correctly.

He kept on dropping it.

When he raised it high, it fell behind him. When he swung it down, it slipped[3] from his hands.

More than once or twice, he had clocked himself in the forehead—and somehow, these were the only times he swung the wooden sword correctly, adding insult to injury.

For Shichika Yasuri, the kaleidoscopic footwork of Kyotoryu Form Seven, the Kakitsubata, was a piece of cake, but somehow the second he picked up a wooden sword, he stepped on his own toes, and would have looked inelegant beside a toddler.

He was so bad he made it look like he was doing it on purpose.

And yet he was simply listening to Togame, setting aside his deep pride in the Kyotoryu, for the time being, to receive the teachings of the Heartland

---

[1] 突っ撥ねる　TSUPPANERU　shove aside
[2] 心底苦手　SHINSOKO NIGATE　"averse from the bottom of one's heart"
[3] 零す　KOBOSU　spill

School from Kiguchi.

Although.

If they had been here even six months earlier—Shichika never would have agreed to join another school, even if Togame was the one asking.

He had been raised to be a sword and to obey his owner's every wish, but the idea that there were orders he could only follow now that he had become more than just a sword—was new for him.

"That's good for now, Master Shichika."

Kiguchi called it a day.[4]

Her pupil had once again failed to show any sign of progress. She handed Shichika a tenugui, which he used to wipe his sweaty body.

Luckily, we might say, Shichika was blessed with endless energy, allowing him to endure Kiguchi's brutal training regimen without a peep (not that he was learning any)—but by extension, this demonstrated that Kiguchi's own stamina rivaled Shichika's.

Over the past ten days.

Shichika had paid witness to her *strength*.

First off, she was strong in body.

But she was also strong willed.

Most people would have tossed a pupil so unbelievably inept as Shichika out the door after at most three days.[5]

"Sorry for being such a bad teacher," Kiguchi took the blame. "The fact is, I've never taught someone before—I'm probably messing up all kinds of things. You'll just have to bear with me."

"..."

Zanki is way too serious, thought Shichika.

Really—the rest of them were nothing like this.

How can this lady be the owner of a Shikizaki blade?

Shichika tried to insinuate as much (although examining things objectively, what came out of his mouth was fairly direct after all, tactless as he was).

"Nothing of the sort," Kiguchi said, shaking her head. "I know that Madame Togame is asking me to hand over Oto the Cured for the sake of the nation, but I'm too immature to act against my personal concerns."[6]

"Sake of the nation, huh."

Since obviously Togame could not tell Kiguchi she was doing this to further her career, and to eventually exact revenge on the entire bakufu, she had given her the usual spiel, in their first session of diplomacy, about the Sword Hunt for the Twelve Possessed of Kiki Shikizaki being carried out for the "sake of the nation," but as it turned out, Kiguchi took her stated purpose at face value.

The opposite of Ginkaku Uneri, despite both of them being swordsman.

The idea that no one who speaks on behalf of the nation is up to any good—

---

[4] ひと段落して　HITO DANRAKU SHITE　(stop at) a good breaking point
[5] 三日　MIKKA　"three days" evokes　三日坊主　MIKKA BŌZU　"monk for three days"
[6] 私心　SHISHIN　"one's own heart"

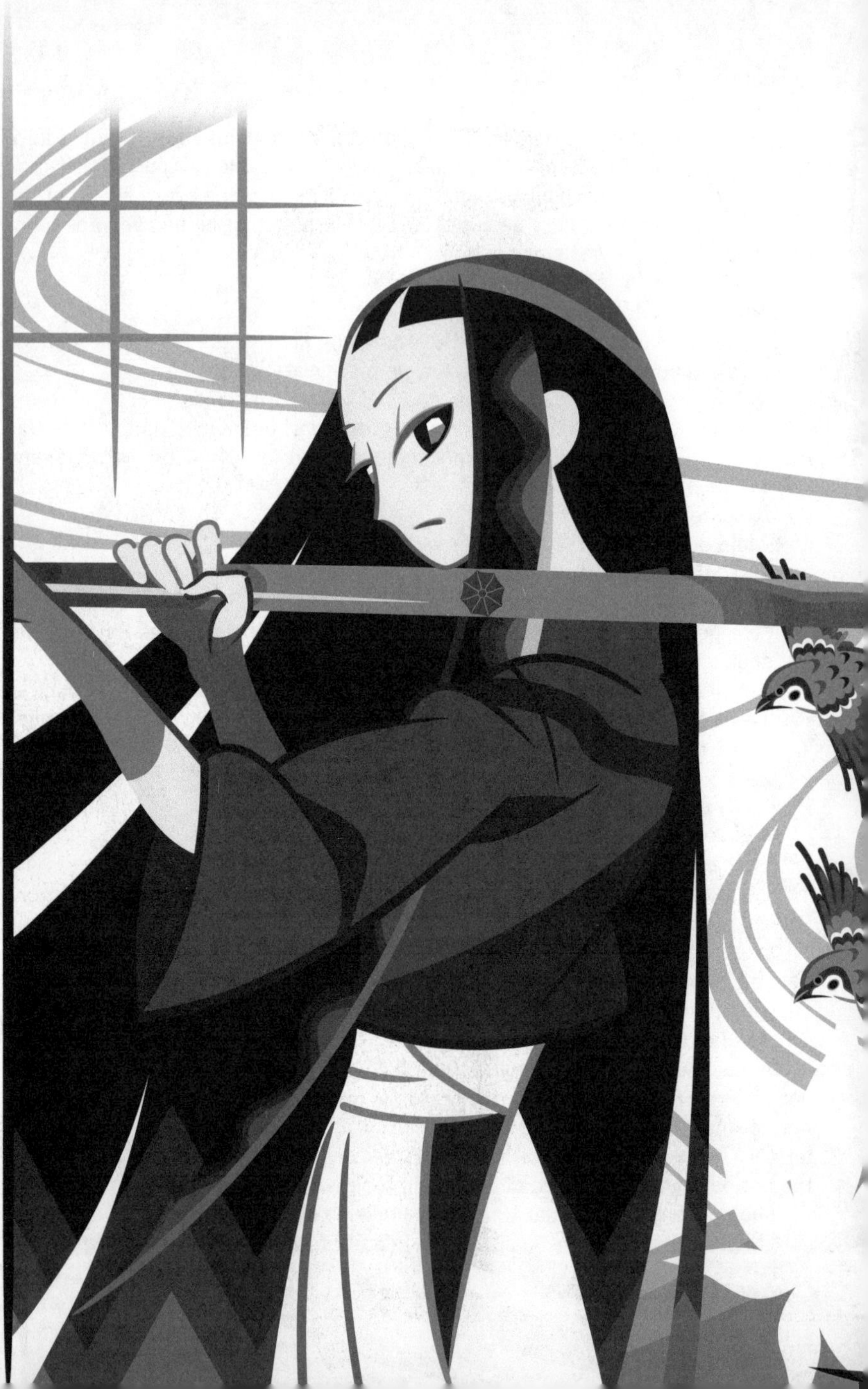

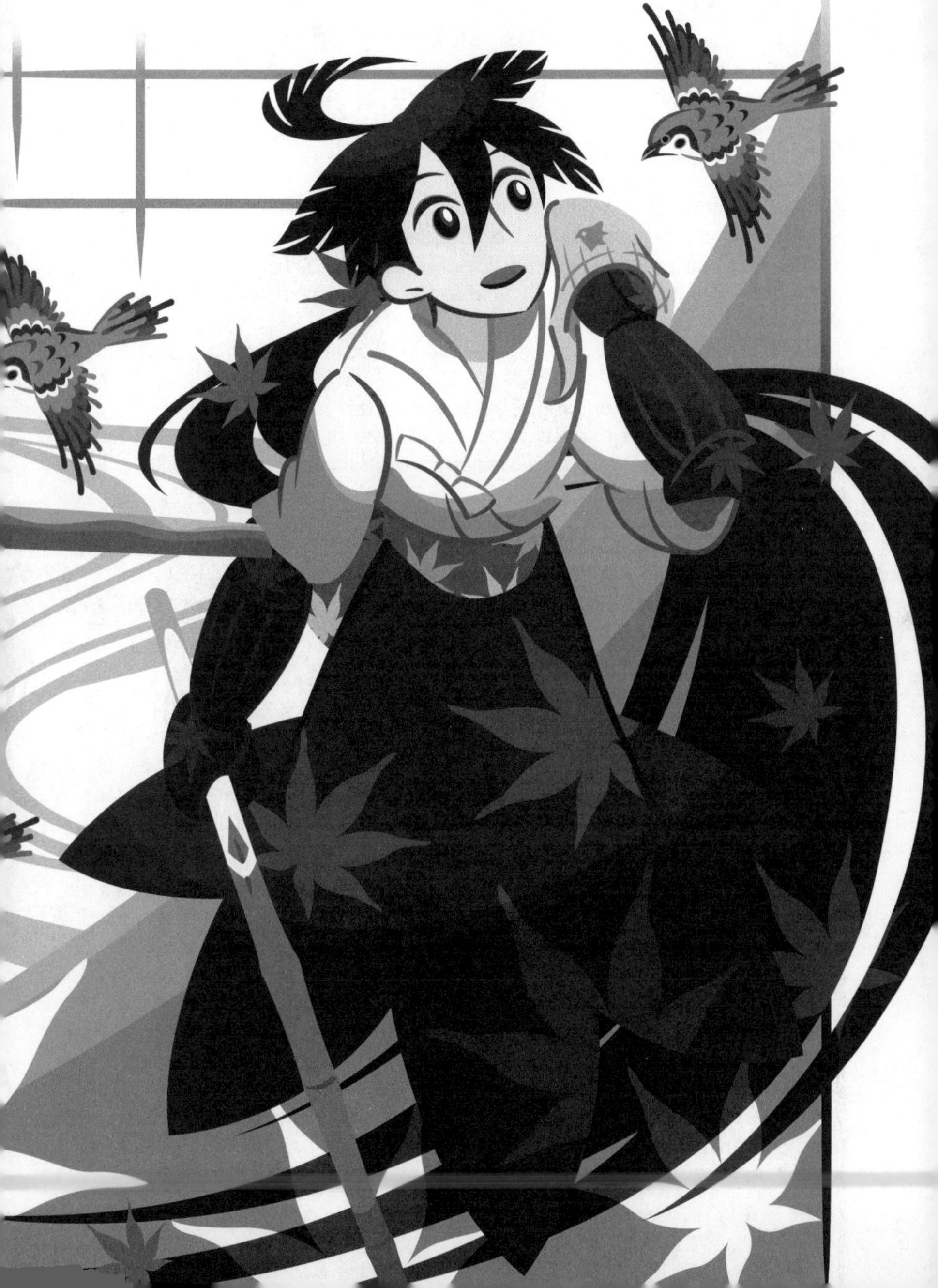

would never have crossed her mind.

"Please try to understand—Oto the Cured is both the trademark of Heartland Dojo and verification of my identity."

"I know the sword was passed down through the generations and all," Shichika said, changing the subject, "but what went down during the Great Sword Hunt launched by the Old Shogun? How did the Heartland School protect the Cured?"

"At the time, Oto the Cured was not in the possession of the Heartland School," Kiguchi explained with that same serious look on her face.

The fact that she was no less gracious, even now that Shichika had been cast in the role of pupil, and thus Kiguchi in the role of instructor,[7] shows you the kind of person that she was.

"If I remember correctly, Oto the Cured became our property under the Eighth Master."

"So, like—your father's father's father's father?"

"No, it's true that I took over the school from my grandfather—but for the most part, the Heartland School has not been passed down through a bloodline."

"Oh, okay."

Unlike the Kyotoryu, thought Shichika.

"Then maybe you don't know exactly how the Eighth Master came to own Oto the Cured?"

"Let alone exactly, I have no clue. I know it was more recent than the Great Sword Hunt, but it still happened quite some time ago."

"Hmm."

Maybe—it didn't matter.

All that mattered was that it was here now.

"In my mind..."

Then.

Zanki Kiguchi—had something to say.

"I am nowhere near as honest a person as you say, Master Shichika."

"Yeah, you mentioned that."

"Indeed. I still have a long way to go—but you should have seen me as a kid. I slacked on my training, and spent all of my time[8] out in the village, playing shogi. The late master and I were always getting into fights about my behavior."

"Wow."

Hard to imagine, from Kiguchi today.

But she was a teenager, too, once upon a time.

On a side note, this would appear to explain why she had decent enough shogi skills to pass muster with Togame.

"When my grandfather passed—I had no interest whatsoever in taking over the dojo, which by then had no more followers, but things changed entirely once I held Oto the Cured. It was so validating."

---

[7] 師範　SHIHAN　teacher　often used in a martial arts context
[8] 明け暮れて　AKEKURETE　"from dawn to dusk"

Kiguchi held Oto the Cured up sideways in front of her face.

"I felt my entire body firming up[9]—if that makes sense. Today, if I'm any better of a person than I was before, I think I owe it all to Oto the Cured."

"..."

In that case, perhaps her intense dedication to her training was an attempt to make amends and recover the losses of her youth.

"Actually, in a similar way, my grandfather used to say that when he took over the Cured from his own master, it gave him a new lease on life—Shangri-Oto,[10] he called it."

"Shangri-Oto..."

This got Shichika thinking: *What if this was what made the Cured special?*

Not only lacking venom, but going further, leaching the venom from whomsoever owned it, a Mutant Blade invested with *the power to detoxify*—

Of course, Shichika didn't strike upon the idea yet.

Could not strike upon the idea yet—that Dokuto the Basilisk, currently held by Hohoh Maniwa and supersaturated with the thewiest[11] of venom, was in fact the polar opposite of the Cured.

Oto the Cured.

Shangri-Oto...

"Man, what Meisai Tsuruga would have done to get her hands on this."

"Huh? Who is this Meisai Tsuruga that you speak of?"

"Uh—no one."

Shichika scrambled[12] to divert the subject.

"But yeah, I mean, if you were able to get a brand-new start[13] thanks to this wooden sword, that's pretty cool."

"Who knows. Because I'm too worldly,[14] not a day goes by where I don't think about the other options that I could have had in life."

"Other options?"

"Surely I could have lived for love."

Kiguchi spoke with extreme sincerity—you could hear it in her voice.

"When I see you beside Madame Togame, I'm unable to suppress this feeling of resignation."

"What's wrong with being a master swordsman, though?"

"In this day and age, swordplay has been rendered useless," Kiguchi stated matter-of-factly—no hint of self-derision,[15] no undertones of irony. "I dare say the Heartland School will end with me—in which case, I genuinely hope to do good by my predecessors as a swordsman. Still, I have to wonder if the way I'm

---

[9] 引き締まる　HIKISHIMARU　"pull tight"　grow tense
[10] 王刀楽土　ŌTŌ RAKUDO　"Paradise of Oto the Cured"
　　　　　　pun on　王道楽土　ŌDŌ RAKUDO　"royal-road paradise"　(i.e. realm ruled by a good king)
[11] 強大　KYŌDAI　"massively strong"
[12] 慌てて　AWATETE　rushed, hurried
[13] 更生　KŌSEI　"renew life"　rehabilitate
[14] 俗物　ZOKUBUTSU　"vulgar thing"　philistine
[15] 自嘲気味　JICHŌ GIMI　"touch of self-mockery"

obsessing over this has more to do with my inability to let go[16] than anything else."

"That sounds..."

That sounds like me—is what Shichika wanted to say.

After all, if Togame had never shown up on Haphazard Island and conscripted Shichika into her Sword Hunt, the story of the Kyotoryu would have been over, dying a quiet[17] death on that desert island in the waters off of Tango.

Ending with Shichika.

Hence his thought, *That sounds like me*.

But he had stopped short of telling her as much—because at this stage of the game, he could hardly claim that his entire life revolved around his school of swordplay.

His life revolved around Togame.

Like Kiguchi said, he lived for love.

In that sense—he was impure.

Lacking the purity—of Zanki Kiguchi.

He had nothing—like her perfect posture.

"..."

"Are you alright, Master Shichika?"

"I mean...that all sounds fine to me. The Cured wasn't made for killing, right? And isn't the Heartland School all about giving life? I wouldn't call that useless, even in these times of peace and order."

"Master Shichika."

It was then—that her tone became self-deprecating.[18] Her face was stern as ever, no smile or smirk, but her self-derision was clearly audible.

"Even a wooden sword can kill, if you hit somebody on the head."

"..."

"A hit to the forearms cracks their bones, a hit to the torso bursts their innards, and a jab to the throat ruptures their windpipe. That is why we wear pads when we spar. It's just that the Heartland School can't cut you down—while it was not made for taking life, it can kill."

■ ■

"Hey, Togame. Boy, did I learn some interesting stuff today! I know I still suck pretty bad, but it feels great to get some exercise. You know, I could get used to training at the Heartland Dojo."

"Cheerio!"

When Shichika arrived home to the inn that night with these good tidings,

---

[16] 未練　MIREN　lingering attachment
[17] むなしく　MUNASHIKU　in vain (also written 虚しく with first character in 虚刀流 KYOTŌRYŪ)
[18] 自虐的　JIGYAKUTEKI　"self-abusing" vs. 被虐的 HIGYAKUTEKI masochistic

Togame greeted him with her familiar cry, delivering a flying backwards roundhouse kick to his face. An incongruous attack from someone who eschewed all armaments and lacked any ability in the martial arts, this was questionable behavior to be sure, but after what Shichika had declared, perhaps she could be forgiven for her exaggerated reaction.

"Get used to it? Hello! What happened to the proud Master of the Kyotoryu?"

"Whoa...I'm pretty sure you were the one who forced me into this...but damn, you sure can kick for someone wearing all those bulky clothes..."

Per usual, Shichika had made no attempt to dodge Togame, taking her abuse full force, but her flying backwards roundhouse kick had evidently caught him by surprise.

"Now that my hair's cropped short, I'm light as can be. Like I might soar into the sky."

"Ahh."

Fine with this explanation, Shichika plopped down on the floor.

In turn, Togame hitched up her "bulky clothes" that looked like twice a dozen layers of flamboyant finery, and sat down in front of Shichika.

"Well then, I know it's taken me a while—but I've come up with something," Togame cut to the chase.

Not giving Shichika a chance to rest after another long day of training.

But as her faithful servant, he had no complaints. "Come up with what?"

"A scheme, dummy. What else would I come up with?"

"I hope you're exaggerating about that."

"At any rate, I've looked at this from every angle, and I think there's only one realistic way for you to beat Zanki Kiguchi."

"So there's only one way for me to beat Kiguchi, huh..."

"At least, so long as you're stuck wearing pads, armed with a wooden sword, and following her rules. Granted, if you could be yourself and fight her barefoot, stripped to the waist, without your arm guards, I have the utmost confidence that you would win. But given who we're dealing with, that won't be possible."

"Not possible, huh."

"I thought through countless ways that you could try to beat her, under those conditions—but up against a person as absurdly serious as Kiguchi, things are bound to go the same direction every time."

"You think Oto the Cured is what's making her so serious? Kiguchi said so herself."

"Oh? Interesting perspective—that's kind of deep. Either way, though, it's clear that this time around, we need to focus on Kiguchi much more than the Mutant Blade."

"So? What's your scheme for me to beat her?"

"*Lean into your weakness*," Togame said simply, aiming her pointer finger[19] at Shichika's face. "I assume you have not forgotten the way Konayuki beat you atop Mt. Odori? In your first defeat of the entire Sword Hunt—"

---

[19] ひとさし指でさして HITO SASHI YUBI DE SASHITE "pointing with the person-pointing finger"

"Yeah, don't remind me."

"Copy her."[20]

"Copy?" Shichika looked at her askance, like he had no idea what she was saying. "What do you mean? I don't have the monstrous strength of Konayuki. I mean, I'm confident in my abilities—"

"This isn't about monstrous strength. Remember what made Konayuki fearsome? It had nothing to do with her monstrous strength. It was the fact she was a *total amateur*."

Shichika Yasuri, Seventh Master of the Kyotoryu versus Konayuki Itezora, sole surviving member of the Itezora Clan.

The main reason why Konayuki had beaten Shichika in their first fight was the huge *disparity* between their skillsets—Konayuki knew nothing of the ways of battle, lacking any real experience or training in the art of war, since she was just a little girl, but that turned out to be precisely why she won.

As an amateur, her moves were unexpected.

As an amateur, her moves were unpredictable.

And due to this enormous disparity in skill—

Shichika lost miserably.

"Take a cue from Konayuki—this time, you're going to beat Zanki Kiguchi, master of the wooden sword, *because you're the amateur*."

"Hmm..." Shichika nodded, attempting to digest[21] this proclamation from his owner. "Still," he said, once he had caught the gist of her idea. "Remember how you said me losing to Konayuki was no more than a fluke accident?"

"Yes?"

"Yes, you say... I mean, don't fluke accidents happen on their own? Trust me, I think your idea is amazing, the sort of thing that only you could see—but how are we supposed to guarantee an accident will happen?"

"You could search the world wide over and never find that kind of guarantee," Togame scoffed. "Even against Konayuki, the odds of you losing by a fluke were one to ten, or even poorer."

"Uh...in that case, isn't it a bad idea to bet on such low odds?"

"Of course. This is just the basic premise[22] of the scheme—I've also come up with ancillary measures to make it happen."

"Like what?"

"Here's what I have in mind—for starters, you can sit tight while I battle Kiguchi."

"You mean shogi, right?"

"Clearly."

Shichika had just been checking, but Togame assured him resolutely—although perhaps she could save such resoluteness for other occasions.

"Wait, though, isn't Kiguchi the one asking for a rematch? What reason does

---

[20] 踏襲 TŌSHŪ follow suit
[21] 咀嚼 SOSHAKU chew
[22] さわり SAWARI highlight

she have to play another game of shogi?"

"None yet, but we'll give her one. I'll show her a fair fight[23]... Specifically... this would all depend on how negotiations go, but in terms of my blueprint, I'm thinking I'll propose a nine-game showdown."

"Nine games...sounds like a lot."

"Don't say that too loud around here, or they'll laugh us out of town."

"Alright, but isn't nine a little random? Why not play ten?"

"It has to be odd to avoid a draw. Since eleven is even more random, we're going with nine. And here's where it gets interesting—*the final score* determines the number of bouts."

"Number of bouts?"

"Between you and Kiguchi. If I win five out of nine games, you get to fight her once. If I win six, you'll fight her three times. At seven, it'll be five times. At eight, it'll be seven. And if I win all nine games, you'll get to fight her nine. But regardless of the number of bouts, all you have to do is beat her once, and we go home with Oto the Cured. Those are our terms."

"Okay, got it—way more involved[24] than last time."

If Togame had asked Kiguchi to give Shichika nine chances at winning—she never would have gone along with it, but by adding in the smokescreen of the shogi showdown, Togame hoped to *smooth things over.*[25]

All Kiguchi had to do was win five times or more, meaning the majority of the games, to ensure Oto the Cured stayed in her possession—and if she lost the majority and had to battle Shichika a few times, they could expect her to take full responsibility.

But even if she had to fight Shichika a hundred times, she would still probably go in assuming that at day's end, Oto the Cured would still be hers.

"I know you didn't exactly go easy on her, but last time you played Kiguchi, you sort of acted like it was closer than it was, right? Not saying you're gonna win all nine rounds necessarily, but I can see you winning eight—in that case, I'd get seven chances to beat Kiguchi. That's pretty good. Seven bouts gives us a decent chance of a fluke happening—"

"Shichika," Togame the Schemer—summarily negated Shichika's view of the situation. "I'm not trying to win that many games—*my aim is to win five.*"

"Huh?" Shichika was baffled, unable to ken her meaning.

"There's always the chance things won't go according to plan. I could wind up winning six—but regardless, I need for you to beat Zanki Kiguchi on the first bout."

"H-How come?"

"Because we're here to win by fluke—it's not the same as rolling dice. The fewer chances, the better."

"B-But..."

---

[23] 負荷を[...]背負ってもらう FUKA WO[...]SEWOTTE MORAU have someone take on a burden
                                          in this case, to even things out

[24] 発展版 HATTENBAN "developed version"

[25] 印象をぼやかせる INSHŌ WO BOYAKASERU obscure the impression

Shichika was hopelessly confused.

"Then why should you play Kiguchi again at all? Like I said, as long as it's one round, I think she would agree to fight right away."

"Because the shogi showdown has outsize importance."

"Outsize importance? What do you mean by—"

"Listen—actually, never mind. I'm not telling," she left Shichika hanging, without so much as a clue. "Thinking it over, I think it's best for you to go in blind."[26]

"Huhhhhh?"

"I don't suspect that telling you would change the outcome, but just in case—leave it to me. That is, unless not knowing means you're unable to trust my scheme?"

"N-No..."

Who could answer yes to that?

Especially when she insisted things would go more smoothly if he went in blind.

"I'll take your word for it. You don't need to tell me. Let me ask you this, though. How much do these ancillary measures, the ones you're keeping to yourself, boost my odds?"

"I'd say it'll be fifty-fifty."

A little low for her to say, *Leave it to me.*

Not exactly what you call a boost.

In a sense those odds were not half bad, considering how weak Shichika became once he picked up a sword—but Togame was painfully aware the odds were miserable.

"I spent ten days hashing out ideas, but this sloppy, clumsy scheme is still the best that I could do—somehow, it feels like we're working harder than necessary. Like we're making problems for ourselves, taking the long way around, oblivious—but know this, Shichika. I'm not sure whether she has the Cured to thank for this, but Kiguchi is not like anybody else—this once, and only once, I'm making an exception. To the best of our ability, I want for us to protect her honor."[27]

"Hmph."

Shichika felt the same.

Train under somebody for ten days straight, day in day out, hour after hour, and some degree of bonding is inevitable—the last thing Shichika wanted was a dirty fight[28] against Kiguchi, culminating in a bloodbath.[29] If doing things her way won them another of the Twelve Possessed, and safely, what could be better?

The more he thought it over,[30] the more Shichika regretted the way he had

---

[26] 事前には知らぬほうがよい JIZEN NI WA SHIRANU HŌ GA YOI better not to know in advance
[27] 顔を[...]立てて KAO WO[...]TATETE allow her to save face
[28] 泥仕合 DORO JIAI "mud match"
[29] 殺し合い KOROSHI AI "killing each other" (or attempting to)
[30] 返す返すも KAESU GAESU MO returning again and again

behaved until just recently.

Does this mean I've gotten stronger—or that I've gone soft?

"Wh-What do you mean you *bonded*... Don't tell me you've had another change of heart! Wh-What exactly were you two doing in the dojo anyway?! To think I trusted you enough to let you spend all this time alone with her! That's it. I'm fed up with your philandering!"

"...I'm the one who's fed up. With your jealousy."

Togame had spun this out of thin air. What a mess.

But then.

Although by no thanks to this outburst from Togame, Shichika noticed something weird about the plan she had proposed.

"Togame, I think we have a problem."[31]

"Problem? I'll admit that I was out of line to force you to train at another school, and certainly regret it, now that you love someone new, but I did the best I could, all things considered. The least you could do is honor that."

"I mean, I think that's a lost cause."

"Lost cause! This is our chance to set things straight! What gives you the right to singlehandedly dismantle everything we've built together?"

She was really going after him.

What was a man supposed to do?

"I meant, uh, there's a problem with your scheme."

"Huh? You did? In that case...we're okay."

"I'm not sure I'd say that we're okay..."

Despite having spent nine months traveling with Togame the Schemer, Shichika felt as if he barely understood the woman.

"Anyway, your scheme depends on me being an amateur with swords, right? Who knows about ten days ago, but while you were working on this scheme, I've been practicing like crazy, directly under Kiguchi, a master swordsman—doesn't that mean I'm not an amateur anymore?"

"Uh..."

"Honestly, it's kind of amazing how bad I am at handling a sword—even a wooden one. Without exaggeration, I've made almost no progress with the basic moves. But the rules and codes of her school are a different story. She's sat me down and drilled[32] me on those pretty good—at this point, I have a decent understanding of her style."

"Hmm..."

Apparently, this was not something Togame had considered. For a moment, she was pensive.[33] Shichika pressed his case.

"As you know well, Togame, I'm not so bright—so maybe saying that I understand her school is overdoing it, but hold on, because there's something else. I may have made a fool of myself training, but I also spent ten days watching

---

[31] やばいかもしれない YABAI KAMO SHIRENAI "this might be dangerous"
[32] 座学 ZAGAKU "seated study" classroom learning, as opposed to practical training
[33] 思案顔 SHIAN GAO "thinking face"

Kiguchi practice like the master that she is. Not like I can watch and learn like sis or anything, but I think I know a lot more about fighting with a wooden sword than I did ten days ago. Isn't this scheme less effective the more I know? If that's the case, I have a feeling the odds aren't as high as fifty-fifty."

"Right," Togame nodded, taking in this insight from Shichika. "I failed to think of that. My mistake—but I know what to do."

With that.

Walking on her knees like it was second nature, Togame scooched right up to Shichika and rested both her outstretched hands upon his tousled hair.

While seriously confused, Shichika held still.

Not even twitching.

For Shichika Yasuri never dodged an *attack* from his owner, taking every hit in stride—

"Mwah."[34]

Togame pressed her lips to his.

What was she doing to him?

Shichika was slow on the uptake.

But before he knew it, Togame had slipped back to where she was before.

From the look on her face, it was like nothing ever happened.

"Do you remember anything about it now?" she asked.

"..."

Shichika shook his head no.

Then finally spoke.

"I forgot all of it."

---

[34] ちゅう CHŪ onomatopoeia for kissing

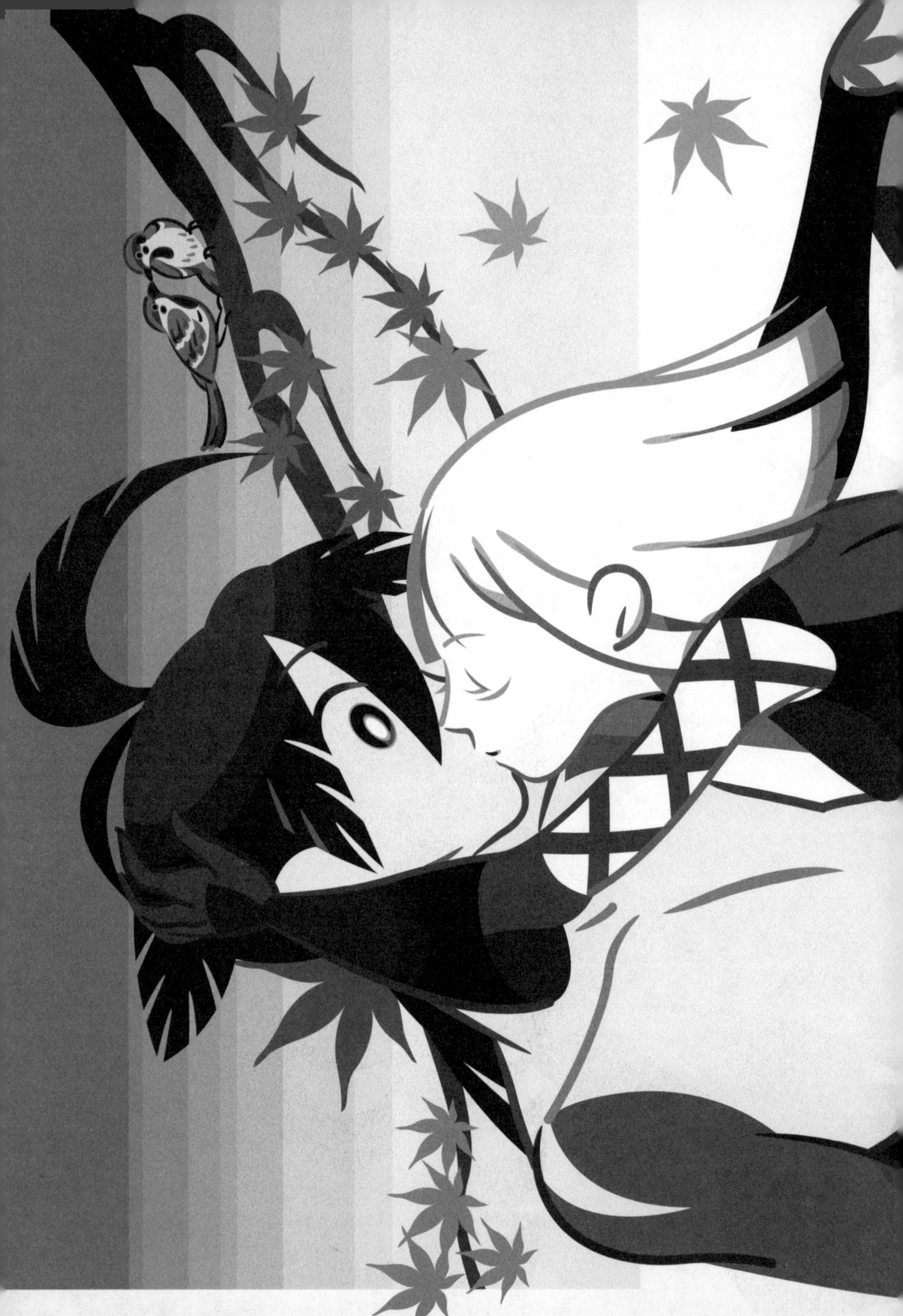

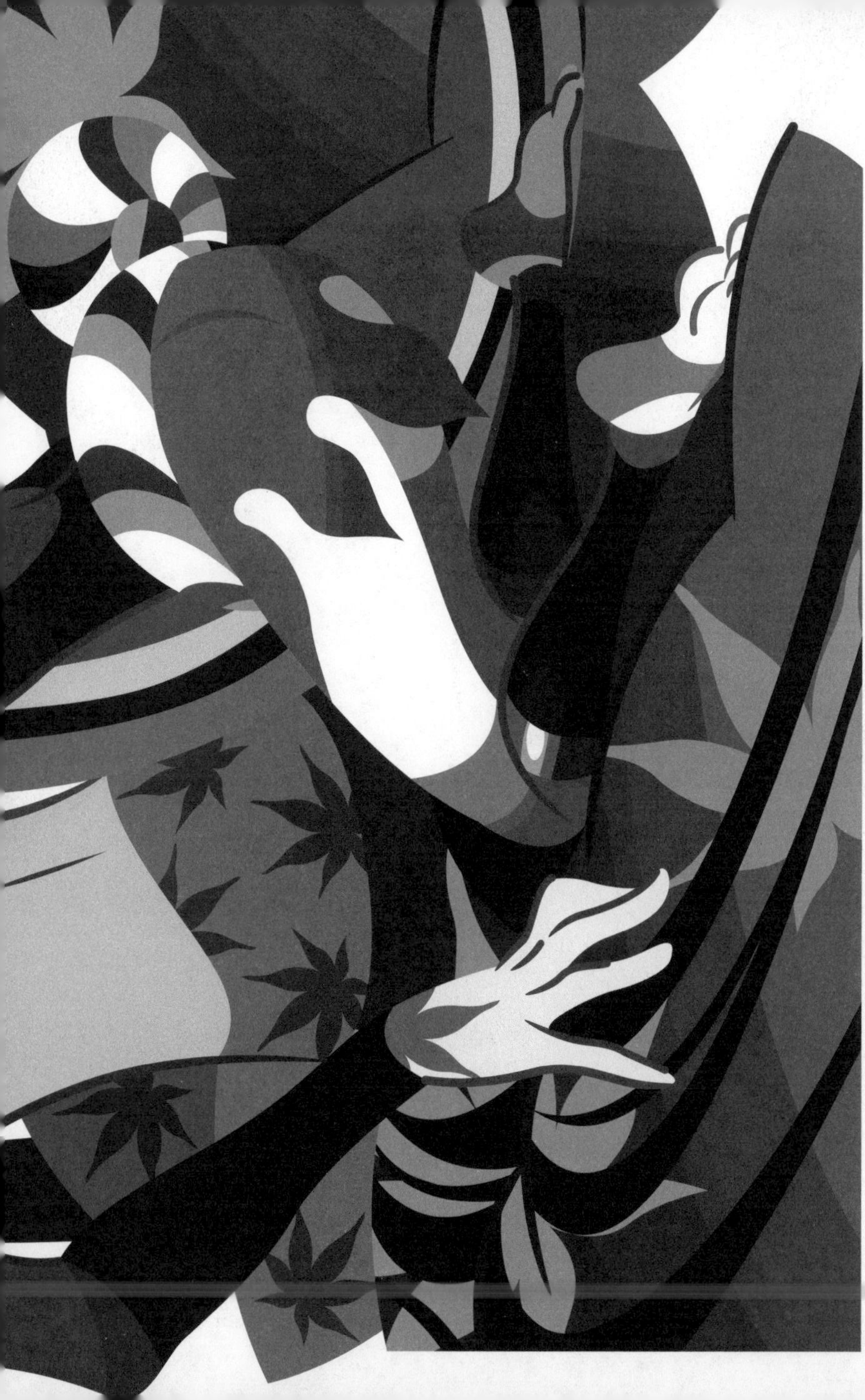

CHAPTER SIX

BLIND SHOGI

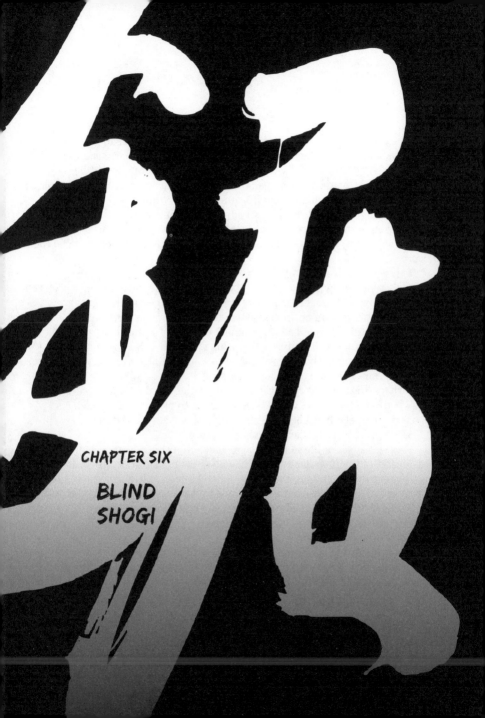

■ ■

The next day.

Albeit after a few twists and turns—things were proceeding according to the plan set forth by Togame the Schemer. Their greatest obstacle was Kiguchi's insistence that Shichika was not yet ready to face off against her—which was the honest truth, since he had made essentially no progress in the course of their ten days of training...but Togame talked her into it.

"Declining to face off against an adversary, citing a perceived difference in ability, is quite the show of arrogance, Madame Kiguchi—nothing is so absolute in swordplay. Any gap in skill is neutralized, once both parties have raised their swords."

This was sophistry.

If Togame really believed this rubbish, she should have spoken up eleven days ago; nevertheless, her sophistry was enough to persuade Kiguchi.

She was preying on her seriousness, her oh-so-serious nature.

Further still, Togame had successfully convinced Kiguchi to partake in the shogi showdown, which reaffirmed Shichika's faith in her powers of diplomacy. She'd gone in saying that negotiating with a person like Kiguchi was impossible—but things worked out in her favor.

Perhaps Togame had deliberately gone for the narrow chance.

"I had been hoping we would have a chance to play another round."

Or perhaps she had a hunch—that Kiguchi would take the bait.

All disputes were settled over shogi.

This was a fact of life in the village where Kiguchi came of age, and becoming Master of the Heartland School had no effect on her affection for the game.

Turning things around, this made Shichika feel as if Kiguchi had little interest in their rematch—but if that was how it was, he had to grin and bear it.[1]

Kiguchi had but one condition—once this was all over, she asked to abandon any further efforts to obtain Oto the Cured.

There would be no next time.

She made it clear that this would be their final try.

Coming from a person like Kiguchi, a declaration of this sort was not open to interpretation.[2] To Shichika, whose assigned strategy was riding on a fluke, giving him at best only a fifty-fifty chance of winning, the statement was unsettling.

"Affirmative.[3] Let's play."

Thus.

---

[1] ぐっと我慢 GUTTO GAMAN suppress a strong emotion
[2] 言葉を曲げる KOTOBA WO MAGERU bend words, i.e. go back on them
[3] 委細承知 ISAI SHŌCHI "agreed on the details"

Togame accepted her condition.

Whereupon—they played nine games of shogi.

Togame was unstoppable.[4]

That said, she stopped short of an overwhelming victory, instead beating Kiguchi five to four, the very score she had foretold[5] to Shichika.

Togame had performed as follows—1: win, 2: win, 3: loss, 4: loss, 5: win, 6: loss, 7: win, 8: win, 9: loss.

Shichika was simply amazed at her ability to lose on purpose, even if it was for her scheme—but what's more, in terms of how things actually played out, her five wins and four losses were all outstanding. Her winning games, as in her victory eleven days earlier, were neck and neck until the very end, and when she lost, she drew the game out for as long as possible.

Shichika did not understand the rules of shogi.

This made it hard for him to guess how Kiguchi felt about the results—if she had caught on to the fact that Togame had taken pains to win one way and lose another to manipulate the final score, then she'd decided not to bring it up.

Perhaps she thought choosing how to win was the prerogative of whoever was stronger.

—*As with swordplay.*

Either way.

The stage was set as Togame had intended, with one chance at a one-point match.

"Are you ready, Master Shichika?"

Dressed in her pads—wielding her sword of wood, and standing at the starting line, Twelfth Master Zanki Kiguchi checked in with Shichika Yasuri, similarly dressed in pads, wielding a wooden sword, and standing at the starting line.

Though he was not exactly ready for action.

If anything, the opposite.

All the same.

"Ready," Shichika answered. "Let me just say first, though—thanks for everything, over the past ten days. I may have been an awful student who didn't come away with anything of use, but the opportunity meant a lot[6] to me."

"No, you taught me more than I could ever have taught you—I'm afraid this only proves I am unqualified to be a teacher. I owe you an apology for being so incompetent."

"Hold off on the apologies. If I beat you in this match, that proves you did things right after all, know what I mean?"

"I suppose so... Um, Master Shichika, you're holding your sword incorrectly."

"What? Oh, okay."

He fixed his grip.

In forgetting all he knew of kendo, he had gone too far.

[4] 独壇場　DOKUDANJŌ　"stand alone on the dais"　nonpareil
[5] 予告　YOKOKU　say going in
[6] いい経験　II KEIKEN　good experience

Indeed.

Although his victory depended on him being an amateur, there were a number of basic things he would do well to keep in mind—and Togame had drilled them into him afresh the night before.

Specifically, what was off-limits.[7]

It would not do for him to be disqualified.

Kicking was prohibited.

As were throws and grappling moves.

Obviously, he had to hold onto his wooden sword.

No attacks to the lower body—and so on.

That said, because the referee was none other than Togame, she could probably overlook all but the most flagrant[8] violations. Kiguchi likely saw this as a fitting handicap—why else would she allow Togame, companion of the enemy, to play the role of arbitrator?

Or perhaps she honestly believed no *bakufu elite* like Togame the Schemer—liaison of the Military Directorate, would violate the rules.[9]

For her part, Togame was hoping to avoid any stark violations anyway, while leaving a little room for playing favorites.[10]

Togame the Schemer would take the Cured by strategy—it had gotten them this far.

Shichika was beginning to see the big picture—and though Togame told him he was better off going in blind, the way things had turned out made it impossible for him not to think.

As much as thinking was a pain for him.

The nine-game shogi showdown determined the number of bouts between Shichika and Kiguchi—but given this agreement, what had possessed Togame to only beat Kiguchi five to four?

What was the meaning of this feckless, meaningless behavior?

At first the answer was unclear to Shichika—but now that he was facing off against Kiguchi, a guess was taking shape inside his head.

It seemed to him—Togame had used her wins and failures to *evaluate* Zanki Kiguchi.

However much a parlor game.

Shogi remained a game of war—the only thing distinguishing it from the fight at hand being whether the two players wielded swords or pieces.[11] That there was no necessary correlation[12] between proficiency at shogi and proficiency in swordplay was a fact that Togame knew better than anybody out there—but in playing several games against a poet warrior like Zanki Kiguchi, she saw a chance of gleaning something of the strategies that the Master of the

---

[7] 反則行為　HANSOKU KŌI　"rule violations"
[8] あからさまな　AKARASAMA NA　blatant
[9] 不正をする　FUSEI WO SURU　commit wrongdoing
[10] えこひいき　EKO HIIKI　partiality
[11] 駒　KOMA　units whereby boardgames like shogi and chess are played　character cues equine imagery
[12] 法　HŌ　law

Heartland School would use in combat.

In that sense, it didn't matter whether Togame won or lost.

As long as she got to play—*a number of games.*

She wanted to learn how Kiguchi *would operate when faced with different challenges*—to learn *how Kiguchi comported herself in the heat of battle.*

They say a shogi play-by-play bears traces of your personality.

In those nine games, Togame had been trying to learn something about Kiguchi—and to do so, experiencing a good number of failures, namely four, had been essential.

All the more because Togame wanted Shichika to beat Kiguchi in one go—to that end, she craved a mastery of how Kiguchi won and how she lost.

Armed with this knowledge.

Togame—surely planned to use it in the battle between Kiguchi and Shichika.

This was risky business.

That said—they were still in business.[13]

If she was able to predict how Kiguchi would swing, their chances would improve—

—*But then again.*

If I don't understand her strategy, what difference does it make? If she's playing referee, there's no way she could pull me aside, while I'm fighting, and help me out.[14]

But in actuality.

What Shichika had guessed was about half right.

Considering his mental acuity, this level of precision was praiseworthy—but in practice, what Togame had in mind was far more elementary.

It was a scheme that only could have worked in Shogi Village, in these circumstances, and under these conditions—but the very fact that Shichika, who had been told that he was better off not knowing, had been able to deduce that much just goes to show how brazen of a scheme it was.

Though thinking was a pain for him.

He couldn't help but think it over—

"Alright then, Master Shichika, let us begin."

"Hold on," Togame said to this prompt from Kiguchi.

It sort of killed the mood,[15] but she had to say this, or she could never give the signal to begin.

"Just to be clear—is there no other way we can convince you to relinquish Oto the Cured? You swordsmanship is top-notch—I'm sure that many in the bakufu would readily employ the services of the Heartland School."

"I have long since abandoned such ambitions. Who needs a sword these days? I said as much to Master Shichika just yesterday. After devoting my whole life

---

[13] 無理筋　無理ではない　MURISUJI　MURI DE WA NAI　illogical move　not impossible
[14] 助言をする　JOGEN WO SURU　advice, coach
[15] 水を差す　MIZU WO SASU　"throw cold water"　discourage

to this sword, I am prepared to give my life for this sword," Kiguchi turned down Togame's offer summarily—as if her answer were prescribed.

"Only the heart can slay what chokes the heart. Hence the name Zanki. I am Zanki Kiguchi—Twelfth Master of the Heartland School. Show me what you can do."

"Don't worry, I was gonna show you anyway, but you'll probably miss it—*if you're torn to smithereens.*"

Putting aside the fact that his catchphrase had become a bit perfunctory.

Things were certainly heating up—[16]

"Alright," Togame said.

Then gave her standard line.

"May the best sword win—go!"

Hearing the signal—neither of them moved.

Vigilant.

Shichika, the novice, was trying not to dive in recklessly, while Kiguchi, the master, was hesitant to win the fight too quickly.

This, obviously, could be turned to their advantage.

The fact that this fight was the *real deal*,[17] but with *wooden swords*—and steeped in an air of seriousness that came from the relationship of this instructor with her pupil, offered a great advantage to a person like Togame—and so the Schemer.

Added this—in the same tone as her standard referee line.

"Pawn to 7-6."

Announcing her move.

■　■

Capitalizing on a difference in ability and banking on a fluke—this time around, Togame the Schemer was able to come up with no better strategy, but in order to make it happen, there were several conditions they would have to overcome.

Their model was the fight on Mt. Odori versus Konayuki Itezora.

As Togame had assured Shichika time and time again, she was certain that he could have beaten Konayuki if only he had fought her normally.

In that case, why did he lose?

Apart from the fluke, why had he lost? After all, a difference of ability in his favor was not a logical explanation for what happened.

Simply put, he let his guard down—Togame had instructed him to take it easy on her, since she was just a little kid and everything.

If you stay focused—and brace yourself for action, you usually obtain a result commensurate with your ability.

[16] 機は[...]熟した　KI WA[...]JUKU SHITA　the time is ripe
[17] 真剣勝負　SHINKEN SHŌBU　"match with real swords"　a serious fight

Which brings us to Zanki Kiguchi.

Would somebody with such powers of focus that she failed to notice two intruders in her dojo—let her guard down against Shichika Yasuri, even when his difference in ability was so pronounced?

Most likely not.

Her school of swordsmanship gave life.

Only the heart can slay what chokes the heart.

She was not fighting Shichika, so much as herself—what reason would she have to let her guard down?

Her focus was impeccable—so why not peck away[18] at it?

Sneak up on her and yell, make things go bang—such ploys are usually enough to break somebody's focus, but an obnoxious disturbance[19] was nothing to Kiguchi.

Something quieter, however, might do the trick.

To that end.

In the last of her nine games against Kiguchi, Togame had *lost*, in order to go first in a tenth game!

"Pawn to 7-6."

Hearing these words.

Zanki Kiguchi froze.

An avid gamer in her teens, Zanki Kiguchi, after taking on her name of shame, lived only for the Heartland School of swordplay, but she was anything but slow on the uptake.[20]

In fact, she prided herself on her intellect.

She knew exactly what Togame was up to.

Kiguchi fully understood how scary it was to fight an amateur—in part, perhaps, because the Kyotoryu was geared toward mortal combat, whereas the Heartland School was geared toward sporting practice.

She would not let her guard down.

She had braced herself, so as not to overthink the way Shichika moved or to get confused by unfamiliar movements.

Though compelled to look out for her pupil—she had no plans to break her focus.

So, when Togame called out her move, Kiguchi understood that she was trying to distract her—and recognized that the Schemer had thrown the final game intentionally—in order to be accorded the first move in the next.

Nevertheless.

When she heard those words.

Pawn to 7-6.

Kiguchi could not help but think about her countermove—*not thinking intentionally*, but automatically. After all, Zanki Kiguchi was born and raised in

---

[18] 乱れはない 乱せばいい MIDARE WA NAI MIDASEBA II no disturbance then just disturb
[19] 妨害 BŌGAI "obtrusive obstacle"
[20] 鈍い NIBUI dull (sword); stupid

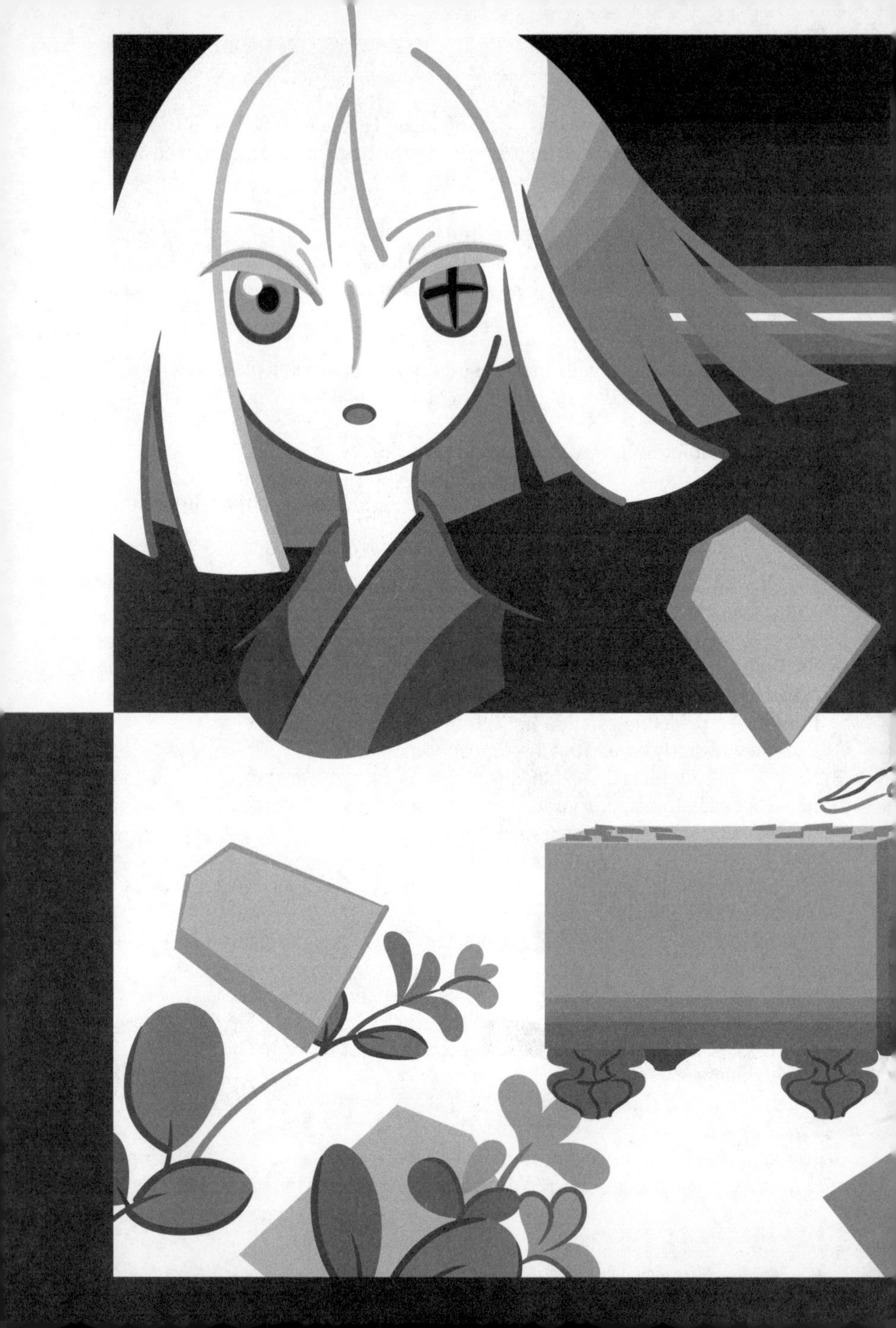

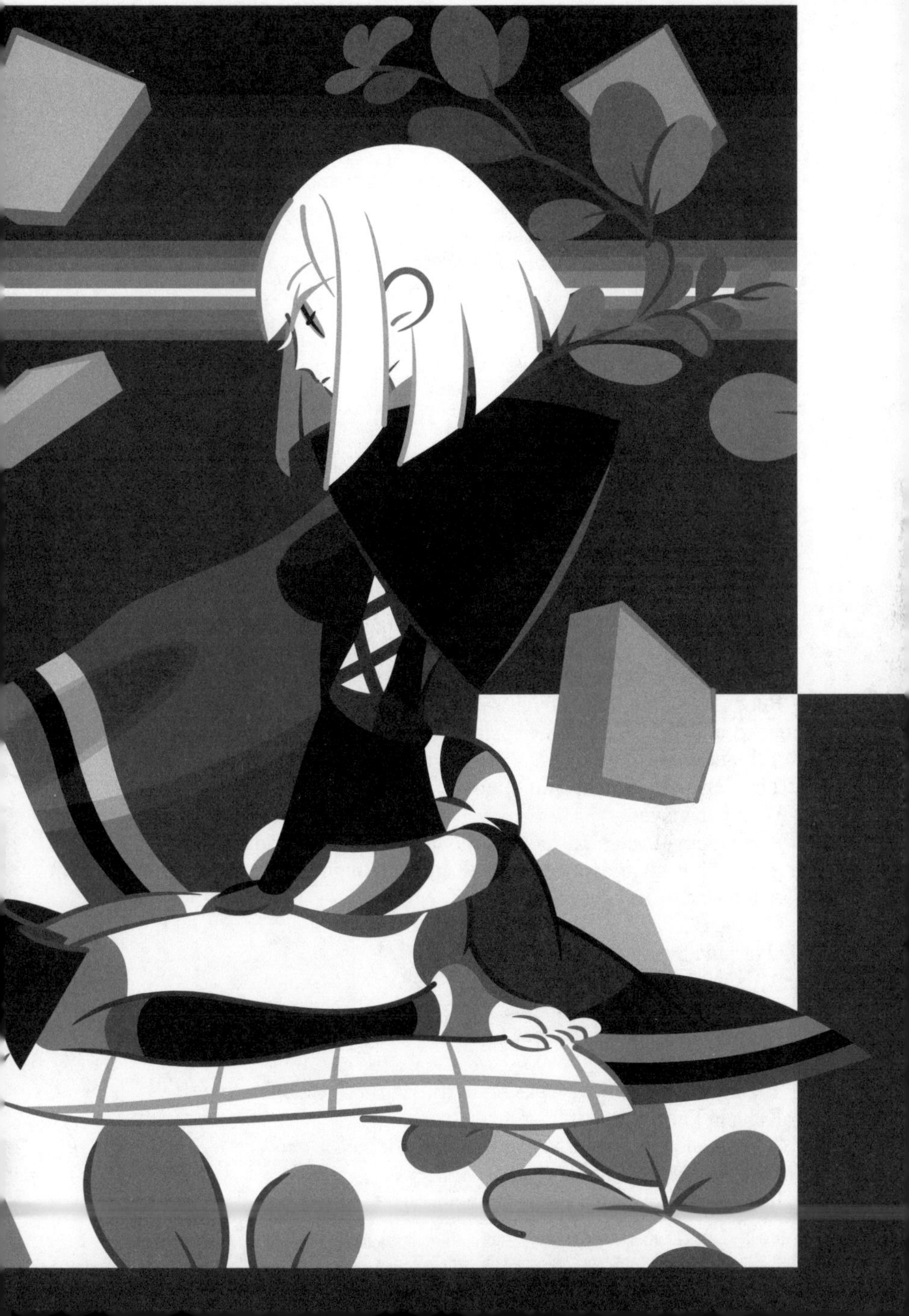

Shogi Village—
    —*If she does that.*
    I'll go with: Pawn to 3-4.
    "Bishop to 2-2."
    No sooner than she thought it—Togame announced her move to follow.
    Swapping bishops with her out of nowhere.
    A hasty move—but wait a second.
    —*T-Take with Silver General.*
    "Silver General to 8-8."
    With that.
    Togame moved her silver general as well, balancing the vertical symmetry of the board.
    —*It's like...*
    She can see my moves before I make them.
    This was blind shogi.
    A way of playing that requires two competitors of unaverage ability—but not a shogi board. The game is played with the imagination, a test of memory as much as skill. This was obviously no easy feat, but almost anybody from the village could play this way, to some degree.
    Back in her teens, Kiguchi used to do this all the time.
    But Togame's version—was *another thing entirely.*
    Kiguchi was not saying her moves out loud—she was *only thinking them.* Saying them inside her head.
    But as if reading her thoughts—as if seeing every single move that she was going to make. Like she was seeing everything, even the thoughts leading up to each decision—
    The Schemer launched an offensive.[21]
    With her moves.
    Announcing each next move—the instant Kiguchi had decided.
    And with each announcement—Kiguchi thought only of her countermove.
    After which, Togame moved again.
    On and on.
    Over and over—chipping away.
    At her focus.
    Breaking her down—wearing her out.
    At this point, she was about to blow[22]—
    "Bishop to 5-5."
    Togame was relentless—as if she'd read those thoughts too.
    Kiguchi knew.
    The simplest way to disrupt Togame's strategy—*all she had to do was not think about the next move.*
    It takes two to play a game of shogi.

[21] 切り込んでくる KIRIKONDE KURU "come cutting in" ironic, since no swords are involved
[22] 自滅 JIMETSU self-destruct, dig one's own grave

If one player walks away from the game, there cannot be a winner.

And yet—it was exactly as Princess Negative had proclaimed at Mansion Negative in Owari, though speaking on a topic unrelated to this match.

People can think all they want.

Not thinking, though, is strangely difficult.

Even Shichika, who had a hard time thinking about anything, had an even harder time thinking about nothing; this was only truer for a poet warrior like Kiguchi.

Nay.

The Schemer was—*urging* her to think.

Thinking of anything except the fight was tantamount to[23] letting down your guard—

—*Alright then.*

Gold General to 7-2.

Kiguchi purposely made a weak move—one which wouldn't come to life down along the line, but didn't hurt either, in effect passing.

—*Let's see her act on this.*

"Bishop on 9-5."

Togame somehow saw through even this and responded accordingly—speaking softly, almost in a whisper.

Indeed, her voice was quiet.

At that volume, she could distract Kiguchi without distracting Shichika.

Reason being—*Shichika knew nothing about how shogi was played.*

Let alone blind shogi.

He couldn't even tell you how a rook moved.

In contrast to the grand scheme that she had used against his genius sister, Nanami Yasuri, at Seiryoin Gokenji Temple, which had kept both Shichika and Nanami in the dark—this was the exact opposite, a terribly small scheme.

It would have failed on anyone but Kiguchi.

On anybody but Zanki Kiguchi, the poet warrior!

"Khh..."

—*Alright, Lance on 5-8!*

The move—defied all reason.

Moreover, she was placing a captured piece—no way it could be read.

This made it check, too.

Unless Togame took the lance, it was Kiguchi's game—but there was no way that the Schemer could expect her to just throw away a piece like that—

"Take with King."

—*She got me.*

Togame seized the lance like it was nothing.

—*So that's why.*

That's why we played nine games.

It didn't matter whether she had won or lost.

---

[23] 同義 DŌGI "same significance"

As long as she got to play—a number of games.
Hence—why Shichika's guess was about half right.
Her approach to the shogi board—
How she responded to certain moves.
Over the course of those nine games—or actually, ten games, if you include their first match eleven days before, Togame had been sizing up Kiguchi.
Hence how she saw her "Gold General to 7-2" and "Lance on 5-8."
—*Who is she?*
Some mindreading wight?[24]
After all, they had only played those ten games.
Even if she had been playing not to win, but to size up Kiguchi—one game had at most two hundred moves.
Ten games would be two thousand.
Hardly enough to cover every pattern that could cross the board.
Had the Schemer—filled in any blanks with her imagination, gaining a total mastery of how Zanki Kiguchi played the game?
It takes two to play a game of shogi.
But at present—Togame the Schemer was running the show solo.
Like she was working through a shogi problem—from the first move, she had been forcing Kiguchi through the game, coercing her into each move!
Wh-Who does that?
Her focus had been cracked.
No—more like, her focus had been *diverted* to a game of shogi.
Just stop thinking.
Just stop thinking.
Why can't I stop!
"Pawn to 5-6."
Knight to 3-3.
"Knight to 7-7."
Rook to 8-4.
"Gold General to 4-7."
Silver General to 4-2.
"Lance on 5-5."
Pawn to 9-4.
"Head."
Huh?
Shichika's wooden sword—smacked Kiguchi on the forehead.
Shichika Yasuri, Seventh Master of the Kyotoryu versus Zanki Kiguchi, Twelfth Master of the Heartland School.
A quiet, abrupt, and unceremonious ending.
Believe it or not, it had been difficult for Shichika to hit Kiguchi, even with her standing right in front of him.
But now that he had, he did manage to stand fast for her counterstrike.

[24] 覚りの妖怪 SATORI NO YŌKAI "monster of consciousness" rooted in Japanese folklore

EPILOGUE

■ ■

"What? You dummy. Of course I couldn't have."

Togame the Schemer.

On their way back to Owari from Shogi Village, leaving behind Tendo and Dewa, Shichika asked Togame whether she could have maintained her spectacle of blind shogi with Kiguchi, predicting all her moves, for an entire game.

"It's only possible to predict the other player's moves reliably in the first stages of the game, when force of habit and temperament shine most brightly. I'd say that I had fifty moves in me. Once you move into the latter stages of the game, the board gets so mixed up there's no use trying to guess. All you can do is bet on the most likely option."

"Huh..."

"Like I told Kiguchi after the fact...shogi is too complex a game to learn everything about a player in ten rounds. But once you start calling out your moves like that, in rapid fire, the other player feels as if you're reading them like a book. The fact they aren't saying their moves out loud works to your advantage—since they must at least have considered the move I predicted. Basically, it's a kind of psychological warfare."

"Psychological warfare, huh. Count me outta that. Makes me wish you'd pulled those guns out when I fought Meisai Tsuruga."

"Fool. Battle is your bailiwick. Today was a very special case."

"Yeah, you're right. My bad.[1] But wait, if you're able to get under her skin like that, did we really need a lucky break? I could've beaten her regardless. She was a sitting duck. Anybody could have beaten her."

"That's tempting to think, now that you've won, but I assure you that you won because you were the amateur. My greatest fear about this strategy was obviously that Kiguchi would finish things before we had our chance—but I was also worried about her more ingrained abilities, the muscle memory created by her constant training. That realm is not my forte, but when warriors head into battle, their body does a large part of the thinking on its own, without the mind, wouldn't you say?"

"Yeah."

"I could distract Kiguchi all I wanted, but if you were just some average swordsman, swinging your sword normally, she likely would have snapped back out of reflex, with her muscle memory. Hence why your amateurish nature, unpolluted by the standard precepts, was essential to this scheme."

"You think I like being called an amateur? Personally, it's depressing. But yeah, I get how someone would have to rely on reason in order to respond to an unexpected move. And with Konayuki—well, I did my best. Still..."

[1] 面目ねえ MENBOKU NEH "no face or eyes"

There was something else that had been bothering Shichika.
But he hadn't had the nerve to ask until they were a good distance away from Tendo.
"Strictly speaking, wasn't that a violation of the rules? Interfering with the fight by bothering one of the players feels kinda unfair."
"Did you really just ask me that?" Togame was astonished. "Of course it was unfair."
"..."
"We had to think outside the board. She went into the fight assuming it would be quiet on the sidelines. But guess what. That fight was really two versus one—and that was more than Kiguchi could handle. I'm always refereeing fights for you, but I thought I'd play my trump card, just this once—although in all fairness, it is a card that never should be played."
"You'd think that she'd say something, though. Kiguchi was a stickler[2] for rules—"
"But remember, Shichika, who made that violation?" Togame asked. "Me, the referee."
"...Right."
Her rebuttal left him speechless.
She could probably overlook all but the most flagrant violations—
But what could be more flagrantly unfair?
"I thought—Schemers won through strategy."
"Well, yes. So if Kiguchi thought that I was out of line, she should have spoken up."
"But—she didn't."
"Don't you see why?"
Here, Togame.
Laughed maniacally.
She sounds like sis, Shichika thought. It was disturbing.
"*In that town—proposing a game of shogi could never be seen as a violation.*"
"Ahh..."
The holy land of shogi players.
It would be analogous to banning swordplay from that holy land of swordsmen, Seiryoin Gokenji Temple, back in Tosa.
Right.
That's what made it—a strategy.
"Alright. So, you're saying that if you'd given me advice or started screaming or whatever, she probably would've called you out on it."
"It would have made no difference. Kiguchi is a top-notch swordsman—once she's in her element, facing an adversary, I daresay she blocks out everything, background noise or otherwise. Any attempts to distract her by yelling or trying to confuse her, which was out of the question anyway, would never have broken

[2] うるさい URUSAI (usually) loud; (here) finnicky, annoying

her attention. The sole exception—being shogi."

"Gotcha... She grew up in the shogi capital of Japan. *How could she say no to shogi?*"

"That's it."

That's it, huh? thought Shichika.

Zanki Kiguchi was unable to dismiss[3] a shogi challenge.

She said that in her teens she was an avid player—but she must have been in love.

Which explains how even after devoting her whole life to swordplay—those memories had yet to fade.

Explains—why she agreed to play Togame in the first place, although she must have realized that the Schemer was up to something when things escalated to the nine-game showdown.

To recap—in the wake of the battle for Oto the Cured...

Zanki Kiguchi had one more go-around with both Togame the Schemer and Shichika Yasuri, battling each independently.

Her first fight being a final bout of shogi with Togame.

This time, however, they agreed—to play with no holds barred.

"Give me everything you've got," Kiguchi told Togame.

After that last scheme of hers, it was all too apparent that Togame had been holding back—but at this point, there was no reason to pull punches.[4] As requested, Togame went all out—and schooled Zanki Kiguchi.

In a mere forty-two moves, Kiguchi, who had the first move, gave up the game.

This, she felt, was the actual[5] Togame. Kiguchi's voice, when she declared *I'm out*, was more brisk than in any prior bout.

And so onto the second fight. A final duel against Shichika Yasuri.

This, obviously, being a test of swordsmanship—but with no pads or boundaries.

Kiguchi armed with Oto the Cured.

Shichika swordless and barefoot, ready for action.

While Togame played the role of referee, this one-point match was *strictly casual*[6]—

Kiguchi balked at the idea of fighting an unpadded opponent, but it was up to Shichika, as the victor, and he insisted.

Since they were only having fun, a little postgame[7] event, they agreed to take it easy, unlike the final bout of shogi between Kiguchi and Togame.

Dialing it back to about six tenths.

Restraining themselves.

And so, may the best sword win—*go*.

[3] ないがしろに NAIGASHIRO NI make light of
[4] 手を抜く TE WO NUKU "pull back the hand" give less than your best
[5] 真髄 SHINZUI "true marrow" essence
[6] かたいこと言いっこなし KATAI KOTO IIKKO NASHI cast formalities aside
[7] 決闘後 KETTŌGO "after battle"

Shichika was victorious.

His clincher[8] being Hyakka Ryoran playing off Form Three, the Tsutsuji. The Fatal Orchid he had used against that Sword Saint, Hakuhei Sabi—which goes to show how strong a foe Zanki Kiguchi proved to be for Shichika.

"I admit defeat."

Lowering her wooden sword at Hyakka Ryoran, which Shichika had reeled in just in time, Kiguchi knelt down on the dojo floor and bowed her head to meet her hands.

Her posture—marvelous.

"I underestimated you, Master Shichika. Please forgive me for treating a fantastic swordsman like yourself as if you were an unschooled pupil."

"Whoa—there's nothing to be sorry about. Come on, don't apologize. There's nothing wrong with any of your swordplay."

On the contrary.

If something was wrong with this picture—it was Shichika.

"Being weaker with a sword—feels like some kind of curse."

Her words hit home, surprisingly hard.

At any rate—they were done clashing with Kiguchi.

No more shogi, no more swordplay.

Which is why.

"As promised, I now relinquish Oto the Cured."

"Hey, thanks. But..."

Perhaps this would have been better left unsaid.

Yet Shichika said it without thinking.

"Are you sure? I mean, doesn't it verify you as the master or whatever?"

"I no longer have the right to wield this sword—or maybe it's the opposite. I have received more than my fair share of strength from the Cured. At some point, you need to let go. It's about time—I left home.[9] Every baby bird needs to hop out of the nest someday."

"..."

"You may use it for the sake of the nation, or you may break it in two and throw it away. The Cured is yours now, to do with as you please."

With that.

Saying nothing whatsoever, unlike Shichika—Togame the Schemer accepted the wooden sword that Kiguchi proffered.

Saying nothing—though she must have wanted to.

"Come back and visit anytime. And when you do, I'll have the shogi board ready to go. Until then, I'll look forward to it, safeguarding the trademark of the Heartland School."

"Trademark...but I thought Oto the Cured was the trademark?"

"Only the heart can slay what chokes the heart. Hence the name Zanki. From now on, I am the trademark of the school."

---

[8] 決まり手 KIMARI TE "decisive hand" winning move
[9] 親離れ OYA BANARE "distance yourself from your parents"

As Kiguchi spoke, her stoic mien relaxed, ever so slightly.

"The face of the brand."[10]

Needless to say...

Shichika hoped that someday he would have the chance to fight another swordsman like Kiguchi—this, too, being an observation that he would not have made a short time ago.

As it turns out.

Zanki Kiguchi had kind of a goofy side...

Didn't realize she liked puns...

"Looks like there's only three swords left—you think the Maniwacs beat us to all three of them?" asked Shichika.

"I'm not so sure. Those guys don't have what it takes...though I wouldn't be surprised if one of them fell into their hands."

Having thus obtained Oto the Cured, for the time being Togame the Schemer had secured her political reputation—they could now return to Owari without shame.

The Cured, of course, they shipped first-class ahead of them.

Allowing them to make the trek home unencumbered.[11]

These walks home were essentially their only downtime—back in Owari, there would be no time to rest.

Especially with Princess Negative around. And Emonzaemon Soda. Not to mention the Maniwa.

Out of the Twelve Possessed of Kiki Shikizaki—three remained.

"So, Shichika. This last adventure brought up something that we have to deal with going forward, as much as I wish we could ignore it."

"Huh? Oh, you mean that I become a total wuss when I pick up a sword? I mean, there's no way this same circumstance is gonna happen twice—"

"No, although that is a serious concern... It's about the Old Shogun."

"The Old Shogun? What makes him a concern out of the blue? Didn't he die forever ago?"

"It may have been forever ago, but I can't stop thinking about the Great Sword Hunt. I had this question on my mind these past ten days, the whole time I was working on my scheme: *How come the Old Shogun was unable to capture Oto the Cured?*"

"How come..."

"Lacking venom—or leaching venom—all that stuff aside, it's just a wooden sword. No razor edge, not really heavy—a wooden sword, plain and simple. So how did the historic owner of Oto the Cured repel the forces of the Old Shogun? The only thing that slowed us down this time was accommodating Kiguchi's way of doing things—compared to all the other months, don't you think this month was pretty easy?"

"Uh...when I asked her something similar, she told me that the Heartland

---

[10] 看板娘　KANBAN MUSUME　"sign girl"　woman employed by a shop to attract customers
[11] のんびり、徒歩での　NONBIRI, TOHO DE NO　leisurely, and on foot

School didn't actually own the sword back then."

"It makes no difference whether the sword was owned by them or someone else. That fails to explain why the Old Shogun was unable to capture it."

Shichika had no idea how to respond to this.

Togame was exactly right.

What had stopped the Old Shogun from capturing Oto the Cured?

But were they sure—he hadn't captured it?

"In enacting the Great Sword Hunt—the Old Shogun's official motive was to build the Katana Buddha. His ulterior motive was to hunt down all the swordsmen. His true motive was to collect all of the Mutant Blades of Kiki Shikizaki—but in light of this new information, there is a strong possibility that he was harboring an additional true motive, deeper than the first. Here I am, thinking that we've come this far from learning from the Old Shogun's mistakes...but maybe his Great Sword Hunt failed for a different reason entirely."

"Okay. Therefore?"

"Therefore—never mind." Halfway through her sentence, Togame shook her head. "It's just a possibility. Not worth getting worked up about. Forget about it."

"Forget it? Pretty tough, when you just leave me hanging[12] like that..."

"Oh, what's this?"

Togame laughed.

A laugh fraught with obscenity.

"Are you asking me to make you forget everything again?"

■　■

The two of them arrived back at the Schemer Mansion eight days later—but they were barely there at all before they set off for their next destination.

On the trail of Seito the Garland. Heading off—to Oshu.

Indeed, the childhood home of Togame the Schemer, though known as such to almost no one, was the very place they hoped to find Seito the Garland, their next target of the Twelve Possessed—thus bringing her back to her hometown, after nearly twenty years away.

Oto the Cured: Check
End of Book Nine
To Be Continued

---

[12] 気になること　KI NI NARU KOTO　a thing or words "becoming spirit"　stuck in one's head

CHARACTER INDEX 8

ZANKI KIGUCHI

AGE	Twenty-four
OCCUPATION	Swordsman
AFFILIATION	Heartland School
STATUS	Master
POSSESSED	Oto the Cured
HEIGHT	5' 5"
WEIGHT	105 lbs.
HOBBY	Practicing

LIST OF SPECIAL MOVES

SHANGRI-OTO	(PERPETUALLY ACTIVE)
BEYOND BOUNDARY	⇨⇨ THRUST
ONLY WOOD	⇧⇗⇨ SLASH
ARMOR UP	⇩⇘⇨ KICK (RAPID FIRE)
GIVING LIFE	⇦ (HOLD) ⇨ SLASH + THRUST + KICK

OPPONENT	Rinne Higaki
OBJECTIVE	Seito the Garland
VENUE	Mutsu: Hyakkeijo

AFTER(S)WORD

In real life, a person of inferior powers taking down a person of superior powers, or a person of superior powers getting taken out by a person of inferior powers, is perhaps not very common, but it is by no means rare. The eventual winner and loser are not always obvious right off the bat, and sudden reversals and major upsets happen with surprising frequency. Thinking this over, most of the time, it points to something overlooked in your initial observations, meaning that the person you thought was superior is actually the weaker one, and the person you thought inferior the stronger one. This turning of the tables can be pretty moving for anyone on the sidelines. Saying "whoever should win will win, no ifs ands or buts, and no reason to overanalyze things" would be going way too far, but we certainly have a tendency to think this way nowadays. We expect the stronger person to win, and so we have no reason to applaud them, and expect the weaker person to lose, and as such see no need to blame them; if the stronger person wins, that makes them lazy, but if the weaker person wins, then it's a miracle. To a certain degree, yes, but in seeing things this way, the simple facts of winning and losing become entangled with some truly complicated implications. Being seen as strong can be a handicap, while being taken for a weakling can turn into an opportunity for victory. Turned around, I guess this points to the idea that true strength has the ability to brush away the aforementioned implications.

The present volume constitutes Book Nine of *Katanagatari*. Book Nine, already? At this point there are just a few books left, which is to say that there are only three months left in the journey of Togame the Schemer and Shichika Yasuri, Seventh Master of the Kyotoryu, and as their author, I can already tell this is going to be a difficult goodbye. Starting off from Kyoto in January, they went to Tottori in February, Shimane in March, Yamaguchi in April, Kagoshima in May, Hokkaido in June, Kochi in July, Tokyo in August, and Yamagata in September. I'm now realizing we've been all over Japan. It's already decided where the two of them will travel in the next three months, but it seems like the plot is becoming quite intricate. Speaking genuinely here, I didn't have the